MEDICAL

Pulse-racing passion

A Daddy For The Midwife's Twins?

Tina Beckett

Cinderella's Kiss With The ER Doc

Scarlet Wilson

MILLS & BOON

A DADDY FOR THE MIDWIFE'S TWINS?
© 2023 by Tina Beckett
Philippine Copyright 2023
Australian Copyright 2023
New Zealand Copyright 2023

First Published 2023
First Australian Paperback Edition 2023
ISBN 978 1 867 29809 0

CINDERELLA'S KISS WITH THE ER DOC
© 2023 by Scarlet Wilson
Philippine Copyright 2023
Australian Copyright 2023
New Zealand Copyright 2023

First Published 2023
First Australian Paperback Edition 2023
ISBN 978 1 867 29809 0

Published by
Harlequin Mills & Boon
An imprint of Harlequin Enterprises (Australia) Pty Limited (ABN 47 001 180 918), a subsidiary of HarperCollins Publishers Australia Pty Limited
(ABN 36 009 913 517)
Level 19, 201 Elizabeth Street
SYDNEY NSW 2000 AUSTRALIA

Printed and bound in Australia by McPherson's Printing Group

A Daddy For The Midwife's Twins?

Tina Beckett

MILLS & BOON

Three-time Golden Heart® Award finalist **Tina Beckett** learned to pack her suitcases almost before she learned to read. Born to a military family, she has lived in the United States, Puerto Rico, Portugal and Brazil. In addition to travelling, Tina loves to cuddle with her pug, Alex; spend time with her family; and hit the trails on her horse. Learn more about Tina from her website or friend her on Facebook.

Visit the Author Profile page
at millsandboon.com.au for more titles.

Dear Reader,

What is your greatest fear? Loss? Financial insecurity? Being alone?

Saraia Jones knows firsthand about loss. She lost her husband to an infection when their twin girls were only three months old. And years later, the man she was dating walked out on her. Since then, she's battled with the fear of loss. Enter Eoin Mulvey, whose good looks and compassion tempt her to try again. But Eoin has a secret that could destroy any chance they have of being together.

Thank you for joining Sari and Eoin as they battle through the fear of loss and learn to make hard choices. This special couple won my heart from the moment they stepped onto the pages of this book. I hope you love reading about their journey as much as I loved writing it.

Love,

Tina Beckett

DEDICATION

For my family. I love you.

PROLOGUE

EOIN MULVEY HELD the envelope in his hand. He didn't open it...already knew the words inside by heart. It was the twentieth such envelope he'd received. One for every year since his diagnosis when he'd been eighteen years old. And every year he had a choice—continue storage or sign the paperwork to discontinue it altogether.

At thirty-eight, Eoin was pretty sure he wasn't going to suddenly get the urge to have biological children of his own. And since he didn't seem to have the best track record in the relationship department, why should he think he'd be any better at being a father?

He'd mentally given himself until he was forty to decide one way or the other. But that deadline was rapidly approaching. Would two more years really make that much of a difference in his life? More importantly, was it what he wanted?

He'd thought it was when he and his girlfriend, Lucy, had met and gotten together. But then she'd pressured him to make that decision last year, just before their breakup—saying if he wanted children now was the time. But suddenly he hadn't felt ready. And it looked like now that that had been the right choice. Because they'd called it quits less than two months later. Not necessarily over the banked sperm, but it sure hadn't won him any points.

Going over to his stack of mail that was his "take care of later" pile, he tossed the envelope onto the top. He was pretty sure it was just going to end up being shredded and thrown in the trash, but he'd give himself a day or two to decide whether or not to take action. He could donate the sperm, but he wasn't sure he wanted to do that either. He'd always thought that someday he'd be a father, that someday he'd know when the time was right to have kids of his own.

But when Lucy had tried to insist, something had held him back. Maybe it was the thought of being somehow tied to the same woman for the rest of his life. And if he'd agreed to have a baby with her, that was exactly what would have happened. Because he would never abandon his own child.

It was a moot point because they hadn't pursued that path. So for now, he would simply continue to help deliver other peoples' babies and live that joy vicariously through them.

It was enough. It had to be. Because, at the moment, he saw no other viable options.

CHAPTER ONE

"I THINK HE'S HERE!"

The clinic had been quieter than normal this morning, with no actively laboring moms. Just the usual prenatal appointments. But that could change at any time.

Saraia Jones glanced up from the text she'd just gotten from one of her twins' preschool teachers and looked at the receptionist. "Who's here?"

"The new doctor. He's a cute one too." The happily married mother of four grinned. "Better be careful, Sari. This one isn't on the brink of retirement."

Rolling her eyes, she gave her friend a look that she hoped conveyed her disapproval with this line of discussion.

The clinic's last obstetrician had retired last month, and they'd had a devil of a time getting another one to take them on. After all, a free—well, almost free—birthing center didn't bring in a whole lot of revenue other than grants and fundraising efforts, so they couldn't offer the huge salaries that some of the hospitals in the Charleston area could afford.

So when one of the largest teaching hospitals in the city had said they had a doctor who was willing to donate a portion of his time—until the clinic found someone more permanent—she'd been more than thrilled. Especially since she'd heard of the man—whose expertise in difficult deliveries was well known, even to Sari, who partnered with women who wanted to go the midwife/doula route. Almost all of them did, since that was one of Grandview Birthing Center's major draws: as few interventions as possible for a safe delivery. An option she wished she'd had when she'd been giving birth to her own girls.

Before either of them could say anything else, the front door swung open, and Saraia did her best not to do a double take. Heidi was right. The man was…well, a hunk. There was no lab coat in sight, but she was pretty sure that even if he wasn't dressed in snug black jeans and a maroon polo shirt, he would have garnered the same reaction. With wavy brown hair that fell over his forehead and a craggy line emblazoned in one cheek, there was something about him that made her eyes want to visit the various landmarks in his face for far longer than they should.

Forcing herself to maintain eye contact instead, she walked over to him. "Dr. Mulvey?"

"Yes. That's me." He paused, that line in his cheek going into action as he obviously waited for her to identify herself. And although she had earned her Doctor of Nursing practice degree as well as being a certified midwife, she didn't use the title of *Doctor*. She was proud to be a nurse midwife and didn't need anything other than knowing she was well equipped to help her patients.

"I'm Saraia Jones, and this is Heidi Midland. Thanks for being willing to come."

He nodded, acknowledging the other woman. "Nice to meet you both. I'm here to help—so, saying that, I'm ready to jump in with both feet. So which one of you can tell me how to do that?"

Sari had to admire his work ethic, but she needed to set him straight. "That would be me. And I'm glad to hear you're ready to go to work, but I do want to warn you that you probably won't see as much action as you would at your hospital. We hope that yours is more of an advisory role."

"Advisory."

"Most of our laboring patients have educated and prepped themselves from the moment they decided to use midwives. They want a more natural birthing experience," she explained. "We have a system that works for us, and things normally run according to plan. It's when they don't, for whatever reason, that we like to have an ob-gyn on hand to assist. We'd rather not have to transport our patients unless absolutely necessary."

"I see. And how many times have you found it…necessary?"

One of his brows raised in a way that made her stiffen. They did not willfully withhold treatment options from their patients, if that was what he was insinuating. Sari wanted a good outcome on each and every delivery.

"Not often," she said. "We have a surgical suite and an anesthesiologist on the premises, in case there's an emergency. We can even do C-sections, if needed."

"Good to know. And if there's more than one emergency at the same time?"

She blinked and did her best not to let his questioning offend her—because he was right. If two women went into crisis at the same time, it would be difficult to handle. But they screened their expectant moms pretty carefully and did their best to space them out so that they didn't have twenty women all due in the same month. When their docket was full, it was full, and as much as she hated to turn moms away, she did so on a regular basis, referring them to another birthing center in the area.

"So far that hasn't happened. Again, we have a system in place to try to avoid those kinds of scenarios. I'll explain all that to you as we tour the facility."

Out of the corner of her eye she saw Heidi sidestepping back to her post, as if trying to get out of range. Evidently Sari hadn't done as good a job as she'd thought of hiding her slight tickle of irritation. She didn't even know the man and she was already expecting him to try to take over. Maybe because the previous doctor had been so on board with their mission that Sari had a hard time believing that any other obstetrician could be as easygoing. Especially one who she'd heard specialized in surgical delivery techniques. Where his expertise had thrilled her moments earlier, it now made her wary. Would he somehow imagine an emergency lurking around every corner?

From her experience some doctors viewed birthing centers as direct competition to hospitals. And maybe they were. But that wasn't her intention. Sari tended to see it as more of a partnership where they both could help their patients have the best experience possible.

She wasn't trying to put hospital maternity wards out of business. She simply wanted to offer another option. One that she wanted every woman to have available to her. The only "right" delivery was a safe one. One where the mother felt most comfortable and in charge of her body. Her own hospital delivery had been less than optimal. Her baby girls had been delivered in a cold surgical environment that had focused on "safe and sanitary" but had done very little to accommodate her own wishes, which had been a quiet room in which she could labor with her husband. Instead the constant checks and hustle and bustle had made her feel like she had no control over anything, not even whether or not to have the C-section where her twins had been delivered.

She didn't want that for her patients.

And since Dr. Mulvey was here, he must've agreed with that philosophy, right? At least in part. So maybe she should cut him some slack. Especially if she expected him to do the same.

Options were good, right? At least her one and only romantic partner since her husband's death had thought so when he'd come to her one night and said he'd thought they should keep their options open as far as dating other people. Sari had taken that as a euphemism for saying they were at a dead end ahead as far their relationship went, and since she wasn't interested in being a "booty call" when no one else was available, she'd broken things off. When he'd called her a few weeks later, she simply hadn't answered. Or any of the other times he'd tried to contact her.

Her girls had been devastated at losing someone who'd seemed fun to be around. They would be even more devastated if they learned that they had been part of the reason

Max had balked. He hadn't been sure he'd wanted a ready-made family. At least that was the feeling she'd gotten when her babysitter had gotten sick one night and they'd ended up having to take the girls with them to the movies. Max hadn't been happy, although he'd done his best to hide it. But their very next date had ended with the "options open" suggestion. She would never do that to her girls ever again.

"Are you ready?"

Dr. Mulvey's voice pulled her from her thoughts, and she forced a smile. "Of course."

Time to play nice with the doctor. She was proud of their little facility, and as they walked she pointed out the things they'd worked so hard to achieve in the four years they'd been here in Charleston. "We have five labor-and-delivery rooms and four exam rooms."

"Have you ever had five patients laboring at one time?"

"Have you ever been able to convince a baby not to come at a certain time?"

He grinned. "Well, I've tried a time or two, but they're usually pretty insistent."

His smile made something shift inside of

her, and she couldn't stop her own lips from curving. "Same here. But in answer to your question we don't typically have someone in every room, unless they're all at different stages of labor," she said. "And we have four other midwives who work at the clinic—you'll meet Miranda, who is due in at ten. We normally have two midwives on duty at any one time, and one is on call. We do that so that we all have at least one true day off a week."

"And where do I fit in with that roster?"

This was where it got a little tricky. Despite the hectic schedules that came with being a doctor, most didn't do well with just sitting around twiddling their thumbs. "If I say 'hopefully nowhere,' will it bother you? Although you might have a line of patients outside of your little cubicle once they realize you're working here."

He shot her a look, and she realized how that last comment had sounded. She certainly hadn't meant to imply that his looks might have something to do with that—although the thought had sure as heck crossed her mind.

"And just why might they be lining up outside of my cubicle?" he asked.

Heat rushed into her face. He'd caught her meaning. Oh, Lord, this tour was not going like she'd envisioned it. Heidi would've been gleeful if she could see them.

Sari decided to tweak what she'd said. "It was a joke. There aren't a whole lot of men who go into midwifery. But seriously," she said, "you might be called in to do prenatal exam *if* one of us has a questionable presentation. But most of our moms want to see the midwife who will eventually deliver her baby, so we try not to switch it up. The goal is to have the same midwife follow their patient from the beginning until delivery. It's the one reason we'll call someone in on their day off. And all four of us are fine with that."

"All four of you. I see."

Sari realized she'd inadvertently made it sound like an "us versus you" atmosphere. That wasn't what she'd wanted to impart. And the last thing she wanted to do was start this off as an adversarial relationship. She wanted them to be a team working toward the same goal: accommodating the mother's wishes while having a safe and healthy delivery. She was making a mess of this whole thing, and that wasn't like her. Maybe Heidi was right.

Maybe his looks were affecting her—and not in a good way.

She cleared her throat and tried not to look at him. "I promise we will pull you in if we have any questions about a patient's well-being. Our goal is to offer a stress-free environment for both mom and baby. But if safely providing that becomes impossible, we won't hesitate to transfer her care to you."

"I'd rather not be sitting here all day doing nothing, when I could be back at the hospital helping patients," Dr. Mulvey said. "Is there a reason you don't just have an on-call doctor?"

"We've tried that. But sometimes there's a need for immediate intervention. Trying to wait even fifteen minutes to get someone here would put lives in danger. I'm sorry if your hospital didn't make that clearer, and I'll understand if you decide this isn't for you."

She held her breath. It had been so hard to find someone willing to help—she would be upset with herself if she inadvertently chased him off.

"No, that's not it," he said. "And you'll find that once I commit to something I follow it through to the end."

Unlike Max, who'd professed his undying

love for her and her girls and then decided he'd wanted to see what else was out there?

God, this was nothing like that. Why did she keep making those kinds of comparisons? Maybe because Eoin Mulvey seemed less than thrilled with what his relationship with the clinic would be.

Again, that had nothing to do with her, other than work environment. If he truly had a problem with his role with the clinic, he'd have to take that up with his hospital.

But that would leave them without a doctor again. And part of the requirements of the board was that they had a doctor physically at the clinic for a certain number of hours a week and that one would be on call for the remainder of the time. The on-call doctors they had no trouble finding, since they weren't called into the clinic except for on rare occasions. But they'd had trouble finding one who was willing to hang out there for very little pay and very little action. Maybe she should at least try to make it sound like she wanted him.

Her face heated again at how her brain had put together that last sentence.

Dr. Mulvey's head tilted as he studied her. "What?"

"Just thinking." What else could she say? "I'd be happy for you to be in the room for the exams and deliveries for the next couple of weeks, if you'd like. That way you can get a better feel for what the clinic does and how we screen patients."

He seemed to mull that over for a few seconds before responding. "That would work. And what would I do during the deliveries?"

"Honestly?" She waited.

"Preferably." Again that line in his face deepened as his lips twitched.

"The fewer medical interventions we have, the better. At least as far as the clinic's mission statement goes. But maybe you can observe some of our different options—at least if the patient doesn't object to your presence. Maybe you'll find some tools you can add to your tool belt."

"Maybe."

He didn't sound convinced, and she couldn't blame him. His training dealt with difficult scenarios, and she was pretty sure he was always thinking three steps ahead in every delivery he participated in. It was probably etched in his DNA by now.

"If you disagree with a decision, maybe hold that thought—unless it's a life-or-death situation—until you're able to talk to one of us in private about it," she said. "I'd rather our patients not feel we're at odds with each other, even though we might be at times." This time she allowed a smile of her own to seep through.

"What? I can't even imagine that happening." The heavy irony infusing those words made her laugh. Then he added, "But I think I can live with your suggestion."

Those words made her relax. She couldn't ask for more than that. "Great, then let's take that tour I promised you."

"Since I'm yours for the day, that sounds like a plan."

She swallowed. He wasn't hers. He was the clinic's. And no matter how devastatingly attractive he might be, Sari needed to remember that. Especially since Evie had evidently started crying this morning and told her teacher that she missed Max. Her teacher had sent her a concerned text. And now Sari had to write back and explain the situation. A situation that should have been over and done six months ago, when they'd broken up. But evidently for at least one of her daughters it wasn't that simple.

Of course it wasn't. But she wouldn't make the same mistake twice. And that mistake was introducing Evie and Hannah to someone who could hurt them. Again.

Eoin was actually impressed with the facility, although he'd had his doubts when he'd originally agreed to volunteer. But he'd always been curious as to how birthing centers like these operated, and he prided himself on being open-minded and non-judgmental. Although his preconceived notions were coming through. He'd heard them a couple of times when he'd commented on this or that or asked a question. Each time it had happened, he'd cringed, realizing he wasn't as impartial as he'd claimed he was. Surprisingly, although Saraia Jones had thrown him a peeved-looking glance when they'd first started out, she hadn't snapped at him, even when he might have deserved it. In fact, she'd seemed to relax, her dark hair sliding across her face when she'd glanced up at him a time or two, making something tighten in him.

But he forced himself to concentrate on what she'd said about the clinic. And it was impressive. The place was immaculate, although the plants propped on shelves or lining the hallways made him tilt his head. His hospital did the fancy bedding and so forth quite well, but even he could admit it didn't look as cozy or inviting as the birthing rooms at Grandview. All of their medical equipment was tucked out of sight, like the lights that were rolled behind screens or the other paraphernalia that was closed inside of a big antique-looking hutch.

If someone walked into one of these rooms, they would swear that it was an ordinary bedroom, not a room where extraordinary things happened. Maybe Saraia was right. Maybe there was a tool or two that he was missing in his own practice. But he was geared to dealing with births where time was of the essence, and having to stop and pull something out of its hiding place? He wasn't quite sold on that. At least not yet.

"You said you have water births as well?" Eoin asked.

"Yep, it's just in this last room."

Saraia unlocked a door on their right and waited for him to go ahead of her. He did and then stopped. This room looked like some kind of cabana. The tile on the floor had the appearance of wood planking, which extended halfway up the walls, giving it a warm and inviting look and yet was undoubtedly easy to sterilize. There were soft curtain-like fabrics draped around the space and an acrylic birthing pool placed in the middle of the room. Again, it didn't look like any delivery room he'd ever seen.

As if expecting the question, Saraia spoke up. "The soft-scaping—such as the draperies—are taken down and replaced with sanitized ones after the completion of each birth. And the moms can wear their own clothing—or not. Whatever makes them the most comfortable."

"And the benches around the tub are for…?"

"They're a place where family members can sit and observe or participate in the birth experience, which many families choose to do."

Eoin's brows went up. "How often is this room used?"

"It depends on the month. It's not quite as popular as some of the other rooms, but we felt it important to offer it as an option."

Which didn't answer his question. As if she realized that, she went on to say, "We probably use this room twice a week at the moment. Sometimes more."

"And changing out those 'softscapes,' as you put it. Who does that?"

Saraia glanced around the room. "Our cleaning crew. The same ones who change the bed linens and towels. They're sent out to a laundry service."

"So if this room starts being used daily, you have enough staff to keep up with the demand?" The words came out sounding like a challenge, and he hadn't meant them to.

She frowned. "We try to keep our numbers pretty steady, although we do have more patients some months than others. For their own safety, we have a cap on how many we babies we can deliver at any given time. I'll admit it's a juggling act, but hospitals sometimes find themselves scrambling too when an unexpected number of patients go into labor at the same time."

"Yes, I agree. That probably wasn't a fair question."

Saraia's face tilted, and there went that hair slide again. It looked soft and touchable, and his fingers tingled. Eoin forced them to curl at his sides.

"No, it was fair. And I want to present a realistic picture to anyone who walks through those doors. It's one reason we don't have a blowup-style birthing pool. It's easier to clean the room and the pool when it's hard acrylic."

He'd figured that might be the case, although most of the ones he'd seen were a taller version of an inflatable kiddie pool. Unlike the beds that could be stripped and remade, a pool seemed like a more complicated process to sanitize. But this didn't look that way. Solid white, it was cloverleaf in shape, each leaflet having what looked like a separate function with different configurations that would support a laboring mom in various positions.

But there was a picture hanging on the wall of how the room might look when it was in use. Eoin walked over to it, seeing a smiling family gathered around water that looked a little bluer than it might in real life. His mouth twisted in amusement. "I take it you don't tint the water with food coloring."

She sighed. "No. That was probably artistic license—although I never really noticed that before. It was actually the photo used by the pool manufacturer. We just liked the design so much that we tried to recreate the scene. In real life, things don't stay as pretty as they do in pictures."

That was the truth. Eoin had just discarded some pictures of him with Lucy. In all of them, they'd been smiling, either holding hands or with his arm draped around her shoulders. They'd been true enough representations of them at the time, but like Saraia had said, things didn't stay that way.

"No, they don't."

Maybe it was the way he'd said it, but he noticed she gave him a look that seemed to pierce right through the wall he'd erected around himself over the last several months.

Not what he wanted, so he quickly changed the subject. "So do you use a hose to fill the pool?"

Thankfully the tactic worked, and Saraia

went into a detailed explanation of how they'd had to retrofit the room with plumbing last year in order to be able to have a permanent pool. "And just around here is an exam table. That way we don't have to move patients from room to room." She pulled back part of the draperies to reveal another bed like the ones in other rooms.

Eoin was surprised. He'd thought those draperies were simply along the walls of the room. "That is pretty ingenious." He couldn't stop the words from coming out, even though he wasn't fully sold on things he had minimal experience with. He'd have to see it in action before he could pronounce judgment on it one way or the other.

"We thought so," she replied. "Like I said, we copied what they had in the showroom. We really want to keep distractions to a minimum for our patients. We want them to focus on the experience at hand. Part of that is providing a calm, soothing atmosphere where they can do that. But the bed is here in case we need to intervene in some way or when they first come in. I hope my girls can one day have all these options if they ever become moms."

She had children. He hadn't seen a ring on her hand, although that didn't mean anything. She could have a partner. Or maybe she'd chosen to have kids in her own way, such as IVF treatments or something.

"How old are they? Your kids, I mean." Eoin wasn't sure why he'd asked the question, but he couldn't retract it now.

And the smile she gave him was nothing short of dazzling, her white teeth coming down on her lip in a way that cut right through him.

"They're five. Identical twins, actually."

Identical. Probably not IVF, then. Twins were common enough in fertility treatments, but they were normally fraternal twins. "They must keep you busy."

"They do. But in a good way." Saraia glanced around the room. "And it's one of the reasons I'm so passionate about the birthing center. It has all of the things I wish I'd been able to have when I was in labor."

This time he did frown. Pregnancies with twins brought a whole host of possible complications. "You deliver twins here?"

"Some. We screen them carefully. And it's one of the reasons we want an ob-gyn on the premises," she explained. "When I learned I was pregnant, I was scheduled for a C-section...was told it was the safest option. I didn't research that claim. I was already a nurse with a master's degree at a huge hospital at the time, and I trusted my doctor implicitly. But afterward, I heard little murmurs about his Cesarean rate. Evidently it was higher than the average doctor's. It made me sit up and take notice, and then my hus— Well, my life situation changed, and I decided to go back to school and become a midwife."

She touched Eoin's arm, her fingers soft and warm. "I truly believe in this place, and that is not just a line coming from someone who works here."

Her voice rang with a sincerity that seemed to come from deep inside of her. The hand on his arm dropped away, and he found he missed it. So much so that he needed to turn his mind back to why he was here at the clinic. "I believe you," he said. "I hope you'll give me the chance to come to my own conclusions."

"Of course. I wouldn't have it any other way."

Eoin couldn't ask for more than that. And

he hoped she was right about how smoothly things went here. Because all he could think was how it would only take one emergency situation—one death, of mother or baby—to turn this place on its head and undo whatever inroads they'd made with the community.

And when or if that happened, it wouldn't be him who'd be on the street corner proclaiming the benefits of natural childbirth, even though he knew in his heart of hearts that women had been giving birth for a lot longer than the term *ob-gyn* had been around. And it probably wasn't going to come to a screeching halt just because he had some concerns about safety.

So all he could do was sit back and listen—and try to keep everything wrapped up in a nice pretty bow that had nothing to do with his questionable responses to Saraia as a person. It was what he'd come to the birthing center to do. And he would do his damnedest to keep his focus on that.

As long as Saraia and her partners kept safe deliveries as the bedrock of their clinic. If he ever saw something that jeopardized that…

all bets were off. He'd be the first one out the door, and he'd ask his hospital to never partner with them again.

CHAPTER TWO

IT WAS SARAIA'S day off, but one of her patients had unexpectedly gone into labor in the middle of the night. Things had been stable until this morning, but her phone rang at 6:00 a.m. when it became evident that this baby was coming today, whether anyone liked it or not. Since it was Saturday, Evie and Hannah's preschool was closed, and her mom hadn't been available, so she'd packed the girls up and brought them into the center.

It was times like this that she missed David's calm demeanor. He would have sent her on her way and spent the day playing with their daughters. But he wasn't. And sometimes the weight of raising them alone threatened to crush her.

But it was what it was, and Saraia was going to do right by them. Not just for David—from the moment she'd found out she was pregnant she'd committed to doing whatever it took to make sure their needs were met. She just hadn't expected to be doing that alone.

But she was.

Pulling her mind back to the exhausted mother whose pushing phase was going longer than she'd anticipated, Saraia said, "Janie, I'm going to need you to pull your knees to your belly to see if we can give your baby a little more room."

Her patient groaned but did as asked.

"Good. Now, when the next contraction comes, give me a big push."

Within a minute, the baby's head appeared. "Okay, baby's making an appearance, so..."

Before she could get the next words out, the head suddenly disappeared back into the canal. Saraia tensed.

Janie must have sensed something. "What's wrong?"

"Baby's just being a little stubborn." But she knew it could be more than that. The turtle sign, where the head emerged during a contraction but retracted afterward, could be a symptom of shoulder dystocia, where one of the baby's shoulders was trapped behind the pubic bone.

The next contraction came, and the head reappeared but didn't stay there. "Janie, this is very important—I'm going to need you to breathe through the next contraction. Don't push."

She hurriedly pressed the button on the side table that would call for assistance. Heidi, who'd also come in on her day off would know what to do.

Sure enough, her voice came through the intercom. "What can I help with?"

"I need someone in here to assist, and see if you can get Dr. Mulvaney on the line. I'm pretty sure we have a baby whose shoulder is just a bit wedged." She phrased it in a way that hopefully wouldn't alarm the mom but would get across that this was an emergency.

Heidi's voice lowered. "Actually, he's here. He's doing puzzles in the staff lounge with your girls."

Saraia blinked before pushing past the tickle of worry that he was interacting with her daughters and went straight to relief that he was in the building. "Can you ask him to come in here?"

"On it."

She turned her attention back to Janie. "I'm

going to have our doctor come in and check on us, okay? If he gives us the all clear, we'll keep on going as we have been. But we may need to reposition you again and to give that baby a little help."

"A cesarean?" Janie got the words out just before the next contraction hit.

Sari helped her breathe through it before she answered. "I'm not going to lie and say it's not a possibility. But I promise we'll see if we can coax your little one to cooperate before we jump to that option, okay?"

Just as she was finishing the explanation, Eoin appeared in the doorway, faded jeans and a T-shirt that emphasized his broad shoulders and toned arms making her pause for a minute. He wasted no time with chitchat. "What have you got?"

"Possible shoulder dystocia."

Damn. This was not the first delivery she wanted the man to see. She'd wanted a smooth, problem-free, homey atmosphere that would sell him on their clinic's mission statement.

But when had things ever been that easy? And right now was not the time to worry about it, since Eoin had immediately gone to scrub up in the sink.

"Is your surgical suite kept at the ready?" he asked.

"Of course." She glanced at Janie just as the woman's hand gripped hers hard while she did her best not to push as the next contraction hit. The woman was too wrapped up in what was happening with her body to notice what the obstetrician had said.

Eoin dried his hands and snapped on a pair of gloves. "Tell me."

She knew exactly what he meant, and she ran through what was happening: prolonged pushing followed by the turtle sign. "Pregnancy and the early stages of labor went like clockwork."

He nodded. "Shoulder dystocia is one of those that sneaks up on you. The baby isn't oversized?"

"No. We wouldn't have delivered her if that were the case. She weighed just over seven pounds at the last exam. And she's just a few days shy of her delivery date."

"What's her name?"

"Janie."

He came up by her head. "Janie, I'm going

to examine you, and then we're probably going to have to reposition you. It's not going to be comfortable, but I'll do my best to be careful. We all want a healthy baby. Do you know what the sex is yet?"

"N-no…we wanted it to be a surprise. My husband is deployed overseas and couldn't be…" Janie dissolved into tears.

It wasn't Eoin. His words had been surprisingly even and gentle. None of the barking orders that she'd seen from a few of the doctors she'd dealt with when doing her rotations. Not all of them, certainly—most of them were great. But she'd actually heard a doctor ask a patient if she was going to pull him away from his son's soccer game to do the delivery. He'd said it in a joking manner but had griped to the nurses about it outside of the room, asking them to only call him back if absolutely needed.

Saraia got it. Being a doctor was hard. Really hard. So was being a midwife. After all, she'd had to bring her kids to the clinic with her for this delivery, but she wouldn't dream of saying that to Janie. When she'd gone into this profession she'd known what was involved. And she'd talked with Evie and

Hannah a lot about her job. And she loved it. All of it. Whenever it interfered with plans she'd made with her girls, she would seek permission from the newborn's parents to get a picture of the baby and show it to the girls. They always oohed and aahed over the baby.

She kept hold of Janie's hand as Eoin performed his exam. "If we can get the baby rotated just a bit more, we might be able to free up the shoulder."

"I thought the same," Saraia said. "And I will say the baby's presentation was normal last time I examined her. She wasn't sunny-side up, or I would have worked to change things up then."

She sounded defensive, and she hadn't meant it to. Saraia just did not want the obstetrician thinking that she would willingly overlook a glaring red flag. Not that the baby was sunny-side up at this point either. So she wasn't sure why she was even saying anything.

"I didn't imply that you wouldn't." He turned back to the patient. "We're going to help you get up onto all fours."

"I don't think I can."

"We're all going to work together, okay?

Keep your knees bent, and we'll just roll you onto them."

He made it sound so easy. And there still wasn't an ounce of panic in his voice. He'd probably seen so much worse than this. But any time a presentation wasn't absolutely normal, Saraia's heart started pounding—much like it was now. But when that happened, her training tended to kick in and she just pushed through it, doing whatever she had to to make sure the outcome was as good as she could possibly make it. But it sure felt good having him here. A little too good.

Eoin chose that moment to glance at her, his eyes narrowing for a second. "I'll get on the other side of the bed," he said. "See if you can roll her up toward me."

"Got it. Let's do it before the next contraction starts."

Sari pushed with all her might, even as Janie's agonized groans tore at her heart. It would be even worse if Eoin had to go in vaginally to try to turn the baby to dislodge its shoulder.

Once Janie was on her hands and knees, Eoin found the controls that would lower the bed without Sari's help and used his hands to apply firm pressure onto their patient's belly. He stopped when the next contraction came as Sari coached her through it. The all-fours position could open the pelvis more and would hopefully help tip that shoulder off the pelvic bone. They rocked her a couple of times.

"Janie, I'm going to raise the head of the bed," he said. "Keep your knees apart and grip the top of the mattress, okay? And as soon as the next contraction comes, I want you to go ahead and push nice and steady. We're going to see if that baby has worked his or herself loose."

He was putting her into more of a squatting position. It was exactly what Sari would have done, but having a second set of hands was a godsend, especially if the technique didn't work and they had to go to some of the more aggressive maneuvers.

Once their patient was in place, Eoin glanced up at Sari. "Go ahead and get behind her. If the baby progresses, we'll just go with it. If not, we'll need to apply pressure over the pubic bone."

Which would require another repositioning and would hurt like hell. She sent up a quick prayer that what they'd already done would work.

"It's coming," Janie said. This time there was more than a hint of fear in her voice.

The obstetrician nodded to her, and Sari didn't hesitate taking back the lead.

"It's okay, Janie—we're right here. I want you to push slow and easy. Nothing too hard until we make sure the baby is ready to come."

The mom didn't reply but pushed, as Sari leaned an elbow on the mattress behind her and felt for the head. There it was. "Just a little more."

Another push had the head all the way out. Her patient breathed out a loud gasping breath, and Sari's heart was in her throat as she waited to make sure the head would stay out this time.

"It worked." She glanced at Eoin in time to see him nod and step away from the bed.

What? Was he leaving? No. He was just fully handing the reins back to her, and she was grateful. Not only for herself, but for her patient.

"Breathe slow and steady until the next contraction, Janie. We're almost there."

"Are you sure?" The exhaustion was evident in her voice, in the shaking of her limbs as she held herself where she was. A second later, the next contraction was on her and she couldn't say anything else.

"Push." Sari started to slowly count to ten even as she helped ease one shoulder out and then the next. "One more big push. As hard as you can."

Janie did as requested, and things happened really fast now that the shoulders were both delivered. The baby slipped out and into Sari's waiting hands. "And we have a baby."

The new mom sagged, her upper body leaning against the mattress in relief. Which was fine, but Sari didn't want her sitting completely on her knees. Not just yet. "Go ahead and rest, but don't sit."

"Is the baby okay?"

Sari smiled even as the baby squirmed for a second before letting out a loud yowling sound as she took her first breath. "I would say so. You have a little girl, Janie."

"Jacob wanted a girl, wanted to name her Martha after my own mom." Emotions seemed to overwhelm her, and Janie gave a sobbing breath, even as Sari waited for the cord to stop pulsing. Once it did, she clamped it in two spots and then cut it.

"Martha is a beautiful name. You mom would have loved her so much."

Sari learned so much about a patient during the course of a delivery. Like the fact that Janie's mom had died of cancer five years ago at the age of forty-five and that she was missed terribly. But her dad was still living and looking forward to being a grandpa.

"Eoin, can you put the bed back to its normal position so we can help her lie down?"

Sari could do it on her own, but since the obstetrician was in the room, she was going to take advantage of his presence. They put the head of the mattress back down and helped Janie lie on her back. Only then did she put the baby against her mom so they could have some skin-to-skin bonding time. She could clean her up after the afterbirth was delivered.

Which happened in a few minutes. Sari was so busy with what she was doing that when she looked up again, Eoin was gone—it was as if he'd never been here. But she'd never been so glad for someone's presence as she'd been a few moments earlier.

Why was he here anyway? He was only

scheduled for two days a week, and Saturday was definitely not one of them. She hoped he was still in the building so she could thank him and have kind of a debriefing session to unpack what had just happened. All she could hope was that he'd approved of her actions and could see that she wasn't going to overlook symptoms if there was even a hint of a problem. The reality was deliveries could either go without a hitch or things could get dicey very, very quickly. She believed wholeheartedly in what she did. But she believed even more in having a live baby and mom at the end of the day.

With the afterbirth delivered and the baby cleaned up, Sari asked Janie what her plans were for the night. They did have the capability of monitoring mom and baby overnight if the new mom simply needed some rest and peace and quiet. Or if things looked good, she could opt to go home as soon as she was ready. Most of the time, insurance allowed for overnight stays.

"I have a friend who's going to come pick us up as soon as she gets off work." Janie shrugged. "She offered to be my birth coach, but the idea of having someone other than my mom or Jacob next to me… Well, I just couldn't do it."

"I understand. And it's fine—you needed to do what you felt the most comfortable with."

"Thank you." She propped the baby into the crook of her arm and grabbed Sari's hand. "I was so afraid I was going to have to have a cesarean once the doctor came into the room."

"I didn't want that for you," Sari said. "But if he thought it was necessary, I would have deferred to his expertise. But only because I wanted Martha to make it into this world in one piece."

"Me too." Janie glanced around the room. "Did he leave?"

"I think he wanted your delivery to finish the way it started—with just us in the room." At least she hoped that was it. It was one of the reasons she wanted to chat with him.

"Well, please thank him for me if I don't see him again."

"I will." Sari smiled. "Do you want something? A drink? Something to eat?"

"Some yogurt sounds good, if you have some."

"We actually do." The clinic kept a small supply of snacks and drinks on hand to give their new mothers a way to replenish calories lost during delivery. "I'll be back with it in a few minutes, if you're okay."

Janie glanced at her baby, who had already latched onto her mom's breast. "I'm more than okay. I can never thank you enough. Can I have my purse so I can try to video chat with Jacob to give him the news?"

"Absolutely." Sari handed her her purse and waited as she fished her phone out of it. "I'll give you some time alone. Just press the button on the side table if you need me for something. And I'll knock before I come back into the room."

"Thanks again for everything."

"You're more than welcome. I hope you can reach him."

"Yeah. Me too."

With that Sari left the room and went to the front desk, where Heidi was still waiting. "I thought you would have gone home by now."

"No way," Heidi said. "Not without hearing that everything ended up being okay. Eoin says it did."

"And he actually was a great help. Is he still around?"

She nodded at the door to the staff lounge. "I think you-know-who have conned him into coloring with them now."

Saraia stiffened. "He's in with the girls? Again?"

She wasn't sure why it mattered, since he'd already done puzzles with them earlier. But for some reason a little twinge of alarm went through her. Or was that alarm at her own reactions to the man?

"Yep. Evie saw him walk by and stuck her head out to call him over." Heidi grinned. "I don't think it took too much convincing. It's pretty damned adorable of him, if you ask me."

Ugh! Sari didn't want the man to be adorable or in any way attractive to her daughters. She gave an internal laugh because she'd already been affected by him.

But she had seen what could happen when she let a man into their lives. Except she hadn't let this one in, and there wasn't much of a chance that he would be involved in their lives in any meaningful way, other than just some stranger who popped in to do a puzzle with them or color a page from a coloring book.

"Well, I'll happily relieve him of his duties."

"What? Did it not go well in there with Janie?"

She realized Heidi thought she'd meant they weren't going to keep him on at the clinic. And maybe it would have been better if he'd been a pompous, arrogant bastard who snatched at control wherever he went. Well, he had taken charge in there. But only because she'd been glad to let him. And he'd let go of it as soon as he'd seen the crisis was over. She couldn't fault him there. It was what Dr. Eric had done during his time at the clinic, but she hadn't expected Dr. Mulvey to have handed things back over to her so quickly—and without even waiting for the patient to thank him.

A shard of respect worked its way under her skin, and it bothered her for some reason. Maybe because she'd been defensive and on guard when she'd first met him. Did she have a problem with trusting doctors because of what had happened to her during her own birth? She hadn't thought so, but maybe it was something that was swirling around in there without her even being aware of it. It had even taken Dr. Eric some time to gain her confidence, and after he had, she'd been convinced he was an outlier as far as obstetricians went, even though in her head she knew that was probably not the case. There were plenty of obstetricians who worked with hospital midwives on a regular basis. But she'd convinced herself that only happened when it was still in a hospital setting.

A birthing center that was not on hospital property was a different animal. At least that was what she'd told herself.

But right now, she had to go in and rescue Eoin from her daughters before they had his thick wavy hair caught up in multiple rubber bands. She bit her lip at that image.

David would have loved that. But he wasn't here. And Eoin definitely wasn't vying for a position as a significant other for Sari or her girls. Nor did she want him to. She straightened her back and headed to the door of the lounge, taking a deep breath before pushing it open.

No rubber bands in sight. But what was in sight was a tall lanky man hunched over a child-sized table in the corner with a red crayon in his hand.

Her breath left her for a moment as she let herself stare at the sight. And from what she could see, he was coloring a picture of a heart. Sari swallowed, allowing herself to take in the sight for a few seconds more. Max had never deigned to color with her daughters, always telling them he was no good at it and that he wanted them to show them their masterpieces after they were done. But looking back, she was pretty sure he'd just been feeding them a line to get out of interacting with them, although he'd made a show out of telling them how good their pictures looked.

Sari's heart ached over memories that she was now able to see for what they'd been: pretense. Wanting to replace what she'd had with David?

When Hannah and Evie had given Max some pictures to take home, she'd thought it was sweet that he'd folded them up and put them into his pocket. But she'd never seen them displayed in his apartment. Looking back there were so many signs that she'd just ignored because she'd been attracted to the man. She'd only seen what she'd wanted to see.

But not again. Maybe Evie or Hannah had just hounded Eoin into coloring with them. But even if they hadn't, she wasn't going to take any chances. Not this time. Especially with how seeing him there was turning her insides to goo.

She cleared her throat and watched as all their heads jerked around to look at her. She suddenly lost her train of thought as that line in Eoin's face deepened and a tinge of color appeared in his cheeks. Embarrassed to have been caught clutching a crayon? Or sitting at a kiddie table?

Somehow it made the act even more endearing.

Oh, hell. She did not need this. Banishing the softness that was crouched in a corner waiting to infect her heart, Sari nodded at him. "Can I talk to you for a minute?"

A slight furrowing of his brows said it wasn't what he'd expected her to say. But he simply replied, "Sure," before looking at her girls. "I'll have to take a rain check on drawing a unicorn."

"What's a rain check?" asked Hannah.

"It means no."

Evie's response made Sari want to cry. How many times had Max used that term? And Evie was right—it had basically meant he hadn't wanted to do whatever it was they'd been asking him to do.

Eoin slashed a look at her before turning back to Evie. "It actually means it's something I want to do but can't right now. But that I'll do it later."

Hannah tilted her head at him, her smile beaming. "So you'll draw me a unicorn later?"

"I will. The next time I see you with crayons. I promise."

Oh, no. He was *not* going to promise them anything. She wouldn't let him. "Girls, you need to let Dr. Mulvey go. I need to talk to him, and I'm sure he has something to do after that."

He stared at her for a minute before finally nodding. "It would seem that I do." He glanced back at the twins. "Thanks for letting me color with you."

Uncurling his long form from the chair, he paused when Evie jumped to her feet and handed him the paper. "Don't forget to take your heart with you."

He took the colored sheet and smiled. But when he turned away and raised a brow at Sari, it made her feel like he wasn't the one who'd forgotten his heart. She had. Had she turned that hard?

Maybe. But it was for her daughters' own good. After all, she didn't want to end up explaining her relationship status to Evie's and Hannah's teachers every time there was a breakup. Because she didn't expect there to be another one anytime soon. At least not until her girls were at a point when they could understand things a little bit better. Maybe not even then.

She moved into the hallway with him and motioned him out of earshot of Heidi—not that she was one to purposely listen in on conversations. But Sari also didn't want her getting any ideas about Eoin being good dating material or anything.

"Everything okay with Janie and the baby?" he asked.

"Yes, everything went wonderfully. I just wanted to thank you for helping."

"You're welcome. But that's not what this little talk is about, is it?"

Sari bit her lip. How did she ask him not to

color with her daughters without making it sound like she thought he was some kind of pervert? So she decided to evade the subject.

"It is, actually," she said. "I really did appreciate the way you did what you did. You didn't immediately insist on surgery."

He eyed her for a second. "Let's get one thing straight. If I'd come into that room and felt she needed a cesarean, I wouldn't have hesitated to say so."

Lord, how did she always make such a mess of every conversation she had with this man? "I know. But the fact that you were willing to wait and size things up is huge for our patients and means a lot. For me, personally. And with your specialty being at-risk pregnancies, it would be easy to jump right on that bandwagon."

Eoin motioned to one of the benches that flanked the hallway. Once she was seated he sat beside her, hands between his knees, the picture he'd drawn still clutched in one of them. "And maybe my specialty lets me discern between a true medical emergency and a situation where we have a little more time before deciding that surgery is the only way."

She hadn't really thought of it that way.

And she could admit when she was wrong. At least about that.

"I will admit that once you mentioned our surgical suite, I thought you would want to head right in that direction," she said. "I'm glad I was wrong."

"Maybe we can agree to give each other the benefit of the doubt," he said, "since I expected you to fight my suggestions at every turn and was honestly surprised when you didn't."

That made her smile. "Believe me, if I thought you were wrong, you would have heard about it in no uncertain terms."

"I do. Believe you."

They looked at each other, and Sari felt an awareness come into the space that made her swallow. God, she did not want to be attracted to this man. At all. But it was hard when he was just so…unexpected. At every turn. Well, she'd better jump right back onto her high horse and gallop away before things got out of hand.

She nodded at his picture. "Anyway, thanks for entertaining them. But I don't expect you to. They only came today because I couldn't make any other arrangements."

"I know you don't expect me to. But it wasn't like they were asking me to buy them a car. It was just coloring."

Just coloring. Didn't he realize how big that was? And how rarely Evie and Hannah had ever had an adult male sit down and pick up a crayon and interact with them? Or a toy. It was huge. And Evie's response to Hannah's question about a rain check was telling. Her daughter didn't expect anything out of a man. Not anymore.

And neither did Sari. And that made her want to weep. Right now, she just didn't have it in her to tell Eoin to not talk to her girls or to play with them. She couldn't find a way to say it nicely without having to explain why she thought it was such a bad idea for them to get to know him.

Or maybe it was that she couldn't find a way to tell herself that exact thing: That getting to know him—*really* know him—would be a very bad idea. For both her and the girls.

So she settled for a quick informational speech about how Janie and her daughter were progressing and thanked him again for his help. It sounded stilted even to her own ears, but it was all she had. For now.

Or at least until she needed to give him a real warning. And if she did, nothing or no one would stop her from saying what she had to say.

CHAPTER THREE

EOIN SPENT THE next two days doing his regular shift at the hospital. But he had to admit, he kind of missed the calm, laidback atmosphere of Grandview. His days could be rushed and frenetic, with very little time to get to know his patients since they were normally already in crisis by the time he was called in.

When was the last time he'd been able to sit and do puzzles with a child? The last time he'd been able to work side by side with a midwife who was so fiercely protective of her patients? Actually, he rarely worked with midwives at all, but not because he was necessarily against it. But it was just because he was normally rushing someone into the operating room in an attempt to save two lives. And sometimes that wasn't even possible. Every once in a while, it was a matter of deciding who could be saved—mother or baby. Whether it was a car accident where the mom was critically injured or a case where the fetus was in such dire distress that the odds of saving it were astronomical, he could not ever remember being able to turn the situation back over to the referring physician. Or midwife, in this case.

And she'd seemed just as surprised by that as he'd been. Walking out of that room without knowing the outcome had gone against every grain of his being, but somehow he'd sensed it was the right thing—as hard as it had been to do it.

It was as if Saraia had expected him to yank her patient away from her without a second glance. He'd never had to yank anyone. They were normally handed over gladly by a medical professional who would rather not have control over an outcome that sometimes promised only heartache.

And although he'd been busy yesterday and today, it had somehow been harder to face the same cases that he'd once considered a challenge. Seeing the relief on Saraia's face when that baby had slid into her waiting hands, seeing the tearful emotion on Janie's face when she'd realized all was well had done a number on him. He was so used to hardening his heart in order to get the job done that he'd had a hard time allowing it to be softened again when there was a need for it.

And when one of Sari's daughters had asked him to draw a heart, it had been as if the universe had been sending him a reminder that it was okay to sometimes wear his heart on his sleeve. That there were times when it was even good and appropriate to let his feelings show.

It was why that picture was now hanging on his refrigerator, although putting his own crude artwork on display seemed kind of strange. But it was as if he was sending a nod back at some deity, that he would try harder to do just that.

But today had not been the day. He'd just lost a baby whose mom had had an undiagnosed autoimmune disorder.

He sat at the desk in his office, steepled hands supporting his head, and told himself not to try to make sense of it. At seven months' gestation, the baby had been capable of surviving outside of the womb with help. And he'd tried to give that help. The baby girl had been tiny and perfect. So perfect, he'd continued attempts to revive her for several minutes after someone had suggested calling it. Saying those words had been much harder than it might have been just two days ago. Before he'd assisted that mom at Grandview.

Afterward, he'd carried the baby's tiny form to the room where her mother had lain sobbing into her pillow. It had hurt to hand her over, had hurt to witness how carefully she'd cradled her deceased child. To tell her that she could carry another child to term once her condition was under control had been out of the question. At least right then, when the pain of loss had been so real. So raw. So he'd left her there and come back to his office, where he'd dissected his every move during the C-section over and over again. But no matter what scenario he played, he didn't see it ending any differently.

But that didn't help.

Right now, he really wanted to run over to the birthing center and watch a baby being born without a care in the world. Where things ran—mostly—according to plan. Even if he hadn't assisted in the shoulder dystocia, he was reasonably certain that Saraia would have been able to dislodge the baby on her own. But neither of them had known that for a fact. And having a second person nearby had been the right call. One she hadn't hesitated to make, which had surprised him, although he was starting to learn it shouldn't have. Everything he'd heard about Saraia Jones said that she put her patients first. Always.

And yet there were those who said standalone birthing centers put lives at risk. Maybe it was part of the reason he'd volunteered to donate his time—so that he could make up his own mind, rather than go by the thoughts and opinions of others. And it was still too early in the game to call it one way or the other.

He'd seen nothing he disapproved of. Yet. Whether it would still be that way in one month's time or one year's time was yet to be decided.

And Saraia's two daughters had been adorable. Although when one twin had asked the other what *rain check* meant and she'd said, "It means no," it had made him tense. Hopefully their mother hadn't given them that idea. He'd wanted to ask why either child would think that but had known he'd be out of line.

After all, he didn't have children, so why would he think he could tell her how to parent her kids?

He glanced at his calendar. He had nothing else pressing, and he was past his scheduled time. Maybe that was why he was so tired and mentally spent. He'd been here for over nine hours. It was time to go home.

Where that heart on the refrigerator could remind him of all the reasons why it was okay to feel emotions. Because right now, he couldn't think of any. Not even one.

Saraia stuck a thumbtack into the picture of a mom with a tiny newborn in her arms. Beside her was her own smiling face as she'd stooped down to the woman's level to let Heidi snap a picture of them.

It was Janie and her new baby. She'd stopped by the clinic to drop off the picture in person, saying she'd left the baby with Jacob's mom in order to come, but she'd wanted to thank Saraia in person. Which she'd done, hugging her and telling her how grateful she was.

Sari smiled, touching the photo with her fingers. It was one picture in a sea of similar outcomes, so why did this delivery seem so special?

"Is that our dystocia patient?"

The low words from behind her made her whirl around, although she already knew who the voice belonged to.

Eoin stood there. This time, rather than faded jeans, he was dressed in khaki slacks and a blue button-down shirt. He looked cool and casual and especially yummy today, his perpetually disheveled hair pushed back from his forehead. A shiver went over her as her eyes tracked over him.

Was that why Janie's delivery had seemed extra important? Because he'd assisted her? If so, she'd better figure out a way to introduce a dose of reality to the memory. Because that delivery had been no more special than any other one had. She couldn't afford to let it be.

It didn't help that her girls had talked non-stop about the nice doctor they'd met a few days ago. The doctor who'd put together puzzles and colored with them.

Heidi had done a lot of that with them whenever she'd had to bring them to work. Evie and Hannah didn't think twice about that. Maybe because it was a normal part of the clinic. But let a handsome man come in and spend some time with them and it seemed to make an instant impact on them.

Well, he'd made an instant impact on her too. And she didn't like it. Because she was noticing far more about him than she should've: the way he looked, the craggy lines in his face when he smiled…the sound of his voice. And starting anything with him was out of the question. She'd done that with one other man, and it had ended up being a disaster. One that seemed to still be affecting Evie.

Sari realized Eoin was still waiting for an answer to his question. "Yes, that is Janie and Martha."

His eyes turned from her to the picture. "How are they doing?"

"Incredibly well, thanks to you. You just missed her by a few minutes. She wanted me to express her gratitude to you."

His eyes turned a shade darker. "Well, you win some, you lose some."

Shock spiked through her system. What an extremely weird thing to say. *"Excuse me?"* She couldn't keep the incredulity out of her voice—along with a hint of anger over how blasé and completely inappropriate his words seemed.

So much for an instant attraction. This was exactly why she didn't let men close.

"Oh, hell, Saraia—I don't mean that," Eoin said. "It's just been a shitty day, and seeing Janie's happy face just hit me in the gut."

She looked at him closer, and all of her anger melted when she saw what looked like a pinpoint of pain in his eyes. She touched his hand. "Hey, did something happen?"

He dragged a hand though his hair, mussing it even more. Her finger itched to smooth it back into place, to ease the line that had formed between his brows.

"I helped deliver a dead baby today."

You win some, you lose some.

Those words took on a horrible and sad new meaning. "Oh, Eoin, I'm so sorry. Do you want to talk about it?" Her fingers twined around his, seeking to somehow comfort him, but was that even possible? She couldn't even imagine what he was going through.

"Yes. No. Dammit, I don't know," he said. "You talked about my job and how specialized it is. I hadn't really even thought about it that way. I just know that by the time I'm called in, the odds aren't looking quite as rosy as they are when you step into a delivery room here at Grandview." He glanced at her. "And I'm not trying to minimize what you do, I just want you to know—hell, I don't even know what I'm trying to say. Do you want to get some coffee?"

She frowned, letting go of his hand when a little voice inside of her whispered that she shouldn't risk it, that she'd told herself over and over that she was immune to the charms of the opposite sex. But this wasn't about being charmed by him. Eoin was hurting, and to brush him off would seem callous. No, it would *be* callous.

Besides, he'd invited her to *coffee*. Not a wedding. And he needed to talk. And honestly, she wanted to help—or to at least be a listening ear. Wasn't she called on to do that with the women she served over the course of their pregnancies? This was really no different.

"Of course," Sari told him. "There's a coffee shop right around the corner. That way I can get back in less than two minutes if a patient comes in."

"Do you have someone scheduled for today?"

She blinked, then smiled. "My patients aren't always as predictable—time wise—as yours might be."

"I didn't mean that. I meant as in prenatal appointments."

Of course he did. "That makes sense. Sorry. And no, I don't have any appointments until later anyway."

"No kiddos with you today?"

She tensed slightly at the mention of her daughters. "Nope, they're in preschool. They don't get off until four, when I have to pick them up."

"I thought maybe they were in kindergarten already."

"This next year. They're excited but sad about leaving some of their friends behind."

He nodded. "I imagine it's sad to leave anyone behind."

"It is." It had been incredibly hard to leave David in the past, to realize that while she could hold his memory in her heart, she couldn't stay back there with him. For her daughters' sake she'd had to remain among the living, no matter how much she might want to wallow in the pain. To surround herself with memories of what they'd had and mourn him forever.

Leaving Max behind had been easier for her, since they'd not been together for that long. It had been harder for the twins. He'd been the only man they'd grown to know, not that they'd really known *him* in any meaningful way. They'd only seen the nice side of Max. The funny side, the tender side. But the man who'd mentioned wanting to leave his options open had been a total stranger. Sari thought back on that moment with a shiver. Talk about callous…

Her girls had seen the rosy picture, whereas Sari had been forced to face the reality. The cold, hard facts. That she and the girls hadn't meant nearly as much to him as she'd thought. And then trying to explain to them that he was never coming back… It had been hard. It was why Evie still got emotional even six months after the breakup.

Had it only been six months? It seemed so much longer. But now was not the time to dwell on that, especially since she'd agreed to go to coffee with Eoin. But at least her daughters would be nowhere around this time. If she ever dated again, she would leave Evie and Hannah out of the equation until she was very sure of the person she was seeing. That had been her biggest mistake with Max. But she wasn't that naive any longer.

Was she sure of that?

Ten minutes later they were in a quaint coffee shop that offered a choice of tables, either on the sidewalk, reminiscent of a French café, or in a covered patio around back. That was what she'd chosen, maybe because she hadn't wanted to risk anyone she knew passing by and seeing her there with him.

Not that she knew all that many people. Sari tended to keep to herself more than she had when David had been alive. He'd been an extrovert, never meeting a stranger. He'd been funny and charming and so very good at making people feel special. Whether it was her or some stranger off the street. Sari had always joked that without him, she'd probably wind up a hermit.

Except she hadn't. Their daughters had prevented her from hiding in a cave somewhere, mourning his loss forever. And surprisingly, she'd met some great people along the way. And she now worked with some amazing women who were as passionate about midwifery as she was.

Stirring creamer into her coffee, she looked at the doctor across from her. "I don't know how you do what you do, Eoin."

"How I do what?"

"Treat people who don't have happy outcomes."

His brows went up. "You can't guarantee those outcomes for anyone. Even at Grandview."

"True. I guess I should have said *people who are in crisis*. Do you lose a patient every day?" Once she'd said the words, she realized how cold they might have sounded. Those women were people, dealing with very real losses. But she didn't know how to take back the question.

"Not every day, no," he said. "But enough that it's hard to walk into that operating room when you're pretty sure it's not going to be a win/win situation, when you're faced with a molar pregnancy or birth defects that are incompatible with life."

She'd never faced a molar pregnancy before, where instead of a placenta, the egg and sperm produced a mass of fluid-filled cysts.

If there was an embryo in there, it couldn't survive. Sari couldn't imagine going to a doctor after having a positive pregnancy test, only to learn that not only were you *not* having a baby but that if you didn't get treatment immediately, you could very well die.

"What made you want to go into that field?"

"Obstetrics?"

"Not that so much. But taking on risky pregnancies."

"I don't know, really. Once I learned I couldn't..." He shook his head. "I think I liked the idea that I might be able to take something where the odds seem insurmountable and prove the world wrong."

"Except you can't always do that, can you?" She knew that well enough with her husband, who had remained in a coma for almost three weeks before finally succumbing to multiple-organ failure from an illness that had turned into sepsis. She'd prayed that, no matter what the doctors had said, he might beat the odds. But he hadn't. And it didn't give her a lot of faith in trying to win anything when the odds were stacked against her. Like fighting for her relationship with Max?

No, that had been an unwinnable situation. Like the ones Eoin said he faced on a daily basis. And fighting for someone who had no interest in staying? It would have only prolonged the inevitable and ended in disaster for everyone. Including Max. Including her children.

"No. You can't," Eoin said.

"And you don't regret choosing to specialize in at-risk pregnancies?" she asked. "Would you go back and change where you practice if you could?"

"There are times when I wish I had." He seemed to think for a minute before continuing. "But then there's that one baby who pulls through against all odds. Or that mom on life support that fights her way back to her family."

David had tried to fight, early on. Until the illness had consumed everything in its path. Wow, why was she thinking so much about this all of a sudden? The twins had been just three months old when he'd died. They had no memory of their dad outside of pictures, and to them that was all they were. Just images that had no real meaning to their young eyes.

Sari mulled over Eoin's response. "And

having one win for every twenty patients makes it worthwhile?"

He gave her a slight smile. "No. Not always. Not today. But tomorrow I might have a different answer. And that's what I have to keep thinking. That there are days when it really is worth it. Those are what keep me holding on, that keep me from throwing in the towel and walking away from it all."

"And those are the people who need you. *Really* need you." Her words were soft. She wasn't thinking of those critical patients, she was thinking of Janie. Janie, who hadn't been so much on the verge of death as she had been on the verge of losing it emotionally. Then Eoin had entered the picture with his soft words and calm manner and had brought her back from the brink and given her the strength to keep on trying, to roll onto her knees and trust what he'd said. It might not have seemed like much to anyone else, but to that patient it had meant everything. And she had a healthy baby to show for it.

"Sometimes I wonder."

Sari reached out and touched his hand. "Don't. Don't wonder. Believe it. You made a huge difference to Janie. And sometimes those 'wins' keep us going even when things seem bleak. When the going is so tough you're not sure you can go on one more day."

Was she talking to herself or to him?

Whatever it was, it must have resonated because his fingers captured hers and squeezed tight. "I needed to hear that today," he said. "More than you think."

His thumb trailed across the top of her hand, making tiny flames dance along her nerve endings. For several seconds she didn't move. Couldn't think.

Her eyes sought his and found that the blue was swirling with darker undertones that seemed to capture her. Draw her in.

Sari hadn't felt this strange sense of inevitability in a long, long time.

She only knew that she didn't want to move her hand away from his. Several seconds went by, and when she blinked they were both closer than they'd been seconds earlier.

How had that happened? If she leaned in another couple of inches she could very gently put her lips—

"Saraia Jones?"

The loud voice that came from somewhere over her head made her jerk back in her seat.

She looked up, halfway expecting to see a fiery figure emerge from the heavens asking what exactly she thought she was doing. But the only figure was a young man in an apron bearing the logo Grounded by Joe, the name of the coffee shop, whose owner was coincidentally named… Joe.

"Yes, I'm Saraia Jones."

"You're needed back at some birthing center." The man's glance went to her midsection as if expecting to see some kind of sign of pregnancy. Her face burned, especially after what she'd just been thinking about.

She reached in her pocket to feel for her phone, but there was nothing there. Oh God, what had she done with it?

"Okay, thank you. I'll go right now." Her glance went to Eoin, who was now sitting back in his seat, an inscrutable expression on his face. No sign of what she'd thought she'd seen in his eyes seconds earlier.

God! She'd probably imagined the whole thing. The burning in her face grew until she was sure it would burst into flames. Sari jerked her hand away and lurched to her feet, hoping beyond hope that she wouldn't have to walk beside him all the way back to Grandview.

"I'll follow you back in a few minutes." His voice was as cool as it had ever been.

Okay, well, evidently he was not as anxious to remain in her company as she was to stay in his. And somehow that was even worse because all she could hear was Max's voice as he'd said he'd wanted them to keep their options open.

"All right, sounds good." Maybe it really had been God telling her to wake the hell up. She'd known the man less than a week, and she was pretty sure if he'd tried to kiss her, she would have been a more than enthusiastic participant. And that scared her on a deeper level. Because it had been *her* who had been thinking of kissing him.

Thank God that hadn't happened. She didn't see how she'd be able to face him again if he'd reeled back in shock and dismay. Instead she reeled back—in dismay at her thoughts a few minutes ago.

Somehow she was able to walk out of the coffee shop on legs that were shaking—almost as much as her confidence in her ability to maintain a celibate lifestyle. Because the moment he'd stroked her hand, the moment he'd given her that look…celibacy had been the furthest thing from her mind.

Had she been crazy to think he'd felt the same thing?

But sex and relationships weren't synonymous, right? If she slept with a man, she wasn't bound to him for life—or until he wanted more options—right? Maybe she'd been looking at this thing all wrong. Max had been a pretty good vaccine when it came to repeating the same mistakes.

So what if she slept with someone? Maybe it would even be good for her.

Oh, no. It would not be good—if she was thinking in terms of Eoin. Oh, it might be *good* as far as the sex went. She was pretty sure it would be, in fact. But for some reason she was almost certain she'd have a hard time keeping her heart out of it if she went that route, and she wasn't sure why that was.

Because he was an attractive man? Maybe. Because she'd seen a vulnerable side to him that she hadn't expected to see when he'd talked about losing that baby? Yes, that was exactly it. His pain had been evident, if only for a few brief seconds. But it had been long enough that she was going to have a hard time banishing it from her thoughts.

But if she couldn't separate the two, then she had no business thinking about him in any way other than as a work colleague. She certainly shouldn't be imagining having sex with the man. She had a feeling he was no more interested in being in a relationship than she was. Although maybe he was already in one.

With the way his thumb had trailed over her skin? Not hardly. She might not have known him well, but she sensed he was not someone who would step out on a wife or girlfriend.

While that should have given her some comfort, it didn't. Because a taken Eoin was a whole lot safer than an available one.

The sudden spring in her step put paid to any such thoughts. Because the man *had* touched her. And that meant she might not have been imagining those molten glances he'd sent her way. And for some reason, it gave her a boost of confidence that had been lacking ever since Max had walked out of her life.

And that couldn't be a bad thing. Yes, she

was going to choose to look at it in a positive light. A man like Eoin might've been attracted to her. And she was attracted to him. As long as she didn't do anything about it, she could at least enjoy the fantasy of it. And boy, that fantasy promised to be almost as good as the reality of it. A very sexy reality if looks were any indication.

A few minutes later when she entered Grandview, Heidi caught her inside. "I've been trying to call your cell. So has the school."

"School? I thought I had my phone with me, but it must be in my jacket. Wait. Did you say school?"

"Yes. It's Evie," Heidi said. "The preschool tried to reach you, and when they couldn't they called here. She fell off some playground equipment and bumped her head pretty hard. They've taken her to the hospital."

"To the hospital?" Sheer panic gripped Sari, and she could only repeat the words back to her friend.

In a daze she realized Eoin had come in during the last part of their conversation. "Come on. I'll take you." He glanced at Heidi. "Which hospital?"

"Portland Lakes."

She heard the words. They clanged through her head again and again. Evie had fallen. Her baby. And now she was at Portland.

Oh, God! Please not again.

Minutes later, she was in Eoin's car and they were headed to the hospital where he worked.

By the time they arrived, more than her legs were shaking.

Was God punishing her for her earlier thoughts?

Stop it, Sari! she told herself. *None of that is important. The only thing that matters is Evie.*

Eoin pulled up to the emergency entrance and told her to go in while he parked the car. This was what it would've been like if David were still alive. He would've told her what to do and stood beside her.

But this wasn't David. And she didn't need anyone to stand with her. She'd been doing this alone for a very long time. With that thought in mind, she clicked off her seat belt, opened the door and, without a backward glance, got out of the car.

CHAPTER FOUR

Saraia's face was closed off by the time Eoin got inside. No sign of the fear or uncertainty that he'd seen back at Grandview.

"How is she?" he asked.

"I don't know. They said she's undergoing an MRI. A doctor is supposed to be out any minute to talk to me."

An MRI. This wasn't just a little bump on the head, then. "I'll wait with you," he said.

"You don't have to." Her words were quiet, but there was a flicker across the still planes of her face that he recognized from countless numbers of his patients. Fear.

There was no way he was going to let her go through this alone. Except maybe there was someone else she wanted here.

"It's okay—I want to." Well, he might not have wanted to, but he sure as hell was not going to leave her here by herself. "Is there someone I can call? A significant other? Evie's father?"

She gave him this look. This strange, pained expression that made him feel like he had missed something important. Knowing him, he probably had.

"Her father is dead," she said. "He died in this very hospital."

Shock held Eoin still for a minute, then formed a ball of unexpected emotion that he forced himself to swallow down. He'd assumed she was divorced.

"I'm sorry, Sari—I had no idea." He gripped her hand. "Come sit down."

He'd lagged behind her at the coffee shop because her words about people needing him had whispered to a place deep inside of him that he'd thought he'd cemented shut after breaking up with Lucy. He'd looked at Sari, and suddenly all he'd wanted to do was tug her toward himself. And do what? Kiss her?

He wasn't sure.

When that employee had come up and told her she was needed at the clinic, whatever spell that had been woven around them had broken, and he'd been glad she'd been called away. *Glad!*

And that probably damned him to a very special place in hell.

They sat in hard plastic chairs that were easy to sanitize but did nothing to provide any comfort to families waiting to hear news of any kind.

Like Saraia when she'd gotten the news that the twins' father had died?

He wrapped his arm around her in an attempt to do what the chairs could not. And she leaned her head against his shoulder for a second before popping up to look at him in panic. "I need to call my mother-in-law and ask her to pick up Hannah. And I don't know where my phone..."

"Use mine." The man who'd died had not only been the twins' father but Sari's husband.

Eoin placed his phone into her palm and watched as she stared at it before covering her mouth with her hand, tears dripping down her cheeks. "I can't... I don't know..."

He got it. In this day and age of just pressing a button, most people had stopped memorizing phone numbers. He took the phone back and called Grandview.

Heidi picked up immediately. "How is she?"

"No word yet," he said, "but Sari doesn't have her phone with her. Is there any way you have her list of emergency contacts there on the computer?"

"Yes, of course. Is she wanting to call Peggy?"

"Is that her mother-in-law?"

"Yes. Wait just a second..." Heidi's voice came back a second later. "Here it is..."

She rattled off a series of numbers that he typed into his phone. "Got it—thanks."

He pressed Call and handed the phone to Sari, who clutched it and put it to her ear.

A second later, she said, "No, it's me, Sari. I don't have my phone with me."

She glanced at him before continuing. "I'm okay, but Evie's been hurt. I'm at Portland Lakes. Is there any way you can pick up Hannah from preschool and take her home with you?"

Evidently Peggy said something because Sari quickly added, "No, please, just take her home. I'll call you as soon as I know something. She'll just be scared if she comes here."

Something else was said, then Sari relaxed in her seat, giving Eoin a slight smile. "Thank you so much. I'll call as soon as I know something. She's being examined right now."

She pressed the End button and handed the phone back to him. "Thanks for coming in with me."

"Not a problem." But he didn't put his arm back around her, nor did she attempt to put her head back onto his shoulder. But even without that, he felt this weird connection that he couldn't remember feeling before. Was this what it would be like to have a wife? A family?

That yearly letter slid back through his mind, and he quickly dismissed it.

Sari wasn't his wife and Evie wasn't his daughter. Even when he'd been with Lucy, he hadn't given thought to wondering about what it might be like to have children with her. Until she had started pushing. And Eoin hadn't liked the future he'd seen between them.

He wasn't sure why he was even thinking about Sari and fatherhood all of a sudden. Whatever it was, he'd better nip those thoughts in the bud before they started growing. He'd been in a vulnerable place this morning, and Sari had talked him through it. He was pretty sure that was what this was all about.

But Sari was just a colleague. A temporary one at that—because he wouldn't be at Grandview forever. Although he hadn't set a termination date on the volunteer form, he'd somehow had it in his mind that this gig would last a year at most. Until Grandview could find someone more permanent. Any physician at the birthing center would have little more than a desk job, as it didn't sound like emergencies came up all that often. And Eoin couldn't see himself doing something like that long term.

Like Sari had said, people at Portland Lakes needed him. And in all honestly, he probably needed them too, despite the heartache that all too often came with the job.

Dr. Sidle, one of the pediatric neurosurgeons at the hospital, came out. He shook hands with him, a question in the man's eyes that made Eoin tense, then he turned to Sari. "Are you Evie's mom?"

"I am. How is she?"

"We suspect a concussion, but there's no immediate evidence of a brain bleed. She's over in imaging just to make sure. And we'll want to keep her for the night just as a precaution after a fall like that. She has a pretty big goose egg on the back of her head."

Sari's eyes closed before looking at Eoin again. "I can't thank you enough for bringing me or for letting me use your phone..."

"Don't mention it." She didn't realize it, but she'd just given Sidle a plausible explanation for their being together.

Plausible? Hell, it was actually the real explanation. There was no "plausible" about it.

Sidle looked at him again, and Eoin felt the need to say, "Sari is a midwife at Grandview, where I'm volunteering."

"I see. Good thing you were there," Sidle said. He didn't ask why she hadn't driven herself here in her own car or why she didn't have her cell phone with her. And if he knew the neurosurgeon, he wouldn't ask later either. They were colleagues but not drinking buddies. And right now, Eoin was glad of it.

"When can I see her?" Sari asked.

"It'll be about a half hour or so," he said. "Once they're finished doing the MRI, we'll get her in a room. As soon as that happens, one of the nurses will come out and get you."

She stood and held out her hand. "Thank you so much."

When the doctor left, she dropped back in her seat, and Eoin said, "I'm so glad she's okay."

"Me too. I'm sorry for snapping at you when you asked about her dad. I just… When I heard she was here, my brain stopped working. I was so afraid."

"I get it," he said. "Do you want to call Peggy and tell her?"

"I need to go back and get my phone and my purse, and…"

He shook his head. "No, you don't. I'll drive back to Grandview and get them. Do you want a ride home?"

"I'll probably stay the night until she's discharged. Peggy will come and get me when we're ready." She leaned over and kissed his cheek. "Thank you for everything."

She didn't know it, but somehow she just had. That kiss made him feel warm and tight and…what was it that she'd said at the coffee shop? Needed. He'd felt needed in a way that went beyond the hospital walls.

"Do you want to go for a walk? It might be good for you to get some fresh air," he said.

"We won't go far, and I can give the nurse's station my number if they get her in a room sooner than expected."

"That would be wonderful," Sari said. "I don't know how to repay you for bringing me here. I'm not sure I was capable of driving."

"No repayment necessary. Do you want to call your mother-in-law before we go?"

"Yes—thanks."

When she ended the call, Eoin was more than ready to go out and get a breath or two of fresh air. Anything other than sit here and think about what could have happened with Evie, what could have happened between him and Sari in that coffee shop.

And yet he was about to go on a walk with her? It was just a walk.

They found themselves in the large courtyard that lay between the wings of the hospital. Two magnolias stretched high overhead providing shade to the benches below. They wouldn't bloom for several more months, but they were still beautiful.

"Do you want to walk?" Eoin asked. "Or sit?"

"Could we walk, please?" she said. "I'm not

sure sitting still out here would be any better than being in the hospital."

"Of course."

A stone pathway wound its way between flower beds that were awash with color, and before Eoin could think of something to say, Sari glanced up at him. "I can't imagine losing one of my girls, I'm not sure I could..." Her voice trailed away.

Was this what being a parent would be like? That clawing fear of losing someone. He'd seen his own parents overcome with emotion more times than he cared to remember when he'd been going through his own treatments. Eoin had carried such guilt over putting them through everything, and yet he knew it hadn't been his fault. They'd told him that every time they'd had to rush to the hospital and he'd whispered how sorry he was. In the end, it had bound them closer together, and although they now lived in Florida, they talked on the phone at least once a week and his parents traveled to Charleston most Christmases.

He reached down and gripped Sari's hand. "She's going to be fine—you heard the doctor."

"I know," she said. "The thoughts just race through my head, and I can't seem to stop them. Maybe I pushed them too hard to try new things, to be adventurous. Maybe I—"

Threading his fingers through hers, Eoin gave her a soft squeeze. "Stop. It was an accident. Nothing you did caused this. Kids get hurt, no matter how hard you try to shield them."

This time, she smiled up at him. "Thanks. And a lot of it is just the fear of the unknown."

"I get it," he said. "I'm not a parent, but I've seen it with my own folks."

"I think we all must go through that. I'm pretty sure even after we grow up, our parents don't lose that fear."

Eoin wasn't a parent and might never be one. It was something he was careful not to talk about with his own mom and dad. He was sure they would've loved to be grandparents, but unlike Lucy they'd never asked about his banked sperm or what he intended to do. At this point, they'd probably given up hope of him actually becoming a father.

"I'm sure when you're a single parent it's even harder," Eoin continued. "How long ago did you lose him?"

He didn't say who he was talking about, and he wasn't sure why he'd even brought it up, other than the shock of hearing that she'd lost her husband.

"David died when the girls were just three months old," she said.

"And you've been doing this alone ever since."

Sari looked up at him, her eyes soft. "Sometimes. But it's surprising how often people step up to help, even when they don't know about David."

Was she talking about him? Hell, he hadn't done anything other than bring her to the hospital. But he had stayed, even when a voice inside of him had been telling him to leave.

Because of what had happened in the coffee shop?

Yes. It would have just been a kiss. Nothing more than what she'd given him on the cheek in the hospital.

Seriously? Because what he'd wanted to do went way beyond that. Way beyond the meeting of two sets of lips. And that scared the hell out of him.

"There are a lot of people who care about

you, from what I've seen," he said. "Heidi. The other midwives. Your mother-in-law."

He left out himself because even the thought of including himself in that contingent was enough to make him want to turn around and walk away. But how could you meet someone like Sari and not care about her? He'd cared about plenty of his patients. All of them, if he really sat down and thought about it.

And maybe this was part of the reason he'd been drawn to her. Maybe he'd sensed something in her that said there was more to her than the cool, competent midwife he'd seen his first day at Grandview.

"I know a lot of good people," she said.

"Yes, you do."

They walked in silence for several more minutes before she stopped and faced him, letting go of his hand. "I just want to say thank-you. Not just for now, but for coming to Grandview, even when you weren't so sure about us."

He smiled. "I wasn't. But I think you're in the process of convincing me."

"Am I?"

There it was again. That softness that beckoned him to move closer to her, to take her into his arms and hold her close. But he wasn't going to. Not because of her words that he knew had been said half in jest, but because of how those words made him feel. Like he wanted her to convince him of a lot of other things. Things he had no business thinking about. Especially at a time like then when Sari's daughter lay in a hospital bed.

So he tried to put some mental separation between them. "All of you are," he said. "And you should be proud of the work you all do at Grandview."

She gave a slight frown. "We are. It's a great team."

This time she didn't say how glad she was that Eoin was part of that team, and he was glad. He needed to put a little distance between his emotions and Sari. Because they were becoming a little too convoluted.

Or did he mean complicated?

It didn't matter. All he knew was that he did not need to put himself in a position where he would have a hard time letting go when the time came. And he had a feeling it might prove a little more difficult than he wanted to believe.

So he needed to make a conscious effort to keep things professional, to keep his work life and his personal life separate before he—

His phone buzzed, and he looked down at it. It was the number to the hospital. "Hello?"

He glanced at Sari as the nurse relayed the message that Evie was now in a room and she could go see her. "Okay, thanks."

"Evie's all set. She's in room 321."

She nodded. "Thank you again, for staying with me. I really do appreciate it. But I'm good."

"Are you sure?"

"I am," she said. "And Peggy will come get me in the morning."

"Okay, I'll run back to Grandview and get your phone," Eoin offered. "Please tell Evie I said hi."

She didn't respond, but then again he hadn't expected her to. Maybe by the time he got back, he'd be able to get his head together and stop thinking thoughts that shouldn't even be on the horizon. At least not on his horizon.

Eoin came back with Sari's purse and her phone about a half hour later, but instead of coming up to the room, he'd thankfully waited for her at the nurse's station. And when she got there, he barely said ten words to her beyond asking how Evie was doing and if Sari was sure they didn't need a ride when she got discharged.

When she said she had it all figured out, he left it at that and headed up the elevator of the hospital, probably going to wherever his office was located. Compared to the behemoth that was Portland Lakes, Grandview was a tiny speck on the map when it came to hospitals and clinics.

Sari remembered the feeling of being lost when David had been here. She could never seem to locate his room, and when she had, the sheer number of machines keeping him alive had boggled her mind.

In the end, they hadn't kept him alive, though. His body had been weary and so, so sick, and it had finally signaled that it had been done fighting. She'd been one of the fortunate ones who hadn't needed to decide when enough was enough. His heart had stopped in the middle of the night, in spite of the work of the ventilator, in spite of the crazy number of tubes and IVs huddled around his bed.

She remembered squeezing his hand and telling him that she loved him before she'd sent him off to whatever the next step had been in his journey. His babies had been right there beside her, the way they'd been for all those days and nights of uncertainty.

At least she wasn't sending one of her daughters off to that unknown place. Evie was okay. She'd been lucky, everyone told Sari. Yes, she had been. But so had Hannah and Sari and Peggy. To lose someone else would have been unimaginable.

One thing she wasn't going to do was tell Evie that Eoin had said hi. She didn't want to see a sheen of excitement in her girl's eyes over a man ever again. At least not one who was only in their lives temporarily and as nothing more than her work colleague.

By the time she got back to Evie's room, her daughter was awake, hands going to the big white bandage around her head. When her daughter smiled at her, Sari lost it, tears she'd been holding back for the last hour pouring from her eyes.

"Mommy? What's wrong?"

"I'm just so happy to see you, baby." She went to the chair beside the bed and perched in it as close as she could get to her daughter. "Does your head hurt a lot?"

"Not anymore. They gave me a shot with a needle that was this long..." Evie held her hands as far apart as they would go.

It was then that Sari truly believed her daughter would be okay. It was such an Evie thing to exaggerate and make a molehill into a Mount Everest.

"Where's Grammy and Hannah?" she asked.

"They're at home," Sari said. "But I'll call them and tell them how big that needle was."

"Aren't they coming to the hospital to see me?"

She gripped her daughter's hand. "I think it might scare Hannah and Grammy to see you in here." She didn't want to say that Peggy might have a hard time facing this hospital after losing her son here, even after all these years. "But they'll come pick us up tomorrow morning, okay? Hannah is excited that she'll have to miss a day of preschool. And if you're up to it, we'll get some ice cream on the way home."

Evie drew a deep breath and let it out in a

sigh before yawning. "Can I have the chocolate swirlie thing?"

"Of course. It's what you always get." She drew her daughter's hand to her mouth and kissed it. "You get some rest, and I'll be right here when you wake up, okay?"

"Okay. I love you, Mommy."

Out of the corner of Sari's eyes, something moved in the doorway. She turned to look and was just in time to see someone turning away from the room and walking away.

She could have sworn from the hair that it had been Eoin, but she'd been sure from the way he'd left her standing at the nurse's desk that he'd been on his way somewhere else. Maybe it hadn't been him, maybe it had been someone who'd simply had the wrong room. But she replayed the scene in her head over and over again as her daughter slept in the bed beside her chair. If it had been Eoin, maybe he simply hadn't wanted to interrupt them.

In the end it didn't matter who it had been. Because Evie was alive and she was safe. And Sari wouldn't take that for granted ever again.

Eoin couldn't get the picture of Sari kissing her daughter's hand out of his head. He'd gone up to his office, then on impulse had descended back to where the pediatrics wing was located and stopped by the room to check in and see how things were going. He'd been just in time to see the emotional scene. His eyes had burned, and he'd turned away, deciding then had not been a good time to stop in for a chat. Or anything else. Because the scene had threatened to draw him in, to make him a part of it when he wasn't.

The shock of learning that Sari's husband had died at Eoin's hospital had nearly unraveled him, especially after finding out how young his daughters had been. Eoin could only imagine how it felt for her to walk back through those doors. But she'd done it. Not that she'd had a choice.

The fact that she loved her daughters fiercely had never been more obvious. And raising them alone? People did it all the time, so why was this any different?

Eoin didn't know. All he knew was that when he'd stood in that doorway, he'd wanted to help her in some way. A way that went far beyond just walking with her in the hospital courtyard. He'd wanted to relieve her of a tiny amount of her burden. But why? He knew her from work.

It's called compassion, Mulvey. Nothing more.

A couple of hours went by before he got up the courage to go back to the room and look in on them. He'd hoped to find Sari asleep in the chair, but no such luck. The second he appeared in the doorway, she turned to look, her mouth forming an O shape as if surprised by something.

"It was you before."

The whispered words barely reached him.

Hell, so she had seen him. Had she seen his reaction too? He hoped not.

He kept his voice low so as not to wake Evie up. The quiet snoring sounds from her bed made him smile and wonder if Evie's mother sounded like that too. He quickly shook the thought off. "I did peek in earlier just to see if you needed anything," he said, "but you were talking, and I didn't want to disturb you guys. She's still doing okay?"

Sari shook her head, her smile big and wondrous. "She's… Evie. I've never been so happy to hear someone laugh."

"I can imagine." And he could. Not as a parent, but he'd witnessed his own mom and dad's heartache when he'd been diagnosed and treated for his cancer. And he'd witnessed other people's pain, had seen it in Sari's eyes when she'd told him that Evie's father was dead. "Is there anything you need?"

"No. Are you not working today?"

"I have some paperwork to do. Nothing that can't wait." It was a little white lie, but he somehow didn't want to leave the hospital knowing she was sitting in vigil beside her daughter's bed, so he'd put it off.

"Do you want to...sit with us for a while?"

He hadn't expected the question. In fact, he wasn't quite sure Sari had meant to ask it, wasn't quite sure how to answer. He went back to his earlier thoughts about wanting to relieve her of a tiny bit of her burden.

She quickly said, "You don't have to. Please don't feel—"

The strain in her voice made up his mind. "No, of course I'll sit with you. Like I said, I don't have anything pressing right now." He doubted anyone would, since they'd expected him to be long home by now. He didn't want to leave. But he wasn't sure how smart it was to stay. "Do you want me to bring you a coffee?"

"That would be wonderful—thank you."

"Cream and sugar, right?"

Her brows went up as if surprised. "Yes."

"I'll be right back."

Taking the elevator to his office, where his coffee maker was, Eoin made two cups of coffee, adding cream and sugar to hers and leaving his black. While going through the motions, he quickly worked out two things. First of all, he was doing something any colleague might do: sit with a friend who was going through a hard time. And secondly, he wasn't sure he was cut out to be a father. Oh, bringing kids into the world, he was all about that. But he always handed them off to someone else to care for. To find out your child could have died during an accident on the playground?

Judging from his visceral reaction to seeing Evie lying on that bed—a girl he'd only met one time in his life—he could only imagine what he would have done had she been his. He'd have broken down completely.

Was that so wrong? He thought for a minute. Maybe not for someone else, but Eoin had always kept a tight rein on his emotions. He'd learned to as he'd gone through his treatment for cancer. He'd always felt he had to be strong for his mom and dad. He'd smiled his way through chemo, even while inside he'd been so terrified that he was going to die. When he'd been so sick he could barely lift his head but had somehow managed to do just that so that he wouldn't scare his parents.

Which was why when he'd lost that baby this morning and then had to talk about it with Sari, he'd felt a vulnerability he didn't often show to the world. It felt alien—almost wrong, somehow. And then right on the heels of that he'd heard about Evie's accident and watched as Sari had cried silent tears over her daughter's bed. It was too hard.

Other people could evidently cope with letting their feelings out, but he couldn't. Because he'd always been the strong one.

And having a kid? He was certain his facade would crack and fall off in chunks, leaving the real him exposed to the world. He was pretty sure that moms and dads had to be even stronger than he'd been as a young man who'd been faced with his own mortality. He'd kept it together. Then. For his family.

Locking those thoughts behind the door of his office, Eoin headed back down the elevator with both mugs in his hands. When he reached the door of Evie's room again, he went through and started to hand Sari her coffee before stopping mid reach. Her head was thrown back against the chair, her hand still clutching her daughter's. But her eyes were closed, and there, in soft quiet tones, were the echoes of her daughter's snuffling snores. Only they weren't from Evie this time.

He smiled, and the weight and heaviness of his thoughts seemed to fall away as he sat back down in his seat and enjoyed the guilty pleasure of listening to them both. Like mother, like daughter. He was sure that Sari would be horrified to know he'd just discovered the answer to one of his questions. Saraia Jones, midwife extraordinaire, did indeed snore.

Eoin was gone when Sari woke up to sunlight pouring into the window of Evie's hospital room. In fact, she couldn't remember him coming back with her coffee, for which she was mortified. There was no sign of the coffee or of him. But he'd left a simple note, and she smiled when she read it.

Call if you need something. I'll be around.
E.M.

And that was it. But it was enough. She appreciated everything he'd done during her crisis. Although hopefully he hadn't stuck around and watched her sleep because she was pretty sure her mouth had been hanging wide open when she'd woken up.

And Evie had a roaring headache today but still wanted the ice cream Sari had promised her. Her daughter seemed no worse for wear, otherwise, after her tumble off the playground equipment. And the doctors said after two or three days she could go back to preschool, which had surprised Sari. For some reason she'd thought it would be longer...or maybe she'd just hoped to be able to sit with her daughter at home and prove to herself that Evie really was okay.

At that moment, Peggy peeked in the room followed by Hannah. "How are we doing?"

Hannah rushed over to hug her, clinging to her hand, while Evie squealed.

"Grammy! Mom said we could go get some ice cream, 'cause of the fact my head hurts."

Sari's mother-in-law gave her a quick look that spoke of worry.

She shook her head. "Just a headache. The tests don't indicate anything other than a mild concussion. They said her head would probably hurt for the next day or two."

"Thank God."

"About the ice cream. You don't have to—"

"Nonsense," Peggy went over and kissed Evie's head. "If my granddaughter wants ice cream, ice cream she'll get."

That made Sari smile. David's mother had been so wonderful to them, even though the girls had to be a constant reminder that she'd lost her son. But on the other hand, they were all that remained of David. And while she could have been clinging and controlling, she never had been. She'd been a source of wisdom when Sari had asked for advice. But she'd also never pushed her opinion onto Sari, for which she was grateful.

"Okay, but we won't stay long."

Peggy smiled and gave her a quick hug. "We'll take as long as you need."

Raw emotion swept over Sari and her eyes

prickled in warning, but somehow she kept the tears from spilling over. But her voice did break as she said thank-you.

Fortunately, her mother-in-law acted like she hadn't even heard it. She just helped her gather her daughter's paperwork and held her hand out for Hannah, while Evie clutched her mom's hand.

They chose a shop about twenty minutes from the hospital and one of her daughters' favorite ice cream places. Stepping out of the car, the humidity of Charleston encased them in a moist hug that wouldn't let go. Going into the air-conditioned shop was a relief.

Located not too far from one of the local beaches, Beverly's Cream and Gelato boasted white clapboard siding. Colorful caladiums and flowers spilled from two window boxes that flanked a white door, and café-style tables sat on the sidewalk for those willing to brave the heat of the day. Today, Sari was thankful for the tables that lined the walls inside the establishment.

They ordered sundaes for the girls, and Sari got a simple vanilla milkshake. Peggy opted for her favorite blackberry gelato. Finding their seats, they slid into the booths with the girls in the inside.

Peggy reached across and squeezed Sari's hand. "She's going to be okay, you know. I'm just sorry you were there by yourself until this morning. I would have come up last night."

"Eoin stayed with me until Evie was settled into her room," she said.

Hearing her name, her daughter piped up. "I didn't get to say goodbye to him."

Sari smiled. "Because you were asleep, silly."

But something in her regretted that she hadn't been awake when he'd returned with her coffee. Because she, too, would have liked to have said goodbye.

"Eoin...?" Peggy asked.

"The doctor that Grandview hired."

"I remember you telling me about him. But I think you used his title."

Sari felt her face flush, even though there was no reason to feel guilty. Peggy had heard her call all of her colleagues by their first names plenty of times.

"I probably did."

Her mother-in-law's head tilted, and she

studied her for a moment. "Well, I'm glad he was there for you."

Evie spoke up. "He colored with us at the clinic. He's super nice."

"Super nice," Hannah repeated.

"Yes, he is." Sari's face heated even more. Why did it sound like they were all infatuated with him? She wasn't. At all.

And that little scene at the coffee shop?

What scene? Nothing had happened. Nor was it likely to. She'd simply felt badly for what had happened to his patient.

Really, Sari?

Yes, really.

"I can tell." Peggy gave a quick laugh. "You need to get out more, Sari. In some ways I feel like you closed yourself off after everything that happened with..." She lowered her voice to a whisper and leaned closer. "Max."

Sari glanced sharply at Evie to make sure she hadn't heard. But her daughter was happily chattering with Hannah about the hospital and the "tube" ride she'd had to go in.

"Can you blame me? I have them to worry about." She tilted her head toward the girls to indicate who she was talking about. "I have one who is still grieving that loss."

She immediately regretted her choice of words, since Peggy carried a grief even greater than the loss of a relationship. She'd lost her son. Sari squeezed the fingers that still gripped hers. "I'm sorry. That didn't come out the way I wanted it to."

"Oh, honey, it's okay," Peggy said. "And more than anything, David would want you to be happy. It might not have happened with that last…guy. But some day the right one will come along."

Sari wasn't so sure. She no longer allowed herself to think along those lines. Not because of David, who Peggy was right about. He wouldn't want her to hold on to his memory and stop living. And realistically, she couldn't. She had his daughters to raise.

"Well, so far he hasn't," she said. "So I'm not going to worry about anything other than getting Evie home and making sure she's okay."

"Please don't let what I said upset you." Peggy glanced past her. "And it looks like they may be about ready."

"I'm not upset. I'm grateful for you each and every day." Sari gave her a smile that she hoped took any sting out of her earlier words.

She knew Peggy meant well and that the selflessness that it took to want her daughter-in-law to be happy with someone other than her son was probably a rare quality. One that she treasured.

They left the shop, and the ride home was filled with talk that had nothing to do with relationships and everything to do with the girls and their preschool activities. Sari tried to relax in her seat, but a thought kept breaking through.

What would Peggy think if she knew that Sari had almost kissed a man she barely knew? She'd probably be ecstatic, since as she'd said, David wouldn't want her to sit around and mourn him forever. Although sometimes Sari thought that might be the wisest course. Dating Max and then breaking up with him hadn't been the easiest thing to do, and there was no guarantee that the same thing wouldn't happen the next time and the next and the next. And then there was Evie's response to Max walking away from them. She'd been traumatized for months.

But Sari wasn't going to worry about any of that. She was going to go back to work tomorrow, and on Eoin's next day at the clinic, she was going to treat him like a colleague and nothing more. She was pretty sure he didn't want more than that either. Yes, they'd held hands after he'd shared with her about the loss of that preemie during the cesarean section. And again in the hospital courtyard. They'd each been hurting, although for different reasons. People often turned to someone for support during difficult times, didn't they? It was also the reason she'd asked him to sit with them when Evie had lain in that hospital bed. So they'd both reached out to whoever had been nearby for comfort. It had just happened to be each other.

It was an easy enough thing to understand and didn't mean anything. Which was a relief. Because despite her earlier thoughts about sex, the last thing she needed was a messy fling or anything else from someone who she wasn't even sure shared her values about midwifery and natural childbirth.

So with that thought in mind, she was going to concentrate on getting home, where she could put all of her foolish thoughts to rest once and for all. From here on out, she was going to jump back onto the train of professionalism—and make sure that train clung to the tracks like its life depended on it.

CHAPTER FIVE

SARI HADN'T CALLED HIM. He hadn't really expected her to, and a part of him was glad. And yet he'd wanted to know how Evie was doing. Her daughters had gotten under his skin. They were cute and outgoing and weren't afraid to speak their minds. They reminded him of their mama.

He'd had a few days to think about their interactions, both at the café and later at the hospital. He decided to chalk it up to the stress they'd both been under. It was probably a normal thing when you started working with someone attractive to wonder what they were like in other ways.

Other ways? Seriously, Mulvey, are you twelve?

And then to learn that her husband had died at Portland Lakes had been a blow. The temptation had been there to ask someone about it, but that would be violating HIPAA rules. Besides, it was none of his business. None.

So, after some deliberation, he decided to do…nothing. And today he was due in the clinic in a half hour. More and more he was thinking that volunteering there had been a mistake.

No, not a mistake. Maybe he'd needed this time in a labor-and-delivery center where patients were screened to avoid as many surprises as he encountered. For a while now he'd felt like his job involved running headlong into a hurricane and doing his best to snatch people out alive. And when he finished one day, he woke up the next and did it all over again.

At the birthing center, he could slow down and maybe enjoy the process. If they let him into the room. That had been a shock to find out that they wanted more of a desk jockey than a real doctor. But maybe they'd made that clear to his hospital administrator and the man hadn't relayed their expectations. Although Eoin had been glad to be there for Janie's delivery.

Walking through the clinic doors, he spotted Heidi and Saraia along with another woman who was wearing scrubs that sported tiny diapers all over them. They were all looking down at something. Heidi and the other woman both looked up when he drew near and smiled.

The woman in scrubs came over to him and held out her hand. He grasped it and let go.

"You must be Dr. Mulvey. I'm Miranda Brady. Sorry I haven't gotten to greet you yet. I ended up helping with a home birth your first day here that took longer than expected and didn't make it in. I heard you helped Sari with Janie Magee's delivery, though. Thanks for that."

Evidently here at Grandview they were a little looser with patient information. Although since it was a much smaller, more specialized clinic, the midwives probably saw most of the patients at some point or other.

"I have no doubt that Saraia would have handled it just fine, had I not been here," Eoin said.

Miranda tilted her head. "Sari thinks differently—said you swooped in and saved the day."

This time Saraia's head popped up, eyes wide. "I didn't quite put it like that."

The other midwife laughed. "It's called dramatic license, Sari. Anyway, she said you were a 'big help.'" She surrounded the last two words with air quotes and turned and eyed the other woman. "Better?"

Color flared in Saraia's cheeks, something he'd noticed happened whenever she seemed flustered. He liked that characteristic. And the way her silky dark hair accentuated her delicate features.

Her twins had her dark hair as well.

And why was he even thinking about that? Time to move to a different subject. "How's she doing? Janie, that is."

Okay, now it sounded like he was avoiding asking about Evie, and that wasn't what he'd wanted. He'd meant to come in and ask Saraia about it right away but had gotten sidetracked.

"Did you see the picture she brought in?" Miranda went over to their huge corkboard and pointed to the snapshot. "They're doing great. And she got in with her pediatrician for an early appointment this morning and let us know that there was no sign of nerve damage from the shoulder dystocia."

"Good to hear." This time he looked at Sari, who was looking everywhere but at him. She seemed as ill at ease as he did. But he had to push through it, or this arrangement was not going to work. "How is Evie doing?"

"She's fine. My mother-in-law is keeping them home today, just in case, even though the doctor cleared her to go back to preschool."

"Already?" Eoin's brows went up, but he wasn't about to question the pediatrician's advice. "I'm sure she'll enjoy her day with Peggy."

Miranda's eyes swiveled back to him. "You've met Peggy?"

This time Heidi piped up. "Sari went to the hospital and forgot her phone, so she had to call her using Eoin's phone."

"Dr. Mulvey was there with you? At the hospital?"

"Call me Eoin—everyone does." He smiled. "I offered to take her since she had no idea how badly injured her daughter was."

Saraia dragged fingers through her hair, and he watched it sift back into place, every lock looking soft and touchable. "I was in shock. And Heidi needed to stay here at the clinic."

"I get it," Miranda said. "At least now. Sari just left out a whole swath of the story."

Had she? Why? It wasn't like they'd been on a date or anything. It had been an emergency situation. Eoin decided another change of subject was a good idea.

"What were you looking at when I came in?"

Miranda turned a sheet of paper to face him. "Our schedule for the week. We normally have patient appointments on Monday through Thursday. Fridays we try to keep the schedule a little lighter so we can rotate Fridays off and each get a long weekend once a month." She fixed him with a glance. "Have you sat in on any appointments yet?"

"No, not yet." He shot Sari a look. Which she deftly avoided.

"Dr. Eric didn't sit in on appointments," Miranda said, "but he'd been here for a few years. I'm sure he probably did initially to see how we handled things."

Saraia spoke up. "I did mention doing that for the first couple of weeks. But it kind of slipped my mind since we normally do them on our own." She glanced his way. "Sorry about that."

He gave her a slow smile. Somehow he didn't think she'd forgotten. She'd been pretty prickly about her patients that first day. But he thought he could see why. Maybe some ob-gyns would come in and try to take charge, since it was what they normally did at the hospital. They had the last say in almost everything. Which was different from how things worked here. And maybe that was a good thing. Maybe these patients didn't need an authority figure stepping in for a few minutes and then leaving until it was time to catch the baby. Maybe these women wanted more of a partner and found that in these midwives.

"We can check with our patients, to be sure, but the majority should be fine with having you in there. If that's something you want to do," Miranda said. "Dr. Eric knew how things ran and chose to sit out appointments. It's a system that worked for us. But if you come on board for longer you'll have to decide what part you want to play in the clinic. I can almost guarantee it's not as exciting as your current position."

Saraia was now watching him with interest. Maybe trying to see how he was digesting this new information from Miranda. And as far as staying for longer than he'd agreed for? The jury was still out on that.

But he had just gotten done thinking that volunteering at Grandview might be just what he needed. A kind of counterbalance for what he did the rest of the week. "I agreed to do whatever needed doing here. But yes, I would be interested in sitting in on at least a few appointments."

"Well, take a look at the schedule. The first couple of patients are Saraia's. So as long as she and the patient are good with you being there, then I say go for it."

Sari gave a strained smile. "Of course I am. When they check in, I'll ask them and then call you in."

"That sounds good to me."

Miranda pointed to three appointments in the afternoon. "And I'm pretty sure my patients will be fine with your presence as well."

"And the ones later in the week?"

Sari came around to look. "Those are Kat's patients. You haven't met her yet since she's normally only here on those days. She does the bulk of our home births and sees most of her patients there."

"So there are three of you in all?" He thought he remembered Sari giving him a number, but things were a bit foggy about that first meeting. So much had happened since then.

Heidi spoke up. "Five, really. A couple are on-call midwives who come in as they can. Normally on their days off from their other jobs." She punched a couple of keys on the computer at the desk and turned the screen toward him. A spreadsheet came into view with color coding. "Each color represents one of our on-call midwives and their availability."

Okay, wow. They did quite a juggling act here. "And this system works well?"

Sari laughed. "Not always. But so far it's done a pretty good job of keeping us straight. There are weeks when everyone wants to be born at once and weeks where we feel we are twiddling our thumbs, but both of those extremes would be the exception to the rule. It's normally pretty steady. And speaking of steady, here comes our first patient."

The three women scattered, leaving Eoin standing at the desk by himself. He was pretty sure he hadn't been hired as a greeter, so he went back to the micro-office they'd given to him. At six by six, the space was definitely small. Just big enough for a desk which took up half the space and two chairs, one on either side of it. There was no computer. Nothing at all in it except for those three items of furniture. There weren't even any pictures on the walls. He couldn't hide a smile. It was as if they didn't want their resident doctor to get too comfortable. But he got it. He wasn't the important figure when it came to the clinic. It was these midwives who supported their patients both physically and emotionally. They were the ones who took center stage. And from what he could see, they did an admirable job of it.

Eoin took his cell phone out of his pocket and placed it onto the desk. He halfway wondered if Sari would even call him in for her appointments. She'd told the truth and had made the offer, but she hadn't seemed very eager to have him in there with her when they'd spoken on that first day. But he got it. She was probably a little bit suspicious of his profession, given her own personal experience with one giving birth. But just like every midwife was different, so was every doctor. They each had their own quirks and preferences. It was what made them human. But most of them truly cared for their patients and wanted the best for them.

His phone buzzed. He punched answer and then put it up to his ear. "Hello?"

"If you want to step in, I'm in exam room one." The phone went dead. Okay, it was Sari's voice, though she still didn't sound overly thrilled. But he would take her invitation at face value. At least she'd asked the patient. She could have just ignored him and left him sitting in his cubicle.

He headed for the exam room, then knocked, waiting for a response.

When he got one, he slid into the room, closing the door behind him.

Sari glanced over at him. "Mabel, this is Dr. Mulvey. He's the obstetrician who's partnering with the clinic at the moment."

Eoin smiled at the woman. "Nice to meet you. I'm just here to observe, if that's okay."

"Yep, fine with me."

Sari went through the motions, doing a lot of what happened in the hospital. The difference was she did a lot more conversing about life and families than he might have done had he been the one in charge of this exam. But he was pretty sure that was what these women were here for.

"Charles is working today, so he couldn't make it," Mabel said. "But he's already asked off for my next appointment. After all, the baby is getting close."

Watching as Sari measured the woman's belly, he would guess she was at eight month's gestation. "I bet he's excited."

"He is. We all are."

Eoin took up a post toward the back of the room, since he was only here as an observer.

"The baby's still active?"

"Yes." Mabel rubbed her belly. "She's wants to be a soccer player, from the way she's kicking."

So this woman had opted to know the sex of her baby, unlike Janie.

"Oops! There she goes again."

Saraia laughed. "I saw that one. It looks like she's moved into the head-down position already. She's getting ready. Did you get the nursery done? I know you said Charles was working on it the last time you were here."

"He still is. But she'll be staying in our

room for a bit to make it easier, so we still have some time yet."

"Yes, you do." She reached out a helping hand, and Mabel grasped it, sitting upright. "It looks like everything is on track. Baby is a good size, but not overly so. So next month we'll switch to every week so we can track the changes in your cervix and get a better idea of when she might want to put in an appearance."

"Thank you. At this point, I'm ready for it to be over."

Sari smiled. "I get it, but not much longer."

The woman slid off the table and put her flip-flops back on, glancing at him. "It was nice to meet you, Doctor. Thanks for being our 'just in case.'"

Okay, well, it was the first time he'd been called that. By anyone.

But he got what she'd meant. After all it was why he'd banked some of his sperm—just in case. And most of the women who walked through the clinic wouldn't need his services. Just like he might never use what he'd saved. It was why that letter came year after year. As a reminder that it was there.

Just in case.

Sari walked Mabel out to the front, and Eoin stood there for a minute staring at the table. Maybe it was time to check a box on his "just in case" letter and make the decision he'd been putting off. If he ever did decide to have a child, there were other ways of doing that. Adoption, for one. Would it limit his prospects as far as partners went? Maybe, but this was his choice to make. Not theirs.

Going over to the table, he started the cleanup process, stripping the paper off and discarding it. He found a spray bottle of sanitizer and spritzed the table and wiped it down before pulling a fresh strip of paper over the table.

"Hey, what are you doing?" Sari asked.

He stopped before turning around. "I thought I could at least do this, if nothing else."

She frowned. "We don't expect you to clean exam rooms."

"So, you have a cleaning crew to do it or a nurse's aide?" He softened the words with a smile.

"Well...no. But..."

"So that leaves who? You?"

She smiled back. “Well, yes. But I’m a woman of many talents.”

“So I’ve seen.” It was better not to elaborate on those words, so he simply added, “It’s kind of nice to have a break from my normal day, so if you’re okay with it, I’ll pitch in where I can.”

“Does that include washing windows?”

He was pretty sure she was joking, but to be safe he gave an honest answer. “If needed.”

“I’m not quite sure if you’re being serious or not.” She said it in a dubious way, as if she expected there to be a catch. But there wasn’t one. And what he’d said was absolutely true—it was nice to have a break from his frenetic schedule. The atmosphere here at the clinic gave itself to that. It had a calm soothing presence, and Eoin couldn’t quite put a finger on the reason for that. Maybe it was the midwives who worked here.

If so, he could only hope some of it rubbed off on him and that he could carry it with him through the rest of his week. He was scheduled to deliver a hydrocephalic baby on Wednesday, which promised to be a tricky affair as the neonate would need surgery as soon as it was born.

It. He hadn't asked the sex of the baby. Hadn't even wondered if the parents knew. And maybe that was a failing on his part. He did think of his tiny patients as people. But he wondered if it was his way of remaining aloof and doing his best not to let them touch any deeper than his skin, which was pretty damned thick. Except for that baby last week—the one who'd somehow reached inside of him and yanked at a part of him that he hadn't been sure still existed.

Evidently it did. And he wasn't sure that was a good thing.

He glanced at Sari, who was still standing there. "I'm very serious. I really do want to help, you know. I didn't come here to change the way you do things. Maybe you can even teach this old dog new tricks."

"Old dog. Hardly." Her nose squinshed in a way that was pretty damned adorable.

"Try living in my skin for a day."

She sighed. "I get it, believe me. There are days when we all feel like it. The trick is just to keep going until the feeling passes."

Sari had more reason than most to feel world weary and tired. She'd lost her husband and, from what Eoin could surmise, was raising her twins without help from anyone but Peggy. And yet she still felt genuine empathy for her patients and their babies. She still managed to get through the days when she felt unsteady. He had done his best to bolster her on the one day he'd seen her struggle. When Evie had been hurt.

He took a deep breath and let it out. She'd ended up bolstering him earlier that same day, when he'd been emotionally shaky after losing his patient.

"I really am glad that Evie is okay," he said.

"Me too. It could have been so much worse."

Something flashed in her eyes that said she knew exactly how much worse it could be. Her husband had died in the hospital. So yeah. She did know.

"Was it hard being at the hospital?"

He immediately regretted asking the question. Of course it had been.

"So very hard," she said. "I told Peggy to stay in the car so that she wouldn't have to face coming in when Evie was discharged. And I didn't want Hannah in there. But of course, Peggy wouldn't hear of it and insisted on coming up to help us get down to the car. She's a strong woman. Far stronger than I am."

Shock rolled through him. There was no way those girls would even have any memory of him. That had to be hard too. "Hell, I'm sorry, Sari," he said. "I can't imagine what it was like to go through something like that."

It was true, even though he'd gone through a pretty tough time himself when he'd been eighteen.

"It was pretty terrible. David picked up an infection from somewhere and turned septic. He was in a coma for a few weeks and never woke up from it."

From what Eoin remembered, the twins had only been three months old at the time. So there she'd been with two infants while her husband had been dying from an illness that hadn't responded to treatment. Portland Lakes was a world-class hospital, so if they couldn't figure it out it was doubtful anyone could have.

"Were you already a nurse midwife at the time?" he asked.

Sari leaned against the wall, head tipped back. "I was already a nurse. But I decided to go back and study midwifery because of how uncomfortable I was with my own birth experience. I ended up getting my doctorate-in-nursing degree." She glanced at him. "So why'd you go into obstetrics?"

That was trickier because it meant going back to his cancer diagnosis and the possibility that he'd never have biological children. It wasn't something he wanted to revisit. Not right now. "You know, it just felt right when I was going through school. All through my rotations I had this idea that obstetrics was where I would end up. And it was." It sounded so simple when he said it in those terms. And in a way it was. It was as if he'd been born to be in this profession. And if he'd never had cancer? That was a question he couldn't answer because his life experiences weren't something he could make disappear.

"Yes, it was. And from what I can tell, your patients are very lucky." She paused. "And I think we are too."

Something warmed in Eoin's chest. He'd had people compliment him before, but coming from someone who had been so prickly toward him at first? It meant a lot. A whole lot. If he wasn't careful, he was going to get stuck in an emotional quicksand that he'd have a hard time escaping. So time to get busy doing something. Anything.

He forced a smile. "You're just saying that to be nice."

"When have you ever known me to just be nice?" She rolled her eyes, and her nose crinkled again. It was just as cute the second time. "Wait—don't answer that."

"You can be nice. When you want to."

This time she laughed. "I thought I told you not to answer that."

Just like that the seriousness of the moment disappeared and they were in lighter territory. And Eoin found himself enjoying the back and forth between them, wishing it could go on a little longer.

So he lobbed her earlier words back at her. "When have you ever known me to do what I'm told to do?"

"Touché, Dr. Mulvey."

He reached and gave her hand a light squeeze before releasing it. "When is your next appointment?"

"In about twenty minutes. Do you want to sit in again?"

He found he wanted to, especially with how open to the idea she seemed to be. It was light-years from the way they'd started off their relationship. Strike that—it wasn't a relationship. But he found he liked being with her, liked watching her work. "If it's okay with you," he said.

Sari tilted her head and studied him for a second before smiling again. "Sure. It's a first-time mom, and this is her first visit, so it'll be a lot lengthier than the last appointment."

"It's fine."

"Sounds good." She glanced around the room. "And since you've so expertly prepped this room, we'll see her in here. After all, I'd hate for all of your hard work to go to waste."

Yep. He definitely liked being with her. And that should've sent up a warning flag in his head. But it didn't. At least not one that he was willing to acknowledge. Instead, he'd just take today for what it was: A chance to learn a little more about what she did. And why she did it.

Eoin had surprised her, and that wasn't easy to do. When Sari had gone into that exam room, she'd been prepared to clean the room herself before her next patient arrived. But to see him wiping down the table had been somewhat of a shock. Dr. Eric had certainly never offered to do any of those things. But then again, he'd been close to retirement and it had probably never crossed his mind to clean exam rooms since he didn't sit in on appointments.

And for Eoin to joke about it had made her heart lighten. It had been a while since she'd been able to joke with someone of the opposite sex.

She hadn't even joked that much with Max—which, looking back on their relationship, didn't seem normal. And she certainly hadn't with Dr. Eric, who'd, in her mind, been kind of an Eeyore figure. In fact, he was the one who'd asked them to call him Dr. Eric, since that's what he'd had his patients call him.

In the time Sari had been at the clinic, the former obstetrician only been pressed into action a handful of times. In fact if the crisis with Janie had happened during the time when Eric Reynolds had been here, she probably would have bypassed him and called one of the other midwives for assistance. It was just the way they did things. She wasn't even sure why she'd called Eoin in, but it had worked. He'd surprised her there too by not continuing to take charge once the emergency had been over.

Her respect for the matter-of-fact way he was able to laugh at himself grew as they waited for their next patient—who came sailing into the room with her husband at that very moment. Cassidy was all smiles over the wonder of their impending entry into parenthood. They were newlyweds who'd wanted to have children right away and who, it looked like, had hit the jackpot. Unlike Sari, who'd had trouble getting pregnant while married to David and had opted to see a fertility specialist. It hadn't been a fun time, and her fluctuating hormones had turned her into something of a monster. In the end, when the process had consumed them and started to affect their relationship, she'd opted to discontinue treatment and surprisingly had gotten pregnant with Evie and Hannah six months later.

She greeted the pair. "Hello, I'm Saraia Jones, and this is Dr. Mulvey. He is our clinic's new resident doctor. Do you mind if he sits in on this first visit? He's getting on track with how we operate."

They looked at each other, and then Cassidy shrugged. "It's okay with me. We'll still have natural childbirth, right?"

"Absolutely—if everything checks out okay for that," she said. "The next couple of appointments we'll be doing a lot of measuring and tracking and I'll be asking a lot of questions, just to make sure you have the safest delivery possible. So let's get started, shall we?"

Eoin stood at the back of the room as Sari took Cassidy's weight and measurements and asked a barrage of questions about the couple's medical and familial histories. No inherited problems from what they said, no history of twins on either side of the family. And Cassidy's pelvis was wide enough to accommodate an average-sized baby, from what Sari could determine.

"I'd like to do a transvaginal ultrasound, if you're okay with that. I want to see where baby implanted and see if we can hear any signs of a heartbeat."

"A heartbeat?" Cassidy looked at her husband. "I didn't even expect to hear that today."

"Well, there are no guarantees," she said. "But since you think you're closer to eight weeks pregnant, we might be able to sneak up on the little one and coax a preview."

She prepped the patient for the procedure and told them what to expect, then rolled the machine over and set the parameters on the screen. Then she introduced the wand and searched for the baby. It didn't take long. "There. The baby has implanted nice and high in the uterus, which is what we like to see." She nodded at the monitor.

Sari clicked on either end of the fetus, measuring its length. Within normal ranges for a pregnancy of eight weeks. Then she heard it. The thready *bub-bub-bub* that signaled the beginnings of cardiac activity.

"Is that...?" Cassidy's voice contained awe and a little bit of surprise.

"Yes, it is. Your baby's heartbeat."

The new mom grabbed her husband's hand. "Oh, Brett..." Her voice choked up, and she couldn't say anything else.

When Sari looked over at Eoin, she noted that he was staring down at his feet. In boredom? This must've seemed pretty blasé to someone who had heart-stopping cases that kept him on his toes. But when he glanced up, she swore that there was something in his face other than indifference. It looked more like what she'd seen in her patient's expression. He looked away so fast, though, that she wasn't even sure what it was that she'd seen.

Turning her attention back to her patient, she finished up the exam and printed off a copy of the sonogram before pulling the curtain back around the pair so Cassidy could get cleaned up and dressed. She had already done a tour of the facility and stated her dream was to have a water birth. Sari had confirmed that was still their goal. And if everything she'd seen today held steady Cassidy might very well have her chance to have that. They still needed to see the blood and urine results that they'd send the pair to get.

Once they came out, Sari asked if they had any questions, and when there were none, she sent them out to Heidi's desk to get scheduled for her next exam in a couple of weeks' time.

Then she turned to Eoin. "So what did you think?"

"It was…something."

She frowned. That was a weird response. "I'm not sure what that means."

"By the time a pregnancy arrives on my doorstep, no one is smiling and I'm facing a set of very worried parents. And a whole lot of questions—some that I can't answer. To be on this side of things and to see such… Well, happiness is a change for me."

"It's a nice change, though, right?"

His mouth canted up on one side. "I want to think so. But a big part of me is waiting for the other shoe to drop. For something to go wrong. It's so ingrained in my DNA as a doctor who sees at-risk patients at every turn that it's hard for me to believe that 'normal' will stay that way. Even your shoulder-dystocia patient had a few minutes when things could have gone badly—"

"But they didn't. And at Grandview 'normal,' as you put it, happens the vast majority of the time."

That sexy line in his cheek deepened. "Will it make you mad if I say I have to see it to believe it?"

"Mad? No. Because I hope you'll see the things that I've seen each and every day of my career. A sense of happiness and expectancy in my patients that makes me love coming to work." She took a step closer. "I get that it's unnerving for you, but we're serving up joy and light here at Grandview, so don't bring any of your 'anti-joy' into my exam room, okay?"

"Anti-joy?" His brows shot up.

She'd meant it as a joke but realized it could have come across as super insensitive since he dealt with the opposite side of the spectrum in his practice. "Sorry—I phrased that badly."

"I get it. And truly, I try not to bring any of that to my own cases. In fact, I strive to bring hope to some pretty heartbreaking cases, but it's not always possible." He gave a half shrug. "But I'll try to make sure I'm happiness and light personified when I'm here."

Happiness and light personified. She wasn't sure she would ever describe him as that. There was an air of broodiness and… yes, sadness to the man, but she could also believe that he would try to find hope in the hardest of situations, and she had to respect him for that.

"Glad to hear it," Sari said. "Now, I don't know about you, but my stomach is growling. Are you up for some lunch?"

"I am. Where did you have in mind?"

"I'll tell you. But first we're going to put

your newfound skills to work and get this room prepped for the next patient."

He gave her what could be a fake scowl. At least she hoped it was fake.

"Happiness and light personified, remember?" he said. "Happiness and light."

When laughter bubbled up from somewhere deep inside her, she couldn't stop it from coming out. "Just keep on saying that, Eoin, and everything will be fine."

CHAPTER SIX

TRAVOLI'S WAS A little Italian eatery just off Charleston's famed Broad Street. Within sight of the crisp white steeple from St. Michael's Church, the area was both beautiful and crowded, bustling with tourists who loved to shop along the palm-tree-lined street. The wait hadn't been long, but the line behind them was growing by the minute. It was good that Sari had suggested arriving a little earlier than noon.

"Have you ever been here before?" she asked.

"No, this is a little hike from Portland Lakes. I normally just try to grab something from the hospital cafeteria."

She made a face. "Ouch. Well, once you eat here you may never go back to your normal routine again. It's a little distance from Grandview too, so I don't usually take my lunch breaks here. But it's great for a treat. Evie and Hannah love it here too."

"Well, then, it must be good. Did you hear from Peggy? How is Evie doing?"

"She's good. They're already begging to be allowed to spend the night. Grandma spoils them."

Eoin couldn't hold back a smile. "I can't blame her. They're a pretty cute pair. At least they were when I saw them last week."

"Thanks. They can be a handful, but I love them more than anything."

What would it be like to have little human beings that made you feel that way? From the little time he'd spent doing puzzles and coloring with the twins, it was easy to see how they could win your heart. They'd done a number on his. A few days ago, he'd been pretty sure he was going to opt not to save his sperm, but he was wavering. Again. Just like he did every year.

There was just such a permanence to the decision. Once he told them to destroy the samples, there would be no going back. The chemo all those years ago had destroyed any chance of him producing any more sperm. It was why he'd held on to the stored batch for so long, why he'd made no move to finalize things, even though he'd been wavering about the decision for the last five years. And if he did the same this year, it would make six. Six years of vacillating between two possible futures: one without kids, and one with.

But he hadn't wanted to have those kids with Lucy—that much was obvious. He'd thought the problem had been about fatherhood at the time, but looking back, it had been more than that. What had seemed so right when they'd met on a blind date, when they'd started dating in earnest had turned sour when she'd started in on how much Eoin would love it if they had a child together. And he'd never been quite sure why things had turned so bad so quickly, but they had. He'd never once looked back and wished things could have turned out differently. And breaking things off had been a relief.

And since Lucy was no longer in the picture, that left surrogacy or adoption as the only options. That would mean raising a child on his own, unless his relationship status changed anytime soon. And he didn't see that happening. He glanced at Sari and gave an internal shake of his head.

Don't get any ideas, Mulvey.

Once seated at their table, Eoin decided to forgo the wine menu since they were still working and had a soda instead. Sari did the same.

She opened her menu, and the light from a nearby window spilled through the locks of her dark hair, giving her an ethereal air that tugged at his heart. He caught himself studying her, admiring the way her brown eyes were intently perusing the options she found on the page in front of her.

"Mm..." Her teeth came down on a corner of her lip. "Okay, Eoin, what sounds good to you?"

His mouth suddenly went dry at the incredibly sexy sound she'd just made. At how she'd paired it with his name, making all kinds of things come to mind.

Things he should not have been thinking. Maybe it had just been too long since he'd been with someone in any meaningful way.

Yes, that had to be it. Except that weird attraction kept popping up when he least expected it to. Lurking just below the surface in the things Sari said. At the unexpected way she'd touched his hand when he'd been struggling to make sense of the loss of one of his patients.

He could admit there was some chemistry here. But working together brought far too many complications to risk venturing down that particular path.

Maybe he should try to meet other women. Although how to go about that when he rarely went anywhere except the hospital was a big question. He was normally too exhausted.

And yet right now he felt pretty energized. Because he was here with Sari?

Damn!

He forced himself to study the menu. "I think I may go with a simple chicken parmigiana."

"That does look good," Sari said. "I normally get the ravioli Florentine. Maybe I'd better stick with something I know I'll like."

And there it was again. The words that he could twist around at will and make into something that had an entirely different meaning.

Thank God their waiter came and took their orders, then brought their drinks. Eoin took a big swig of his, wishing he'd ordered beer or something stronger instead. If ever he'd needed a drink, it was now. But he never drank alcohol while working. And then there was the case of having no social life, so he rarely drank *ever*.

Maybe he really did need to make an effort to put himself out there. But he wasn't sure he even knew how after all this time. And telling someone about his cancer diagnosis and sperm-bank deposit seemed like a real mood killer.

"Mommy, Mommy!"

Sari's head came up in a flash and jerked to look toward the right. Two little rockets hurtled toward them, and she turned just in time to brace herself for their impact.

The girls planted kisses on their mother's face before one of them turned in his direction. "Oh, it's you! Yay! Do you still have your heart?"

It took him a second to realize what she was asking. Not about his literal heart but about the picture he'd colored. He nodded. "I still have it."

Sari shot him a look.

"I'll explain later."

The midwife glanced past the girls. "Where's Grammy?"

"She's picking up our food because we begged her to come here. But she said only if she could take it home. She said Evie still needed her rest."

So the speaker was Hannah. It would take a while for him to be able to tell them apart. Not that he had that kind of time. Because he wouldn't be seeing them on a regular basis. And strangely that made him feel a little bit weird inside. Because they were sweet and funny, and he could see how they would keep their mom on her toes.

"Does Grammy know where you are?" Sari asked.

Hannah glanced over her shoulder. "Yes. She saw you first and said we could come over."

As if summoned, Peggy appeared carrying a white plastic bag containing what was probably their lunch. She glanced at Eoin and her brows lifted slightly. "Sorry to interrupt your lunch, but they would have been devastated if they'd known you were here and didn't get a chance to come over."

"It's okay." Sari gave him a glance that had a wary look to it. The same look she'd given him when she'd found him coloring with the twins in the clinic lounge. Did she not trust him with them?

God, he hoped that wasn't the case. He wouldn't do anything to hurt either one of these kids. Wasn't it obvious by his profession that he loved children?

But he got it. In today's world it wasn't always easy to know who to trust around those who were so precious to you. Maybe he should talk to her about it.

And say what? That he wasn't the kind of horrible person that you heard about on the news?

He could say it, but how would she know, really?

So he decided to just let it go. He wouldn't be spending hours alone in their company anyway.

Sari motioned to him. "Mom, you remember Dr. Mulvey, don't you? He took me to the hospital after Evie's accident."

"Eoin, right? I do," Peggy said. "I'm glad you were there to help my granddaughter. She means the world to me."

He was surprised she knew his first name, but then of course Sari would have talked about her colleagues. He also liked the way she called her mother-in-law "Mom." But it seemed like something she would do…making those in her life feel important and loved. "I know she does. And I'm glad she's okay."

"Me too." She motioned to the twins. "Well, girls, we need to go and let Mom eat so she can get back to work. I assume you're not off yet."

Sari's face turned pink. "No, not off."

"Mom, Grammy said we could spend the night with her if it's okay with you. *Ple-e-e-ease?*" One of the twins broke in and saved them from having to explain further.

Sari glanced at Peggy. "Are you sure? You've had them all day already."

"I'm sure. I never get tired of having them around. I have extra clothes and pj's at the house." She stroked Hannah's hair, while her arm held Evie close to her side.

Yes, Eoin's parents would have loved to have grandkids. His heart tightened in his chest. If things ran true to course, they might never get that chance.

"Okay," Sari said. "I'll be by to pick them up for preschool in the morning."

"Sounds perfect. I'll make breakfast for all of us."

"Oh, you don't have to—"

Peggy made a shushing sound. "I want to. Please let me."

There was a tremulous quality to her voice that made his gut tighten. It was easy to forget that not only had Sari lost her husband but Peggy had lost her son as well. And from what he could see there wasn't a significant other in the older woman's life.

Sari reached out and grabbed her hand. "Thank you. You do so much for us."

"You're family." The simple words were said with a smile before Peggy gathered the twins together and hustled them back through the restaurant. One of the girls kept looking back and throwing kisses to her mom.

"They're adorable, you know." The words came before he could stop them.

She looked at him with a smile that made his heart cramp with some strange emotion. "Thank you. Like I said, they're my world."

Their waiter chose that time to come and set their artfully plated food in front of them. Soon the conversation turned back to work and their different fields, comparing notes on how they each did things.

Sari asked what his most memorable happy ending was.

Eoin told her, leaning forward as he remembered different aspects of a woman who'd come in expecting to hear that her baby had an inoperable problem with one of his kidneys, only to have Eoin share that he'd found a specialist who had treated a similar case in utero. And while he hadn't performed the actual surgery, he'd observed, and when it had come time to deliver the baby, she'd been healthy and strong, with no sign that there had been a problem at all, except for a small incision on her back that would fade with time.

"That's wonderful," Sari said. "I'm sure times like that make the harder cases a little easier to bear."

He thought for a minute about his last tragic case. "Maybe not easier, but if they were all hopeless, I might change my specialty. Maybe those sad cases make me celebrate the good outcomes a little more than I might otherwise."

She nodded. "I think I take things like that for granted—those good outcomes. But after meeting you… Well, maybe I won't do that anymore."

"You're blessed" was all he said before remembering that this woman had experienced her own share of heartache.

But if she'd had the same thought, she didn't let on. She just smiled and said, "I know it. I just need to look at life differently sometimes."

"I think we all do."

Her cell phone rang, and she checked it. "Oops—hold that thought. It's the clinic. Just give me a minute."

"Hi, Heidi. What's up?"

She listened for a few minutes before responding again. "Are you sure?"

The other woman said something else, and then Sari said, "Okay. Call me if you need me, then. I'll tell him."

She hung up and then shrugged. "Well, that's a first. My last appointment had to be rescheduled and the clinic has been slow today, so she said for us to take the rest of the day off. They'll call if something comes up."

Eoin chuckled. "Well, that's a first for me too. Not the part about a patient canceling, but I don't think my hospital has ever told me to take the rest of the day off."

"I mean, I have taken the day off before, but it's normally been something planned."

"Are you going to go pick up your kiddos?"

Sari bit her lip. "I think Peggy and the girls would all be disappointed. They normally eat and then curl up on the couch together watching movies for a few hours."

"Well, if you don't have anything pressing, I have an idea," he said.

"Obviously I don't, since I was expecting to be at work the rest of the afternoon. So what did you have in mind?"

Sari wasn't sure how, but they wound up at the end of Folly Beach Pier that stretched out over an expanse of blue ocean. Located on Folly Island, it was southwest of Charleston proper, and the pier along with the white stretch of beach that surrounded it was a popular spot for fishing and tourists alike.

"I haven't been here in ages," she said. "Not since they rebuilt the pier."

Folly Beach Pier's wood pilings had been heavily damaged by shipworms over the years. The decision had been made to close it for two years so that the pier could be reconstructed—this time with concrete support structures that would be impervious to marine worms.

Sari took a deep breath and turned her face toward the sea breeze, letting it whisper past her skin. "I'll have to bring the girls—they'll love it."

David had never been a fan of the ocean—or any bodies of water, really—since he couldn't swim. It was the one thing that they'd differed on. Standing out over water like this would have made his anxiety go through the roof. She'd had the girls in swimming lessons since they'd been old enough to walk for this very reason. They were little fish, loving every minute of their water time. She was pretty sure David would have approved, although it wasn't something they'd talked about during her pregnancy.

Eoin stood by the rail hip, propped against it as he faced her. They'd talked about work and about life in general—something she hadn't done with a man since Max. Since having a brief panic when she'd found the obstetrician coloring with her daughters the other day, she'd come to the conclusion that she was being silly. He was a work colleague, and Evie and Hannah had met plenty of her friends and colleagues over their lifetimes. She and Heidi often did stuff together with them and her own kids. She was like an aunt to them, since Sari had been an only child whose parents had died in a car accident years ago. Maybe Peggy was right—maybe she did need to allow more people into her life.

And Evie seemed to have turned a corner where Max was concerned. There'd been no more crying at school over his absence—something Sari was grateful for.

She glanced at Eoin, loving the way the stiff breeze ruffled his hair and plastered his denim shirt against his torso. Heidi had been right that first day about him being cute. But it went way beyond that. The man was downright gorgeous. From his blue eyes right down to his narrow hips. She was surprised he wasn't married or attached by now. And he wasn't. Or they wouldn't have had that moment at the café last week.

"So how did you know about Folly Pier? Did you grow up in Charleston?" she asked.

"Yes, born and raised here." He smiled. "I used to teach surfing lessons down on this beach while I was in college to help pay for my books."

Her brows went up, and she glanced down at the surrounding waves. "You surf? You know they found an alligator swimming in the water here several years ago."

He chuckled. "I heard about that. I haven't surfed in the last few years, though."

She somehow found that surprising and she wasn't sure why. Maybe she was comparing him to David. But she thought it was more than that. "My girls would probably love to do that someday. As you can tell from Evie's fall, they're kind of daredevils."

Sari wondered if that too wasn't because of their dad's fears. If maybe she hadn't pushed them to do things that he might have been afraid of. When the school had called about Evie's fall, Sari had poured herself a stiff dose of guilt, wondering if it had been partially her fault. But, like Eoin had said, kids fell, right? They got hurt, right? She couldn't wrap them in bubble wrap and coddle them.

What was with this sudden dissecting of her late husband? She and David had been happy enough, despite the water thing.

"I think I was surfing almost from the time I could walk."

Somehow the image of Eoin in diapers riding the waves made her laugh.

He tilted his head. "What?"

"It's nothing."

He reached over and touched her hand. "No, seriously, what? Is the idea of my surfing that ludicrous? It got me through some tough times."

What kind of tough times?

"No, of course not. I was just picturing you in diapers on a surfboard." She shrugged. "See? It was silly."

He smiled but didn't move his hand. "I'm sure I was potty trained at an early age."

"Oh, you were, were you?" she teased. "You remember that far back?"

"No. But I'll remember this," he said. "Thanks for coming out here with me. I needed this more than I realized."

"Did you? Because I think I did too."

The atmosphere on the pier slowly shifted as they looked at each other. Her laughter dried up, and something rose to take its place. The dozens of people milling around them faded to nothing as her glance dropped to his lips, her tongue moistening her own.

His fingers tightened on hers before someone bumped her from behind with a muttered apology. But it shuffled her closer to Eoin until she was just inches away from him. Where she swore she could see into his very soul. Those blue eyes glimmered with some kind of light from within, and she couldn't stop herself from staring into them.

"Eoin..."

His free hand went up to the hair at her nape and sifted through it, teasing out a tangle he found there. Then his fingers trailed over her cheeks, down the edge of her jawline. Sari caught her breath and held it, afraid to move. Afraid she would do something to sabotage whatever was happening here.

Everywhere he touched came alive as if she were being rebuilt from the ground up, just like the pier had been a few years ago.

She suddenly wanted him to kiss her with a desperation that left her shaky. She hadn't wanted something this much in... She couldn't remember when. She lifted her face toward him.

As if Eoin understood her silent plea, he closed the distance between them and canted his mouth across hers, a light touch that could barely be considered a kiss. But it set her on fire. She edged closer, going up onto tiptoe in an effort to reach him. Then his fingers tunneled deep into her hair and his mouth covered hers again, this time leaving no uncertainty that he wanted to do this.

And she loved it, kissed him back in a way that said she could give as good as she got. It was sexy, fun, and she wanted it to last forever.

But of course, it couldn't, and when Eoin eased back to look down at her, his palms cupped her face. She braced herself for an apology or some kind of rational explanation for what had happened. Except his gaze contained a heat that found its equal inside of her.

"I want so much more of that."

The low words were nothing like the ones she'd expected him to say, and she relaxed into his embrace.

"Me too."

"Do you?"

When she nodded, he leaned down to kiss her again. "But not here. Not where everyone can see us."

She knew what he was asking. And it wasn't about kissing. It was about so much more. Without hesitation, she traced the line in his cheek and nodded. "Let's go, then."

"My place?" he said. "It's just a few blocks from here."

Somehow she managed to get the word "Okay" out. She couldn't believe she was doing this, couldn't believe she was about to go back to Eoin's place. Sari wasn't an impulsive person. Or...at least not anymore. When she'd been younger, yes, absolutely. But after David's death and later the breakup with Max, she'd become a more sober person, thinking through each and every decision she made.

But this felt good. It wasn't hurting anyone, and for once she was going to do something wild and impetuous...something just for her and her own pleasure.

At least she hoped that was what Eoin was planning. If he just wanted to sit and talk, she was going to be sorely disappointed.

But when he dropped another searing kiss onto her mouth, she knew it had nothing to do with talking and everything to do with action.

The return trip down the pier seemed to take forever as he towed her behind him, steering around people who were out fishing or just gathered together in groups. Sari vaguely wondered how many other people had been bewitched by the beauty of the pier and had made the same trek back to their houses to make love.

Make love?

You could call it that, even when there was no love involved, right? This time it wasn't about a relationship. It was about pure need. Unadulterated craving.

She realized she'd been sizing him up for this since that first day in the clinic, although she would have been mortified if anyone had noticed. Especially Eoin. But he hadn't. At least she'd seen nothing in his demeanor that said he'd witnessed her surreptitious glances.

He loaded her into the car and finally let go of her hand long enough to go around to his side. Since his vehicle had manual transmission, he had to work the stick shift in the heavy beach traffic. But there was something about the way his fingers slid over the mechanism that made her think about how his hands would soon be sliding over her body. It made her shiver.

He must have noticed because he fiddled with the climate-control knobs. Except her reaction had nothing to do with being cold and everything to do with the heat that was sliding over her, a heat that was tightening her nipples while softening other parts of her body. In preparation…

God! If the clinic called now, she was going to scream in frustration.

She just wouldn't answer the phone.

No, of course she would. Because that wasn't who she was. She might say that she was going to take this for herself, but it was hard to remember a time when she hadn't had so many responsibilities weighing down on her.

Her job. Her girls…

No! Don't think about that now, she told herself. *Just enjoy the fact that a handsome man wants you. And you want him back.*

She did. So very, very much. "How much further?"

She hadn't meant to say the words out loud, had meant them to be trapped with the other dialogue that was singing inside her head.

Eoin glanced at her and smiled. "Just a few more blocks. I promise." He reached over and squeezed her hand until he reached another intersection.

Then they were pulling into the lot of an apartment building a few miles from the beach.

"Wow, you must love living this close to the ocean," Sari said.

The building was painted in a sea-washed blue that looked perfect in this setting.

"I don't go as often as you might think."

He parked and came around to let her out of the car. Keys in hand, he walked up a flight of stairs to the second floor. He opened the door and let her walk in ahead of him before closing it behind them.

She could feel his eyes on her as she took in the space. It didn't have the dark leather sofa and huge television screen that she would expect in a bachelor pad. Instead, the furnishings were light and airy and perfect for a beach retreat. And it was neat. Really neat. As if this wasn't where his life happened.

"No TV?" she asked.

"There's one in the bedroom." He took her hand and tugged her toward him. "And no, we're not going to watch it."

She smiled and leaned into him, the scent of ocean air still clinging to his clothes. And his hair was a wreck. A very sexy wreck. She reached up to twirl a lock around her finger. "I would be very disappointed if you said we were. I might even have to wrestle the remote out of your hand."

"I might like to see that, actually." His arm wrapped around her waist and held her against him, where she could feel every hard line. "Not the remote part. But you and me… wrestling on the bed."

Sari would definitely like to experience that. Lots and lots of wrestling.

This time when Eoin kissed her, he kept her pinned to his body and squirmed to get nearer. She loved his masculinity and confidence. Because she needed this, needed to be swept away by someone in a way that hadn't happened in a long time. Max had been all about the sex in the beginning of their relationship, but as time had gone on and the girls had become more involved in their lives, he'd spent more time in front of the television than anything. And she wondered if it had been because he hadn't wanted a ready-made family.

Not something she should've been thinking about right now. Not when she was being kissed by a sexy man in the living room of his house.

He lifted his head. "Do you want a drink?"

Of him? Absolutely. Of anything else? "No."

"In that case..." He swept her up into his arms and carried her down a short hallway to a bedroom. This one was masculine, with a bed that had dark heavy posts and looked like it could withstand any amount of wrestling. "We have to be quiet, though. I have an eighty-nine-year-old woman living in the apartment below mine who might be scandalized."

Sari's brow shot up, and he laughed. "I'm kidding. I'm assured that the soundproofing in these apartments is top notch. So you can be as loud as you'd like."

Hot color swept across her cheeks right before she was dumped unceremoniously onto the bed. Eoin followed her right down, leaning over her, weight resting on his elbows. He brushed a lock of hair off her forehead. "You are truly beautiful—did you know that?"

She smiled. "And if I said so are you?"

"It might not be as much of a compliment," he said.

"Okay, how about a ruggedly handsome surfer dude?"

He settled in for a long, soft kiss before lifting his head. "Surfer dude, huh? Aren't those all in California?"

"This one isn't. And he's the only one I'm concerned with right now."

"In that case, I hope you're very, very concerned."

She nibbled his lip. "Let me show you exactly how concerned I am."

CHAPTER SEVEN

His fingers were sliding over Sari's body in a way that made her quivery. With every touch, kiss and look he'd given her, she'd soared just a little bit higher.

She'd meant to show Eoin how much she wanted him, and he'd beaten her to the punch. But it was time to show him she had a few little tricks up her sleeve as well.

Pushing at his shoulders, she succeeded in rolling him onto his back, where he looked up at her in puzzlement. "Everything okay?"

"Uh-uh."

But when it looked like he was going to say something else, she straddled him, watching the delicious surprise that went across his face, a surprise that changed to need when she pulled the top of her scrubs over her head, leaving her in a bra and her pants. This was where she got a little bit anxious, since she had a cesarean scar on her abdomen along with stretch marks from carrying twins. But she pushed that from her mind. If he didn't like the way she looked, he wouldn't be here with her right now.

His fingers curved around her waist, thumbs stroking her abs in a way that made her muscles ripple. Halfway between tickly and super sexy.

His palms slid slowly upward, thumbs moving higher and higher until they reached the bottom edge of her bra. She held her breath when his fingers went behind to find her clasp and undo it, easing the garment off until her breasts were free. Then he cupped them both in one sensuous move that was almost her undoing.

He sat up in a rush, wrapping his arms around her. Being tangled up together with him like this was heaven. And they hadn't even stepped out onto any of those clouds yet, hadn't even experienced what her body was yearning for.

Eoin palmed her cheeks like he'd done on the pier and kissed her. Slowly, thoroughly, until she wasn't sure who was initiating what. All she knew was that she was squeezed up against him, straining to get closer even when they were pressed tight to each other.

Two becoming one. She understood what that meant now.

But you aren't one.

The words whispered through her head, but she tossed them away. She didn't care. Just wanted to be with him in whatever way she could. She could unpack all the other stuff later.

He kissed her once more, then eased away. "Sari, I want you to stand up for me."

"Stand up? Why?"

One finger brushed over her nipple, making her shudder. "Because I'm dying here, and I need to undress you."

Eoin set her on her feet beside the bed, but when he went to reach for the waistband of her scrubs, she held his hands. "I—I need to tell you… My scar, it's…"

He paused before evidently realizing what she was worried about.

"It's okay, Sari. I have a scar too. Look." He hauled his shirt over his head and tossed it aside. Then he put her palm over a scar on his torso. "Does this change what you want to do with me?"

"No, of course not." She traced the faded white mark with her fingertips, finding it as sexy as the rest of him. "How did you get it?"

"Surgery when I was younger. It's all healed now."

He didn't say what kind of surgery, and she didn't ask. It didn't matter.

His thumb rubbed over her tummy right above her elastic waistband. "I've shown you mine. Will you let me see yours?"

That made her smile. Then she nodded, her fingers going to her pants and pushing them down her hips and beyond. Her panties weren't super high waisted, and while some of her stretch marks were visible above them, they weren't low enough to expose her incision.

Still she felt self-conscious for a few seconds before he traced one of those marks made by her pregnancy. "You are gorgeous, Sari. Every last inch of you."

He climbed out of bed and stood behind her, his chin on her shoulder as he reached around and cupped her breasts. The feel of his naked chest against her bare back was exquisite. Then one hand slid down her belly and dipped below her panties, moving lower until it found the spot that had been aching for his touch for what seemed like forever.

Her eyes fluttered shut, and she moaned, pressing into his caress, her arms curling back around his neck and holding him against her. He was right—her scar and stretch marks didn't matter, if what she felt against her backside was any indication. He wanted her as much as she wanted him.

But if he didn't stop soon…

She twisted around in his arms. "Eoin…"

"I know." He shucked the rest of his clothing, going over to a side table to pull a condom from a drawer. And when he turned back toward her.

God! He was like an Adonis, striding toward her, rolling the condom over his length as he came closer. He flipped her back onto the bed and removed the last of her clothing, bending down to kiss her scar in a shivery move that took her by surprise. Then he was on top of her, his knee parting her legs. Sari braced herself for the wall of pleasure that would come the second he filled her.

But he didn't enter in a rush like she'd expected him to do. Like she'd wanted him to do. And she squirmed in protest.

"Shh...just wait."

Instead, Eoin used his length to trace over her most sensitive area, in much the same way as his fingers had stroked her earlier. Slowly. Thoroughly. And even with the protection between them, the sensation was crazy. Perfect. Maddening.

She couldn't think beyond one-word descriptions right now, and she didn't care.

Her hips shifted to move with the rhythm he was setting up, just as he bent forward and took one of her nipples into his mouth, sending a surge of pleasure through her. Her body jolted against his. She needed him so badly.

"Please, Eoin."

That was all it took. He entered her, and it was every bit as good as she'd dreamed it might be. She was full, so gorgeously full of him that she couldn't speak. Couldn't think. Could only feel what he was doing to her.

With each thrust, her body moved beneath his, and she could feel the softness of his quilt beneath her, the slight scratchiness of his chest hair above her. And throughout it all, her heart was pounding out a rhythm she hadn't felt in far too long.

He changed his angle slightly, and she was

suddenly transported to a world where sights and sounds didn't matter anymore. She let herself get lost in the feeling of his skin sliding over hers. In the rasp of his breathing as it washed across her cheek. In the low sexy words that were meant for her alone.

If anyone had told her sex could be like this she would have laughed. She wasn't sure she had ever experienced this level of intensity before. Her whole being became a pinpoint of feeling as something happened inside of her. A slow coiling in her belly that ratcheted tighter and tighter and tighter until…

Oh, God!

Her head craned back as a cascade of raw pleasure exploded all around her, her hips bucking hard as if trying to reach even greater heights.

"Sari…!" Eoin thrust again and again before straining against her, his own face a mask of what she'd just felt, and she welcomed him in.

God, it was good. So very, very good.

Even as she slowly came down. Even as her breathing leveled out. Even as his movements slowed. She wrapped her arms around him and held him to her. Satiated and yet feeling like something was lacking. Like she needed something more. Had reached for more before snatching her emotions back in a sudden panic.

But she wasn't going to analyze anything right now, not with him slowly withdrawing, making her wince. She hadn't been quite ready for that, had wanted that connection to last just a little longer.

He kissed her forehead, coming up onto his elbows. "Are you okay?"

"Do I look okay?" She realized that wasn't quite what she'd meant when he frowned. "No—I mean, my hair is probably a mess and—"

"You're beautiful, Sari. Truly beautiful." His thumb rubbed over the point of her chin. "Do you have to be back home tonight? The girls?"

"Girls?"

Oh, yes. Her children. What on earth had made her forget them for even a second? Eoin, that's what. And she wasn't sure if that was from what she'd just physically experienced or from something a little more insidious. A trickle of something that might be a little more than she'd expected or wanted.

But she couldn't think about that right now because he was waiting for an answer. And right now, she really didn't want to worry about anyone but herself. Couldn't she do that just this once? Evie and Hannah wouldn't know anything about it. She wasn't even going to tell Peggy. This would be her one secret.

"No. I don't have to be back."

"Then stay with me?" he asked. "Just for the night. I'll take you home in the morning."

That was right. He'd driven her here. Even more of a reason to spend the night. After all, she didn't want to make him get dressed when he could be…

Could be what, Saraia? Making you feel more of what you just sampled?

"I can stay."

He leaned down to kiss her. "I was hoping you'd say that. Because I'm not quite ready to let you go. Not yet."

And she wasn't quite ready to be let go of.

So she lost herself in his kiss and tried not to think of anything outside of what was happening on this bed.

With Eoin.

* * *

"Sari?"

Even as he sat up in bed the next morning and called her name, Eoin knew there'd be no response. She was gone. But how?

But more to the point, why?

They'd had fun, but he hadn't thought either of them expected more than that, although they hadn't talked about it. They'd just made love twice more before falling asleep in each other's arms. All had seemed fine.

So why had she left without a word?

Climbing out of bed took a little longer than usual because the bedclothes were a tangled mess, but he finally succeeded in kicking them off and leaving the room. The bathroom door was open, and the rest of the lights in the place were off. So he was right. She was gone.

The drawer to the nightstand was open, and the package of condoms seemed to laugh at him. It was kind of ridiculous to use them, since he couldn't get anyone pregnant. But there were things other than sperm that could be passed from one person to another, and he never wanted anyone to feel unsafe being with him.

Moving to the kitchen to get himself a drink of water, Eoin paused when he got to the refrigerator. The heart that he'd colored with Sari's daughters was askew, as if someone had taken it off to look at it before putting it back under the magnet. Maybe he'd moved it when he'd gotten into the fridge the last time. The truth was he'd gotten so used to it being there that it had kind of become invisible. Until it wasn't.

Surely Sari wouldn't be upset by it being there. She'd seen him coloring with them and hadn't said anything.

He was overreacting. She'd probably just woken up early this morning and decided to catch a cab back to… He didn't actually know where she lived in Charleston.

Actually, he didn't know all that much about her life outside of the clinic.

But he'd learned a lot yesterday. That she loved water. Loved the beach. That her husband had died of an infection at his hospital.

That was the one big thing he knew about her.

And yet on the flip side, what had he told her about himself? Not much. She didn't know that he'd had cancer. That the scar he'd shown her last night was the result of a splenectomy he'd had during his cancer treatment. She'd actually asked him what it was, and he'd avoided telling her. Why?

Eoin shrugged to himself. He hadn't wanted to ruin the mood with unimportant information.

And yet she'd shared something really vulnerable about herself just moments before—that she'd been worried about him being turned off by her scar, by the signs that she'd had babies.

So what had held him back?

Maybe the fact that you only shared stuff like that with a person you cared about.

So he didn't care about her?

Actually, he did. He'd already admitted that to himself when Evie had been hurt. And maybe that was exactly why he hadn't told her anything about that physical battle he'd fought. Maybe he was afraid that with every revelation, it would bind him a little more to her.

And after what had happened with Lucy, he wasn't sure he wanted to share all those details of his life again. Even if he cared about the person. Because he hadn't wanted to get that "real" with a person ever again.

Until now? Until this morning after having the best sex of his life?

Maybe. And that scared the hell out of him.

As well it should. Because he still hadn't made the decision about biological children. And being with Sari had shown him that he didn't need sperm to be a father. She had two adorable, beautiful girls who would make any man proud to carry the title of *Dad*.

For a split second Eoin allowed himself to fantasize over what it would be like to be her husband, to raise those precious twins.

Hell! He shook himself back to reality.

Thinking like that didn't help anything. It didn't help him make a decision about whether or not to let go of having a child who came from his own cells.

And that choice needed to be made without adding the face of an actual person to the mix. Did *he* want biological children? Yes or no? Maybe it was time to figure that out.

He had a couple of days before he was due back at Grandview, so maybe he should do a little soul-searching about what he wanted in life. Did he want a family? Did he want to remain single for the rest of his life? Neither choice was right or wrong. He just needed to decide what was right for him.

So his goal for the next three days was to make one big decision. Leave kids on the table? Or take them off it forever—at least when it came to his banked sperm. In sending the facility a yearly check, he'd basically been coasting, putting off a decision that he really did need to make.

So that was what he was going to do. He was either going to write a check or give the sperm bank permission to destroy his samples. Once he did that, maybe he would have the freedom he'd never felt. The freedom to move forward with his life and his future.

Sari felt like she was moving in a vacuum. Her days went like they always did, a mixture of calm one minute, frenetic the next. Her night with Eoin felt like it had happened in a dream world.

A sexy, terrifying dream. But one she might repeat, given the chance. Except for that one thing that made an uneasy lump form in her chest.

Eoin had kept that heart he'd colored with

her girls. Why? She'd gotten up early in the morning with the idea of getting a drink and then climbing back into bed, but then she'd seen his refrigerator door. There'd been no question about what that thing on it was. It had been right there at eye level. He had to see it each and every time he opened that door.

Why keep it? Why not just toss it before he'd left Grandview that day? The sight had kind of spooked her, and she'd suddenly felt the need to get out of there. It had been a wakeup call about what she stood to gain and what she stood to lose. Or actually, what her girls stood to lose if she continued down this track.

If Sari let herself get involved with Eoin or any other man, she risked not only her heart but those of her girls.

It was as if the universe had sent her a big old reminder of what was at stake—in the form of an actual heart. So maybe she should thank him for hanging that thing up. Because it had scooted her butt out of that apartment and into an Uber, whose driver had thankfully asked no questions about what she was doing requesting his services before six in the morning.

But she hadn't wanted Eoin to wake up. Hadn't thought she could handle any kind of small talk or worse…breakfast, with that heart staring at her from across the kitchen.

So she'd skedaddled. And not only had Eoin not tried to contact her since she'd fled his place three days ago, she was going to have to face him later this morning when he came into work. She could only hope one of her patients unexpectedly went into labor and needed to be seen immediately.

But what was the likelihood of that happening? Never. It never happened when you wanted it to.

Worse, Hannah had asked about Eoin when Sari had picked them up from preschool the day after her sexy rendezvous with the obstetrician. She hadn't wanted him to make an impression on them, but evidently it was too late for that. So all she could hope was that the curiosity would burn itself out by extinction. If they rarely saw him, they wouldn't think he was anything special, right?

Had her own curiosity about him burned itself out? She'd once wondered if it would if she ever got the chance to experience him. Well, now she had her answer.

Not only had it *not* burned itself out, she wanted to know more. She wanted to know exactly what that scar on his torso was from, even though she knew it was none of her business. If he'd wanted her to know he would have said so. But she felt a little unevenly matched since he knew exactly what her scar was from.

And he'd been so exquisitely tender about the whole thing, even making her smile with his "I showed you mine, now show me yours" challenge. He'd known exactly what to say to put her at ease. And she loved that about him.

No. *Love* wasn't the right word. She *liked* that about him. There. That was better.

Just then, the door opened and in strolled Eoin, looking damnably good in jeans and a navy T-shirt. He was dressed a little more casually than he usually was, but none of them dressed up for this job. And he actually looked like all was right with the world, which made Sari feel kind of miserable.

Heidi took one look at her face and made an excuse to leave. Was it that obvious that something about the man was bothering her?

He came over to her and smiled. "You disappeared."

She knew exactly what he was talking about. And she didn't really want to discuss it out here in the foyer. "Can we go into your office for a minute?"

He shot her a look. "Sure."

Eoin led the way to the minute space, and they both squeezed inside. Maybe this was a mistake because the way he filled this room was reminiscent of the way he filled…

Uh-oh. Stop, she told herself. *Right now.*

He didn't wait for her to say anything—he spoke up instead. "I would have taken you home, you know."

"I didn't want to put you out." Liar. Was this really how she wanted this conversation to go? "No, scratch that. I felt funny about what had happened and decided to sneak out while you were sleeping."

"I kind of realized that when you weren't there the next morning." He paused. "You felt funny how?"

"I don't know. I dated someone a while back and let him get involved in my girls' lives, and then we broke up. They were devastated. I swore I would never go down that road again with anyone. And I was afraid if I stayed…"

"You were afraid if you stayed that I might ask that of you," he said.

"Simply put, yes."

He came around his desk until he stood in front of her. "I would never put you in that kind of position, Sari. You control who your daughters interact with, and you absolutely have that right. I promise I won't try to worm my way into their lives behind your back."

"It's not just behind my back," she said. "I…well, I don't want to make another mistake."

"Neither do I," he said. "I was in a bad relationship a while back as well. And I'm not in a hurry to jump back into one either. Why don't we agree that what we did was fun? And if we want to do it again, it's okay."

She nodded. "I can live with that."

"And while we're being honest…" He rubbed his hand over an area on his midriff. "That scar I showed you is from a splenectomy."

"A splenectomy? Were you in a car accident?" Most splenectomies she'd heard about had been the result of some kind of injury to the organ that could cause it to swell with blood until it burst, a life-threatening event.

"No. I wasn't in an accident. I had Hodgkin's lymphoma almost twenty years ago. They had to take my spleen because of it."

Shock went through her. "Eoin, I'm sorry. I had no idea."

"I know. And I'm not sure why I didn't tell you that night. Maybe because talking about your cancer isn't the sexiest thing in the world."

That made her laugh. "And talking about stretch marks is?"

"Yes." He touched her hand. "Because yours are very, very sexy."

Sari bit her lip. "Okay, maybe we should change directions. So we agree that everything is okay and nothing is weird?"

"'Nothing is weird' as in nothing is off limits?"

She swatted his arm. "You know what I meant." But she loved that he could joke about it. It made running off like she had seem a little bit ridiculous. He was showing her there was nothing to be afraid of.

"I did. But your face turns pink right here

in a way that fascinates me." His fingers slid over her cheek.

Wow. She fascinated him?

Well, he certainly fascinated her as well.

"And your cancer is cured?" The words came out before she could stop them. And she wasn't sure why they even came to mind.

"That's what they tell me," Eoin said. "There's been no sign of it recurring anyway, although a splenectomy means I might get some other type of lymphoma at a later date."

He was so matter-of-fact about it, as if it weren't important. And maybe if you'd been facing something like this your whole life, it became almost normal.

But it wasn't. And "some other type of lymphoma" probably meant one that was more aggressive, although he hadn't specified that. It wasn't her area of expertise and she didn't feel right grilling him with questions about his health, so she decided to leave it be.

After all, like he'd said, they were just having fun. There was no commitment. No need to wonder about what their future together might hold. Or might not.

In a way it was freeing. Because with Max, she'd been constantly analyzing everything he'd said as things started heading south between them.

She didn't need to do that here. And Eoin had promised to keep Evie and Hannah out of it if that was what she wanted. It was. She thought so anyway.

"Well, I'm glad you beat it. Because I can't imagine the world without you, Eoin Mulvey."

She hadn't been able to imagine the world without David either, but there you had it. You didn't always get your wish.

"Thanks," he said. "I'm kind of glad to still be here in it. Even if beautiful women run out on me in the middle of the night."

She laughed. "It was morning, mister!"

"Same difference." His face turned serious. "I woke up, and you were gone. I didn't much like that feeling, so please don't do it again."

Said as if they might spend the night together again. She liked that, although her daughters didn't spend the night with Peggy more than about once a month. And it would be hard to ask her to without offering up some kind of explanation. But Sari also didn't want to say no to him. So she took some middle ground.

"If I'm ever at your place again, I promise not to leave next time without at least waking you up before I go-go."

Eoin groaned as he realized she'd recited some song lyrics. Then he took her hands in his. "I hope there is a next time."

"I hope so too." She squeezed his hands and then let go. "So we're good?"

"We're good. Now, we should probably get out of here before Heidi or one of your other midwives get the wrong idea about us." He raised a brow. "Except it wouldn't exactly be wrong, would it?"

"No, which means we definitely should leave while we each still have some plausible deniability," she said.

Eoin pulled her in for a quick peck on the cheek. "I have to tell you—I'd be hard pressed to deny anything that happened the other night."

But he reached around her and pulled the door open. "So what's on the docket today?"

As they left his office, the conversation turned back to what the clinic's schedule looked like today. And Sari was glad. So very glad that they'd gotten things settled between them.

Even if they were no closer to putting a definition to what they'd done than they had four days ago. Other than "fun."

Their night together had been fun. And maybe there was no need to define it past that. At least not for today.

CHAPTER EIGHT

EOIN HAD SURVIVED his first water birth.

Well, *he* hadn't, but Sari's patients had. Both of them. They'd offered to let him observe, and Sari had taken him aside and asked him to make sure that he didn't put on his doctor hat unless she specifically asked him to.

He had to admit it was a nerve-racking experience, even as an observer. He'd held his breath the whole time the baby had been born beneath the water's surface, even though he'd mentally known that the cord had been providing all the oxygen that the baby had needed. And the infant had been out of the water and onto his mom's chest pretty quickly.

Water births weren't new by any means. His own hospital was even thinking of putting in a birthing tub in the maternity ward. But Eoin would never get to use one. Not because he disagreed with them, but because by the time the patients reached his office, any kind of natural birth was off the table. Survival was the name of the game.

The method was certainly not without its critics. And many of those detractors were in his own field.

It was obvious that Sari really believed in this. She'd coached the mom through the whole process, all the way down to letting the mom and dad catch their own baby.

Watching her in that role was amazing. Her passion. Her belief. The way she tirelessly advocated for her patient. It made something in Eoin tighten with some unknown emotion. But he felt damned proud that he'd been here to witness this.

Everyone seemed healthy and happy with the process. Sari measured and weighed the baby once the mom was ready. Skin-on-skin time was very important at the clinic, and she let them set their own time frame as far as how long that lasted. If it had taken hours, Eoin had no doubt that she would have been fine with that.

Once everyone was out of the tub, the mom glanced his way, and he stepped forward and congratulated them, thanking them for letting him be in the room during this special occasion.

"Was it what you expected?" she asked.

"No, but it was a beautiful process, and I'm glad Grandview offers the option."

"We are too." She smiled. "We're so happy a friend recommended we check it out. And Saraia has been wonderful throughout the whole pregnancy. We'll probably have our next child here as well."

Next child. As if that were just a given. He'd thought all week about what to do with his banked sperm, and after his thoughts about Sari and being a dad, he realized he wasn't as opposed to it as he'd been back when he and Lucy had been together. In fact it had looked damned attractive the morning after he and Sari had made love. And he realized with the right person, he might just want to don that *Dad* title. So he'd decided to pay for another year. Not just to put off deciding like he'd done in the past, but to really use this as a springboard for what the future could hold.

Might that have been partly because of his night with Sari?

Yes, he thought so. Thought it might actually happen someday. But what he wasn't saying was that he was pinning any of his hopes on Sari. Because he wasn't. Even this morning, she'd been honest, saying she wasn't sure she wanted someone in her girls' lives—now or maybe ever. And he could respect that.

Once he and Sari left the room to let the new little family get acquainted, she said, "So, what did you really think?"

"I'm thinking it was pretty far out of my comfort zone. But certainly not out of theirs. Or yours."

"I don't do a ton of these, but no matter how a baby is born, it's always a pretty miraculous event," she said. "Mine wasn't ideal, but I'm still glad for the experience. Still glad for two healthy girls."

"Do you think you'll ever have more children?" he asked.

She paused, as if not sure how to answer. "I don't know, honestly. Next year, when I turn thirty-five, I'll be considered a higher-risk patient in most obstetricians' books."

"How about in most midwives' books?"

"It's not out of the realm of possibility to still give birth at Grandview, but there would be tests to check for birth defects. And after a C-section it's riskier to have a natural birth. It depends on the state of my uterus, especially after twins. It's not something I let myself think a lot about." She shrugged. "Maybe it's another reason I went into midwifery. To help other women get what I didn't."

"I can definitely understand that," Eoin said.

She smiled and touched his hand. "I'm glad. Now, I need to go and get some paperwork done on this birth. See you later?"

"I'll be around."

With that, Sari sauntered down the hallway, looking like she didn't have a care in the world. But he did. Because despite the little pep talk he'd given himself about kids and not letting himself get caught up in casting Sari into any kind of role in that, he suddenly realized he might have already done so. And if that were the case, he was in big trouble.

He might have said not even five hours ago that they were just having fun, but after watching her partner with that couple, he realized it was no longer true. Because during that water birth, something else had been born as he'd watched Sari work, as he'd watched her absolutely take care of her patients with a compassion that made them want to come back and experience it all over again.

Just like him. He wanted to experience her again. Not just the sex. But the whole package.

And exactly what was that?

He wasn't sure. But maybe he'd just gotten his answer about whether or not he wanted to be a father. He did. And it didn't involve sperm stored in some kind of ice vault.

The way his heart had been for the last twenty years? Lucy hadn't been able to chisel her way to it, but he was pretty sure Sari—in the short time he'd known her—had done exactly that without even trying. Without even wanting to.

Hell. *He* hadn't wanted her to either, but… it was done. And what was done couldn't be undone, no matter how much he might wish otherwise.

He loved her. He'd done something he'd promised himself he wouldn't do: fall for someone without giving it just as much consideration as he'd given his banked sperm.

Only this was more important than whether or not he chose to have children in the future.

This was about his future itself. His and Saraia's.

She'd made it pretty clear how she felt about men coming into her girls' lives. It would take a certainty that he wasn't going to just disappear like her ex. Or her late husband. And Eoin wasn't sure he was the one who'd be able to give that to her. After all he'd had cancer once. He was at a higher risk for a recurrence. She might not even want to take a chance on being with him.

Time would tell. But one thing he wasn't going to do was put his feelings into the driver's seat and let himself pressure Sari into giving more than she wanted to give. This was her life, her choice. And in the end, all he could do was let her decide how far she allowed him in her life, how close she allowed him to get to Evie and Hannah. And that would take time and trust. Two things he wasn't quite sure he'd earned yet.

Sari took her time filling out her paperwork. Eoin had taken that water birth a whole lot better than she'd expected him to. What she hadn't expected, though, was for him to ask her about whether or not she wanted children in the future. Was it just an idle curiosity?

Sitting at her open cubicle, she pulled up information on Hodgkin's lymphoma. She was surprised at how very little she actually knew about it. For example, she was surprised that they'd taken his spleen.

Resting her chin in her palm, she started to read through the information, but just then she spotted Eoin walking down the hallway and quickly shut down the screen. For some reason she'd thought he'd be in his office. But why? He didn't really have anything he needed to do there, unless they called him into service.

He spotted her and came over, and her chin dropped off her hand. Sari felt guilty, as if she'd just done a Google search on the man himself, looking for dirt. She hadn't been, but it might be crossing a line of prying into his personal life, even though she hadn't been going through his specific medical records.

She forced a smile when his glance went to the computer screen. "Hey, what's up?"

"I need to go back to Portland Lakes."

Her heart jolted. "Permanently?" She wasn't sure why she'd said that. She just knew that she was rapidly getting used to his presence at the clinic. A little too used to it.

"No." This time Eoin frowned as he looked at her a little bit more closely. "I have a patient with twins who thinks she might be experiencing labor before her planned delivery date. I need to go check her."

"Is she having a cesarean?"

"Yes, it's her second set of twins and she has some fibroids that weren't removed near her cervix, making it tricky to get the babies out past them."

"I see." And she really did.

"Do you want to watch the birth if it comes down to the fact that she really is in early labor?" he asked. "We have an observation room over the surgical suite. It might give you more of an idea of what I do and why I do it."

Sari glanced at her watch. It was just past two. "Can you call me if it comes down to it? I need to pick the girls up from preschool at four. If it looks like it might be later than that, I can see if Peggy might be available to watch them. She does sometimes if I have a patient who comes in during my off hours."

"I'll leave that up to you. Just thought you might be interested," he said. "But if watching a cesarean brings back bad memories, I'll completely understand."

"No, I don't think it will. I've come to think of every live birth as a success story. I just want moms to be able to have some say in the birthing process itself. But I know in some cases that isn't feasible or even possible."

"This is one of those, I promise," Eoin said. "I don't ever take the lazy way out. If I ever did, it would mean I've been doing this too long and need to hand the reins over to someone else. But I hope that doesn't happen for a long time."

"I don't think it will." She couldn't imagine him being lazy about anything. Especially not his job. "Let me know about your patient, and make sure she's okay with someone watching. And I'll get in contact with Peggy."

"Sounds good. See you."

"See you." She reached and squeezed his hand, holding it for a bit longer than necessary. "And good luck."

As soon as he was gone Sari hesitated, her finger over the button that would restore the screen she'd been reading. She bit her lip. Was what she was doing right?

Hadn't she mulled over how she'd become

so much more sober and cautious in the last little while and how she needed to maybe throw some of that to the wind and allow a little impulsivity to peek through periodically? Hadn't Peggy hinted at that during their visit to Beverly's ice cream shop?

Maybe. But Sari wanted her impulsiveness to be tempered with reality and to weigh her decisions in light of that reality.

So she clicked open the screen and began to read. Lymphoma and other cancers were certainly on the radar after Hodgkin's lymphoma, depending on the treatment that had been used. And evidently the spleen wasn't always removed after the diagnosis was made. But according to the article, lymphoma cells could enter the spleen and cause it to swell to a dangerous point, and so a splenectomy was sometimes advised.

The word *splenectomy* was in blue font, meaning she could click on it to learn more. She almost scrolled past it, but something made her aim the cursor in its direction and push a button.

Up came a new screen that gave the information on splenectomy.

There was a bunch of technical stuff about

how and why the organ was removed and the risks of the surgery itself. Nothing helpful here. Sari started to go back to the previous page, when something caught her eye.

There was a section on precautions to take after having a splenectomy. At first she thought it was more postoperative information, but no, it wasn't. It was information on how to prevent infections. There was a whole laundry list of items ranging from wearing gardening gloves while working in the yard to getting a flu shot and carrying a card that identified you as being asplenic…or not having a spleen. Because without a spleen you were at risk of getting a serious infection. The type of infection that could rapidly progress to…*sepsis*.

Sari blanked out the screen before any more words could penetrate her brain. God! Even seeing that word in print brought back memories that were too painful to bear. Of David lying in that hospital bed. Of the hopelessness of his condition.

She closed her eyes and wished she had never looked, had never even typed *lymphoma* into her search engine.

But Eoin wasn't David, and he'd lived for

twenty years without having a serious infection. At least he'd never mentioned one. But who knew if he had or hadn't.

She pulled in a deep breath. Okay, she needed to stop before her mind sent her to dark places she didn't want to visit. Eoin was fine. He was healthy. She was going to leave it at that. And since she wasn't going to let her involvement with him go more than skin deep, she was going to paint a fantasy that ended with him having a good long life. And them having a night or two of passion that would stay with her for the rest of her life. If Eoin wasn't worried, then she wasn't going to let herself be either.

No more Google searches for you, Sari. You're cut off. Starting now.

"Are you sure you want to do this?"

For a second she tensed, thinking he was talking about their personal life. Especially since she'd just googled his cancer—something that made her feel inexplicably guilty. So much so that she had a hard time meeting his eyes.

"You mean watch the surgery?"

"What else would I be talking about?" Eoin

tilted his head and looked at her for a moment. "What's wrong, Sari?"

"Nothing. I'm just a little distracted," she said. "But yes, I do want to watch the surgery."

Despite what she'd found out, she still wanted to learn about what Eoin did on this side of the birthing spectrum. Looking back at the day she'd first met him, she realized how dismissive she'd been about him…about obstetricians in general. And she could see how wrong she'd been. He cared about his patients just as much as she did. She'd seen it in the way he'd grieved over losing one of his patients not all that long ago. And yet he had to keep pushing forward.

The same way she did. Each and every day.

"Okay, I need to go scrub in for surgery, and then I'll meet you afterward in the lobby, okay?" he said.

She nodded before impulsively going up on tiptoe and kissing him on the cheek. "Good luck."

Eoin gave her a smile that made her swallow. It was filled with something she couldn't quite identify. Anticipation of the surgery maybe? That had to be it.

"Thanks, Sari. I'll see you when it's done. Pray for a successful delivery."

"I will." It wasn't just a line. She would be praying. For him. For the mom. And for those tiny babies who were waiting to come into this world.

As he turned to leave, she stood there staring after him for a moment or two before finally moving toward the door that would lead her to the observation room a short distance away.

Sari's emotions were all over the place an hour later as she met Eoin in the lobby. But more than anything, there was a happiness that bordered on euphoria. She refrained from rushing over to hug him, but just barely. Instead, she clasped her hands in front of her and took a deep breath before letting it out. Then words started rushing out as well.

"God, Eoin, that was amazing. I'm so, *so* glad things went well for that couple. I can't tell you how many times my heart leapt into my throat during that."

Her searching the internet seemed insignificant compared to what she'd just seen in real life. And it made her reaction to the splenectomy information feel kind of ridiculous. She'd looked closely, and there'd been no sign of worry in Eoin's demeanor or actions. So she'd breathed a sigh of relief and given herself over to what had happened in that surgical suite.

Both mom and babies had come through the surgery without any issue. Eoin had asked if it would bring back bad memories of her own cesarean, but it hadn't. It wasn't as if her surgery had been horrifying—she'd just felt a loss of control that had bothered her.

But Eoin had been so kind with his patient, and Sari could tell he'd listened to her at length because they'd exchanged a few words before she'd been put under anesthesia and her hand had reached to grip his. The same way that Sari had reached for his hand in the courtyard that day. Wow, that seemed like so long ago, but really it wasn't.

Even so, she felt the same kind of trust that his patient had seemed to feel. And it made her smile.

"Things went well," Eoin said. "These are the cases that make things worthwhile."

And just like the patient had done less than an hour ago, Sari gripped his hand. "I can see that. Thanks for helping me push aside some of my preconceived notions. All obstetricians are not ogres."

She was joking. She knew plenty of doctors who were wonderful. Her work was just a different facet of the same goal: a safe delivery.

"So *I'm* not an ogre? Or I am? I'm not quite getting where I stand in this particular assessment."

She pivoted to face him, hand still clasping his. "You're definitely in the not ogre category. You're too good-looking to be an ogre."

"So you're saying I'm not hideous."

"Not hideous," she agreed.

His finger came out to stroke her cheek. "Well, that's a relief."

"Is it? And why is that?"

"Because you wouldn't want to be seen out and about with someone who barely misses the ogre mark."

That made her laugh. "I don't know. It depends what you mean by 'out and about.' Because I was thinking more about staying in."

Had she really just said that? It had to be the rush of adrenaline and relief over things going so well—because it was making her thoughts head in all kinds of dangerous directions.

"Staying in?"

"Mm...the girls are at Peggy's for the night." Wow. She was actually propositioning the man.

But something in her was humming, and Dr. Google suddenly seemed a long way away. What did he know anyway?

"They are?" Eoin said. "What did you have in mind?"

Not that he didn't already know by now. But she loved listening to him talk, and drawing this out a little longer was making her want to yank him into the nearest exam room and...

"What do you think I have in mind?"

"I'm not sure, but I know what I have in mind." He leaned down to whisper. "I want to tangle my hands in your hair and feel your tongue slide over my skin."

He didn't specify where, but her imagination was inventing all kinds of places she could lick. And they were all fascinating. But he hadn't stopped there. He continued to murmur things that made her face heat and her body ignite.

When he pulled back to glance at her, he laughed. "I think I'd better stop before someone notices."

He nudged her thigh, and her eyes went wide, catching his. Eoin nodded. "It's definitely not a mouse."

She licked her lips. "It's definitely not the size of one either."

His arm came around her, and he grabbed her to him, making her thankful that they were in a dark corner where no patient's families were in sight.

"Lord, Sari. What you do to me."

"I haven't even started yet," she said. "So the sooner we get out of here..."

They used his car again to head back to his house, and memories of their last time there were swirling around her. None of them had faded. They were all just as stunning and brilliant as the real thing had been.

Because it had been real. And she'd been with him. And it was so far beyond any fantasy that she might have had about him that she had nothing to compare it to.

She let her hand rest on his thigh as he drove, her thumb stroking over the corded muscles beneath the fabric of his slacks. How could so much gorgeousness be housed in one human form?

His hand came down on hers. “Careful. I want to get there in one piece.”

The fact that a simple caress could turn him on was heady. Too heady. And she was suddenly desperate to get to the apartment.

Fortunately, five minutes later, they’d rolled into his parking lot and left the car behind. In the elevator, Eoin put his arms around her and pulled her back against him, leaning down to nuzzle the side of her neck. Her eyes closed as sensations washed over her, just like last time. He knew just how to touch her to make her come alive.

Then they were in his apartment, and Sari’s eyes automatically went to his refrigerator to see if that red heart was still there on display. It was. But this time its presence didn’t shock her like it had the last time. Maybe because she’d already geared herself up to seeing it again.

“Do you want something to drink?”

“A glass of wine, if you have it?” She wasn’t sure why, but she wanted to slow this down just a little now that she was here. Their last time together had been so frantic and all-consuming that she wanted her brain to be a little more engaged this time. By asking for wine? That made no sense whatsoever. But it was all she could think of.

Eoin went over to a bar area in the corner and went behind it. "Red or white?"

"Red."

He poured her a wine, then poured himself some amber-colored liquid from a decanter. He motioned her to the couch. She chose a spot and hoped to hell that he sat next to her, which he did.

They sipped together in silence for a moment or two before he glanced at her. "Sari… are you sure you want to be here? I can always take you back to the hospital."

Did he think she'd changed her mind? "No, I just…" How could she put into words what she hadn't even realized until she stepped into his home again? "I don't want it to go by too fast."

His body seemed to relax into the sofa. "That I can understand. I don't want it to go by too fast either. We can take things nice and slow." Eoin smiled. "After all, we have all night. You set the pace."

Maybe if she didn't let herself lose total

control, she wouldn't feel so panicked when it was over. Was that from the fear of him disappearing from her life? She wasn't sure. What she did realize was that something more than that picture had spooked her last time. Maybe her fear of caring too much.

Too late. She was pretty sure she already cared far too much. But he was letting her set the pace. Maybe not just for tonight, but for where things led after tonight. She still wasn't sure about that part, but what she did know was that she wanted to be here, wanted him to make love to her. And she would accept the consequences for that decision.

Hopefully, like Eoin's surgery tonight, whatever happened would have a successful outcome. One that she wouldn't look back on and regret.

Taking one last sip of her wine, she set it down on the coffee table and turned toward him. "So it's okay to go slow?"

"It's okay." He set his own drink down and linked his fingers with hers. "Because slow or fast, we've already proven it can be good. So very good."

With that, he kissed her, slow and easy, and suddenly she knew he was right, knew that tonight was going to overwhelm her the way it had the last time they'd been together. But like that picture on the refrigerator, this time she was prepared for that possibility. And she was ready to face it, come what may.

Eoin rolled off Sari, his breath rasping in his lungs, but tugged her so that she wound up on top of him. He couldn't stand not being in close contact with her. Couldn't stand not touching her, even after what they'd just done. He reached up to kiss her earlobe, still trying to suck down enough air to speak. "That... was...phenomenal."

She laughed. "Do you always do this after a successful delivery?" She trailed her fingertips across his cheeks and down the sides of his face, using short soft strokes. The light pressure felt wonderful. And hell, if she didn't sound a whole lot more composed than he felt.

"Mm...feels good." She'd asked him something. Oh, yeah, about what he did after surgery. "No. Almost never. I'm too wiped out, normally."

She kept up her ministrations, leaning over,

her breasts coming tantalizingly close to his mouth. "But not this time?"

"No. You energize me." It was true. He'd been on a high from those two babies emerging from their mother, squalling and kicking and pink. There'd been a few tense moments when the uterus had started to show signs of failure and they'd needed to get in there quickly and take the babies. It all had turned out well. But the parents had determined this would be their last pregnancy, and he affirmed them in that decision. The mother's fibroids would continue to give her problems, and the next time they might not be so lucky.

"I do, do I?" Sari asked.

"Yes, you do." He tunneled his fingers into her hair and gently massaged her scalp. Eoin was having a hard time finding words that weren't trite or over the top. But he'd come to a decision over the course of the day—he wanted Sari in his life.

The thing was he wasn't sure she wanted the same thing. And he had no idea how to even go about asking. If she didn't want more children, that was fine. He wasn't married to that concept. What he was becoming married to was the idea of sharing his life with her and Evie and Hannah. If he could get past her fears and convince her that he wanted all of them. Not just her.

He wasn't sure why her ex had made the decision to walk away, but he was damned sure he wouldn't do the same thing, unless she gave him no other choice. It might've been early, but Eoin was ready and willing to stand and fight for her affection. He just needed to know that there was at least a chance for them, that she would at least consider the idea.

She leaned into his touch. "You're good at more than just surgery."

"Am I?" He moved his hand to her back, using a gentle touch to stroke down her spine, all the way to the top of her buttocks.

"You know you are. But if you're not careful..."

He reached down to cup her behind and settle her more firmly against him. "Do you want me to be careful?"

Sari buried her face against his shoulder. "I think I want you however I can get you."

He went still, wondering if she was saying more than she realized. "Do you mean that?"

Up came her head, and she met his eyes.

The tiniest flash of wariness showed as shallow furrows between her brows. “Are we still talking about sex?”

Eoin needed to pick his words carefully, but they suddenly all seemed out of reach. He finally settled for, “We are. But I also want to talk about more than just sex.”

He held his breath as he watched her face. The smile he’d hoped for didn’t appear, but something did change in her expression. He just couldn’t tell what it meant.

“More. As in…”

“As in do you think you’ll ever want more than this? With me.”

Sari sat up in a hurry, and his hands fell away. “I thought we’d talked about this. Or at least agreed that neither of us were anxious to be back in a relationship.”

Damn. He’d bungled it. He should have kept his thoughts to himself. But in reality, he wasn’t sure—despite what they’d talked about—that he wanted to continue just having casual encounters with her if there was no chance of more. He loved her, and his heart was becoming more and more entangled in that emotion, to the point that he wanted to include the girls in any future outings they had. And he'd love the opportunity to teach them to love the water as much as he did. Even wanted to teach them to surf, if they were interested in that.

"We did talk about it," he said. "I just… care about you and would like to explore where that might take us. What a future together might look like."

Sari gave a visible swallow and pulled the sheet up to cover herself. A sign of protecting herself? "I can't think about this right now, Eoin. I just can't." Her eyes went to the door, and he knew she was looking to escape again.

Was this what she would do every time they were together, as soon as they finished having sex? Look like she couldn't wait to get away from him?

Not so good for Eoin's ego. But more than that, this time it was like a knife to the heart. Especially since she'd said she wouldn't do it again, wouldn't disappear into the night.

Maybe he should just cut his losses while he could. "You talked about your fear with the girls and what happened with your ex, and I get that. But is it possible to leave them out of it for the moment and just explore things between us?"

"There are things that I can't…risk, Eoin."

"Like what?" Maybe if he understood what she was so afraid of, they could work through it together. "Tell me. Maybe I can help."

"You can't. And I can't afford not to take Evie and Hannah into consideration for whatever move I make. It's not fair to them," she said. "They've already suffered so much… loss. To go through that again, well… God, I knew this was a mistake."

She got up and started getting dressed, her movements jerky and fast. The top of her scrubs was inside out, and she had to take the garment off and right it before putting it on again. "This isn't a good idea. For either of us." She shook her head, the shimmer of tears visible in her eyes.

He got out of bed and took her hand. "Slow down for a minute, Sari. Can we at least talk about this?"

"No. Just no. Talking won't change reality."

"The reality of what?"

She didn't answer, just shoved her feet into her shoes and hurried into the living room. Eoin could hear her collecting her purse and knew he should go offer her a ride. But he already knew she'd turn him down if he even tried.

It was like last time, and yet it wasn't. Because this time he was wide awake, but he wasn't going to make a move to stop her. Because if she couldn't get past whatever she was so scared of, there was no future for them. Now or ever. And the sooner he accepted that, the sooner he could move past her and do his best to forget tonight had ever happened.

CHAPTER NINE

TWO DAYS LATER, Eoin had evidently called the clinic and said he couldn't make it in that day. He didn't give an explanation or a return date, and Heidi and Miranda were throwing possible explanations for his absence back and forth.

Sari was almost certain she knew, and if she was right, he probably wouldn't come back to Grandview. Ever. She hadn't thought about what the repercussions of their last night together might hold for the clinic. She'd naively thought they could just go their separate ways and work on how to go back to being colleagues.

Except on some level, she'd thought he might try to call and coax her to think about it some more. But that wouldn't help. Because the more she thought, the more terrified she became. Not only because of Evie and Hannah, but for herself.

The implications of Eoin's splenectomy made her realize just how scary it would be to live with—or be married to—him. She'd lived through the loss of one husband. She didn't think she'd survive losing a second one. All it would take was one stray microbe, one instance of not being careful enough, of not taking precautions. It could even be something she carried to him from the clinic.

Her initial fears about Eoin had centered around Max's leaving, and in her mind, that had been a legitimate concern. But after her Google search that fear had turned monstrous, growing into a huge mountain that she wasn't sure she had the strength to climb. Because it wasn't just about him walking out on them—it had to do with him dying on them. Could she put the girls through that? They had no memory of what had happened with their dad. But if something happened to Eoin, they would very much remember it.

She finally realized two sets of eyes were staring at her.

"What?"

Heidi tilted her head. "Miranda asked

if you had any idea what is going on with Eoin. But I think we just got our answer." She stared at Sari. "It's you, isn't it?"

Could she be any more transparent? If they could see through her, then Eoin would too. And how did you tell a man that his cancer made you not want him? Especially since it wasn't true. She did want him. She was just too scared to take the risk.

Sari gave a miserable nod of her head and dropped into a seat in the waiting area. "Yes, I think so. I was stupid and let myself get swept up in a fantasy that..." That what? Could never be based on reality? But that was because she said it couldn't be.

"Oh, my God, it's even worse than I thought. You slept with him, didn't you?" Miranda's eyes went huge. "Was it that terrible? Is he so embarrassed by his performance that he's afraid to show his face around here again?"

She waved her hands at them, trying to ward off any more comments. "No, it wasn't horrible. And maybe that's part of the problem. It was fantastic. All of it. So much so that I think I care about him."

"And the jerk doesn't reciprocate? Spill the

beans, Sari." Heidi sat down next to her, followed by Miranda.

"He's not a jerk, and he does. At least he says he does. But I'm just not sure I can do this. Not after David. Not after Max."

"But Eoin isn't either of those men. How do you know it won't work out with him?" Miranda asked.

She didn't know. And that was part of the problem. What if life with him was wonderful and then tragedy struck? "All I know is that it could very well end up in heartache for me and the girls," she said.

Heidi put her arm around her. "Hey, don't we face that with each birth we assist with? No one knows exactly how they'll turn out. Whether there will be a celebration or mourning when it's all said and done. We've sent patients over to the hospital with babies who have died in utero. Nothing is guaranteed in this life."

"I know that," she said. "At least my head does. I just don't think my heart is willing to take that risk."

"I get it, Sari." Miranda leaned forward. "But if you *don't* take the risk you might never get the chance again. You might never feel this way again. With anyone."

They were right. Both of them. But her thoughts were so jumbled right now that nothing she said seemed to make sense. "I guess I just need some time to work through things."

"You've got it," she added. "Maybe. But his absence today tells me he is weighing his options, just like you are. And if you let it go too long, the opportunity may be gone forever."

And that was the problem. She just wasn't sure she could walk away from him completely. But he'd made it sound like he wasn't willing to continue on like they'd been, and she wasn't sure she could bear to walk into an uncertain future.

So she'd better decide one way or the other—and quickly.

After not coming in at all the week he'd called off, Eoin had finally opted to call the clinic and ask to switch his future volunteer days to the days Sari normally had off, simply stating that he'd had a change to his schedule at work and leaving it at that. It was true—it had changed. Because he had been the one to change it. But he couldn't go on seeing Sari each and every week after the way they'd left things the last time they'd been together. He thought switching days would be the easiest solution for everyone involved. But after trying it, he wasn't so sure.

Two weeks had passed since he'd last seen her. And in those two weeks he'd been pretty miserable. The total opposite of how he'd felt when Lucy had left.

Maybe he should get a dog or something. But he doubted even that would help fill the void he felt right now. That empty space was a vast cavernous wasteland where nothing appealed to him. Not his job. Not volunteering at Grandview. Maybe he should throw in the towel as far as going there went. But it wasn't fair to Miranda, Heidi, Kat or the others at the clinic to leave everyone in the lurch after they'd worked so hard to replace their last obstetrician.

They'd consulted with him a couple of times when a presentation hadn't looked exactly like he'd expected it to. And he liked knowing he was helping such a good cause.

If only Sari didn't come with the package. Surprisingly no one had asked him about his schedule changing the way it had. It was like they'd just accepted it with no questions asked. Nor did they pass along any little messages like Sari saying hello.

Today, Miranda had pulled him in to see one of Saraia's patients, saying the midwife had a previous commitment that she couldn't get out of.

Yeah, a commitment to avoiding him. Eoin was fairly sure of it. And yet what could he do? He was pretty much doing the same thing. He'd laid his heart on the table, only to have it tossed back at him. Maybe he should unpin that heart from his refrigerator and give it to her. Maybe there was something about that that had unnerved her. Looking back, he rarely ate at home, so opening his refrigerator was not something he did all the time, unless it was to crack open a beer.

Maybe he should ask her point-blank if she wanted him to quit, wanted him out of her life even on a superficial level. Except he'd been the one to change his hours, not her. Which told him she thought maybe they could work together. She hadn't contacted him to say so, though. And he hadn't seen her girls at the clinic again either.

Because he wasn't at Grandview at the

same time she was. The other midwives, if they knew anything about what was happening between him and Sari, were playing things close to the vest. But they would be. They were all good friends. Whatever weirdness that was between him and Sari evidently didn't affect the other personnel at the clinic. They were all the same cordial people they'd always been.

But something was going to have to give. At some point they would find themselves at the same place at the same time. Whether it was a fundraising gala or a dinner out as a team, which he'd seen happen from time to time on the calendar in the staff lounge. They would see each other. And it was up to them to set the tone for that encounter. Maybe he really should try to at least talk to her again. Not about pursuing a relationship, but to assure her that he would no longer pressure her into taking their relationship any further.

Okay, now that was a plan he could get behind. Maybe he should try to appear on a day when he knew she would be here. Or maybe he should simply send her a text asking to see her.

No, that wouldn't work. Because she'd just

view it as more of the same and would refuse to see him.

Unless he surprised her. But would that come across as stalkerish? Hell, he didn't know anymore. But one thing he did know was that he had something that he should return to her so that she would no longer worry about him pursuing her. He was going to give her his heart. Not as in the actual one, but the one he'd colored. And then he could simply ask her if she wanted him to leave the clinic. It was a pretty simple question and called for a pretty simple answer.

Now all he had to do was figure out a way that seemed as nonthreatening as possible.

Sari wasn't sure she could do this anymore. And she wasn't sure it was working. She came in each and every day and knew that Eoin wouldn't be there because he'd been there on a different day. And when she was home with her girls, she wondered what he was doing at the clinic. The thought of opening the door to something more still frightened her, but so did the idea of never setting eyes on him again.

Didn't people do cancer treatments all the

time and never have to look it in the face again? There were people who never relapsed—Hodgkin's having one of the highest cure rates of all the lymphomas. And the sepsis risk? It was there. But David had never had cancer, and he'd still contracted an infection that his body couldn't fight off. Any of them could. Evie could have died of her head injury when it came down to it. And yet Sari hadn't thrown her daughter out of her life.

She had a feeling Eoin didn't talk to many people about his cancer. He'd admitted as much, and yet he'd told her the truth, had made himself as vulnerable as she'd made herself. But whereas he'd accepted her, accepted the whole package, she'd put up a big detour sign, motioning him to steer clear of her and her daughters under any circumstances.

It had probably made him feel pretty shitty. No wonder he'd changed his schedule. She wouldn't want to see him either if he'd done something like that to her.

Kind of like Max had done. She'd vilified her ex in every way, and yet she'd walked away from Eoin in just the same manner.

It wasn't fair. And he deserved to know

what exactly she was so afraid of. And then maybe he would at least understand how he'd turned her world upside down with his presence. And she wasn't sure she wanted to—or even *could*—go back to what she'd had before.

So did she take a chance and risk it all? Maybe. Maybe that was the only way for her to know one way or another if she had the courage to face another illness or death.

Perhaps Sari would show up on one of the days he was here and march down to his office and knock on the door. Did she deserve a hearing? Probably not. But she wanted one, so she could put this behind her once and for all. So that she could decide whether her future included him or it didn't.

Just like the expectant moms Sari served at this clinic, it was her choice. She had the power to decide her future. Or at least feel out what it might look like. If Eoin was even talking to her anymore.

So that was what she was going to do. Tomorrow was his day to work, so she'd be there bright and early. And she wasn't going to say a word to Heidi, Miranda or Kat because as much as she loved them, she didn't want them inadvertently tipping Eoin off to the fact that she wanted to talk to him.

Miranda met her at the door Thursday morning, waving her arms in all kinds of weird ways. “What the hell are *you* doing here today?”

“Um… I work here,” Sari said. “Do I need a reason to show up?”

“Well, no…but…it's *today*.”

Something was up. She could tell just by the way the other midwife sounded. “What's going on?”

“Nothing. I'm just waiting on Heidi.”

Sari frowned. “Isn't Eoin supposed to be working here today?”

“He was supposed to, but he called yesterday and said he needed to switch his day to this Friday instead.”

The day she was supposed to be working. “Did he say why?”

This time, her friend avoided her eyes, so Sari stepped in front of her, forcing her to look at her. “Did. He. Say. Why?”

Miranda actually bit her lip and looked horribly guilty. “He said he wanted to talk to you. Whatever it was sounded pretty final.”

Oh, God. "Is he quitting?"

"I don't really think so," Miranda said, "but I couldn't say. He could have just put his notice in with Heidi and been done with it. All I know is that it sounds like he has something pretty important to discuss with you. Just remember what we talked about. Please?"

She had something pretty important to discuss with him too. "Okay, thanks. Please don't say anything to him, though. I'll just show up like normal on Friday and see what happens."

"So you don't want me to mention your coming in today?"

She gave her friend a scowl. "No. I don't. This is something Eoin and I need to work out between ourselves."

"Well, I damn well hope it gives you both a better attitude," Miranda said, "because no one has wanted to be around either of you for the last two weeks."

Sari was immediately contrite. She walked over and gave her friend a hug. "I'm sorry. I guess I have been pretty grouchy."

"Why do you think Heidi headed for the hills when she saw you coming today?"

"Oh, hell. It looks like I owe a couple

of people an apology." She closed her eyes and then opened them again. "Starting with Eoin."

"That's the spirit." Her friend smiled. "I truly hope it works out between the two of you. I can't imagine a cuter couple."

She shrugged. "It'll be what it'll be."

On Friday, Sari entered her cubicle, only to find something on her desk. She frowned and went over to the paper. It was blank on one side, but when she turned it over there was a red heart. Her own heart leaped into her chest because she recognized it. And she had no idea what it meant. Did it mean Eoin was done, that he wasn't holding on to anything that reminded him of her? She was too late. Just like her friends had warned she might be.

She sat down and stared at the piece of paper.

"Sari..."

His voice came from the entryway to her space, as sure and deep as it had always been, as it had been those steamy nights when they'd made love. And she realized then and there that she'd fallen in love with him.

All of him.

Despite his uncertainty over some of the birthing techniques she espoused, he'd been able to keep an open mind about it.

And yet she hadn't done the same for him. She'd shut the door without even looking behind it to see the possibilities. Because she was afraid.

Sari looked up, twining her hands together as she tried to think of the right thing to say. But she came up blank.

Maybe she needed to start with the picture and go from there.

She picked it up and held it so he could see. "I don't understand. What does this mean?"

"It means I don't want to hold on to anything that makes you uncomfortable," he said.

"Uncomfortable?"

"Yes. If you don't want me in your girls' lives, I'll respect that, but I can't go on working here if that's the case," he said. "It would just be too…hard."

Oh, no. It really was too late.

"But why?" she asked.

He stared at her for a long moment. "Isn't it obvious?"

Was it supposed to be? "Maybe to you. But not to me."

He took a step closer. "Okay, I'll spell it out for you, even though it's something you probably don't want to hear," he said. "I love you. I realized it right before last time we were together, but from your reaction it was pretty obvious you don't feel the same way, so…that's that."

She fingered the picture. "Will you sit for a minute and let me explain to you why I said what I did that night?"

"Will it change anything?"

"Maybe," she said. "If I haven't left it for too long."

Something in Eoin's eyes darkened as if trying to weigh her words, but he sat down like she'd asked.

"Let me start by saying I did some reading about Hodgkin's lymphoma and realized I know very little about it. I didn't even know that a splenectomy carries some long-term risks." She bit her lip, struggling to continue. "Like an infection turning septic. The second I read those words, it set off a chain reaction inside of me. It brought back memories of David, as he died of that very thing. But worse was the fear that the same thing could happen to you at some point. That my daughters, who don't remember their dad, would have to live through something horrible happening to you."

She shrugged. "Because I love you too. And I'm so terrified of losing you…" Taking a breath, she somehow got out the rest of the sentence. "I'm so terrified of losing you that I was willing to shut you out of our lives completely."

"Was?"

She nodded. "I'm still afraid. But something finally clicked in my head. None of us are guaranteed tomorrow. I've seen pregnancies sail along without a problem, only to reach an unexpectedly tragic end. But most of the moms I've met wouldn't trade the ability to hold their infant. If I'd known ahead of time David was going to die, I'd have still married him, would still have our beautiful girls. And that is the kicker—am I willing to shut the door on what could be a beautiful thing just because of a picture I've constructed in my head out of fear?"

"What are you saying?" Eoin asked.

"I'm saying that if you'll still have me, I'll try," she said. "If you'll help me work through my moments of doubt and fear. But you have to promise never to walk out on my girls, even if we end up in the divorce courts."

He tipped her chin up and placed a gentle kiss on her mouth. "How about if I promise to never walk away from any of you? And I can tell you right now that I'm as healthy as a horse. I've shown no signs of relapse or serious illness. It's not to say that it couldn't happen. But we all take that chance when we love someone."

"So it's not too late?" Sari asked.

His brows went up. "Honestly? I thought maybe it was. I was pretty sure I was going to hand in my resignation today." He reached across the desk and took one of her hands. "But if you say otherwise, I will walk through that door with you instead of on my own."

"I don't want you to leave."

His eyes closed for a minute before reopening. "God. I never thought I'd hear you say that."

"So you'll stay?" she asked. "And let me make it up to you?"

"I'll stay. But I have one more thing to tell you. And it'll be your decision entirely," he said. "Twenty years ago, when I was undergoing treatment, the doctors asked me to think about whether I'd ever want to have kids. Like most young people, I said of course. But the treatment wiped out my ability to father children naturally."

"I don't care about any of that."

"I do. Because I banked sperm just in case, and it has sat in limbo for all this time," he said. "I went back and forth about what to do about it. Keep it stored? Or have the samples destroyed? A few weeks ago, I finally decided I might want a child someday. But no matter what, I would consider having a ready-made family made up of you, Evie, Hannah and me the biggest privilege of my life."

Sari bit her lip, a sudden train of possibility barreling toward her. "You mean you might want me to have your baby?"

"No, not my baby. *Our* baby," Eoin said. "But hell, I never thought I'd ever be with you, so it's enough that you might want me. Despite your fears."

"I do want you. And I don't know if my body will accept fertility treatments at this stage of the game or if my eggs are even young enough to produce a healthy baby. And that's the most important thing to me—that our baby has a chance at that."

"We'll talk to someone, ask their opinion," he said. "But if it does happen, I want to make something perfectly clear. Your birth process is yours to control. I will support you in whatever you want to do."

Sari's eyes watered at what he was offering her. But she couldn't take it. Not even if she wanted to. "It's ours to control. Just don't throw out the possibility of a vaginal birth unless testing shows it's not possible. I'll take your word at face value, if you feel it's too risky."

"Life is too risky, Sari. And yet..." Eoin went over and tugged her from her chair and held her close, aware on some level that Miranda and Heidi were lurking in the hallway watching them. He laughed. "I think we have an audience."

"We do. Because I showed up here a couple of days ago thinking I would catch you on the day you'd chosen to work, only to have Miranda inform me that you'd changed it to Friday. So here I am." She glanced at her friends and motioned them in no uncertain terms to clear the area because she wanted this man to kiss her senseless, and she didn't want the peanut gallery watching when that happened.

This was for them alone. To work out the details and figure out how to make it happen. After they finished making love in his apartment.

She picked up the heart and gave it back to him. “That’s yours to keep. It’s where this all began. And, Eoin, I never want to forget that. Even for a minute.”

“Agreed,” he said. “I think I may frame it and put it over our bed as a reminder that in the good times and bad times, we share the same heart.”

And with that, Eoin finally did what she’d been hoping he’d do for the last several minutes. He kissed her until she couldn’t breathe.

And then he did it all over again, with a promise that he would continue doing so for the rest of their lives.

EPILOGUE

SARI HAD GIVEN birth to their baby to the great joy of an ever-growing family that included her girls, Peggy and Eoin's folks, who had made several trips up from Florida. They were delighted not to have not just one grandchild but to include Hannah and Evie in that category. She was so blessed. So very, very lucky.

Their baby hadn't been born at Grandview Birthing Center, she'd been born at Portland Lakes Hospital. It wasn't just that she'd thought Eoin would feel more comfortable with the baby being born in a hospital, it was also the fact that she had still been able to use Miranda as her midwife. She'd gotten hospital privileges just for this event.

And things had gone wonderfully. Eoin had kept his "daddy hat" on the entire time, being her supporter, her lover…her friend.

And their girls had been able to be in the room with them. Although their constant questions had made her wonder if it had been the right decision.

But this would be their only baby together. It was something both Sari and her new husband had agreed on. She'd asked the minister who'd officiated at their wedding to strike out the line "in sickness and in health," not because she wouldn't stand by Eoin if anything happened, but because she didn't even want to send those words out into the universe. In the same way that they hadn't been sure she'd be able to get pregnant going through the whole hormone-treatment path, they couldn't predict how anything might go.

And it had taken a lot of work and love for her to really trust in a future together, that Eoin would truly love her girls and not see them as some sort of appendage that he had to accept in order to be with her.

But he did love them. And they were over-the-moon in love with him. Evie hadn't said her ex's name since the day she'd met Eoin that first day at the hospital. Maybe her daughter had somehow known that this man would end up being someone special in their lives.

If so, she'd been right. Sari didn't search for Hodgkin's lymphoma again. She knew enough to know the risks and knew Eoin well enough now to know that he wouldn't take his health for granted.

And *their* girls—it was still hard to think of them that way, because she always thought she'd be raising them alone—had already taken up surfing. Well, not quite. But they'd both paddled around on two small boards that Eoin had bought them as a wedding present.

It had been sweet and thoughtful and was going to be a real bonding experience between them.

And watching her husband up on his own surfboard? Absolute deliciousness. Actually, she had a hard time getting her fill of looking at him, of being with him deep into the night. Everything in her being told her she'd made the right choice. Taking a chance on them wasn't a scary experience. It was a joyful one.

Eoin carried Samantha over to the bed, where Sari was sitting up. She might've been under Portland Lakes's roof, but she was still going to do things her way. At least as much as possible.

Settling the baby into her arms to nurse and kissing her forehead, he went over to color with the girls at a small table in front of the pullout sofa. The sight made her smile.

Miranda came over. “Are you good?”

“The best.”

“I have to say I never thought I’d see you give birth in a big sterile hospital room, but maybe things are changing. No one tried to interfere or bustle around the room when you wanted the lights dimmed and quiet.”

Sari smiled. “I think I’ve made a believer out of Eoin. Oh, I know that what he does is very much needed. And every woman should be able to choose her experience as much as possible. But it worked out. And I think given my age, it made Eoin a little more comfortable having me in his territory.”

“Because you’re so ancient.” Miranda pursed her lips in disgust.

A laugh bubbled out before she could stop it. “There were times during this pregnancy that I felt ancient. This will be our last child. I want to concentrate my energies on the family I have now—and my job.”

"Did Eoin make a decision about…things?"

Sari nodded. "We asked that his remaining samples be made available to a clinic that specializes in helping families that want to have children but who have trouble affording the treatments they need in order to make that happen. There are grants and all kinds of things that I don't understand, but it's helping people."

"I think that's wonderful." Miranda smiled. "Speaking of wonderful, I need to get back to the clinic before rush hour hits."

"Go. We're fine—we're more than fine."

At that moment Eoin rose from his spot on the floor and nodded at Miranda. "Thanks for everything you did. And for not knocking me out when I asked for an update on the baby's vitals."

"You're a dad. And a doctor. It's hard to separate those two, but you did a pretty good job," she said. "Congratulations on Samantha. She's perfect, and I have to say I was right—you guys really are the cutest."

"Cutest. Okay." He made a face. But Sari knew he wasn't serious. He loved them. And she and the girls loved him.

Evie's voice came from across the room. "When can Sammy get her own surfboard?"

"Oh, heavens, honey, let's at least give her a chance to start walking before we talk about that."

"Daddy said we can all surf together."

Daddy. The decision about what to call Eoin hadn't been the easiest, but the girls knew that they had a dad who was in heaven. And between Sari and Peggy, they would make sure that David wasn't forgotten.

"Did he now?" She eyed him with mock irritation. "Has he forgotten that I don't surf?"

"He says you can still learn. That you're not too old."

That one made Sari snort, when Eoin hurried to say, "Let me just say that I never used the word 'old.' Not one single time."

"I'm kidding." She looked across the room at what she'd chosen as her focal point. It wasn't a Picasso or a beautiful island view. It was a simple heart. The one that Eoin had colored with the girls more than a year ago. He'd given it to her and said he knew it might be cheesy but that he meant it with everything he was. With everything he had. And that made it the best gift she could have ever gotten.

Because they had a love that would endure. And their family—now complete—had captured her own heart. And it would stand the test of time. No matter what.

* * * * *

Cinderella's Kiss With The ER Doc

Scarlet Wilson

MILLS & BOON

Scarlet Wilson wrote her first story aged eight and has never stopped. She's worked in the health service for more than thirty years, having trained as a nurse and a health visitor. Scarlet now works in public health and lives on the west coast of Scotland with her fiancé and their two sons. Writing medical romances and contemporary romances is a dream come true for her.

Visit the Author Profile page
at millsandboon.com.au for more titles.

Dear Reader,

It's hard to believe that this is my fifty-first book for Harlequin. Time seems to have passed in a blink of an eye and I can still remember that day I got my call to tell me my first book—*It Started with a Pregnancy*—would be published. The fact that I'm still here shows you all how much fun I'm still having, so if any of you ever have a romance idea and think you might like to write a story, I urge you all to check out the Harlequin website and give it a go!

Cinderella's Kiss with the ER Doc is Skye and Lucas's story with some of my favourite themes. It's set around Christmas and New Year, and involves a surprise secret inheritance that reveals a title and a huge ancestral estate. Letting my characters work through their issues including bereavement, press interference and a self-centred relative before finally reaching their happy-ever-after was so much fun!

Hope you enjoy reading,

Scarlet Wilson

DEDICATION

To my team of girls: Elaine Kerr, Natalie McLeod, Jennifer Reid, Gillian Robertson and Ruth Convery. Is working supposed to be this much fun?

Scarlet Wilson won the 2017 RoNA Rose Award for her book *Christmas in the Boss's Castle.*

CHAPTER ONE

IT ONLY TOOK a few seconds for Skye Carter's Spidey-sense to start tingling. She'd been aware of the low-level tension in the air as she'd dashed between one cubicle and another. A quick scrub change had been required when an elderly patient had vomited on her, and she was pulling her blonde bob back into a scrunchie as she heard the voices escalate.

'He said he'd be back!' an angry man was shouting. 'And that was ten minutes ago.'

Her hair wouldn't comply with her wishes. It was her own fault. In a moment of odd impulse in the hairdresser's she'd asked her stylist to take three inches off her hair. The blonde bob was lovely but touched her shoulders, so didn't quite comply with nursing regulations, meaning she'd spent the last week battling with hair clips and scrunchies in an effort to tie it back.

She gave up and increased her strides as the shouting continued. 'Where on earth is he? This place is a disgrace. You should all be ashamed of yourselves.'

Skye took one glance at the whiteboard nearby to check the name of the patient.

Roan Parrish, three years old, Paeds.

A child. Of course. Relatives were always over-emotional when it was a child that was sick, and she didn't blame them one bit.

'Enough,' she said sharply as she stepped into the cubicle and turned to look at the red-faced man. 'I'm Skye Carter, the A&E sister. What can I do to help you?'

Some people would question her de-escalation technique. But over the years Skye had learned not to go in with a quiet, nice approach. She'd realised when someone was loud, angry and potentially aggressive, to draw a line in the sand straight away. It tended to jerk back people's immediate behaviour, and let them know she wasn't going to be bullied. She certainly wasn't going to put up with bad behaviour towards her staff, but going on to ask how she could help tended to cut straight to the heart of the problem, where people could say exactly what it was they wanted.

The man gave a few short blinks and pointed at the child on the bed. 'He said he was going to be back soon.'

'Who said that?' She picked up the nearest chart to scan what it said. Another glance back at the board told her that although the child had been assigned to Paediatrics, they hadn't yet attended. Great.

'The doctor who was here. Scottish guy.'

She nodded, glancing at a few more notes. Lucas Hastings. She hadn't met him yet as she'd been on leave for a while—but, to be fair, she'd heard good things. He was a new registrar in the A&E department and at his level she would have expected him to have dealt with this child appropriately.

She moved over to Roan, who was lying on the bed with his eyes closed, his dark skin damp. A quick touch of his forehead told her he was running a slight temperature. He was attached to a monitor, so she pressed the button to check his blood pressure again and recorded his readings, pulling an ear thermometer from a drawer to add to the information already gathered.

There was a thudding noise outside and a

guy appeared at the curtains, breathless and carrying a unit of blood in his hand. His brow furrowed as he looked at Skye but, seeing her uniform, he carried on into the cubicle and started to speak quickly.

'Mr Parrish, sorry for the delay, but the lab called me. Roan's blood levels are a concern and we need to start a transfusion as soon as possible.'

It took Skye's brain a few seconds to adjust. The doctor had a thick Scottish burr, and his words came out quickly. She could see something similar happening with Mr Parrish. The man blinked and opened his mouth, but no words came out.

Skye blinked too. Lucas Hastings was more than handsome. Tall, broad-shouldered, with slightly longer dark hair and eyes the colour of an emerald ring she'd once admired in a jeweller's shop. At twenty thousand pounds, it was the kind of thing a girl could only dream of.

Lucas put his hand on the man's upper arm. 'Is there any way to get in touch with Roan's parents? I'd really like to talk to them too.'

Skye moved around behind them and grabbed an IV infusion kit and infusion pump. Her actions were instinctive and automatic. It only took her a few seconds to set them up and run the blood through the line.

This guy wasn't the parent? No wonder he was so worried. She gave him a quick glance. Mr Parrish wore his years well. He could be anything from early fifties to late sixties, and in this day and age it didn't pay to assume anything about who might be a parent.

Mr Parrish shook his head. 'My son and his wife are in the Caribbean. She's from there, and her sister is getting married today. They're only away for four days and Roan is staying with me.'

Lucas gave a nod. 'Was Roan born here?'

Skye tilted her head. Her years of experience meant she knew exactly why Lucas was asking the question. It was smart. But not all doctors got there quite so quickly.

Mr Parrish shook his head. 'No, he was born in Africa. My son was working there at the time. We have family there, and he was helping set up the accounts for the family business.'

'I don't suppose you know if Roan had a heel prick test as a baby?'

Skye could tell Mr Parrish was starting to get agitated again. He shook his head and tugged at the collar of his polo shirt. 'I have no idea. Does it matter?'

Skye handed over the electronic prescribing tablet to Lucas, indicating to him to prescribe the blood transfusion. It couldn't be set up until it was prescribed and they'd both double-checked the labelling. Experience had told her exactly where this conversation was heading.

'Have a seat, Mr Parrish,' she said gently.

'Is it bad?' His dark eyes were full of anguish as he turned towards her. Skye's stomach twisted. He was terrified for his grandson.

'It's manageable,' she replied. She was always completely honest with her patients.

Lucas's green eyes met hers. She'd never worked with this guy before, and had no idea about his patient skills or techniques. But somehow he seemed like a safe pair of hands.

He looked as if he might want to say something to her, but instead his fingers moved quickly over the prescribing tablet, then set it down next to Mr Parrish. He took a breath. 'Have you heard of sickle cell disease?'

The man's nose and brow wrinkled. He gave a slow nod but still had a look of confusion on his face. That told Skye a lot. He clearly didn't have someone in his family already affected by this disease.

Lucas continued. 'Our tests show that Roan has sickle cell disease. In the UK, all new babies are checked with a heel prick test after they are born. Because Roan was born in Africa, it's likely he missed that. It would have picked up the fact that Roan might be affected by sickle cell disease. It's why the lab phoned me, and I went to get the blood.'

Mr Parrish pulled out his phone. His hands were shaking. 'Is this going to help my grandson?'

Lucas nodded. 'We'll get him started on treatment. I'm really sorry the paediatricians haven't seen him yet. But this can't wait. We'll start this now, and I can give you a basic outline.'

Mr Parrish shook his head. He was still fumbling with his phone and Skye put her hand on his shoulder. 'Is it your son you want to get hold of?'

He nodded and she closed her hand over his. 'Would you like me to do it for you?'

His bottom lip trembled and he nodded again.

She waited until he slid the phone open, then glanced at Roan's electronic record for his dad's name. She dabbed her initials into the electronic prescribing tablet, gestured for Lucas to do the same and held the blood label where they could both check it.

She read the details out loud, waited for him to confirm, then also confirmed the run rate for the IV infusion. Within seconds, it was set up and running.

She gave them both a smile. 'Mr Parrish, I'll step outside and speak to your son.'

She just knew that he wasn't going to be in a position to absorb anything she told him right now. So she found the number, adjusted the dialling code to connect with the Caribbean and took a deep breath.

After a few seconds of hesitation, the call connected and was answered after a few long rings, to sounds of music. 'Dad?' came the yell.

'Sean Parrish? My name is Skye Carter. I'm a sister at A&E in The Harlington Hospital, London.'

It took Lucas five attempts to find the new mystery sister. He tried the nurses' station, the treatment room, the office, the sluice and then the linen closet before he was finally pointed in the direction of the staffroom. It could be hard to find a quiet space in one of the busiest A&Es in London.

As he pushed the door open he could hear her talking calmly. She was explaining in clear terms what sickle cell disease was, how they were currently treating Roan and what the paediatricians would do next. This clearly wasn't her first rodeo, and he was impressed by her knowledge of something that wouldn't be routine in A&E.

He waited until she'd ended the call before he picked up a packet of biscuits and sat down next to her, passing them to her. 'Thanks for that.'

She picked out the top digestive and took a bite. 'No problem. Is someone with Mr Parrish right now?'

He nodded. 'One of your staff, Leona, is keeping an eye on Roan's obs and sitting with Mr Parrish. The paed has just arrived. They had an arrest. That's why they were so long.'

Skye's eyebrows raised. 'In Paeds? Everything okay?'

Lucas leaned back against the slightly battered chair. 'Severe allergic reaction. Transferred to PICU on an adrenaline infusion.'

They both sat for a few moments. No one

liked it when kids were sick. An arrest in an adult was difficult enough, but in a child?

He held out his hand. 'Lucas Hastings,' he said. 'I've been here a few months. I don't think we've met before.'

'I haven't been here,' she said quickly, before sliding her hand into his. 'Skye Carter.'

She didn't expand on why she hadn't been there, and even though he was curious he wasn't going to ask. Her warm hand felt good in his and she had a firm grip that she pulled away a little quicker than he hoped for.

'Where did you work before, Lucas?'

'Liverpool, Glasgow, and a short spell in East Anglia with the air ambulance service.'

That seemed to catch her attention and she frowned. 'How did you land that?'

'A friend was sick at short notice,' he said. 'He asked me to cover and it suited them, and me.'

She took another bite of her biscuit. 'Good experience.' She gave an approving nod.

He pulled a face. 'Yes, and no. Sea and mountain rescue were certainly interesting. A lot of farming accidents. But the worst part was always being first on scene at some of the country road traffic accidents.'

She closed her eyes for a second and he

could see her shudder. If she'd worked here a while, she'd likely seen just as many horrors as he had. He was trying to figure this new colleague out.

It had been a surprise to sprint back into the hospital cubicle and see the unfamiliar blonde, holding her own with an air of authority. Her swift movements and how she'd just spoken to Roan Parrish's dad told him that she had experience that matched his own. He was curious about her. Skye? The staff here were friendly enough but no one had mentioned a missing sister.

'Cool accent,' she said unexpectedly. 'Which part of Scotland are you from?'

He gave a brief laugh. 'All of it, and none of it.' Her nose wrinkled and he continued. 'I was born somewhere near London, but then my mum moved to Dumfries. We stayed in Glasgow, Ayrshire, Edinburgh, even the Shetland Islands at one point, then we moved to Europe for a while. Spain, Gibraltar and Portugal, before coming back to Scotland so I could finish secondary school.'

Skye gave a wide smile. 'Wow, what a childhood.' There was a wistful light in her eyes. 'It's been London and London for me, and I always wanted to try someplace else.'

'Another country?'

She shrugged. 'Maybe. Or even another part of this country.' She took a breath and her smile tightened a little. 'I had family ties so had to stay put, but that's changed now, so it might be time for a change.' Her eyes looked off to the far wall, and he could tell she was seeing images in her mind. 'Where's your mum now?' she asked, the smile reappearing.

He got the oddest sense of vulnerability from her. Family ties that had changed? It was clear she was trying to change the subject and he understood that.

He said the words he'd said a number of times before. 'Not actually sure right now. Let's just say she's always been a bit of a wanderer.'

Skye gave him an odd look. 'Don't you keep in touch?'

'I try to,' he said, instantly knowing that Skye would pick up the implication. 'She's an independent woman, always moving onto the next place, and the next circle of friends. My friends at university nicknamed her the Scarlet Pimpernel.'

Skye let out a laugh. 'What do you mean?'

'You know the phrase: *They seek him here, they seek him there...*? My mum is a bit like that. I never know where she will pop up next.' He smiled as he remembered the late-night calls declaring she was in a part of the world that he'd sometimes never even heard of.

Skye took the last bite of her biscuit. 'Straight over my head. Guess I'm not cultured enough. We didn't do *The Scarlet Pimpernel* at school. We did *Romeo and Juliet* and I had definite issues with it.'

Lucas raised his eyebrows and felt a little spark of...something. He couldn't remember the last time he'd enjoyed a conversation like this. In theory, he'd always said he wouldn't date a colleague, but maybe it was time to reconsider?

He folded his arms and prayed his pager wouldn't sound any second. 'What were your issues?'

She threw up her hands. 'Where to start? Their age. The lies. The drama. Why are fifty per cent of all stories just about people not talking to each other and being truthful? They knew each other for a day. Young as she is, Juliet is on the rebound. And Romeo wasn't really romantic, more like—' she lifted her fingers into the air '—creepy.'

Lucas started to laugh. 'A million teenage hearts are breaking all over the world right now.'

Skye raised her eyebrows, giving him a clear view of her bright blue eyes, which exactly matched her scrubs. 'Fools.'

The door opened behind them and one of the other staff members gave them a quick glance. 'Can you two cover Resus? Ambulance on the way with an older man who's been attacked and is apparently in a bad way.'

They were on their feet in seconds, no hesitation, just a quick march down the corridor, where Skye washed her hands and donned a plastic apron. As she moved aside to make way for Lucas, she had a quick check over the equipment. She couldn't deny her sense of pride in her staff. Even after a few major incidents in Resus today, everything was restocked and in place, exactly as it should be.

She'd missed the familiar surroundings, and the familiar faces. She'd missed hearing the stories of teenage sons or baby granddaughters. Of Vixen the very wicked cat, or Albus, the not too bright sausage dog, belonging to one of her staff. For the last seven years this place and these people had been like an extended family to her.

Coming back hadn't been difficult. But her future thoughts might be. The rush of London was dulling. The Saturday night drunks and stabbings were certainly wearing her down. From the moment Skye Carter had her first nurse placement in A&E she'd known it was the place for her. But now? She was beginning to wonder what else might be out there. There was nothing to limit nurses these days, from advanced practice to specialisms. Skye just had to decide what direction she wanted to go in.

The approaching sound of a siren drew both her and Lucas to the receiving doors of the A&E unit. As the ambulance backed up, Lucas opened the back doors and Skye saw a familiar face.

'What you got, Nalin?'

Her Sri Lankan friend looked up and his face broke into a wide smile as he manoeuvred the stretcher towards them both. 'How's my favourite A&E sister?'

'Good.' She nodded as the wheels of the stretcher dropped down as it glided from the ambulance.

The other paramedic strolled round from the front of the ambulance and slung an arm around her shoulder, dropping a quick kiss on her head. 'Great to see you back, Skye.'

'Thanks, Jim.'

Her heart swelled. Both were good friends, and she knew their sentiments were entirely genuine. Over the years they'd seen some sights together, from major road traffic accidents, building collapses and train collisions. She'd trust these men with her life, and even though only a few seconds had passed she could sense the curious gaze from Lucas.

Nalin started talking. 'This is Albert Cunningham. Eighty-one. We think he was mugged and attacked, then run over by a car.'

Skye winced as she fell into step beside the stretcher as they wheeled it inside, her eyes on the portable monitor. 'Bad day,' she said quietly.

Nalin continued. 'We suspect a left fractured femur, with possible tib and fib fractures too. Head injury, Glasgow Coma Scale four at present. Rib injuries. Possible internal injuries too. BP is low at ninety over sixty, tachycardic at one hundred and forty. Only thing normal is his temperature.' As they pushed him into Resus, Nalin gave a sad sigh. 'He hasn't been conscious at all since we reached him.' He handed over a chart. 'At this point, know that we haven't given him any analgesics so far and I imagine he's going to need some.'

'Police been called?' asked Lucas.

Jim nodded. 'They were at the scene and are following us in. They have his personal effects.'

'Who would do this to an old guy?' Skye sighed as she looked down at him. The overcoat he was wearing was thick and elegant, the suit underneath probably from a Savile Row tailor, and the leather shoes on his feet had likely been handcrafted. Like a number of people in London, this man was well dressed. She was likely going to have to cut off clothes that cost more than she earned in a few months.

Lucas continued his examination as Skye slid the man's arm out of his coat and drew some blood from the crook of his elbow.

'Mr Cunningham?' She spoke gently but there was no response.

Two dark figures appeared at the door and Skye recognised one. 'Hi, Laura,' she said, and smiled.

'Skye, you're back. Nice to see you.' The

police sergeant was carrying a large bag with a number of items and was wearing a pair of gloves. 'I see you've got Mr Cunningham.'

The two paramedics were retrieving their equipment and getting ready to leave.

Lucas looked up and gave a nod. 'We have. I haven't finished assessing him yet.'

He recorded something in the notes and then looked up again. 'Apologies, we haven't met before. I'm Lucas Hastings.'

The two officers exchanged glances. Laura took a moment to answer. She flipped open her notebook and turned it to face Lucas. 'This Lucas Hastings?'

He glanced at the page and pulled back. 'That's my date of birth and address—what's going on?'

There was a deep furrow in his brow, just as Mr Cunningham gave a little twitch. Skye leaned over him quickly to reassess his neuro obs as the phone beside her rang. Her thoughts were spinning. What on earth was going on? Why had the police turned up here, looking for Lucas? It was more than a little unusual, but she didn't want to start asking questions. She had a patient to take care of, one who might be deteriorating rapidly.

Neither of their police colleagues had a

chance to reply before Lucas answered the phone and said a few short words. 'CT scan is ready for us.' He looked at Skye as Mr Cunningham gave a little twitch again. She was leaning over the patient checking the pupils of his eyes with a pen torch. 'We'll have to go with him. He's too unstable. I'm worried he's going to seize.'

The police exchanged glances. 'What does that mean?'

Skye started unplugging things and moving the monitor onto the edge of the patient trolley. 'It means that Mr Cunningham might have a blood clot on his brain, caused by his injuries, that might cause him to seize. He's starting to show signs. We need him scanned and may need to relieve the pressure on his brain.'

She turned around and opened a few drawers and took some sealed sterile surgical equipment from them.

'Good thinking,' murmured Lucas.

He turned to a healthcare support worker who'd just come into the room. 'We're taking this man to CT. Can you phone Neuro and ask them for an urgent consult? If they can, I'd appreciate it if they can meet us there.'

The healthcare support worker looked at

the name on the tablet Lucas handed him and gave a nod. 'No problem.'

As Lucas and Skye started wheeling the patient trolley down the corridor, Lucas looked over his shoulder towards the police. 'If you still need to speak to me, you'd better come with us.'

Lucas's stomach was knotted as they walked swiftly down the corridor. He wasn't a criminal. He knew he hadn't done anything wrong. So why on earth were there two police colleagues in his A&E department, with a notebook with his details in it?

As far as he was aware, he didn't even have an outstanding parking ticket. He started to think about the traffic around London. Had he unwittingly gone in a lane meant only for either buses or taxis? Had he missed a traffic light? Had he been caught speeding?

Lucas was generally a careful driver. He didn't even drive that often in London, making it even more unlikely. But he couldn't think of another reason for the police to be looking for him. Some unknown traffic infringement was his best guess.

The CT staff were ready for them, and assisted in moving Mr Cunningham into position for the scan.

Lucas, Skye and the two accompanying police officers moved into the viewing room while the scan was taking place. Lucas's eyes were fixed on the screen, suspecting what he might see.

'Who would do this to an old man?' murmured Skye before turning to face the officers. 'Where did you find him, Laura?'

Laura paused before answering. 'Just a few streets away, actually.'

Skye frowned. The hospital didn't have a huge car park as it was in the middle of London, and staff and visitors did sometimes park in the streets round about.

'Was he coming to visit someone?'

'Yes and no,' replied Laura, before casting her eyes in Lucas's direction.

Lucas almost felt her gaze on him. He looked up for a few seconds, shaking his head. 'I don't know him.'

The other officer started speaking. 'We think he was robbed because of his car. Apparently, it's an Aston Martin.'

'Like James Bond?' said Lucas, because that was what he generally associated Aston Martins with.

'More than you know,' replied the officer. 'It was actually his car that was used in one of the films a few years ago.'

'No way,' said Skye, her eyes going between the officers and the scanning screen.

Laura nodded. 'Someone saw the same car speeding away. We suspect he also had a watch and wallet stolen.'

Now Lucas was curious. 'So, if his wallet was stolen, how did you work out who he was so quickly?'

Laura held up a briefcase. 'There was nothing of value in here. Only paperwork. But that's why we're coming to you, Lucas.'

Now, he was thoroughly confused. 'What are you talking about?' As soon as the words were out of his mouth he held up his hand, recognising something on the screen. 'Large subdural haematoma,' he said quickly. As he reached for the phone, a woman in a white coat walked in.

'What have you got for me?' she asked, then glanced at the screen. 'Oh, dear.'

Skye gave a nod towards the officers. 'This is our neurosurgeon, Aasa Sangha.'

Aasa gave a quick glance and raised her eyebrows as Lucas handed her an electronic tablet with all the patient details.

'He's just been admitted after a robbery and assault. Left fractured femur. Tib and fib fractures too. There may be other internal injuries as he was also run over, but we prioritised the head scan due to his GCS reading.'

Aasa nodded. 'I have to relieve the pressure now.' She glanced at the tablet, then at the police officers. 'Do you have next of kin details or are there relatives here?'

Both shook their head. 'Still attempting to find a next of kin.'

Aasa turned to Skye and Lucas. 'In that case, I'm going to take Mr Cunningham straight to surgery. I'll be in touch once surgery is complete and—' she looked at his chart again '—I'll talk to one of the orthopods about the bone injuries.'

Lucas gave a grateful nod. In other circumstances he might have needed to do an emergency burr hole in Mr Cunningham's skull. Thankfully, that was not tonight. As Aasa asked some staff members to assist her and set off towards the theatre, Lucas was left with the distinct feeling that he was currently under the microscope.

He wanted to get back to A&E and continue to see patients.

'You still haven't explained why you're here,' he said bluntly to the two officers.

Laura set down the briefcase and flipped it open, lifting out a stack of papers. 'We haven't had a chance to look at these properly. But Mr Cunningham had your name and place of work in his possession. When we opened his briefcase we found this.' She handed over a large envelope.

If Lucas had been confused before, its contents didn't help.

The Last Will and Testament of Ralph Ignatius Cornwell Hastings, Duke of Mercia.

'Who is this?' he asked. 'And where's Mercia? Is it European? Like Monaco?'

Laura bit her bottom lip and took a deep breath. 'Turn the page.'

Lucas flipped over the page and his eyes scanned the legal jargon that no one understood. He stopped reading at the *only son* point.

He murmured the words out loud. 'Only son, Lucas Harrington Hastings.' He looked up. 'I'm not his only son.'

Laura pulled another paper from the sheaf. 'Birth certificate. This is you, isn't it?'

Lucas's skin prickled. Curiosity had pulled Skye closer, and she was at his elbow now, reading what he was. Lucas Harrington Hastings. His date of birth. His place of birth. Father, Ralph Hastings. Mother, Genevieve Hastings.

Lucas shook his head. 'I never met my father. He died before I was born. But he certainly wasn't a duke. I'm sure my mother would have told me that. My mother and I moved around a lot. But I've never heard of…' he pointed to the address that was listed among the papers '… Costley Hall.' He shook his head again. 'I think Mr Cunningham has got me mixed up with someone else.'

Skye sucked in a deep breath next to him and he realised she'd pulled her phone from her pocket.

'What? What is it?'

Her eyes met his. She turned her phone around slowly. 'You might not have met him…' Her words tailed off and as he saw the image on the screen he realised why. The Duke of Mercia—wherever that was—was literally an older version of him.

He blinked then peered a little closer, looking at the distinct green eyes, skin tone and shape of face. He leaned back.

'This is one of those practical jokes, isn't it? Some con for the new guy in the place.' He looked at Skye. 'Did you do this? We haven't met before—is this how you initiate your new staff?' He was starting to feel a bit angry now. He thrust a hand out. 'Have you looked at the board in A&E? There's no time for this, no matter how good a con you think it is. And here?' He pointed to the now empty scanning room. 'This is hardly the place.'

Skye's face pinched.

'Take a breath,' said Laura from the sidelines. 'Mr Hastings, I think you probably need to sit down.'

'I need to sit down?' He spun around. 'I need to sit down?' His voice was rising in pitch. 'Who even are you guys? Some pranksters? This is ridiculous.'

The male policeman put a very firm grip on Lucas's arm. 'Mr Hastings, calm down.'

Lucas threw out his other arm, sending the paperwork scattering on the floor. He was caught in one of those stupid TV prank shows. Or something even worse. He had patients to see. He had notes to write up. Most of all, he had no time for this. And the fact that the new colleague he'd actually considered attractive a few hours ago was in on it made it even more annoying.

'I have work to do,' he declared.

There was an expletive from the floor at his feet. He looked down. Skye was picking up the papers he had scattered. One was clutched in her hand. She stood up, pushing her hair, which had escaped from her tie, back from her face.

'You bet you do,' she said. The tone of her voice stopped him dead.

The look on her face was stuck between incredulous, scornful and laughing. She held the paper up for him. 'Because if this is true… Lucas Hastings?' She said the word with a question in her voice. 'You're the new Duke of Mercia, and a potential billionaire.'

CHAPTER TWO

SKYE WAS ASTOUNDED. But clearly not as much as Lucas, who stood shaking his head. The paper she held was a letter from Mr Cunningham's solicitors' firm, outlining exactly what the will and testament meant for Lucas. It was clear that his intention had been to give this to Lucas. Unfortunately, it looked like that might not happen for a while.

They'd both gone back to A&E to complete their shift. She'd tried to talk to him about it, but Lucas was either in denial or just wasn't ready to believe it.

In the meantime, Skye was looking around at the place she loved and realising that, for the most part, it had lost its shine for her.

Losing her mum had been a pivotal moment for Skye. She was comfortable at The Harlington. She was comfortable in her rented flat. But did she want to spend the rest of her life feeling comfortable?

A few years before, when she'd been looking to make some savings, she'd tried different kinds of nursing—doing bank shifts for a Harley Street clinic, covering post-operative shifts a couple of weekends a month. It had paid well, and they'd offered her a full-time job. But the clients weren't always particularly nice, treating her more like a servant than a nurse, and she'd known it wasn't for her. So, it was time to look again.

She was sitting in the hospital canteen on a break, scrolling through job adverts on her laptop, when she felt a tap on the shoulder. 'Can I join you?'

For a good-looking guy, Lucas looked awful. He had dark circles under his eyes and it was clear he hadn't slept the last few nights.

'Sure,' she said, then shifted a little when he didn't take the chair opposite her like she expected and instead sat down next to her. He was carrying two cups of coffee and two scones.

'I came prepared,' he said and pulled a face. 'I want to say sorry for accusing you of pulling a fast one on me. I honestly thought this was some kind of joke.' He gave a sigh.

'Turns out the joke is what I thought was my normal life.'

If this had been someone she knew better Skye would already have been hugging him right now. But she'd barely met Lucas. It wouldn't be appropriate, no matter how broken he looked.

She accepted the coffee and scone with a nod. 'I've been a nurse too long not to be suspicious of someone who comes bearing scones.'

He nodded. 'You're entirely right. I'm here to see if I can bend your ear for a bit. Or, as my favourite teacher used to say, have a blether.'

She smiled at the phrase. 'Blether away,' she said as she pushed her laptop away, and started buttering the scone.

'Have you told anyone what happened the other day?' The question was tentative.

'Of course not.' She looked at him. 'That was an entirely personal matter. I wouldn't tell anyone about that.'

He didn't even try to hide the audible sigh of relief.

She nudged him with her elbow. 'Eat your scone.'

She'd just got here and had plenty of time

left on her break. Lucas clearly needed someone to talk to, and even though she was just back at work, and had doubts about a million things, it was kind of flattering that he'd picked her.

Lucas started eating and took a sip of his coffee. His shoulders visibly relaxed and she could tell the tension was starting to leave his body.

'So,' she started, 'should I call you Duke?'

He groaned. 'Don't. I have no idea what's going on.'

'How's Mr Cunningham?'

'Still very sick. The surgery to relieve the pressure on his brain was a success, and he also had further surgery to replace one of his hips and set his fractures. But his lung collapsed and he had to have repair work done on his spleen. Apparently, he's regained consciousness on a few occasions, but they're pretty much keeping him sedated to let him heal.'

She studied Lucas's face. Talking about patients was easy for him, but talking about himself and his own life...?

'Is there someone else in the company that can help you?'

He nodded. 'I have an appointment tomorrow. Hopefully, this has all just been a big mistake.'

She took a slow breath. 'People tend not to make mistakes when it comes to money and titles.' She'd finished one half of her scone and spread some jam on the second half. 'So, have you spoken to your mother?'

He cringed. He actually cringed, before leaning his head on his hand and looking at her. 'So, my mum is a bit of a unique individual.'

Skye couldn't help the small smile that appeared on her face at the unusual description. She set down her coffee cup and looked at him. 'And what does that mean?'

He sighed. 'It means that I've left her sixteen voicemails and emailed half a dozen times. I'm not sure if she's in Italy or Spain right now.'

Skye sat back in her chair. 'Wow,' she said simply, her brain whirling. She'd been close to her mother. It was part of the reason that when her mother had been given a terminal diagnosis, Skye had been determined to nurse her herself. She was wise enough to know that families came in all shapes and sizes with differing dynamics, but she couldn't imagine her mother ever disappearing on her like that.

'Are you close?' she asked, almost afraid of the answer.

He waved one hand. 'We moved about a lot. I think I told you that before. My mother was always wanting to jet off somewhere, so this isn't so unusual.'

Skye shifted on her chair a little. 'You moved around a lot?' she reiterated.

He nodded.

'Why do you think that was?' As soon as she'd asked the question, she almost wanted to pull it back. It was too personal—and definitely none of her business. But, then again, Lucas had asked if he could talk to her.

Because she hadn't been here the last few months, she had no idea how Lucas had settled into his new job and new surroundings. Maybe there hadn't been time yet to strike up any friendships. Was it so wrong to be his listening ear?

Over her years in nursing, Skye had learned that there were times when she should just listen, and there were times when she should ask questions. The questions almost always circled back to whoever she was talking to, in a way that gave them a chance to come to their own conclusions.

Lucas had frozen. He didn't answer. Skye immediately felt guilty. Maybe he wasn't ready for this.

She'd tried to imagine being in his shoes. To have someone appear and ask unexpected questions about family. To impart knowledge that things might not be as she'd always imagined. Then, to throw on top, the chance of some kind of title and estate?

Even Skye had to admit that might feel as though her legs had been swept clean out from under her.

Lucas licked his lips. 'I thought she was just restless,' he admitted. 'That she was always looking for the next adventure, the next place.'

'And now?' she asked.

He lifted his head and stared across at the windows. 'Now, I wonder if she was running. If *we* were running.'

Skye's skin prickled. Of course. It was a natural question to ask.

'I take it you didn't know your mum was married?'

Now, he let out a short laugh. 'Married? Are you joking? My mother has the biggest array of rings you've ever seen. But she never wore a wedding ring. Never wore anything on that finger. She told me my dad had died before I was born, but she also told me that she'd never been married to him. I thought Hastings was my mother's maiden name.' He looked thoughtful for a moment. 'To be honest, I always wondered if my dad was married to someone else and had an affair with my mother. But he just didn't feature in our lives. She barely answered any questions about him, and it was just never a thing.' He was shaking his head now, and Skye was aware that a million other questions would now be circulating.

'So, the Duke? Is it likely that he's your father then?'

'Unless it's normal to look at a photograph of someone and wonder if you're looking in a mirror.' His voice had taken on an exasperated tone.

He gestured towards the laptop. 'Thinking of going somewhere else?'

Skye gave a jerk at the sudden change in topic. Her head had been so into Lucas's internal drama that she'd forgotten she'd left the laptop open. She wasn't even quite sure how to answer. She hadn't really had a chance to talk to any of her colleagues yet about how she was feeling.

'Just thinking about the world in general,' she said blandly.

He gave her a look. A look that told her he was just as smart as she was when it came to listening, and asking the right questions. 'Time for a change?'

She bit her lip. 'It might be. I'm not quite sure yet.' She gave a half-smile. 'My brain can't catch up with the rest of me.'

'You've just got back to work. Do you think you might need time to settle again?'

He hadn't said the words out loud, but somehow she knew he'd heard on the grapevine that her mother had died.

'I don't think I want to settle,' she admitted. 'Settling means getting stuck in a rut. Sometimes the rut gets too comfortable. And if you don't take a step outside, you don't know what opportunities you might miss out on. I tried a few other things before, but they're not what I'm looking for either.'

He gave a slow nod, but his green eyes were fixed on her, looking thoughtful. 'All true. But usually when someone is looking for a new job or a career change…' he paused; it was clear he was choosing his words carefully '…they are enthusiastic about it, or excited?'

Skye let out a hollow laugh. 'Meaning I'm not?'

He held up both hands. 'I wouldn't comment on something I shouldn't. I guess I'm just asking the question.'

She waited for a few moments, mulling things over in her mind. 'I guess I am too.'

He nodded at the other tab that was open—the one that had been revealed when she'd tried to click away from the job adverts. 'And what's the excuse for this then?' He was giving her a most amused grin, showing off his perfect teeth.

She looked back at the screen and sat back in her chair. 'That—' she pointed '—is the dream chair, or maybe it's the dream chaise longue.'

He shuddered. 'Okay, now you're scaring me.'

'What?' she asked, half laughing, half teasing. 'You don't like it?'

She looked back at the image of the Chesterfield chaise longue, covered in dark blue velvet patterned with parrots in red, green, yellow and bright blue. 'It's a work of art,' she argued.

'Of a five-year-old,' he mocked, still grinning at her.

She gave a sigh and waved her hand, then put it on her chest. 'You know how sometimes you just spot something so ridiculous, so unexplainable, but you just love it deep down?'

Now he was looking at her as if she had lost her mind, but she kept going.

'And even though you know that—' she pointed at the price tag '—it's something a million miles out of your league, you tell yourself that if you ever win the lottery and money isn't an object any more, that's what you'd spend it on. Just because.' She loved the expression on his face right now, as if he couldn't really understand if she was joking or not. 'Anyway, you know they're called "feature" chairs or "accent" chairs.'

He leaned a little closer, giving her a really good view of just how green his eyes were, and the fact he had eyelashes some girls might kill for. 'So, you're telling me the parrot feature chair is your lottery ticket?'

She gave him her sincerest nod. 'In a heartbeat,' she said without a second of hesitation.

He sat back in his chair, 'Wow,' he murmured, his eyes flicking back to the screen in bewilderment.

Inside, she was still smiling. There was something nice about such tiny moments of connection, even if they were in jest. As she shifted in her seat and he lowered his hands, her fingers brushed against his. It made her catch her breath, and she glanced at her watch, knowing it was time for her to leave.

'Can I say one thing?'

'Of course,' he said.

'When you get hold of your mum—' her voice trembled a little '—no matter what she says, don't be angry. That time is gone, but you've still got her. Just love her.'

She'd overstepped. She knew she'd overstepped, but she couldn't help how her current position made her feel. She'd give anything for one more hug, one more conversation, even though her mum had died in a comfortable, respectful way, and entirely the way she'd wanted.

He gave a slow nod. She couldn't even guess what the myriad of emotions were that flickered behind his eyes. 'Can you come?' he asked.

She picked up her laptop. 'Where?'

'Tomorrow. To the lawyers. Can you come with me?'

He looked so vulnerable. So torn about everything. Skye was off-duty tomorrow, and she wondered if he already knew that, and this had been why he'd sought her out today.

'Of course,' she replied, writing her number down on a scrap of paper from her pocket. 'Just let me know when, and where.'

As she made to walk away, he pointed at her laptop. 'And don't worry,' he added. 'Your secret is safe with me.'

And as she hugged her laptop close to her chest and headed back to A&E, she somehow knew it was.

He was pacing. Lucas knew he was pacing. He glanced at his watch again and breathed a sigh of relief as he glimpsed a bright red wool coat as Skye emerged from the underground. She pulled her bobble hat from her head and gave him a grin as she tried to fix her hair. The temperature had plummeted in London in the last couple of days and the first few flakes of snow were falling.

'Brr...' Skye shuddered. 'How's Mr Cunningham?'

Lucas gave a nod. 'Improving, but very slowly. They're weaning him off the sedation. He's got a chest infection now too, on top of everything else, but his levels of consciousness are improving.'

Skye gave a nod, her blonde hair already covered in tiny flakes of snow. 'That sounds a bit better. But still in no shape to talk to you?'

He shook his head. 'I wouldn't even go there.' He glanced up at the blue glass building in front of them. 'The lawyers were keen for me to wait until he can deal with things. But I think they're being unrealistic about his recovery time.' He shrugged his shoulders. 'I'm not Mr Cunningham's doctor, so it's not for me to have that conversation with them. I just told them someone else would need to bring me up to speed.'

It struck him that he'd only ever seen Skye in work clothes. Her fitted red coat, black boots and blonde hair were more than enough to turn a few heads in the street. He felt strangely protective of her.

'Thank you for doing this for me,' he said quickly.

'No problem,' she said. 'I've gone through some of this myself already. It's not nice, I can't lie. But hopefully it will help, having someone with you.'

She gave him a curious look. 'Did you get hold of your mum?'

He gave an exasperated sigh. 'Yes, and no. She's apparently in a place with no phone signal. An exclusive yoga resort. But she replied to one of my many emails—' he held up a finger '—with the birth certificate attached, and said that yes, the Duke was my father, but they'd had a falling-out years ago and she didn't want anything to do with him.'

Skye's brow wrinkled. 'There has to be more to it than that.'

'Oh, there is. But she's not telling me any more at the moment. Says it's all in the past, and she'll be back in London soon and we can catch up then.'

Skye stood still for the longest time. He had no idea what was going on in her head, but he saw her give a visible swallow and then a nod. She looked up at the building. 'Shall we go ahead?'

'Let's go.' He held the door open for her, and pushed the buttons when they moved into the lift to climb to the fifth floor.

When the doors opened again it was to a sleek reception desk, where two members of staff in dark suits and with immaculate hair and make-up were waiting for them.

One stood up. 'Your Grace.' She gave a nod

and Lucas felt as if he'd stepped into an alternative universe. He glanced over his shoulder. Nope. No one else here. She'd definitely been talking to him.

A bewildered grin appeared on Skye's face as she started walking after the receptionist. 'Come on,' she prompted in a low voice, keeping the smile in place.

His feet had welded themselves to the polished floor. His mouth was dry. For a few seconds he wondered if he could walk out again. But Skye's red coat was leading the way into another room.

He hurried to catch up, moving into a room with two stern-faced men, a woman with a notepad and a large table that was clearly meant to be intimidating. There were only six chairs in the room, and this table was far too large to only seat six.

Lucas sat in the chair that he was gestured to, and accepted the offer of coffee. Skye slid off her red coat. She'd dressed for the occasion, and he suspected she was better prepared for this than he was. She was wearing tailored black trousers and a cream satin blouse. One of the men half glared across the table at them both.

'Roger Phillips,' he said stiffly. 'And this is my colleague, William Bruce.'

There was an air of disapproval in his tone that Lucas didn't like. Was this the man he'd spoken to on the phone, who'd originally refused to meet him? Lucas wasn't normally short with people, but by the time he'd phoned the lawyers' office to request a meeting he'd been stressed and confused. When he'd been brushed off, he'd mentioned that he was surprised that a London solicitors' had no resilience built in, and surely one man wasn't the only person familiar with each individual case. An appointment had been found, even though it was apparently resented.

'Lucas Hastings,' he replied, 'And this is my colleague, Skye Carter.'

Mr Phillips's brow furrowed so badly Lucas was sure he could plant seeds in it. 'You do realise that everything that is discussed in here today is confidential?' He was actually glaring at Skye, who seemed completely nonplussed.

This woman had worked in one of London's busiest A&Es for seven years. He doubted very much that a grumpy man would have any impact.

He kept his voice level as a steaming cup of coffee was put in front of them, the coffee grounds fragrant in the air. 'I'm a doctor, my colleague is a nurse. Please don't lecture us on confidentiality.'

Mr Bruce gave a short laugh, making both Lucas and Skye turn their heads in his direction. He smiled. 'This might be fun.'

Lucas shifted in his chair, his mind going back to the day he'd been first told about all this and thinking it was some kind of joke. The laughing lawyer felt like a continuation of the joke.

'Honestly,' he muttered, 'it's like being in an alternate reality.'

Skye side-eyed him. 'Better be chocolate in this reality or I'm calling quits,' she said under her breath.

Mr Phillips's face was turning redder by the second.

'Can someone please get to the point?' Lucas sighed.

Mr Phillips started talking in a pompous voice. 'Mr Hastings, we're meeting you today because ten months ago the Duke of Mercia, Ralph Ignatius Cornwell Hastings, died. Our company is the executor of the Duke's will.'

Lucas didn't speak. He didn't have anything to add. He already knew the bones of the story.

'The Duke did not have any other children. Therefore, the majority of his estate has been willed to you, his son, Lucas Harrington Hastings.' His gaze narrowed. 'We will, of course, require a DNA sample to ensure we have the right individual.'

Lucas raised his eyebrows. 'The right person, with the right name, date of birth and birth certificate, which is mine?'

'It's a legal matter,' snapped Mr Phillips.

Mr Bruce leaned over the table. 'Do you have an accountant?'

'What?' Lucas shook his head. This was like an episode of a comedy series. 'I'm a doctor. Of course I don't have an accountant.'

'I can recommend one,' said Mr Bruce with a wave of his hand.

Skye closed her hand over his, clearly trying to centre him back to the madness in the room. 'Can you tell Lucas what is involved in the estate, as you call it?'

A bound collection of papers was passed over to Lucas. He opened it. The first asset listed was Costley Hall, along with its value, running costs and staff. He gulped, trying not to seem overwhelmed.

He turned over the page. Details of a number of vineyards, wineries and associated companies. More pages—more properties. More pages—lands and gardens. More pages—company names, all based in locations he hadn't even heard of.

He looked up and lifted the bound papers. 'So, what does this actually mean for me?'

'There's the issue of inheritance tax,' said Mr Bruce, scribbling a note on a piece of paper and passing it to Lucas. The sum made his eyes water. If he worked as a doctor his entire lifetime he wouldn't be able to earn the sum he was supposed to pay in inheritance tax.

'Is there a timescale to settling the estate?' asked Skye. She was sitting a little straighter now and had a serious look on her face—she'd clearly seen the figure on that piece of paper too.

'Once the DNA sample is confirmed, the monies and legal documents will be handed over to Mr Hastings's team,' said Mr Phillips.

'And if he doesn't have a team?' probed Skye.

Mr Phillips looked up from hooded lids. 'Then he'd better get one.'

Silence in the office while Lucas digested that last statement. He really didn't like this guy.

'So, Mr Cunningham normally deals with all this?'

Mr Bruce nodded. 'Albert Cunningham has been the Duke's solicitor for more than fifty years. He knows everything about the estate and companies.'

'And the title?' Skye's question came out of nowhere and all eyes turned towards her.

Mr Phillips cleared his throat. 'The title passes to the oldest son, which means that, as of ten months ago, Lucas Harrington Hastings has been the Duke of Mercia.'

'Is there a reason you took so long to let him know?' Skye was practically perched on the edge of her chair now.

Mr Phillips waved his hand. 'An estate of this size takes considerable work. Things can't be done overnight.'

But it seemed that Skye had no intention of letting this go.

'I have some experience in these matters,' she said coldly. 'Shouldn't the next of kin be informed of a death in the family as soon as possible?' As the lawyers exchanged glances she kept going. 'Ten months hardly seems right.' She pulled a piece of paper from her pocket and unfolded it. 'In fact, Mr Cunningham had this letter on his person at the time of the attack. It's dated—' she looked at it theatrically before straightening '—eight months ago, informing Lucas of the death of the Duke, the approximate value of the estate and the fact he'd inherited the title.'

Mr Phillips's face was still red. 'Our colleague was presumptuous. Details had to be checked.'

'Eight months is a long time to check details,' Skye observed.

Silence fell again.

'Who has looked after the estate, properties and companies for the last ten months?' asked Lucas.

Mr Bruce gave a half-smile. 'Everyone employed by the Duke's companies has continued in their role. The companies have continued to trade as normal.' He cleared his throat. 'There are a few other factors to consider.'

'Such as?' Lucas's skin prickled. Somehow, he knew this wasn't going to be good.

'The Duke's will also grants properties to some of those who were in his employment. A housekeeper and groundsman at Costley

Hall have inherited a cottage on the grounds. As has the head groom.' He pressed his lips together for a second. 'There is also a spousal maintenance payment.' He looked up, his dark eyes meeting Lucas's.

It took a few seconds for the penny to drop. 'To my mother?'

He'd always wondered how she'd managed to maintain her lifestyle. He'd asked on numerous occasions, because he'd never actually known his mother to work, but she'd waved her hand and spoken about 'family money', saying it in such a way as to imply it had come from her deceased parents.

Now, it seemed it had been coming from the ex-husband and father of Lucas—the man she'd let him think was dead.

'I should mention,' said Mr Bruce quickly, 'that one of the stipulations in the will is that you continue with the payment to your mother.'

Lucas let out a sound he couldn't even decipher himself. Continue to support the mother who'd lied to him and, even now, couldn't bring herself to come home and tell the truth.

'The Duke,' he said suddenly, 'how did he die?'

He was a doctor and it had just occurred to

him that, all of a sudden, he was about to find out about half of his family genetics. He'd always wondered. Toyed with those family DNA tests which could also test for genetic conditions. Lots of things could be inherited. So, this thought had occurred to him like a giant wrecking ball hitting his head side on.

Mr Bruce took a theatrical pause. Lucas—who was used to being calm and collected—was visualising dragging the man across his imposing table.

'The Duke had an abdominal aortic aneurysm. He collapsed at home and died before he reached hospital.'

'Had he been screened?' asked Lucas without hesitation. Abdominal aortic aneurysm screening had been available in England for a number of years for all men over sixty-five.

Mr Bruce gave an uncomfortable shiver. 'That information is not available.'

No. *Unfortunately...* No, *I'm sorry to say.* Mr Bruce didn't even have the curtesy to try and soften his words.

Lucas stood up abruptly. He'd heard enough for today.

Mr Phillips looked startled. 'We've still to make arrangements for the DNA test.'

Skye stood up too. 'And we will. Although—'

she glanced over at Lucas and back to the lawyers '—if you knew the Duke personally, I'm sure you can both see the family resemblance.'

Lucas knew there was a hint of a smile on his face. He'd brought Skye along for moral support, and she'd done that in spades. She was totally unaffected by the attitude in the room, or the amount of money that had been shown on the paperwork they'd both looked at.

She shot the lawyers her brightest smile as she tucked her arm into Lucas's. 'Gentlemen, if you'll excuse us, we have another appointment.'

Mr Phillips was clearly annoyed. It was strange, as he hadn't wanted to meet Lucas in the first place and didn't seem particularly adept at answering any of the questions that had been put to him. It struck Lucas that this company had likely always made a large part of their income from the Duke. Might they have deliberately delayed things to allow that to continue? It wasn't such a ridiculous thought. He couldn't wait to get out of here.

As they headed for the lifts, Mr Phillips followed them, still talking in an indignant voice. The two receptionists at the main desk stood as they walked past and Lucas had a flash of memory.

'Mr Hastings, we have not finished. You still have to be verified...'

Lucas spun around. 'We've already made it clear that we are finished for today.' He kept his voice low and steady. 'I'll be in touch about the DNA test, once I've had some independent advice.'

Mr Phillips made a derisive sound and Lucas knew he'd touched a nerve. Of course he would take some other advice—that was entirely his right, and the only sound thing to do. Mr Phillips gave him a look that could only be described as a sneer, and opened his mouth to speak again. But Lucas cut him dead.

'And in future, Mr Phillips, I would appreciate if you could address me by my proper title, which I believe is—' he raised his eyebrows '—Your Grace.'

And with that he stepped inside the lift alongside Skye and kept his eyes looking straight ahead as the doors slid closed.

CHAPTER THREE

SKYE READ THROUGH the application form for the fifth time and finally pressed send. It was the fourth one she'd completed, and she wasn't entirely sure that any of them would prove to be the right move for her. This one was for a job as a practice nurse in a GP surgery. She'd also applied for district nurse training, to be a nurse lecturer for student nurses, and for a training post as an endoscopy nurse. The whole world was out there, but she just didn't know the path to take.

Part of her wondered if it was running away. Getting away from The Harlington might help clear her thoughts. Because of what had happened with her mum dying, it was almost as if she associated her workplace with all those memories. It was a strange connection, and one other people might not get, but it was definitely in her head.

So, no matter what job came up, a fresh start might just be the change that she needed.

'What's that sigh for?' asked Lucas as he pushed a box of doughnuts under her nose. It was huge. A staff A&E delight, with twenty-four to choose from. She plucked a raspberry one from the box and looked over his shoulder to see if anyone else was around. Thankfully, the staffroom was empty.

'Just finished another application form,' she said.

'You're serious about this?'

She nodded. 'If I were Dorothy, I'd be looking for the Emerald City right now, but not sure of the direction.' She gestured to the computer. 'I've just got to hope that fate will have a hand in where I end up.'

She took a bite of her doughnut and looked at Lucas again. She'd heard a few colleagues talking about him the other day, wondering if he was dating anyone, and she hadn't liked the way it had made her stomach clench. She still found him as good-looking as the first day she'd met him, and when she heard his Scottish accent down the corridor it made the tiny hairs on her arms stand up to attention. The dark circles had disappeared from under his eyes now, and he seemed more chilled.

'Any word from your favourite solicitors?' It had been two weeks since they'd been at the office.

He nodded. 'I got a letter yesterday. The DNA test told them what they needed to know.' He groaned. 'It's also confirmed to me that I now have a one in three chance of developing the same condition as my now confirmed father.'

Skye leaned over and squeezed his hand. 'The danger of knowing too much about family genetics is overthinking it. There's too much that's new right now. Take some time to consider things.'

She was trying to be logical for him, hoping that if the shoe were on the other foot this was the kind of thing he would say to her.

'So, what happens now?'

He sighed. 'Now, I get to go and see Costley Hall. Want to come with me on Saturday?'

They'd fallen into an easy friendship, working alongside each other but still keeping each other's secrets for the past few weeks. Skye was aware that colleagues were likely talking about their secret whispering, but she didn't really care.

Was it too personal to agree and see where the previous Duke had lived?

He nudged her. 'You know you want to.'

She rolled her eyes. 'I do, actually. I was just wondering if I should try and show more decorum.'

'Decorum?' He laughed. 'Have you met me? I'm the guy with the broad Scottish accent. As soon as I set foot on the estate, they'll likely all run screaming from the building. I know nothing about the aristocracy. I have no idea what they actually expect of me—if anything.'

Skye gave him a curious look. 'Why on earth would you feel like that? You're a good guy. A doctor. True, you might not have known your father was a Duke and that it was a title you would inherit but, let's face it, the fault there lies with the adults in your life, not with you.'

He raised one eyebrow and smiled. 'Oh, call it like you see it. Don't hold back.'

Skye swallowed a bite of her doughnut. 'Have you managed to pin your mother down yet?'

They'd talked about this on a few occasions and it was clear to them both that Lucas's mother was using avoidance tactics right now. Skye was beginning to feel annoyed by this woman she'd never met. This was hard enough for Lucas. His mother could at least be truthful and let him know the entire story.

He shook his head and grinned at her. 'I get the distinct impression that if she ever appears you might bodily pin her to the ground yourself.'

Skye nodded. 'It's crossed my mind.' She pinned a smile on her face. 'But let's forget about that. I'd be happy to come along and see Costley Hall on Saturday. Let's just hope we can actually get in.' She tilted her head. 'Have you seen Mr Cunningham?'

Lucas sighed. 'I have—he's much improved, and devastated that he's lost his Aston Martin. It was one of only a few made.'

'You managed to talk about the Aston Martin instead of your father?'

Lucas pulled a face. 'It's hard. I'm not officially his doctor, but I did treat him. I don't think it's right for me to ask him questions when he's still in the hospital. Especially when I think there's something off about his colleagues.'

Skye stood up and brushed some sugar from her uniform. 'Oh, you've got that right. That was one of the strangest meetings I've attended in my life.' She let out a wry laugh. 'And I've been to our Trust's leadership groups.'

He rolled his eyes. 'The ones where they make you all hum, or the ones where they tell you to picture yourself as an animal?'

'Both,' she said, laughing.

'What were you?' he asked.

Skye could feel heat rising in her cheeks. 'Oh, don't.'

'Go on,' he teased. 'Tell me what animal you picked.'

She waved her hand. 'It was a bad day for me. I was running late after a flat tyre on my car, was covered in muck from changing my tyre at the side of the road and had missed out on the coffee. Honestly, when she picked on me and asked me to choose an animal, my mind went entirely blank. You know how that sometimes happens when you go to put your pin number in a card terminal in a shop? Nothing there at all?'

He nodded and she pointed to her chest. 'Well, that was me. Skye Carter. Human being that's been on the planet for thirty entire years, has passed exams, got a degree, rents a house, manages bills and a budget and—' she flicked her fingers in the air '—nothing. A big fat nothing.'

'So, what did you say?'

She laughed. 'Oh, the guy sitting next to me—who I'd never set eyes on before, and have never set eyes on again—did me the favour of mumbling "beaver" under his breath. So that was me. Before my brain started functioning again. I became a beaver.'

Lucas started to laugh.

'Not one of my finest moments.'

His shoulders were twitching up and down. 'Seriously?' He reached a hand up to wipe a tear from his eye.

Skye was still laughing too. 'Seriously. The A&E sister, who is sitting on a Trust leadership course with all these other senior NHS managers, told her colleagues her most associated animal was a beaver.'

She walked over to the sink and washed her hands, glancing over her shoulder at him. 'I try not to talk about it, but I'm pretty sure the rest of those people still tell friends and colleagues that story.'

There was something so nice about this. Just…chatting. Having someone she felt comfortable around. It was hard to ignore how wide his grin was, or the colour of those eyes. But she was doing her best to focus on being a friend for Lucas. He'd had a shock. His main family relationship had changed for ever because of this news. And he was still on a learning curve about what all this meant.

He'd only been in London for a few months, and she'd been on leave for a good part of that, but she got the impression he hadn't yet made any good friends around here. It could be tricky for medical staff, particularly when their training programmes could mean moving every year and working across different cities. Lucas was proving easy to be around.

After the trauma of losing her mum, and the secondary part of working through all the practical issues, having a different focus was good for her. Nursing a parent, and being the only one to deal with everything afterwards, had been draining in a way it was hard to explain. Even before she'd returned to work, some days had seemed as if there was nothing else to focus on.

Now, while she still had a few things to sort out, she could let her thoughts drift into Lucas's crazy situation. She could get angry for him. She could help him plan. And this meant she wasn't constantly thinking about fighting with the gas supplier to get a final bill when they kept telling her they would only speak to the account holder—even though the account holder, her mother, was dead.

Skye gave a small smile. 'Why don't you let me go and talk to Mr Cunningham so you don't feel as if there is a conflict of interest? If I think he's still too unwell I won't ask a thing. But if he's doing better, I could find out some general information for you.'

'Aren't lawyers like doctors—client privilege?'

She pressed her lips together. 'Probably. But your dad was the client, not you. I can ask him some general questions about the Duke and let him know we're going to see the house.' She nodded. 'Let me see what I can do.'

'Oh, no,' said Lucas, folding his arms with a grin. 'You've got that look again.'

'What look?' Skye tried to appear innocent.

'You know exactly what look,' he joked. 'The one that means you're plotting. No one is safe.'

She smiled again as she headed for the door. 'And that's exactly what I want everyone to think.' She winked. 'Keeps them all on their toes.'

* * *

Lucas was feeling strangely nervous. Not the kind of flutters that occasionally came with the first day on a new job. Nope. This was a deep down, heavy sensation in the pit of his stomach.

He was glad he wasn't doing this alone. Skye had jumped into the car with two steaming cups of coffee and some banana loaf that she'd had a go at making herself. 'My mum's recipe,' she said as she handed some over, wrapped in tinfoil. 'To be honest, I'm crap at making it, but I keep trying. It's a bit wonky. I've also got a recipe for yoghurt loaf. And one for lentil soup. But don't you always feel that when you make it yourself, it never tastes as good as when someone else makes it?'

She was talking nineteen-to-the-dozen. Was Skye nervous? Today her hair was skimming her shoulders in soft waves and her lips matched her red coat. A waft of orange and spice drifted in his direction. The perfume suited her. And he couldn't help but smile.

He looked down at the squinty slice of banana loaf on his lap. 'Thanks. I'm sure it will be great.' He broke a piece off and ate it as he pulled back into the traffic.

The journey to Costley Hall took over

ninety minutes. It was just on the outskirts of London, where the mass of buildings started to turn into the green of the countryside.

'I got some gossip,' Skye said as she watched the countryside slip past.

'What?'

'From Mr Cunningham.'

'No way—did you con information out of him?'

Skye grinned. 'I didn't con any information out of him. I asked him about an old friend. I also gave him a warning about his business colleagues, but I suspect he's wise to them. It's maybe why he hasn't retired. He might have referred to them as whippersnappers.'

Lucas laughed out loud. 'What?'

She beamed. 'Whippersnappers. It's a great word. Exactly the kind of word a very well brought up man in his eighties might use.' She leaned back against the leather seats in the car and sighed. 'I think Mr Cunningham might have been a bit of a catch in his day.'

Lucas gave her a surprised look, but she'd turned to face him as she continued. 'Can you imagine him, driving about in his super spy Aston Martin? I bet he was popular.'

Lucas took a sip of his coffee. 'So, the gossip. What did you find out?'

'Oh, yes.' She looked perfectly pleased with herself. 'The Duke of Mercia. Do you know why he's called that?'

'Er, no,' replied Lucas, not taking his eyes off the road.

'Well, Mercia is like Wessex—you know that name that was given to Edward—Earl of Wessex? It's an old England name. In Anglo-Saxon times, from back around the eight hundreds.'

Lucas frowned. 'So where was Mercia? And where was Wessex? I thought dukes were supposed to be named after real places, like Edinburgh or Cornwall.'

She shrugged. 'Wessex—depending on what map you look at, and what point in time—covered, at one point, London, Winchester, most of the south part of England, although I think there was some fighting between the various parts. Mercia, on the other hand—' she nodded and gave a knowing smile '—was bigger. It covered Chester, Lincoln, Worcester—basically a large part of the middle of the country.'

'So, my father was named a duke of some ancient Anglo-Saxon kingdom.' He wrinkled his nose. 'I have told you that I keep thinking this is all just an elaborate joke, haven't I?'

She nodded. 'On multiple occasions. Still not a joke.'

He gave her a sideways glance. 'What else did you find out?'

Skye pulled a face. 'It was a bit of a two-way exchange.'

He raised his eyebrows. 'Sold me out, did you?'

'In a heartbeat.' She smiled, her blue eyes connecting with his. He caught his breath. It was the look on her face. Yes, they were joking. This was how they'd quickly learned to be around each other. But, deep down, and even though he'd only known her a few weeks, he had a good feeling about Skye Carter. She didn't strike him as a girl who would sell anyone out.

'He was a good friend of your father,' she started, then took a breath. 'And I got the general impression that they liked and respected each other.'

There was something in her tone. 'But?' He glanced at her, but her expression was fixed. 'Skye?' They rounded a long curve in the country road. 'What are you not saying?'

She licked her lips and let out a long, slow breath. 'I could be very wrong, but I got a feeling it could have been more—not that Mr Cunningham said that.'

Pieces of the jigsaw puzzle that Lucas hadn't even begun to fit together assembled in his head.

'Oh?' he said as they slotted together. Then, 'Ooh...'

Silence followed in the car and Lucas's nose wrinkled. 'I wonder if that's why my mother isn't saying much.'

Skye looked at him. 'It could be, and I might be entirely wrong. It was just a feeling I got...a sense.'

As they neared the area where Costley Hall was situated Lucas spoke again. 'Did you find out anything else from Mr Cunningham?'

'Just very general things. Costley Hall was always going to be yours. The intention was always that you would inherit the title. They had no idea that your mother had told you that your father was dead. The Duke tried to make contact on frequent occasions, to try and stay in touch, but everything was always on your mother's terms. When you turned eighteen, he tried to find you again, but your mother wouldn't let him know where you were, or what you were doing.'

Lucas had the oddest sensation. As if someone was reaching into his chest and twisting his heart. His father had never been a focus in his life. He'd been told his father was dead, and that had been the end of it. Even when he'd asked questions growing up, his mother had made it clear the conversation was finished. He'd accepted it. There had been no point in pursuing things. He'd had no reason to think there was.

'There!' Skye pointed at a road sign for Costley Hall and Lucas indicated to turn in. They passed through a wide set of iron gates and followed an avenue with trees on either side. It went on for ever.

'Is this place hidden?' asked Skye.

'I have no idea,' said Lucas, finally slowing as a building on the right-hand side of the road emerged. It was a stone cottage, well maintained, painted white, with a bright red door. It was relatively large for a cottage and had clearly been extended over the years.

'Do you think that's where the groundsman and housekeeper live?' Skye asked. 'It looks lovely.'

The car had almost drawn to a halt, and Lucas realised that he and Skye were practically staring into someone's home. He gave himself a shake and continued down the road.

After another few minutes the trees fell away and the grey road changed to a dusky white colour. As they followed the curve of the driveway, they got the full impact of Costley Hall.

It was like a house from a film or TV series. A grand building with three floors and glistening windows. Circular steps were at the front, pillars over the entranceway and wooden doors that looked too big to be practical. Skye let out a breath, and her head nodded up and down as she counted.

'Okay, there's ten sets of windows on either side of the doors—just how big is this place?'

'Don't ask me,' said Lucas as he swallowed uncomfortably. A sign for the stables and gardens indicated another road which branched off around the side of the hall towards the back. The front gardens were pristinely manicured.

'Someone is clearly an expert in topiary around here,' murmured Skye as she pointed to the array of round, spiral and pyramid-shaped bushes and shrubs on display. What was even more attractive was the fact that most of them were tipped with the lightest dusting of snow. She held her hands out. 'Is it time for snow already?'

Lucas smiled. 'Sure is—next you'll be getting your advent calendar out.'

They climbed out of the car and just stood for a moment, both staring up at the hall, which seemed to have blindsided both of them.

Lucas's voice was a little nervous. 'Should we look around?'

They both started walking. Lucas looked back at where he'd parked his car. It looked abandoned near the fountain at the front of the house. The circular road around it was clearly designed to allow cars to turn, but he hadn't been exactly sure where to park. It wasn't obvious.

Skye stopped walking and held up a hand in a stop sign. 'Picture calendar or chocolate calendar?'

It took him just a second to realise she was referring to his previous comment. He was glad. It seemed she was trying to distract him from the hugeness of all this.

'Honestly, I prefer the wine one a friend bought me one year.'

'You had a wine advent calendar?'

He nodded. 'It was delivered to a place I was renting, and was actually addressed to my mother. But she was spending her winter in the Maldives, so I shared it with my roommate.'

As he said the words, something passed across her eyes.

'My male roommate,' he added quickly, then wondered why he'd felt obliged to qualify it.

They were friends. New friends. But would there be a chance of something else? The more time he spent around Skye Carter, the more time he wanted to spend around her. She was smart, fun, and not slow to let anyone know what she thought. She was also a great nurse, with clinical skills he could rely on.

Maybe it was the point they were both at in their lives that was drawing him to her. He knew she'd just returned to work and was contemplating a change. He'd just had a change thrust upon him that he certainly wasn't prepared for.

Having someone by his side was comforting. And the fact it was Skye? Just made it all the better.

Skye gave a shiver and wrapped her red coat around her a little tighter. 'Should we go inside?'

'Sure,' he said, his stomach clenched as

they walked up the steps to the enormous country house he now officially owned.

He paused, wondering whether to just push the door open or to ring the bell. He didn't want to get off on the wrong foot with anyone, so he used the large door knocker.

'There's technology,' Skye whispered, pointing to a doorbell that clearly had a camera attached.

'Let's see if the door knocker works,' he replied with a shrug.

A few seconds later the huge door was pulled open by a woman with bright blonde hair and a nervous smile. 'Your Grace?' she questioned.

Lucas blinked. For all his bravado at the lawyers' office, he was sure this was an address he wouldn't get used to. He nodded and held out his hand. 'Lucas Hastings,' he said. 'And please call me Lucas.'

The woman licked her pink lips, gave a small nod and shook his hand. He wondered why she was so nervous, and again thought about the father he'd never known. Had his father been a bad boss? Made the staff uncomfortable?

'And this is my friend, Skye Carter,' he added quickly as they stepped inside the door.

The woman shook Skye's hand too. 'I'm Olivia Bell, the housekeeper of Costley Hall, and my husband Donald is the groundsman. He'll want to meet you both.' She gave a nervous laugh, and Skye shot Lucas a glance. It was clear they both realised this woman was on edge.

Lucas couldn't help but look upwards. The main entranceway was beyond grand. It reached all the way to the top of the building, where there was a magnificent glass dome. Small yellow, blue and peach-coloured squares of glass decorated the dome, and the sun streaming through made it look as if confetti was dancing on the pale floor.

The walls on the ground floor were wood-panelled, and two magnificent staircases curved up on either side of the entranceway to the first floor. On either side of the entranceway, two gleaming chandeliers lit the way to either side of the house, adding to the otherworldly beauty of the whole place.

It took a moment to take everything in. Lucas glanced at Skye, in part to try and steady his nerves and maintain some normality, but Skye seemed as amazed as he was. She'd already opened her red coat and pushed her blonde hair back from her face. Her eyes were wide and her mouth slightly open.

He took another breath. She was stunning. And it was the first time he'd really noticed. If he'd glanced at her from across the room, he was sure his feet would have been making their way over right now.

'Would you like some tea?' asked Olivia.

'We'd love some tea,' said Skye quickly and the sudden words made Lucas blink away his previous thoughts and focus on what lay ahead.

Olivia nodded. 'I'll show you to the drawing room,' she said, her voice getting slightly higher pitched.

'Actually,' said Lucas, his hand touching her arm gently. 'While we'd love to see round the place, why don't we just follow you to the kitchen and have tea there?'

She seemed a bit worried and Lucas was conscious of trying to put her at ease. He wasn't there to fire them or intimidate them in any way. In an ideal world, he'd like this woman and her husband to be his friends. This was all brand-new, and he wanted to think he could trust the people who were already living in his inherited home.

The housekeeper seemed startled at first,

but then led them through the wide corridors, laid with tiny black and white tiles, to the enormous kitchen. At the heart of the kitchen was a twelve-seated wooden table. The surface of the table was polished, but it held a lifetime's worth of scrapes and dents.

As Olivia hurried around the kitchen Lucas had a look around. The windows looked out over what seemed to be a well-maintained vegetable garden, some greenhouses, and then on to manicured back lawns, with stables off to the side. He sat down at the table with Skye and ran his hand over the surface of the table, wondering if, in another lifetime, he might have made some of these marks and dents.

Skye seemed to read his mind and gently put her hand over his. 'It's a lot,' she said, her smile warm. 'I might need to lie down after seeing all of this place. It feels like what I imagine Cinderella's palace might be like.'

There was the sound of a door opening, and a man appeared, still wearing work clothes. He removed his boots and came over, holding out his hand. 'Your Grace.'

'Lucas,' said Lucas quickly. 'Are you Donald? It's a pleasure to meet you.'

As introductions were made, and Olivia

brought over tea and cakes, she and her husband seemed to hover by the table. Skye gave Lucas a nudge, and he realised what was wrong.

'I'd be delighted if you'd both sit down and join us,' he said quickly. 'I want to hear all about Costley Hall and what you both do here.'

There was a nervous exchange of glances before they both finally sat down. Tea was poured into elegant china cups and saucers, and cake was passed around.

'Tell me about this place,' said Lucas. 'I only know the briefest of details about it, and about my father.'

Donald looked puzzled. 'Albert hasn't told you?'

Lucas cast a quick glance at Skye. They clearly didn't know.

'Albert was injured on his way to the hospital to find me. He's been a patient for a couple of weeks now, and I've had to deal with some of the other lawyers from the practice.'

'You work at the hospital?'

Lucas met their gaze. 'Yes, I'm working at The Harlington. I'm an A&E doctor there, and Skye is one of the charge nurses.'

He could tell from the glances they exchanged that they secretly approved, and he felt an odd sense of relief. He wanted these people to like him.

'Will Albert be okay?' asked Olivia.

Skye smiled. 'He's making a good recovery, but it might be another few weeks. We—' then she looked sideways '—I mean Lucas, hasn't wanted to ask Albert too many questions when he should be focusing on his recovery.'

Donald took a slow breath. 'Well, those lawyers won't have been able to tell you much. The Duke threw them out of here on more than one occasion.'

Lucas looked up sharply and couldn't hide his broad smile. 'I've dealt with them on a few occasions,' he admitted. 'And they haven't become any more palatable.'

This time it was Donald's turn to laugh. 'You're more like your father than anyone expected.'

Lucas's skin prickled. 'I never knew my father,' he said slowly. 'In fact, my mother told me my father was dead. She never said anything about him being a Duke, or that he was even alive.'

Olivia's face pinched. 'Ginny had plans of her own. I've never understood why she didn't let you stay here and grow up in such a wonderful place.'

Lucas tried to remain steady. The fact that Olivia had just referred to his mother as Ginny meant that she'd known her well. He'd only ever heard a few people call her that, and they'd both been old acquaintances. For as long as he could remember, she would introduce herself to people as Genevieve.

He decided not to go down that path. 'What can you tell me about Costley Hall? Obviously, I've never been here before.'

There was another exchange of glances.

'But you were,' said Donald in a soft tone. 'You were here as a baby. But, just before your second birthday, your mother packed her bags and left. The Duke was distraught. Had private investigators searching for you both. Eventually, divorce papers arrived and Albert acted as the Duke's solicitor.'

Olivia gave a small sigh. 'We were surprised. We thought Albert would manage to get you back. To arrange visitation rights for your father. But it just never seemed to happen.'

The air around them was practically flickering. Lucas could sense it, and he knew Skye could too because her hand moved under the table and touched his thigh. Her intention was clearly to keep him calm, but the gesture had the opposite effect. In truth, it took his mind off the conversation they'd just been having and to a completely different place, but this wasn't the time or the place.

He moved his hand over hers and squeezed it.

His thoughts had lingered a few times on Skye applying for other jobs. He didn't like the thought of that. They were a good team at work, and she was the only person who knew about this, and the only person he'd connected with. He didn't want her to leave.

But Lucas knew it wasn't his place to even think about that. He caught a frequent sadness in her eyes at work, and he wondered if it was more about her mother than anything else. Her hand, warm in his, brought him back to the present, and all the things he didn't know about his own life.

'Tell me about the Hall,' he said.

'The history, or the layout?' asked Donald.

'Both,' he replied.

Donald nodded. 'Costley Hall was originally built in the nineteenth century and has changed a number of times over the years. The foundations for this building were laid in 1842 and the internal layout has altered a few times over the years. You'll like this,' he said with the hint of a smile. 'It was used as a hospital in the First World War for wounded soldiers and was run by the then Duchess. In the Second World War it was used as a home for children who were evacuated from London. There are over one hundred rooms, staterooms, bedrooms, two libraries, studies, multiple dining and drawing rooms, as well as a ballroom.'

'Wow, that'll be some heating bill,' said Skye, and as all heads turned towards her, her hand went up to her mouth. 'Oops—' she pulled a face '—did I say that out loud?'

Donald started to laugh. 'You're not joking.' He gave a shrug. 'Just don't ask how many boilers a place like this needs.'

Lucas could feel his skin start to prickle. His hand went up to rub the back of his neck. 'Is there any more help around here?'

Olivia stood up and opened one of the drawers in the dresser, bringing out a large black hardback notebook. She set it down on the table and pushed it towards Lucas.

'We thought you might want some kind of summary. This is a note of everyone employed on the Duke's estate…' She halted suddenly and paused. It was clear she'd forgotten for a moment that the Duke was no longer there. 'Your estate,' she carefully corrected herself. 'It details the groomsmen at the stables, the gardeners, the handymen, the cleaners and bookkeeper, the cook and waiting staff, and all the other staff who are needed around the estate.'

Lucas gulped, and he didn't even pretend to hide it. He flicked through some of the pages. 'Are all of these staff here all of the time?'

Donald shook his head. 'There are a few permanent staff, but Olivia and I are the only ones that stay on site. Some staff are seasonal, some part-time and some sessional.' He went to continue, then also halted his words. 'The former Duke used his cook a few days a week, and she baked for him too. He didn't really like the bother of preparing his own food.'

Lucas held up his hand. 'It's fine,' he said, even though these words seemed strange. 'I have no problem with you both calling my father the Duke; it's how you knew him. I'm not a big person on titles.'

What else could he say? This was all so alien to him. He looked around the kitchen. It didn't matter that it was only one room. It led to a pantry, and a utility room, and what looked like a boot room.

'I can't believe one person owned all this.'

Olivia was twisting her hands together. 'It's been in the family for two hundred years,' she said swiftly. 'And lots of other things happen here. The Duke allowed parts of the house to be used for conferences and weddings. He also hosted a number of dignitaries and guests on behalf of the royal family. He was a huge supporter of a number of charities. Some of the bedrooms are converted to allow guests with disabilities to stay. There's a lift in the left wing, and Costley Hall has regularly been used as a respite facility for families and children. Our event manager takes care of most of these things, and there's also riding lessons from the stables.'

The more he heard, the more he felt swamped.

He was a doctor. Show him a patient—show him the most difficult patient in the world, with the most obscure condition—and Lucas would roll up his sleeves and get to work. But this?

Donald continued. 'Actually, the events manager is anxious to meet you. She wants to check your availability for certain dates and functions.'

Lucas gave a short cough. 'What?'

Skye caught his eye and, under the table, her hand rested on his leg firmly, but even she looked a bit overwhelmed by all this.

'Well, this is all new, of course. And I'm sure Lucas will be able to meet with her, but not today, and not until he's managed to get to grips with his role in the estate.' She gave her brightest smile and Lucas wondered if the others knew it was entirely forced, and on his behalf. 'Remember, he still works full-time at The Harlington and has duties and responsibilities to consider.'

'But you're the Duke now,' said Olivia quickly. 'I'm sure you won't need to bother with being a doctor now. And it really is quite urgent.'

He didn't get a chance to speak because Skye was on her feet, the chair legs screeching on the black and white tiles.

'Well, the estate has managed for the last ten months without a Duke. Lucas will need to decide his own time frames. If you don't mind, we'll go for a look around.'

Olivia spoke immediately. 'The Duke's suite is on the first floor on the left.'

Without wasting another second, Skye reached over and took his hand, keeping the smile on her face as she guided him along the corridor next to her.

CHAPTER FOUR

SKYE WAS DECIDEDLY ignoring the little flashes dancing up her arm as she held Lucas's warm palm and focused on the fact that he was swearing softly under his breath the full length of the corridor.

The swearing didn't stop as she picked a corridor to walk down, glancing from side to side at some rooms before finding one she thought might be suitable, pulling him inside and closing the door firmly behind them both.

To be honest, she was feeling a bit light-headed, and a bit sick—and it was nothing to do with Olivia's cake. It was the enormity of all this. It was all very well finding out Lucas was a duke. The information at the solicitors' had seemed overwhelming, but actually seeing Costley Hall in reality—took things to a whole other level. Lucas seemed so normal. He *was* normal. How would this all change him? All she really knew was that it was a million miles away from where she'd grown up in a council estate in one of the less salubrious parts of London.

The room they'd walked into was a library. It was an exceptionally beautiful room, kitted out in dark wood, lined with rows of bookcases and expensive-looking books, a rolling ladder, a desk and chair, then a fireplace with chesterfield sofas and a dark red rug.

All along one side were wide windows, looking out onto the gardens at the rear and allowing an exceptional amount of light to stream into what would otherwise have been a dark room.

Skye collapsed onto one sofa and waited until Lucas sank into the other. He leaned forward and put his head in his hands, shaking it fiercely. 'No. No way. Absolutely not.'

Skye let him rant. She would have done exactly the same in his shoes, so was in no position to judge.

As they'd sat in the kitchen and asked questions, what had started as a nice introduction had seemed to turn into the biggest list of all time. The expectations of the new Duke were high, and Skye wondered if Lucas might just decide to run for the hills.

She decided to try and play devil's advocate, tamping down her feelings too. 'They seem nice enough,' she said. 'I think they might just have unrealistic expectations of the role you might want to play here.'

He sat up and sighed. She could practically feel the anger emanate from him. 'I don't think I want any role here. The house is beautiful, but why would I actually stay here? I rent a flat in London and that meets my needs. I know nothing about estates, or stables, or how to run a place like this.'

'I get it.' She nodded as she looked around the room, then gave him a cheeky smile. 'But can you just give me five minutes of bliss, please?' She closed her eyes and breathed in heavily.

'Skye, what are you doing?' he asked.

She opened her eyes again and held out her hands. 'Ever since I was tiny, my life's ambition was to have my own library. This place, the smell—' she pointed to the ladder '—that is part of my childhood dream. Look, it's on wheels.' She got up and touched it gently to see if it moved. It stubbornly stayed in one place, so she gave it a tougher shove and it squeaked and moved along the runners at the top and bottom with an uncomfortable noise. Skye ignored it and ran her hand along the spines of the books on the shelves. Red, brown and blue volumes with gold lettering. 'I don't even know what these are,' she said. 'But I want to read them all.' She walked around the room and then she let out a squeak similar to the ladder. 'Oh, look!'

Lucas stood up and wandered over to where she was standing. Her finger was pointing at a large and slightly threadbare pink velvet chaise longue.

'Oh, my,' she said with glee, before positioning herself on it comically. 'I always wanted one of these.'

She laid one hand on her forehead to shield her eyes from the rays of sun that were streaming through the window on this winter's day. After a moment she opened her eyes and said to him, 'Bit of a draught, right enough.'

Lucas laughed and sighed at the same time. 'I appreciate the deflection.' Skye kept smiling at him because he knew exactly what she'd been doing. 'But I imagine this whole house is a bit of a draught. There are probably regulations that say the windows can't be changed.'

'I have a sealant gun,' she said, swinging

her legs off the chaise longue and standing up. They were closer than she'd expected, but he didn't move away. She tilted her head up towards him. 'This whole place is overwhelming, Lucas. Only thing I can say is, don't make any sudden decisions. Like I said, this place has functioned for ten months before they managed to find you and let you know about it. Okay, there will likely be some things outstanding, but I'm sure they can wait a while longer.'

Skye took a breath. Longing to tell him that whilst she found this place a bit magical, she also would likely be scared to touch anything else whilst she was here. And questions were circulating in her head. Would Lucas change, become part of the aristocracy, and next thing she knew he'd be engaged to a princess from somewhere spectacular? It all just seemed too much, but she was determined to keep supporting him, even if she was terrified.

They stayed like that for a few seconds, Skye Carter looking up at him with those bright blue eyes. Her blonde hair was sitting perfectly on her shoulders in a way that wouldn't be allowed in the hospital, and the concern and sincerity in her eyes was genuine.

He knew it instinctively. From the day he'd met her she'd been a genuine soul, with a spark about her. The palm of his hand itched. More than anything, right now he wanted to reach out and touch her. The feelings of attraction he'd been trying to downplay before now—purely because of everything else that was going on for them both—were hard to ignore. As he stood, not moving away, her perfume drifted up around him.

He could picture himself as a child, reading stories about snakes being piped out of a basket by a snake charmer, and that was exactly how he felt.

How would she react if he touched her cheek right now and bent to kiss her? Right now, they were so close they were practically touching, and neither of them seemed inclined to step away. They hadn't talked about taking the next step. Was she waiting for him to make a move?

She blinked, then her phone beeped loudly in her pocket, causing them both to jump. Skye let out a nervous laugh and pulled it out, frowning for a few seconds as she swiped something open and read it.

'Everything okay?' he asked as she finally stepped away and moved closer to the window. On a winter's day like this, the sun was now hidden behind a cloud and the library wasn't well lit.

Her head came up sharply, her expression surprised. 'I... I...' She hesitated, something he wasn't used to seeing in Skye. Her face broke into a smile. 'I've got an interview for a new job.'

His stomach fell. 'You have? Where?'

He couldn't help the first thought that was echoing around his head.

Oh, no. Oh, no. Oh, no.

It didn't matter that it was selfish and pathetic. He genuinely enjoyed working with her, and she was the only person who knew his awkward secret. He wasn't ready for her to step out of his life.

'I told you I'd applied for a few,' she started as he nodded. 'This one is for a practice nurse job in a GP surgery.' She peered out of the window. 'It's in London. But I've applied for another one too, that actually isn't too far from here.'

A tiny wave of relief flowed over him. At least one of the jobs she'd applied for was near here. That was good.

He paused for a second, trying to think

about Skye and not himself. 'You've applied for a few—is this the one that you want?'

She sighed and sat back down on the chaise longue. She shook her head lightly. 'I actually don't know what I want. I just hope that I get invited for an interview somewhere and feel a good vibe. You know how that happens sometimes?'

'Oh, yeah,' he had to agree. 'There have been a few places I've interviewed that I've wanted to walk out five minutes after walking in. Then there are others I get back out to the car and feel jealous of all the people already there.'

'See, you get it,' she said. 'I'm hoping I get that feeling.'

'When's the interview?'

'Next week—know anything about general practice?'

He nodded hesitantly. Even if Skye got the job, she'd still need to work at least a month's notice. He would still see her.

'I have a few friends that have gone into general practice. Want me to ask them what they'd be looking for in a practice nurse?'

Her shoulders visibly relaxed. 'Yes, thanks, that would be great.' She gave a sigh. 'I think I just need to be somewhere different. I've always loved my job and my colleagues, but now, every time I step inside, I remember when I had to go and tell Ross, our boss, about my mum and her diagnosis. And then again when I needed to take time off to nurse her at home.'

He gave a nod of understanding. 'So, you want to make different kinds of memories?'

For a second her eyebrows shot up, and she gave him a mocking look.

He waved his hand. 'You know what I mean.'

She sighed. 'Yes, I do.' She bit her lip. 'Just like you, with this place. You have a chance to make a whole new set of memories here.'

He was just contemplating what she'd said as she started to walk back around the room, running her fingers along the books. 'I'd still love a library some day.' Her smile broadened and she turned back to him. 'Maybe that's the job I should be applying for—a librarian.'

Now it was his turn to laugh. 'You couldn't be an ordinary librarian,' he joked as he took his turn to push the ladder along its rails. 'You'd be the kind of librarian that's in those TV shows. Everyone thinks they're quiet, but they actually have a superhero cape and fight off vampires or have secret rooms that lead into other worlds.'

Skye moved alongside him and raised her eyebrows. 'Are you sure you're a doctor and not a fiction writer?'

He shrugged and smiled. She was definitely making this easier for him. 'Maybe I'm a bit of both?'

'What say we take a good look around?'

He glanced at his watch. 'I think it's going to ice up again soon—not sure we want to stay here too late. The country roads around here probably don't get gritted.'

If she knew he was still feeling a bit out of sorts here she didn't say it, and for a second he thought she might have looked relieved.

'Okay then, what about a quick look around the first floor? We can call it quits after that and come back another day.'

Warmth spread through him. This wasn't just a one-off trip. She intended to come back with him again.

'Sure,' he said quickly and they left the library and walked back to the main entranceway and up one of the curved sets of stairs. Lucas ran his hand up the dark polished wooden banister as they climbed the wide, red-carpeted stairs.

'I wonder how many people have touched this banister over the years,' he said with a hint of melancholy.

'You should be proud,' she said.

He looked at her in surprise. 'What do you mean?'

'You heard the stories that Donald and Olivia told you. Some people will have been patients, some doctors and nurses, some evacuees.' She glanced up to the dome and smiled. Dark clouds had filled the sky above so the delicate glasswork wasn't quite so visible. 'Think of the stories they could tell. And even the last few years—' she gave him a nudge '—I bet there are a few wedding albums that have a shot of the bride and groom taken from below to get that gorgeous dome in the picture. And if it was like earlier, with the sun streaming through, making it look like confetti was on the walls…' She let her voice trail off, a wistful smile on her face.

'Why do you always look on the bright side?' he asked.

'Is that a cue for a song?' she joked.

He shook his head. 'Just an observation.'

Skye took a deep breath as they headed down one of the corridors, opening doors as they went. 'It's not really my nature. I'm faking it. My mum tried to persuade me it was a better frame of mind to adopt. And I vowed that I'd try.'

There was a hint of wobble in her voice and, before he could think about it, Lucas put an arm around her shoulders. They stopped at one of the doors to peer inside.

'I think that sounds good,' he said gently. 'Your mum was obviously a wise woman.'

She looked up at him with slightly damp eyes. 'She'd like that someone said that about her.'

Lucas stayed silent, giving her a moment to collect herself.

Skye took a kind of shuddery breath, then changed the subject. 'It's a bedroom,' she said.

He gave a short laugh. 'Seems so.'

The wide window let some dim light into the larger than average room, with a double bed, wardrobe, dresser and heavy brocade curtains at the window. The room smelt surprisingly fresh and, after a few sniffs, Skye pointed to the air freshener attached to the plug point. Another door led to a bathroom with bath, sink and toilet all in white, with some rather grand taps. The tiling was a little dated but the room was spotless.

'Do you think they're all like this?' Skye asked.

'I have no idea,' Lucas replied and they walked down the hall, opening more doors and peering into other rooms. The layouts were similar, the décor slightly different. They found what looked like an upstairs drawing room, three times the size of the other rooms, with other versions of chesterfield furniture. There were a few bathrooms, what looked like an office, and a few smaller rooms near the end of the corridor.

Then they came to the rooms that Olivia and Donald had mentioned. They were clearly designed for people with additional needs. Adaptations were in place in the bathrooms, the rooms had more modern furniture, special beds and completely flat floors with no rugs or carpets. There was also a lift near these rooms and Skye pressed the button to call it.

'Sorry,' she said with a shrug. 'I was one of those kids that if you put a sign on something saying *Don't Touch*, guess what I did?'

The lift pinged and opened and they bent forward to look inside. 'Wow, it's big,' said Skye.

Lucas nodded. He was starting to understand a little more about the place. He walked back to one of the rooms and went over to the windows. It really was getting dark now, but he tried to imagine what a respite session here might be like for some of the families that had been mentioned. Most of them had probably never stayed anywhere like this before. He still found it hard to believe that he actually had.

If he didn't get his act together, would all this good work fall by the wayside?

'So many rooms,' said Skye as they stood together. 'I wonder how long it takes to clean this place?'

He smiled. 'Why would that be the first thing that comes into your head?'

She paused as she looked at him, and he wondered if she was adjusting what she really wanted to say. She gave a half-shrug. 'Just thinking in days gone by I'd likely have been a scullery maid in a place like this. Think how long it would take to scrub the floors.'

She sounded kind of strange, so he put his arm back around her shoulders. 'You don't need to scrub floors, and you don't need to clean. Maybe you can give me decorating advice?'

They moved back to the staircase and his

hand paused near a door. It was as if Skye knew exactly why he was hesitating.

'The Duke's suite. Do you want to look inside?'

He couldn't pretend he wasn't curious. So, he pushed open the door. The suite was large. There was a sitting room, a dressing room, a huge bedroom and an equally large bathroom. He couldn't help but look at the slightly dated furnishings and run his finger along the dark wood desk, wondering how often his father had sat here. A man he'd never known.

There was a photo on the bureau that stopped him dead. It was his father, his mother and clearly an infant him on a beach somewhere. How long had that photo been here? Just less than thirty years?

He gulped and took another look around. There was a bright red footstool. An elegant cushioned rocking chair. A rainbow stuffed toy which looked decidedly modern. Another photo, this time of his father and Albert on a golf course somewhere. They were laughing heartily and something about that made him want to ask even more questions.

An impulse grabbed him and he opened a large mahogany cupboard and his breath caught somewhere in his throat. His father's clothes were all still hanging there, and a certain aroma of cologne swept towards him.

He lifted his hand and touched the well-cut suits, obviously from Savile Row, along with designer shirts and ties. There was even what looked like a burgundy velvet smoking jacket. Aside from that, it looked as if his father had been a well-turned-out man.

It was the first real pang that he felt, wishing he had known him.

He walked from room to room and Skye just stood back and let him, not speaking, just letting him have this time.

When he'd finished, he knew his eyes were likely shining with the threat of tears. Skye moved beside him.

'This place is pretty much a mirror image of itself—let's look at the other side.'

They moved across the grand staircase to the other side, and opened the opposite suite. It was clean and tidy, but had a neglected air about it. The furnishings were in keeping with the rest of the house, but without the same lived-in feel or individuality.

'Do you think this was your mother's at one point?'

Lucas gave a sad smile as he ran his finger along the top of a full-length mirror that stood next to the wardrobe. 'Oh, I think so,' he said with irony. 'Even though there's a dressing room next door filled with mirrors, she'd still have to have another in here.'

He took a deep breath. 'If I have to stay at some point, I'll probably use these rooms instead of the Duke's.'

'Instead of your father's,' Skye said gently.

He stood for a moment, letting that sink in.

'Instead of my father's,' he repeated as she slid her hand into his. He knew she was doing it to comfort him. But it took his thoughts to another place. One where Skye wasn't only here as his friend.

The more time he spent with her, the more he was attracted to her. At first, he'd just instantly noticed her good looks and admirable don't-mess-with-me manner. But over the last few weeks, as he'd got to know her better, it was her warmth and empathy that had drawn him in, her sense of humour and intelligence. Even now, she seemed to know exactly what to do in this unforeseen situation.

He swallowed, his throat instantly dry.

'Hey, you.' Skye gave a squeeze of his hand. 'Is it time to go?'

Lucas gave a grateful shrug. His head was spinning.

They headed back down the stairs and made their way back to the kitchen. Donald had vanished but Olivia was pacing. She jumped as they walked back in.

'Thanks for letting us have a look around,' Lucas said graciously. 'But it's getting dark and we're going to head back to London.'

'You're not staying?' She seemed genuinely surprised.

He shook his head. 'I'm working again tomorrow. We have to get back.'

He could only describe the look on Olivia's face as disappointed, and he didn't really understand.

'If you could give me your phone number, I'll be in touch when we're going to come back.' Saying 'we' made him feel strangely comfortable.

She pulled open a drawer and brought out a card with the former Duke's details on it, a line drawing of Costley Hall with the address and phone number underneath.

'We can get these changed,' she said apologetically.

He shook his head and stroked the card for the briefest of seconds. 'It's fine, honestly. We'll talk about it some other time.'

Olivia followed them to the main door and

watched them climb into the car, which was covered in a dusting of snow. Lucas started the engine—or at least he tried to start the engine. It turned but didn't catch.

Skye gave him an anxious glance. 'Maybe it's just the cold?'

He tried again; this time the car was silent.

They sat and looked at each other for a few moments, neither of them wanting to say the words out loud.

Skye pulled a face. 'Sorry, don't have any roadside cover.'

Lucas closed his eyes for a second. 'Me neither.' He looked back out at Costley Hall. 'Or maybe they would expect home start from here.'

Both jumped as there was a small knock at the window. Olivia was shivering outside. Lucas opened his door.

'Car trouble?' she asked.

He nodded to the obvious question and climbed out.

'Would you like to borrow a car?' she asked.

Lucas felt his heart leap in his chest. 'You have something I could borrow?'

'Well, it wouldn't be borrowing, exactly.

Because they're all yours. They were your father's cars. He was a bit of a collector.'

Skye shot him a hopeful look.

'I have cars?'

Olivia shivered again, and Lucas remembered himself. 'You should get back inside.' She nodded gratefully and they followed her back into the house.

'Give me a moment,' she said, then disappeared down the back corridor.

'I thought for a minute we were going to be stranded here,' said Skye with a relieved smile. 'Thank goodness there is another car.'

Footsteps echoed along the corridor and Donald appeared in a thick jacket. He gave a nod. 'Come with me, Your Grace.'

Lucas didn't think it was the time to object to the title and they both followed Donald through the dark corridors and out through a door at the back on the right-hand side of the house. It led directly into another dark space, and after a few moments Donald flicked a switch.

Lucas held his breath. The garage was the size of a football pitch and it was filled with a variety of cars, some with gleaming bodywork and some covered and hidden from view. Rolls-Royces, Bentleys, Aston Martins, Mercedes, BMWs in a variety of ages and styles. He gulped. It was like a teenage boy's fantasy.

Donald gave him a few moments, obviously realising this would be some kind of shock.

Lucas's voice came out slightly higher-pitched than normal. 'You didn't mention cars before, Donald.'

The burly man turned and gave a slight bow. 'You didn't need one then, Your Grace.'

Skye started to move. Lucas wasn't sure how much she knew about cars, but her eyes were wide as she ran her fingers lightly along a few of the bonnets and wings.

'How many are there?' she asked.

'Thirty-three,' said Donald smartly. 'The Duke loved his cars, but he reduced his collection over the last few years. He also allowed a few select friends to drive his cars.'

Lucas shivered. 'Was one of those friends Albert Cunningham?'

'Oh, no,' said Skye, her hand going to her mouth. 'The Aston Martin was one of the Duke's cars?'

'What happened to the Aston Martin?' asked Donald with one eyebrow raised.

'We'll talk about it later,' said Lucas with

a wave of his hand. He still couldn't take his eyes off the cars in front in him.

Donald gave a brief nod. 'Which one do you want? I'll get you the keys.'

Lucas blinked. Was that a DeLorean back there? A Ferrari? And if these were on display, what was beneath the covers?

He took a breath. 'I need something that can handle country roads, possibly ice, and we're going back to London, so really I need something that car thieves won't track in the blink of an eye.' He smiled and shook his head. 'Do you have anything normal in here? Something that I can drive in London, where I won't need to worry about dings and scratches?'

This time both eyebrows went up and Donald gestured for them to follow him, going to a safe on the wall and keying in some numbers before pulling out a set of car keys. He threaded his way through the cars and moved over to a gleaming black Range Rover with shaded windows.

'It's top of the range,' said Donald matter-of-factly. 'The Duke wouldn't buy anything less, but it can certainly handle country roads, ice and whatever else is thrown at it.'

'It has *Steal Me* written all over it,' sighed Skye with a smile.

Lucas nodded, then stopped. 'Wait a minute—what about insurance?'

Donald shook his head. 'All the cars are insured under the Costley Hall estate. You're covered to drive it.'

Lucas glanced at the keys in his hand. 'You're sure?'

Donald nodded and folded his arms. 'I still want to know about the Aston Martin.'

Lucas gave a slightly nervous smile. 'Sure, when I get back.'

Donald moved over and flicked another switch and one of the garage doors glided open. Lucas and Skye climbed into the luxurious car, starting the engine and sinking down into the already warming leather seats.

Skye looked at the lights on the dashboard and laughed. 'It's like the Starship Enterprise in here.'

Lucas nodded and moved a few switches to make the lights and windscreen wipers automatic. 'Ready to head back to London?'

She took a deep breath and stared at him for a few moments, her blue eyes fixed on his. 'Thanks,' she said simply.

'What for?' he asked. 'It's you that's been helping me.'

As he moved the car outside the garage and gave a wave to Donald, she wrapped her arms around herself, waiting for the car to heat up. 'No, I think it's pretty equal,' she countered.

'What do you mean?' The driveway was snow-encrusted now and driving along it was like taking a trip through a winter wonderland.

She kept rubbing her arms even though the temperature was rising rapidly.

'All of this,' she said in a quiet voice. 'I know it's a lot, and I know you're overwhelmed by it all, but for me?' She looked at him with sorrow in her eyes. 'I don't mean to be selfish, but it's a distraction. One that I needed.' She looked guilty for a second. She took a juddery breath. 'Going back to work has helped. But every morning, when I wake up, for a few brief moments I feel normal, and then I remember that my mum died and it all crashes back.' Tears slid down her cheeks. 'I should be over this. I should be coping better with this. I got to nurse my mum the way I wanted to, I've had time to sort out all the accounts, the house stuff, and all her things.'

Lucas was trying to keep his eyes on the

road but there was no way he could do that when Skye was clearly crying. He looked for a suitable place to pull over and did so sharply, cutting the engine, turning to face her and unfastening their seatbelts. It only took him a few seconds to pull her into his arms.

'I should be better than this,' she sobbed against him, her warm breath filtering through to his chest. He held her close, stroking the back of her hair and whispering reassuring words. Guilt was sweeping over him. He'd known about her bereavement. Her fellow staff members had warned him to treat her carefully. But because she seemed so self-assured, so strong, it hadn't occurred to him it might all be a front.

Skye was caring and compassionate with patients, and her years in A&E had clearly taught her to take no prisoners. He'd liked that about her. It had been the first thing he'd noticed about her, and the feisty attitude was definitely part of the attraction.

But what if that really wasn't Skye? What if it was just a work persona? He hated to admit he'd been leaning on her throughout all this. She'd been great and had stayed by his side, but all the while she'd been falling apart inside.

'Who says there's a timeline on grief?' he said softly. 'I'm sorry I haven't asked more. I'm sorry I've been relying on you so much when I should have been a better friend. This was your mum, Skye. You've had a whole lifetime with her. You had routines with her. It doesn't go away at once. No matter how hard you try.'

She sniffed and lifted her head, letting him see her tear-filled blue eyes. 'I'm sorry.' She shook her head and pushed herself away from him. The sudden space between them felt cold and empty.

'Skye, I hope by this point you'd consider us friends. You can talk to me, tell me how you're feeling. If you're having a bad day, you should say so. We didn't need to come here today—we could have done something else. Something you wanted to do.'

'But that's just it—' she blinked '—I *did* want to come here. I wanted to be with you. I wanted the distraction. Everything at home, and at work, just tells me I need to look at my life and make a fresh start.'

Lucas took a deep breath. He couldn't pretend he didn't feel guilty.

'Skye, a distraction might be fine. But the trouble was, I got to Costley Hall and just felt overwhelmed by it all. I stopped paying attention to you. My brain was trying to understand how much it costs to heat a place like that, and to keep the businesses and land running. I feel as if I'm not cut out for all this.' He put his hand on his chest. 'I trained as a doctor, not as a duke. I'm not sure I want to spend the time and energy that this will take.'

He reached over and brushed the side of her cheek for the briefest of seconds. 'When what I should be doing is looking after the first friend that I met when I got here.'

There was something there. A definite spark between them. His brain was telling him that now was not the time to act on it. But even as he was looking at her the edges of her lips tilted upwards. Her head moved a little closer and she reached up towards him.

'Thank you,' she breathed, resting her forehead against his.

They stayed in that position for a few moments. He wanted to reach out and take one of her hands and hold it in his. But he also wanted to respect her. They were on a dark, snowy country road. He didn't want to make a move that could make her feel compromised. He'd never do that. Every cell in his body was aware of the breathing rhythm of their bodies that had automatically synched with each other.

'Any time,' he whispered back, and she smiled, before eventually lifting her head and settling back into her seat.

Lucas took the cue and restarted the engine, the windscreen wipers coming on automatically. The snow was falling thick and fast.

Skye peered out into the pitch-black night. 'It's beginning to look a lot like Christmas,' she joked. Then her gaze flicked back to him. 'There's a thought. I didn't see a Christmas tree or decorations in Costley Hall.'

He frowned. 'Come to think of it, I didn't either. I wonder why?' As he steered the car carefully along the twisting roads, he gave a sigh. 'I actually prefer New Year to Christmas. I always offer to work Christmas Day.'

'Me too,' said Skye in surprise. 'Or maybe it's just that I'm not married and don't have kids, so I've always chosen to volunteer to do Christmas to let my colleagues with families have the time off.'

'When did you last have a Christmas off?' he asked.

She shook her head. 'Never. Since I was a student nurse, I've always offered to work. My mum and I used to have Christmas dinner on another day. And I'd just record anything special I wanted to watch from Christmas Day.' She gave him a curious glance. 'Don't you spend Christmas or New Year with your mum?'

'My mum?' he said with amusement in his voice. 'Ever since I was at medical school, my mother has endeavoured to get herself an exotic Christmas and New Year invite—usually to a private island somewhere. I told you, not your typical mother.'

'And you never get an invite?' she asked incredulously.

He laughed out loud. 'Never mind *me* not getting an invite. Half the time I'm quite sure my mother *didn't* get an invite.'

Skye laughed in surprise. 'You're joking?'

He shook his head as the sign ahead indicated the way back to London. 'You haven't met her. You'll understand when you do.'

'I think you mean she hasn't met *me* yet,' said Skye. 'I'm more than a match for your mother.' She was joking—he knew she was—but after a long and stressful day, she still had the ability to make him smile.

'Can't wait to see when that happens,' he responded. 'I definitely want a ringside seat.'

She raised her eyebrows. 'Want to take bets on whether Mr Cunningham might want one too?'

They'd joined the main road into London.

'Ah, the mysterious Mr Cunningham.' Lucas gave a slow nod. 'By all accounts, he's doing a lot better now.' He gave Skye a sideways glance. 'Maybe it's time to go and see him again, this time to talk about Costley Hall.'

Skye nodded in response. 'Your mission, if you choose to accept it…' She let her voice tail off.

'Wanna come with me when I go?' he asked.

'Absolutely,' she replied without hesitation. 'There's no show without Punch.'

He smiled as a warm feeling spread through him. There was no question that he absolutely wanted her to be by his side. But in the capacity of a friend—or something more?

CHAPTER FIVE

SKYE KEPT HER eyes on the board, scanning constantly to try and keep her A&E department viable.

She moved to the desk. 'We have four ambulances that can't unload patients. Every bed and trolley in here is being used. Time for a huddle. Call the emergency page holder.'

She gave a signal and the A&E internal emergency lights flashed twice. They were strategically placed around the department and used for a variety of reasons. An emergency huddle was one of them.

She gave it five minutes, until most of her staff were present, before she started. She could sense Lucas before she even saw him. He came up behind her, the smell of his aftershave instantly recognisable. It was strange how the scent of someone could do strange things to a person.

She could remember the first time she'd noticed it and thought it kind of nice. After the first few times, she'd started to associate it directly with Lucas. Then, after a few weeks, it had started to make her skin tingle and her stomach flutter. Whilst what was going on in Lucas's life was proving a distraction from her own issues, the man himself was enough of a distraction without the prospect of him being a duke being thrown into the equation.

He'd been so nice last week when she'd had a mini meltdown in his car. It had been a long day and things had just seemed to pile up and overwhelm her. It was uncommon for Skye, but then she'd never been in a position like this before.

Dev, the page holder, appeared and Skye gave a nod. 'Right, everyone, we need to clear some room in A&E. We have four ambulances that need to unload, patients we need to treat. Ro, update me on your patients.'

'I have two patients with chest X-ray films to be reported, both elderly, both probable chest infections and both requiring admission to medicine. I also have two Paed patients who can probably go home with medicines, but I can't get a paed down here to see them.'

'I'm waiting on Surgical,' sighed Louise,

another staff member. 'Three patients waiting to be seen.'

'Ortho for me,' said Adam. 'The plaster room is backed up. Hopefully not for much longer. I've six patients waiting on some kind of cast.'

Skye gave a nod. Adam could put a plaster cast on with expertise and quicker than most people could drink a cup of coffee. She knew all her staff were working as hard as possible.

Lucas spoke next. 'I have four drunk and disorderly patients. All with a variety of minor injuries, but none of whom are fit to be safely discharged as yet.'

Skye looked at Dev, whose job was to manage all the beds in the hospital. He had considerable sway, because a hospital with all beds full was a hospital that would have to close to admissions. It was the biggest 'no' that existed in healthcare.

'Tell all specialties that if they aren't down here in the next five minutes we'll be assessing their patients and admitting direct to their wards,' Skye said with a no argument kind of voice. 'Lucas, the two paeds…can you assess and, if safe, send them on their way? And Dev, can you find me a healthcare support worker and an area for our four drunk and disorderly patients to be observed for the next couple of hours?'

She turned back and leaned over the desk. 'I'm going to phone Radiology now and ask for reports on those two chest X-rays.' Then she nodded to one of her ANPs. 'Leigh, please go and assess the patients in the ambulances. If any are urgent, let us know, and we'll clear an area.'

The staff all nodded and walked away quickly. No one liked it when the department was like this. It didn't feel safe for staff or patients, and Skye wasn't prepared to compromise on the care they delivered.

A few minutes later—with a promise of X-ray reports in the next ten minutes, and a few scowls from specialty doctors who'd arrived in A&E—she went to join Lucas with the paediatric patients.

He looked up as she walked in, and handed her a tablet. 'Skye, this is Mikey and his mum Caroline.'

Skye gave them both a smile. Mum was already wrestling Mikey back into his clothes.

'Mikey has a chest infection and I've prescribed some antibiotics for him. Can you ask someone to supply?'

She nodded and signalled to another nurse

walking past. The hospital pharmacy was closed at night, but the most commonly used prescriptions were pre-prepared for supply in A&E. All they needed was the patient's name, and some instructions given.

With a few words of goodbye, Skye and Lucas moved into the other cubicle with the second paediatric patient. As they walked through the curtains the tiny baby in her mother's arms vomited.

Skye moved quickly to assist and her heart skipped a few beats when she saw the colour of the vomit. She looked at the tablet that Lucas had picked up. *Esther Lewis, ten days old, vomiting and excessive crying. Colic. For assessment.*

She turned over the cloth she'd just wiped Esther's face with.

Lucas moved quickly. 'Do you mind if I examine Esther?' he asked her mother, taking the squealing baby and gently laying her on the trolley, before examining her with the tenderest of touches. Little Esther had slight abdominal distension, but as soon as Lucas brushed his fingers against her little belly she squealed. He fastened her to the nearest monitor, which showed a rapid heart rate to match her rapid breathing.

Skye put her arm around mum. She knew the next set of questions.

Esther's mum, Juliette, was in her early twenties. 'It is something, isn't it? My friends thought I was overreacting.'

Skye put her hand over Juliette's as Lucas asked a few questions about feeding and nappies. 'You're not overreacting, Juliette. You're in the right place. We can look after Esther.'

Lucas sat down in the chair opposite. 'I'm so glad you came in, Juliette. I think Esther has a condition called volvulus. It's when the bowel twists so the blood supply gets cut off.' He lifted the cloth and opened it to show Juliette the green bile. 'Is this the first time Esther's vomit has been like this?'

Juliette's eyes widened. 'Yes, it's just been milk up until now.'

He nodded. 'Then all your instincts were spot-on. This is a sign of volvulus. Right now, Esther can't absorb and digest her milk the way she should. I'm going to get a paediatric surgeon to come down right now and do some emergency tests, but it's likely Esther will need surgery in the next few hours. Can I phone someone to come and join you?'

Skye felt Juliette sag against her.

'Surgery? But she's only ten days old. She

can't have surgery.' Her voice was rising in panic.

Lucas stood up and gave Skye a nod. 'Will you be okay for a few minutes while I go and make the calls?'

Skye nodded and wrapped Esther loosely in a blanket, handing her back to Juliette to hold for a few minutes.

'She'll be fine. I know she's tiny, and that she's your whole world. Our surgeons will come and explain everything to you. They've done this operation a number of times. This condition can affect up to one in three thousand babies, boys and girls. Often, they have to do this on preemie babies that are only around twenty-four or twenty-six weeks gestation. Dr Hastings will come back in a few minutes and he'll slip a little needle into Esther's arm so we can keep her hydrated.' She rubbed Juliette's back. 'Now, can I call someone for you?'

Juliette nodded and swiped open her phone with trembling hands. 'Here,' she said. 'Can you call my mum and dad?'

'Absolutely,' she replied as Lucas walked back in. 'That was quick.'

'Mr Amjad has just finished another case.

He's coming along with Claire, the anaesthetist.'

Skye kept the phone in one hand as she pulled over a small trolley with the other, placing the equipment on it that he needed to slip in an IV.

He gave her a nod. 'Let me make a call and I'll be straight back.'

Skye couldn't help but think they made a good team as she quickly spoke to Juliette's mum and dad, who were shocked but said they would be at The Harlington soon.

Within an hour, all Esther's tests were completed, the diagnosis confirmed, and Skye walked the family along to the waiting room at Theatre, supplying them with some tea and biscuits for their wait.

By the time she got back to A&E, the ambulances had cleared and there were five free cubicles. Adam had cleared the plaster room, three patients were waiting on porters to take them up to wards, and the four drunk and disorderly patients had been transferred to another area where all were being observed.

A huge box of twenty-four doughnuts was sitting in the middle of the nurses' station near the centre of A&E.

'I think this is coffee time,' said Lucas, glancing at his watch.

Skye took another quick check around to make sure everyone was okay, picking up a note on the desk for Lucas. 'I agree,' she said, lifting a napkin and selecting her favourite raspberry iced doughnut.

They walked along to the staffroom after Lucas selected a doughnut of his own, then made coffee simultaneously next to each other.

Skye let out a laugh. 'We're like an old married couple.'

Lucas waggled a spoon at her. 'If you touch my doughnut, I want a divorce.'

They sank into the nearby seats and Lucas opened the note that had been left for him. He looked thoughtful and handed it to Skye. It was from the charge nurse on the ward that Mr Cunningham was due to be discharged from in the next few days.

Heard you were on duty tonight. Just to let you know Mr Cunningham is a poor sleeper and likes to chat. I know you want to speak to him again, so if you get a chance come along. Fran

Skye took a bite of her doughnut. 'Well,

there's an offer you can't really refuse. It might give you a chance to get some answers.'

He nodded thoughtfully. She could see a world of questions and doubts on his face. Was he anxious about asking the questions and what he might find out? Part of her wondered if this might make him more determined not to take over all the duties that went along with being a duke.

'Will you come with me?' he asked. 'There's no show without Punch,' he added with a smile.

She couldn't help the answering smile that spread across her face. 'I think we might have some time,' she agreed. 'Do you think Albert might like a doughnut?'

The lights were dim in the corridor as they made their way to the ward where Albert Cunningham was still a patient, Skye carrying a doughnut on a plate.

The nurse at the station looked up and smiled as she was typing some notes on the computer. 'Are you Dr Hastings?' she asked as they approached.

He nodded, 'And this is Skye Carter, the charge nurse from A&E.'

The nurse gave a nod. 'I'm Allie. Fran said

she'd invited you to pop along. I've just made Albert a cup of tea. He's in good spirits, and once he's assessed as safe on the stairs, he'll be discharged home. You can go and see him—he's in the side room around the corner so he can watch TV through the night.'

'Thanks,' said Lucas, then paused a second. 'How did he do on the stairs?' He could tell from the way the nurse had phrased her response that Albert had already been assessed.

She gave a shrug. 'He's still too unsteady. The physio won't let him be discharged until she judges him safe. She's coming back tomorrow, so we'll see what she says.'

Lucas gave a nod. 'Thanks,' before heading down the corridor with Skye at his side.

'You ready for this?' she asked.

'Probably not,' he admitted. 'But it might be the only time I get a version of the truth, so let's go.'

He knocked gently on the already open door. Albert Cunningham was sitting upright in bed, supported by pillows and watching the flickering TV in the corner of the room. He took a few seconds to recognise Lucas, then waved them in, picking up the remote to silence the television.

'Your Grace.' He nodded, and Lucas felt his skin prickle.

He gave a small smile. 'I honestly can't get used to that,' he admitted. 'I keep wanting to look over my shoulder to see if people are talking to someone else.'

Albert smiled, and his eyes had a wicked twinkle in them—something Lucas hadn't had the chance to see the first time they'd met.

Skye sat down and reached over and touched Albert's hand. 'I'm Skye, I work in A&E with Lucas. I was there when you were brought in. In fact—' she glanced at Lucas '—it was our first night working together. So it's nice to see you looking so much better.' She handed over the plate. 'Here, we brought you a doughnut to go with that cup of tea.'

Albert lifted the paper napkin on the plate and looked in approval at the chocolate iced doughnut. 'Perfect pick,' he complimented. 'Thank you so much, and for your care when I was in A&E.'

'You're welcome.' Skye smiled, settling back into her chair.

Lucas took a breath. He was fortunate that he'd already had his first conversation with

Albert, but he hadn't really asked him anything about Costley Hall or his father.

'We went to visit Costley Hall,' he started.

Albert paused mid bite of his doughnut. He set it down on the plate. 'What did you think?' He was trying to hide it, but there was pride in his voice.

Lucas had to be honest. 'It's a beautiful place, but I'm just not sure what I'm supposed to do with it.'

Albert took a bite of his doughnut and chewed with a few nods, as if he were contemplating what to say.

'And my car wouldn't start, so Donald gave me a loan,' said Lucas, humour in his voice.

'What did you pick?' Albert asked without hesitation.

'It was snowing. I had to be practical. We picked a Range Rover. It's beautiful. So easy to drive.'

Albert blinked. 'I was devastated when I heard about the Aston Martin.' He sighed. 'Your father loved that car. Have you heard anything from the police?'

Lucas shook his head. 'Nothing, I'm afraid.'

Albert shook his head too. 'I'm an old fool. I should never have brought it that day. It was in a James Bond movie,' he said, casting a glance at Skye.

She nodded. 'I know. The police mentioned they thought it was likely stolen by some chancers, but has probably now been sold on to a collector, once they realised what they had.'

Albert leaned back against his pillows, a forlorn expression on his face. 'It's such a beauty. London used to feel a much safer place.'

Lucas waited a few moments and then tried to steer the conversation back to Costley Hall. 'I met Donald and Olivia. I'm assuming that for the last few months everyone has been paid as they should?'

Albert's head tilted to one side. He was astute. That much was crystal-clear. 'Of course,' he said quickly.

Lucas gave a slow nod before he met Albert's gaze. 'So, you can see what I do. I'm a doctor, not a duke. I don't see a role for me at Costley Hall. Everyone seems to have managed for the last ten months without any problems. Can things continue the way they are?'

Albert's gaze narrowed, and Lucas felt his heart sink.

'We didn't get a chance to talk before my

accident.' His words were clipped. 'I'm not sure what my partners have covered with you, but I'll be frank because I owe it to your father. I've looked after much of the estate for the last ten months. But I'm not in any condition to keep doing that, and you absolutely cannot trust my colleagues at the firm.'

Skye gave a shocked gasp, then laughed. 'Say it like you see it, Albert.'

His head turned to her. 'Have you met them?'

She nodded.

'Did you like them?'

'Not for a second,' she admitted.

His face broke into a half smile. 'That's what I like about nurses. They tend to be able to see through the veneer.'

Lucas didn't like how this was going. 'So, what does that mean?'

Albert met his gaze again. 'It means that once I introduce you to your accountant, you'll have to take over.'

Lucas shook his head. 'But I can't—and I'm not sure I want to.'

'Why on earth not?' The incredulity in his tone surprised Lucas and he could see Skye trying to hide a smile.

He took a breath. He wasn't sure what to

make of Albert. Was he the family lawyer? His father's best friend? Or something else?

'Albert, you and my father knew of my existence. But I never knew of yours. I know nothing about being a duke or running an estate. I've spent my whole life dreaming of being a doctor, and completing my training.' He pointed to the floor. 'This is where I want to be.'

Albert looked at him as though he'd spoken in another language. 'But you've seen Costley Hall, you've seen the grounds, the cars, and met the staff. It's a home and lifestyle that millions would beg for, and you don't want it?'

Albert was getting angry now. Lucas didn't want to upset the elderly man, but equally he wasn't going to be pushed into something that a few weeks ago he'd known nothing about.

'You have duties, responsibilities,' Albert continued, but Lucas cut in.

'Exactly, I have duties and responsibilities here.'

Albert's head swivelled and his gaze fixed on Skye. The tone of his voice changed completely. 'Is this because of you?' he asked.

Colour flared in Skye's cheeks, but she wasn't flustered. Instead, she looked Albert straight in the eye. 'I don't think it's because of me,' she answered simply, 'because I'm planning on leaving. I'm not keeping Lucas here.'

'That's not fair, Albert,' said Lucas quickly. 'Skye's here because she's my friend.' The primal urge to protect her came out of nowhere.

Albert looked back to Skye. 'You're leaving the hospital?'

She nodded. 'That's my plan. I have one interview for a job as a practice nurse in a GP surgery in London, and one for the district nursing course.' She glanced over at Lucas. 'And I have another interview, for a GP practice near Costley Hall. I just heard about that one,' she added.

Lucas's heart clenched in his chest. Of course, it didn't matter. Of course, he wanted her to be happy, and of course, he should support his friend in her career choices. But the thought of working here and not having Skye alongside him made him ache in a way that didn't match the fact that he'd only known her for a month or so.

He hadn't known about the interview for the job near Costley Hall, and he couldn't pretend it didn't give him a huge wave of relief, but why? He hadn't even agreed he would do anything with the place. Why did he want her to be near there?

He looked down at his watch. 'We should get back,' he said, rising to his feet.

Albert gave a little jolt. 'But we've not finished.'

'I have to get back to work, Albert. Patients are depending on us.'

Skye stood up too and straightened her tunic.

'You have to take over, Lucas. The will is detailed about your responsibilities, those for the title and the estate.' Albert looked out at the dark night sky. 'It's December already. You have to be ready for the New Year's ball.'

Lucas had already started to make his way to the door. He turned back. 'What?'

Albert had an air of panic about him. 'For the last fifty years there has always been a New Year's ball at Costley Hall. It's a giant fundraiser. It usually brings in around fifty per cent of the income for the charities that the Duke supported. It's vital that it takes place. The plans are already in place. Haven't you spoken to Brianna, the events manager? She spends months getting every detail right.'

'Lucas?' Skye asked quietly, her blue eyes fixing on him.

'I think she might have emailed a few times,' he admitted. 'I just haven't had a chance to read them properly.'

'You have to do it,' said Albert, a pleading tone in his voice. 'It's a tradition. And the charities depend on it.'

Lucas felt himself wavering. 'I'll get in touch with her,' he finally relented before excusing himself.

He walked back down the corridor with Skye, stopping as they turned a corner and looking at his watch again. His head was swimming and he had a sudden feeling of claustrophobia, even though they were in the middle of a long corridor.

This place was just too enclosed. Like all hospitals, it had that aroma about it. Disinfectant. Body fluids. Age. Staleness. Death.

Air. He needed air.

'We have around five minutes,' he said, taking a quick look around, opening a nearby door and ducking inside.

'What on earth are you doing?' asked Skye as she followed him inside.

It was one of the laundry rooms, stocked

with sheets, pillowcases, towels, blankets and scrubs for staff.

There was a small window at the other end and Lucas picked his way over the variety of objects on the floor before he reached it and pushed it upwards, letting in a gust of cold December air.

He stuck his head outside and breathed heavily, trying to suck in the chilly air. He felt a rustle beside him, and then Skye's body along the side of his, and her head stuck out next to his.

'Okay,' she said. 'What are we doing? And, whatever it is, it's too bloody cold.' She grinned at him. 'Did I sound Scottish?'

He laughed, and as he did it was like a shake of relief. For all the craziness that was going on in the world all around him, he still had this friend by his side.

'If you want to sound Scottish,' he said, 'then you have to try and say a lot of special words.'

'Like what?' she asked, her breath steaming the air between them. Her eyes and blonde hair were reflecting the orange light of the lamp-post across the street, giving her a warm amber glow.

'Murr...durr...' he started with.

She laughed and copied him. 'Muhurr… durr,' she tried.

'Drookit,' he said next.

Her brow furrowed. 'Drookit,' she mimicked. 'What is that?'

'Very wet. Mauchit.'

The furrow deepened. 'You're making these up now, aren't you?'

He shook his head, 'It kind of goes hand in hand with the last one usually. Try it. Mauchit.'

Her nose wrinkled. 'Mauch…it.'

'It means very dirty.'

Skye looked confused. 'Very wet and very dirty?'

He grinned. 'Remember the weather in Scotland is different from London. When I lived there, we used to say it was common to see four seasons in one day. I'd go out with a friend to play and it would be blazing sunshine. Four hours later, it had rained, sometimes sleeted too. We'd come back and my friend's granny would complain we were drookit and mauchit, and usually a lot more besides.' He gave her a nudge with his elbow. 'She was really a bit crabbit.'

Now Skye laughed. 'Now, that one I do

know. Crabbit. I know a few people I could put on that list.'

He looked at her sideways. 'Am I on that list?'

She gave him a careful stare, then licked her lips and drew back inside.

Lucas pulled back in too. It really was cold out there and the scrubs that they both wore were no match for the cold weather.

Skye hadn't moved away from him. They were only a few inches apart. She rubbed her cold arms. 'Just depends,' she said softly, with a twinkle in her eyes.

There it was again. That glimmer in the air between them. The one he hadn't yet acted on. Would now be the time he would finally take that step?

His voice was low. 'Depends on what?'

She gave a soft smile. 'You know—the time, the place, the patients.'

He stared at her for the longest time. She'd tried to pin her hair up again, and a few unruly strands had escaped to frame her face. She had some make-up on, making her eyelashes longer and her lips peachy pink. But the colour in her cheeks had come from the air outside. It gave her a glow that just seemed to light her up.

'So, what if the time was night and the place was somewhere magnificent?'

'Like a grand old house that secretly looks a bit like a castle?'

He smiled. 'I might know one of those.'

A smile kept teasing the edges of her lips. Even though they weren't touching, he could feel the heat from her body. It was practically reaching out and filling the gap between them.

'Maybe I don't need a grand old house,' she said.

His skin prickled, and it was nothing to do with the still open window.

'How about I tempt you with a linen closet in one of the oldest, and probably haunted, hospitals in London?'

'Are we still talking about being crabbit?' she asked.

He leaned forward. 'I think we're talking about something else entirely,' he whispered.

Skye tilted her head up towards his, reaching her hands up around his neck.

His lips met hers. It was almost as if something flared in him. She tasted sweet. Just the way he'd imagined she would. One of his hands rested on her hip and the other wound its way into her hair, ruining whatever was left of her clipped-up style.

Skye's body pressed against his, the thin scrubs allowing him to feel the curve of her breasts against his chest. Every part of him was yelling inside, his senses overcome.

He couldn't remember ever feeling a connection like this. There had been plenty of kisses in his past. Plenty of flirtations, plenty of short-term relationships.

But none had the inevitability of this one. The glances. The looks. The feeling.

The getting-to-know-you part. He'd wondered if they'd continue to tiptoe around the friend scenario, when his brain was going in another direction entirely, but, thankfully, it seemed as if Skye's thoughts had moved in the same way.

Everything about this felt right. In all the wrong ways. Especially when they were both working, and currently in a linen closet.

He stepped her back against the stacked rails. There was nowhere for them to go. No table to perch on. Only shelves and shelves of supplies.

Skye arched her back as he ran some kisses down her neck and throat. She let out a strangled gasp and started to laugh, just as his fingers snaked into the gap between her scrubs and made contact with her skin.

She laughed and pressed both hands on his shoulders and gently pushed him back while catching her breath.

Lucas started to laugh too, adjusting his scrubs.

She leaned over and pushed the window back down into place with a bang that made both of them jump.

'How to get caught making out in the hospital,' joked Lucas under his breath.

'I'm not getting caught—' Skye laughed as she eyed his scrubs '—but you'd better wait a few minutes.'

'Hey,' he said, reaching out and taking her hand. 'Thank you.'

'For what?'

'For stopping me screaming out of a hospital window.' He raised his eyebrows. 'It might have attracted some attention.'

She gave a cheeky nod. 'So, *that's* what we were doing?'

He sighed as he smiled. 'That's what I would have been doing if you hadn't been with me.'

Their hands were still entwined. 'I'm glad I could distract you.'

'Oh, you certainly did that.'

For a few moments they just stood there, looking at each other. It was the strangest sensation. But Lucas didn't want the moment to end. Right now, it was just him and her, here at work, where they could just be the doctor and nurse that their patients and colleagues expected.

No pressure. No expectations.

'We'd better get back,' said Skye. 'Let me go first.'

He gave a nod.

As she reached for the handle of the door, she turned and gave him a final glance. 'You can teach me more Scottish words later,' she said with a wink, before she disappeared out of the door.

CHAPTER SIX

HER PHONE BEEPED annoyingly and then rang.

Skye sat straight up in bed. The only person who would phone her at this time was her mother.

It took a few seconds for realisation to swamp her like a tidal wave. It couldn't be her mum. Her mum was gone.

So, who could be calling her?

Her brain started to shift into gear. A major incident at the hospital. That was the only reason she would get a call.

She answered immediately. 'Skye Carter.'

'Major incident alert at The Harlington. Please report for duty.'

It wasn't a real voice. The call was automated, but Skye was out of bed, stripping off her pyjamas and pressing the remote on the TV to see if anything was reported as she dressed.

She washed her face, brushed her teeth and pulled on her scrubs in under three minutes. By the time she was sticking her feet into her trainers she could see the yellow ticker tape line scrolling along the bottom of the news feed.

Train derailment in London. Major incident alert.

Her heart sank like a stone as she grabbed her bag and headed to the door. There wasn't time to watch the rest of the news to see where the incident had occurred.

As she jogged along the street it was still dark. The pavements glistened with frost. The roads had pink, purple and green fluorescence, as if oil had been spilled, but likely meant that ice had formed on them.

It would soon be Christmas. Skye couldn't help but fret over how many families' lives might be about to change because of this major incident.

As she reached the crossroads at the bottom of her street, someone gave a wave and stopped their car. Skye opened the passenger door and climbed in gratefully.

Julie, a radiologist, lived about a mile away and had clearly been called in too. 'Should have called you,' said Julie as soon as she pulled the car away again. 'Haven't really woken up yet though.'

'Me neither,' said Skye. 'Heard anything else?'

Julie shook her head. 'Feeling a bit sick to be truthful. Figured I wouldn't turn the radio on in case it was full of rumours. I'll just get a briefing when I get there.'

Skye's phoned beeped again and she pulled it out of her pocket.

Need me to come and get you?

It was Lucas. All staff had been called.

She texted quickly back.

Got a lift, see you there.

Julie shot her a glance. 'Hospital?'

Skye shook her head and answered without thinking. 'One of the docs offering me a lift. He lives really close to The Harlington.'

The words seemed to wake Julie up. 'Lucas Hastings?'

Skye looked at her in surprise. 'How do you know that?'

Julie laughed. 'There's been rumours about

you two for the past few weeks. Darn, wish I'd put a bet on now.'

Skye's stomach did a full forward roll. 'Tell me people are not placing bets on this?'

Julie shrugged. 'You know how the hospital goes. Anyhow, nothing serious, just a box of doughnuts or a round of drinks.' Her hand hit the steering wheel as she sighed. 'It would have been so much better if I'd picked you *both* up.'

Skye sighed and let her tense shoulders release. 'If there wasn't something serious happening, this might have bothered me.'

'Well, it shouldn't. Handsome guy, and not heard anyone say a bad word about him.' She gave Skye a sideways glance. 'You're entitled to some happiness, you know.'

Julie knew all about Skye's mum. Skye gave her a grateful smile. 'I know,' she admitted.

The car pulled into one of the streets around the corner from the hospital and they both jumped out. Skye could see other colleagues pulling up at various spots, all heading in the same direction.

The ambulance bay was empty, and Skye pulled off her jacket before she was even through the door. Two minutes later, her jacket and bag stowed safely in her locker, she reported to the main A&E nurses' station.

'Where do you want me?'

The place was eerily empty. As per the major incident protocol, the patients who had already been in the department had now been decanted to various other places, in preparation for what lay ahead.

Lucas appeared at her side, asking the same question she had. 'Where do you want me?'

The Director of A&E was in place behind the station, his face innately calm. Skye had worked with Ross Colver for years and knew just how good he was. Within a few moments the rest of the staff had assembled and Ross was standing with coloured bibs in his hands for clear identification of roles.

He stood on a chair and addressed them all quickly. 'We've had a major incident called this morning due to a collision of two trains just outside the Fraser Lane stop. Estimates are for around seventy casualties. The Harlington and the Elsborough will share casualties equally. As you can see, our patients are already decanted, and we've sent a team to the site.' He looked at his colleagues. 'Things will get hectic in here, but if you need help, ask for it.' He nodded at Skye. 'Skye and

Lucas will be front door triage.' He handed over red bibs and a pack with coloured triage stickers. 'Allewa will assist.' The experienced admin assistant took the red bib and went to collect a tablet and clipboard.

Ross continued in a steady manner, assigning staff to Resus, Paediatrics, plaster room, cubicles and the waiting area. Skye knew that in all other parts of the hospital—Radiology, labs and some wards, similar decisions would be made. A control room would be set up in the boardroom upstairs to handle the calls, comms and decision-making.

'If you need to eat, drink or pee, do it now,' said Ross as he finished up. 'We're expecting our first ambulance in around ten minutes.'

Skye looked at Lucas. 'I can't think about eating or drinking right now.'

'Me neither.' He grabbed their pack and slipped his bib with *Triage Consultant* over his head.

They headed out to the ambulance bay to take a few minutes before the bedlam began.

'Those poor people,' said Skye as she ran her hands up and down the outside of her arms. 'Catching the train this morning, likely going to work, and thinking it was just going to be another day.'

He slipped his arm around her shoulder. 'If we'd been night shift it's likely we would have been sent out in the primary triage team.'

She shuddered. 'I know. I've done it once before, and is it wrong I'm glad it's not me?'

He shook his head. 'Of course it's not wrong. But equally, I know if you'd been sent you would have done your job just like you should.' He gave her a curious stare. 'Are you sure about the decision you're making—about moving to another job?'

Skye looked out at the dark sky and glowing lights around them. 'You mean will I miss this? Working all the different shifts, and then getting called out in the early hours of the morning?'

He gave an understanding nod. 'I get it.'

'All interviews are in the next few days. And I emailed your GP friend to say thanks for the chat he had with me the other day. It was really useful.'

A distant siren sounded and a fellow colleague with a purple bib appeared. His face was pale. He was one of the paediatricians. 'We might not be able to do all paeds separately,' he warned. 'There were apparently two separate school trips on the trains. There may be too many. I won't be able to assess them all.'

Lucas didn't hesitate. 'Primary or secondary school?'

'Both.'

'You do primary, I'll take secondary,' said Lucas. He gave a nod to Skye and she nodded back in agreement, then turned to Allewa.

'Just get as much info as you can from the kids we triage. Someone at the scene should be co-ordinating where the kids go, but things can get confused, and parents get really upset trying to locate their children.'

Allewa's expression was grave. 'Don't worry, I'll get as much as I can and co-ordinate with the others.'

The blue flashing lights were getting closer and the siren increasing as they approached. Skye took a few breaths. Lucas's warm hand squeezed hers.

'We've got this,' he said with his honest green eyes.

And she believed him. Because she knew he meant it.

Since their kiss they'd spent more time together. They'd gone to the cinema, and for drinks, but still hadn't spent the night together. Skye had previously liked to take things slow in relationships, but she'd never truly felt as comfortable around someone as she did around Lucas. It was the oddest sensation. As if they just fitted together the way they should.

The first ambulance came to a halt and they pulled the doors open. 'Seventy-year-old, impact to chest and head injury, GCS eleven.'

Skye pulled the trolley towards her, with her on one side and Lucas on the other. They worked as a team, assessing the gentleman. His breath sounds on one side were limited, meaning he likely had a collapsed lung. His oxygen levels were adequate whilst he had his mask on, and although his blood pressure was low, it wasn't dangerously so. This man needed treatment and some pain meds but was not in immediate danger.

As they graded him and sent him through, Skye turned to Lucas. 'First time I've not sent a patient with a collapsed lung straight into Resus.'

He reached over and touched her shoulder as they walked to the doors of the next ambulance. 'We only have three Resus beds. He'll get the treatment he needs.'

The doors were already open and their

paed colleague was standing back, as it was clearly a patient for them instead of him.

This time it was a woman. 'Mary Keen, age forty, teacher at Palin Secondary School. She was caught between some seats and has two fractured tib and fibs,' said the paramedic.

Mary's face was so white she was ghost-like and even though Skye could see from her chart she'd been given pain meds, they clearly hadn't had the full effect.

'I need to be back with my class,' she said, wincing as the ambulance trolley moved. 'I don't know how they all are.'

Lucas put his hand over hers. 'Don't worry, our colleagues are there taking good care of them. Let us take care of you.' He assessed her quickly as Allewa took some notes.

The paramedic looked over to the paediatrician. 'There's a few on their way. But most are walking wounded. There are only a few with more serious injuries.' She shook her head and mouthed silently, 'No fatalities that I know of.'

As Lucas graded Mary Keen, Skye could almost feel the relief in the air around them. Her insides had been in knots at the thought of children being on those trains.

Sirens rang in the air again and the first

ambulances moved out of the way to allow others to arrive. It was a steady stream from then on.

Mostly broken bones, and some facial injuries from glass or flying luggage. The majority of the adults were commuters heading into work. A few had been people heading into London to go on to airports, whose trips would now be delayed.

Most of the teenagers had minor injuries. One had their shoulder pinned by a metal part of the window frame of the train and was taken off to Theatre for its safe removal. Another had severe face lacerations from broken glass and was also taken to Theatre by one of the maxillofacial surgeons.

The Harlington was getting busier by the second. Parents, friends and relatives were arriving and, as first suspected, some had been directed to the wrong hospital. Phones were constantly ringing, with workmates trying to find out if their colleagues who hadn't arrived at work had been involved in the accident.

In between all this, the 'normal' ambulances rolled in, since patients hadn't been diverted from the hospital as yet. Pensioners who'd fractured hips on slippery pavements, a young man who'd been stabbed in an early morning mugging and a few people with chest pain, one of whom arrested as soon as the ambulance doors opened.

Police and fire colleagues were also dotted throughout the department, some having attended the scene of the accident and either accompanying patients or having injured themselves. And reporters were everywhere. Most were fine, and followed the instructions from the hospital comms department, but there were always a few rogue reporters, stepping in places they shouldn't or asking questions when they could see people were busy doing their jobs.

All the while, Lucas and Skye were steadily working.

One young girl with a broken arm was part of the *corps de ballet*. She was hysterical as Skye took time to comfort and reassure her. Of course, she wouldn't be able to dance with the cast she would have to wear for the next six weeks. But Skye assured her there would be no reason why she would not be able to continue afterwards. She watched as the young girl was wheeled away in a chair.

'Okay?' asked Lucas at her elbow.

She leaned against him for a few seconds, not really caring who saw. 'Just thinking about her. She's worked so hard to get this place, and this accident could steal that from her.'

'You think?'

'I think that lots of young girls are just waiting for their own chance to make it into the *corps de ballet*. Her worst day is going to be someone else's best.'

She sighed and he slipped an arm around her waist as Ross Colver appeared. If he noticed their position, he didn't mention it.

'You two, coffee and sandwiches in the staffroom. We aren't expecting any more ambulances from the site right now.'

Skye flicked the switch on the machine to give her double the strength of coffee she would normally take. The sandwiches didn't look particularly appetising. Her brain was still in breakfast mode, so she reached for a packet of chocolate digestives instead, settling down next to Lucas on the sofa.

There were a few other people in here that she didn't recognise—likely from other parts of the hospital who had come down to help. She rested her head on his shoulder.

'It's not been too bad,' he said reassuringly, before looking down at a small splatter of blood on his scrubs.

'I can't believe there's no fatalities,' she said wearily. 'It's like a Christmas miracle.'

'I spoke to one of the policemen. They said it was a failure on one of the lines. They were the first trains of the day, and one of the drivers recognised that something wasn't quite right. He'd radioed ahead and both trains had slowed down. It didn't prevent the collision, but things could certainly have been worse.'

She looked up and gave him a smile. 'We worked well together, didn't we?'

'I think so,' he replied, fixing her with those green eyes.

For a few moments it felt as if they were the only people in the room, the others just fading into the background. All she could focus on was the bright green of those eyes, the slight shadow around his jaw line and the slight dark curl of his hair. That, and the way he was totally focused on her.

He was looking at her exactly the way he'd done before they'd shared their first kiss in the linen closet.

'Are you tired?' he asked, his voice barely above a whisper.

She nodded without speaking.

'When we all get stood down, do you want

to come back to mine? You know I'm only a few minutes away from here.'

She knew exactly what he was asking. And she knew exactly what her reply would be. 'Sure, I'd like that.'

His smile widened, and there was a glimmer of something in his eyes. Maybe his face was just reflecting exactly how she felt inside.

'Just think,' she said, 'in three interviews' time, it will be Christmas.'

'Is that how we're counting now?'

'That's how I'm counting,' she said, putting her hand on her chest. 'It's been a long time since I've had an interview. I'm scared I'll blow it.'

'You won't blow it,' he said easily. 'Look at the experience you've got and the skills. You can do bloods, Venflons, IVs, ECGs, set up syringe drivers, dress wounds, diagnose as well as any junior doctor.'

'What about palliative care? There are so many more people choosing to spend their last days at home.' She gulped. 'I only have personal experience of that, or experience where a care package has broken down and someone with end-of-life care ends up in here. GPs and their teams, and district nurses, play a huge role in all that now.'

Her hand was still on her chest, and Lucas put his hand gently over hers. 'And your personal experience is unique. It gives you the knowledge that others might not have, and the perspective of a carer in all this, what they have to take on, and how they can be best supported by the team around them.'

Her eyes flooded with tears. Even when she was having doubts, Lucas could make her feel better, let her recognise her own value in a sea of other potential candidates. The coffee she'd been drinking started to flush through her system, giving her the caffeine kick that her body needed.

'Thank you,' she said, straightening up. 'Ready for the second wave?'

Lucas nodded and they both headed back out into the department. Some parts of the major incident were winding down now. All of the patients from the accident had been taken to the two hospitals. There were still some walking wounded waiting to be seen, but all had minor injuries that would only require some patching up, or a few stitches at most.

The admin staff at The Harlington had kept on top of all patient details, contacting relatives when required, redirecting enquiries and ensuring that all children were accompanied whenever needed. Both schools had also sent extra staff to stay with children whose parents were struggling due to the transport issues the train collision had caused.

Skye set herself alongside another nurse in one of the cubicles and dealt with as many walking wounded as she could. Although the overall number of people injured had been estimated as seventy, the steady stream of walking wounded in The Harlington alone amounted to four hundred.

By the time Skye was pinning her hair up for the umpteenth time, she was truly exhausted.

Lucas appeared around her cubicle a little after six. 'Ross says to go home.' He smiled, and even though she could tell he was just as tired as she was, he still had a sparkle in his eyes.

'What about Ross?' she asked as she pulled her plastic pinny off, deposited it in the bin and washed her hands for the hundredth time.

'What about Ross? If you can persuade that man to go home, then you're a better person than I.'

Skye sighed, realising straight away that

even though Lucas hadn't known Ross as long as she had, he'd certainly got his measure.

She pulled her phone from her pocket. 'Give me five minutes,' she said, disappearing into an office for a moment.

When she came back out, Lucas had his jacket on. 'What were you doing?' he asked as he walked her back to the locker room.

She winked as she grabbed her own jacket and bag. 'Phoning Ross's wife.'

'The big guns?' he joked.

'You know her?' she teased back. 'Biggest heart on the planet, but not to be messed with. She'll persuade him to go home now.'

They walked out, saying goodnight to some fellow colleagues, and Skye felt relieved to finally be getting out of the place.

'Fancy a takeaway?' asked Lucas. 'What about some pizza?'

'Anything,' she said, laying her head against his upper arm. 'I will literally eat anything. And you'd better have some mindless TV for me to watch.'

'Like what?'

'*Friends, Bridgerton, Gilmore Girls, Killing Eve, West Wing, Stranger Things, Star Trek*... Any of the above will do.'

He laughed, 'Oh, I'm sure I'll be able to find you something that will do.'

His phone buzzed and he pulled it out of his pocket and frowned.

'What is it?'

'A message to contact my solicitors as soon as possible.'

Skye stopped walking. 'Is it from Albert?'

Lucas pushed his phone back into his pocket. 'That's what's odd about it. It's from one of those other guys—you remember Mr Bruce?'

She wrinkled her nose. The guy really had been unpleasant and generally quite smug. 'Yeah.' Even the thought of him gave her an uncomfortable feeling.

'Well, he can wait,' said Lucas brusquely.

'What about the other person—the events manager, are you seeing her?'

'Day after tomorrow,' he said, and she could feel him sucking in a big breath. 'And doubtless I'll find out all about the New Year's Eve event.'

Her hand tapped his chest. 'Oh, just as well you'd already offered to work Christmas then, isn't it? You should at least have that night off.'

'I feel as if you're quite amused by this,' he said, a suspicious look in his eyes.

She shrugged and laughed. 'Told you I always prefer New Year. At least we know where the party is, and don't need to hunt one out.'

'How come I instantly feel there's a few stories in there?'

He'd slowed down outside a large glass-fronted apartment block with a concierge at the front door. The dark glass doors slid back without a sound.

'There's more than a few,' she admitted as Lucas nodded at the concierge and led her over to the lifts.

A minute later they arrived on his brightly lit floor and Lucas opened one of four identical dark doors.

He flicked a switch as they walked inside and Skye was struck by how modern and well-maintained the flat was. Somehow, her place on the outskirts just didn't compare.

It was strangely comforting seeing inside his place. The sofas looked comfortable, the kitchen he took her through to had well-stocked cupboards, and as she slid on to one of the comfortable leather stools at the kitchen island, he opened the fridge to offer a variety of drinks.

She shook her head. ‘While I’d love a glass of wine, I think I’d just prefer a coffee to go with the pizza. I’m too tired for anything else and it might wake me up a bit.’

He flicked a switch on a nearby machine and stuck in a pod. The coffee was finished just as the pizza arrived and Lucas joined her on a stool at the island as they ate out of the box.

‘What do you want to watch?’ he asked as they walked through to the living room. The dark windows showed a glittering view of London, and Skye gave a tiny shiver.

‘Can people see in?’ she asked, looking at the dark towers around them.

Lucas frowned, ‘I suppose, in theory, they can. But can you see into anyone else’s place right now?’

Even though it seemed voyeuristic, Skye walked up to the window and stared at the surrounding buildings. She could see warm lights, blinds and blurred outlines. A few figures could be glimpsed up close at windows for a fraction of a second. But everyone was too far away for any details. It gave her a little reassurance.

'I just wondered,' she said, rolling her shoulders back to release some of her tension.

'What? That people might see you sitting on the sofa watching *Gilmore Girls*?'

She laughed and nodded. 'Yeah, that. But I'm feeling kind of sci-fi right now.'

He picked up the remote as they settled on the squishy sofa, her fitting comfortably under his arm as he scrolled the TV menu.

'Before you ask—' he sighed '—yes, I did buy a sofa without actually sitting on it. I didn't realise it was quite so soft.'

'It's certainly comfortable,' she joked. 'I might just not be able to get up again.'

'Well, we wouldn't want that,' he said in a low voice.

She turned her head to face him. They hadn't put on any of the main lights, and the only glow was from the TV screen. Her hand moved up and rested on his chest. 'Maybe I don't really want to get up,' she said, her heart beating fast.

He shifted his body so they were face on. 'So, what do you want to do?' he asked, a teasing note in his voice.

She tilted her head to the side. 'There's this man I've been seeing—' she smiled

'—and it's reached a point…' She let her voice tail off.

Lucas picked it up with an equally teasing smile. 'It's reached a point…?'

His hand had moved around to her back, slipping between the gap in her clothes, and his finger was tracing tiny circles on her bare skin.

She tried not to sigh too hard, her brain leaping *way* forward. Instead, she reached up her hand and let her own finger run down his cheek, stopping at his shadowed jaw line where his stubble was rough against her finger pad.

'To see what comes next,' she whispered. Then she made the first move. Pushing him backwards on the sofa so she was above him. It was easy to lie her body on top of his and start kissing him.

In turn, his hand snaked up inside her top again, stroking her skin and toying with her bra strap as he met her kisses with equal passion.

It seemed as if everything had been leading to this. She was exactly where she wanted to be, with the person she wanted to be with.

And all of a sudden, she wasn't so tired any more.

CHAPTER SEVEN

LUCAS WAS AWOKEN by the sound of his buzzing phone. There was a horrible sense of déjà vu as he realised another phone was buzzing too. Skye's. She was snuggled under his arm, her warm bare skin against his. They'd finally made it through to his bedroom, and both were off work today. Their phones shouldn't be buzzing like this.

He gave her a nudge. 'Skye, your phone,' he mumbled, hating the fact that he was going to have to pull his arm out from under hers to detach himself and retrieve his phone from the floor beside them.

She gave a half-hearted mumble, then, at the next buzz, sat bolt upright in bed. The duvet was clutched to her front.

'You've got to be joking,' she groaned as she leapt from the bed, stark naked, and grabbed her phone from the top of the chest of drawers in his room.

He couldn't help but smile at the brief glimpse of her naked form as she grabbed the phone and pulled the covers back over herself.

'Don't,' she said with a raise of her eyebrows.

Her movement gave him the chance to glimpse his own phone and his brow creased in confusion.

'What?'

There was no emergency text from the hospital. Instead, there were multiple missed calls and a few missed texts. A few were from friends, but most were from the solicitors.

Skye was reading the messages on her own phone. Her mouth was open. Her head whipped around.

'What is all this?' she asked.

She held her phone up so he could read the latest message.

Don't read the headlines. Ignore them all.

It was from Ross, their boss.

Lucas picked up his tablet from his bedside table and flicked on the TV at the same time.

The newsreader was reporting on yesterday's train accident. No fatalities. Eighty-six hospital admissions. More than four hundred requiring treatment. An investigation would be taking place over the next few weeks. It was implied that if it had been slightly later in the day, the numbers would have been much worse.

But the newsreader moved onto quite a different subject as the headlines flashed up on his tablet.

The new Duke of Mercia is London's latest billionaire after inheriting the title from his previously unknown father.

Their heads shot up in horror as the newsreader continued to explain a variety of factual information, alongside a whole host of information that seemed more fiction than fact.

Skye leaned over and glimpsed some of the less flattering headlines on his tablet that were currently adorning the red top papers. These were coupled with some slightly unflattering photos, clearly taken last night on their walk home.

Dashing new Duke caught in nurse's snare!

Is it him she loves? Or is it his billions?

The Harlington's hidden doctor is a secret billionaire!

Too late, ladies—the new Duke is already hooked!

Has Cinderella got her hands on the brand-new Duke?

If the headlines weren't bad enough, the reporting that followed was more than a little questionable.

Skye's head was touching his shoulder as he scrolled through the articles. Some described her as plain or unattractive, accompanied by a blurred photo, clearly from Skye's schooldays, showing her wearing her uniform and with her hair pulled back severely in a ponytail. It was like a million other unflattering school photos.

One claimed she was homeless. Another mentioned she lived in the 'poorest part' of London. What on earth would her neighbours in Tower Hamlets make of that?

There was a 'quote' from a colleague: 'Oh, Skye Carter, yes, she'll wrap herself around any doctor that comes along. But this guy? She'll hang on for dear life. She's always been looking for a rich bloke.'

Lucas flinched. He hated all this, and it felt entirely his fault, even though he'd had no knowledge of it.

Skye stiffened next to Lucas, before reaching over and grabbing last night's used scrub top from the floor. She shook her head. 'What on earth is going on? Who has been talking to the press, and how did they find out about you?'

Lucas's phone started to ring, and he thought about ignoring it for a second before he answered. 'Ross,' was his only reply.

This was a nightmare. Not at all what he'd expected. Why on earth was there any interest in who he was dating? His heart clenched in his chest. He'd felt Skye tense next to him, and he didn't blame her. The reporting was ridiculous and hurtful. The last thing he wanted was for Skye to suffer because they'd started dating. At least he assumed they'd started dating. They hadn't even had a chance to have that conversation yet.

He really, really didn't want anything to spoil this. Even before last night, Skye had found a way into his life and his heart in a way he hadn't imagined possible.

Anger was surging through his veins at the thoughtless words and ridiculous headlines. He wanted to protect her. He wanted her to feel safe around him.

Just like he felt around her.

All those thoughts passed through his head in the blink of an eye, and Ross was speaking. So Lucas started to pay attention.

This was a nightmare. She'd woken up to an actual nightmare. She'd heard about other people being attacked in the press before—but she'd never expected it to be her.

All of a sudden, Skye had a wave of understanding and sympathy for the minor celebrities who found themselves under the spotlight, photographed unexpectedly and with every conversation dissected by the press.

It was terrifying. Was this what dating Lucas would mean? It made her blood run cold.

This was new. It was exciting. They'd had a few weeks to get to know each other, and Skye liked every single thing about him. She knew he wasn't perfect—but neither was she.

That was the beauty of getting to know someone. What she didn't want was lies, figments of people's imagination and misinterpretation of facts being printed about her in the press, or online. She had always valued her privacy. The sense of betrayal from some of her colleagues ran deep.

She listened, wondering what Ross might be saying to Lucas. He was a good boss—his text this morning proved that—but her stomach was still in knots.

After a short time Lucas finished the call and looked at Skye.

'What did he say?' she asked.

'He wanted to check that we were both okay…' Lucas started, then he pulled a face. 'And he asked if I was actually a duke.'

'Did you tell him?'

'He's my boss, I could hardly not. Plus—' he sucked in a breath '—it seems like the whole world knows. It's not like I can keep it a secret.' He shook his head and continued. 'So, we both have the next few days off. He asked me to confirm that I would still cover Christmas, and I said yes, obviously.'

A phone sounded, a different kind of ring, and Lucas picked up a regular-looking phone next to his bed. There was a mumbled exchange. He ran his fingers through his hair and replaced the receiver.

'That was the concierge. He said that the building is surrounded by reporters.'

'What?' Skye glanced at the remainder of her crumpled scrubs on the floor. 'Oh, great.'

Lucas sat on the edge of the bed. 'I'm sorry,' he said in a low voice.

'It's not your fault.' She paused for a moment, doing her best to blink back tears. 'But I do wonder how they found out.'

He put an arm around her shoulder and kissed the side of her head. 'So do I,' he sighed. 'I was a fool to think I could keep this quiet. I'm so sorry you've been exposed to all this.'

She stared at the floor for a few seconds. Now was the time. Now was the time to make the decision if she was in or out.

She looked at him, and she could tell he knew exactly what she was thinking.

He brushed her cheek with the softest of touches. 'Not exactly how I dreamed about our first morning together.'

She stared into his green eyes. 'You dreamed about it?' she asked in a quiet voice.

'Of course I did,' he admitted. 'Didn't you?'

And that was it. As the warm feeling

spread across her belly, she knew her decision was made.

'Can my duke take me away from all this?' she asked.

He gave a shaky sigh. She could sense the relief her words had given him, and he squeezed her hand as he stood.

'It's going to be a nightmare to get out of here. Why don't we just take the car? We can go to Costley Hall.'

Skye felt a bit unsure. Her appearance had already been under scrutiny. All she had was the scrubs she'd been wearing the night before. They'd both been so tired there hadn't been a chance to plan ahead. It would be like doing the walk of shame after a hitch-up on a night out.

But no. She shook that thought from her head. There was no walk of shame. This was Lucas, the man she'd grown to know, and to care for deeply. No matter what they said about her, she was going to hold her head high.

'I'll need to get some clothes.'

'No problem. We'll drop by your place on the way.'

Her heart was heavy. This wasn't the way she'd pictured today going. In her head, she'd wanted to wake up in Lucas's arms and have a nice day together. Relaxing, talking about how things might be and looking forward to what might come next.

Her eyes darted to the tablet again. The headlines were ridiculous and mainly untrue. She was just a nurse. No one special. But within a few hours they'd identified her, found old school pictures and apparently found colleagues with dubious opinions of her.

That, undoubtedly, hurt the most.

She'd dated one orthopaedic doctor, four years ago, for around five months. That was the totality of her relationships with doctors at The Harlington. They'd broken up amicably because things hadn't really clicked between them. That was it. Nothing else.

She slipped on her scrub trousers and collected her jacket and bag while Lucas stuffed some things into a rucksack. He grabbed some toiletries, then gave her a nod. 'Ready?'

A few moments later they were in the lift which took them down to the underground garage. The gleaming black Range Rover was parked in one of the spaces.

'Bet you're glad you didn't give that back,' she murmured as they jumped in.

'My other car is still in the garage getting fixed,' he said, 'or else I would have.' He paused for a moment. 'I really should phone and let them know that we're coming, shouldn't I?'

She grimaced, thinking of Donald and Olivia. 'I guess so.' Her insides twisted, wondering if they would be welcome, or at least if *she'd* be welcome, or whether they might actually believe some of the stuff reported in the news today.

Lucas made the call and they pulled out of the underground garage. As he had to pause to pull out onto the main road, a number of photographers spotted them and snapped away. Half an hour later, as they approached her flat, Skye realised there were another few outside her door.

Lucas shot her an anxious glance. 'Do you want to stop, or just continue on?'

She really wanted to go back into her own home, to get some make-up, toiletries, her charger and favourite clothes if they were going to be away for a few days. But the thought of being snapped by more photographers was too much.

'I guess I might be wearing your things for

a day or so. Darn it, I was halfway through a really good book.'

Lucas gave her a half-smile. 'Haven't you heard I'm a billionaire? I can buy you clothes.' He did a swift U-turn on the road and headed in the other direction.

They both started to laugh and Skye felt an unexpected wash of relief. After a stressful day, a wonderful night and a crummy morning, she needed it.

Then something came into her head. 'Oh, no.'

'What?'

They'd stopped at a set of traffic lights.

'I have an interview. Well, three interviews in the next few days.'

'And I've just met my accountant and now have one of those exclusive Coutts cards—like the Queen had.' He shuffled and pulled his wallet from his back pocket, tossing it on to her lap. 'I'm serious. Buy what you need. A suit, some shirts, some shoes. Costley Hall is the billing address and that's where everything will be sent, so just use my name.'

Skye opened his wallet and pulled out the card. She'd never seen one in person. She held it, palm open, and looked at it suspiciously.

'Are you sure?' Then she shook her head and dug around for her own bag.

'Don't you dare,' he growled. 'It's my fault you're in this position, not yours. I've inherited more money than I know what to do with. You know what I've bought so far?'

She shook her head.

'A new sofa,' he joked. 'And you know how those things take months to arrive? I paid so much… It's coming in three days—two days now.'

She wrinkled her nose. 'For your flat?'

He shook his head. 'No, for Costley Hall. I hated the furniture in the main rooms. I ordered a new bed too—it should arrive today, along with new bedding.' He gave a hollow laugh. 'None of it will be in keeping with the rest of the furnishings, but I figured at least one part of Costley Hall I can decorate myself.'

The words made her skin tingle a little. 'So, you're getting used to the idea?' she asked tentatively.

'I'm buying some time,' he said, and then groaned as he obviously realised how literal those words were. 'I've spoken to the events planner, Brianna, but haven't met her yet. She seems nice. And actually quite fierce. And since I don't have a pre-booked holiday on New Year's Eve, I can't really get out of the ball.' He gave her a sideways glance. 'And I'm kind of hoping that neither can you.'

She gave him a little smile as a warm glow spread through her. 'You're asking me on a date?'

'I'm asking you to be my partner in crime.' He smiled, then paused. 'Yes, I'm asking you on a date.'

She didn't say the words that were currently circling in her head. That sad thought that still kept bubbling up when she least wanted it to. It was nearly Christmas and New Year. This would be her first without her mum. Her first alone.

It actually hurt much more than she'd expected it to. Of course she'd known it would be difficult. But she hadn't realised it was the little things that would catch her unawares. Catching sight of an advert for a TV programme they'd always watched together at Christmas. Pulling out the Christmas decorations and gently touching the ones that her mother had bought for her once she'd got her own place. Unpacking her winter clothes and finding the pink and purple bobble hat that her mother had got her the year before, and the giant bed socks with pom-poms down the front because her feet were always freezing at night. Finishing the last of the lemon marmalade that her mother had always bought especially for her, from goodness knew where, because none of the supermarkets seemed to stock it these days.

Being somewhere different—somewhere new—at New Year's Eve would be a blessing. Being there with Lucas might be something else entirely.

It was almost as if Lucas was reading her thoughts, sensing her mood right now.

'Ever wanted to do something completely mad? Throw all caution to the wind? Well, that's what I want you to do for the next hour. Order everything that you want. Your make-up. Your perfume—everything you would have brought from home and couldn't collect. All you need for your interviews. A new laptop. And a ballgown, because you'll need one. The book you were half reading. Order it all. And then order more.'

He was lifting his hands from the steering wheel now, throwing them outwards in enthusiasm.

She laughed at him. 'It's a wonderful idea, but I'm not sure I'm designed that way.'

'Order the parrot chair!' he shouted, and she jumped in her seat. 'Order the chaise longue too!'

Her skin tingled at the thought. How to go wild? To just spend money without worrying? Skye had never been in that position. Living in London made that impossible, except for the very rich. She had a budget she stuck to. She always made sure her bills were paid and her rent was covered. She saved if she wanted something. She wasn't poor, but she didn't have thousands stashed in the bank either. Her mother had taken out life insurance nine years before she'd died and whilst she was still in good health, so Skye knew that eventually, when everything was settled, she might have a little inheritance, but that was it. No golden goose. No big nest egg.

'Go on, Skye, why not? I probably earn more in interest than some people get paid. I haven't decided what to do with the money yet. But I can guarantee you that anything you spend in the next hour won't even scratch the surface.'

He was holding this imaginary gift in front of her, dangling it, where she could reach out and touch it.

'I don't have anywhere to put a chaise longue,' she said simply.

'Then pick a room at Costley Hall,' he said. 'It will brighten the place up. Go for it.'

Her mouth opened, and then closed again. She did need some make-up and clothes for the next few days. This could be fun. Even if she only did it for five minutes. She gulped. 'I'll get some essentials.'

As they continued through the London streets, Lucas started playing some music. Skye bought her usual make-up, underwear, one pair of jeans, a jacket, four tops and a pair of pyjamas—though she wasn't entirely sure she would need those. All from the regular high street stores where she usually shopped. Then she took a breath and ordered a black suit jacket and skirt, a pair of black court shoes and a bright pink and identical red shirt for her interviews.

These things were slightly different. They weren't identical to what she had at home. She'd planned to buy some new shirts, to wear alongside a slightly tired suit she had from a few years ago. Again, she bought from a high street store she favoured, rather than any of the fancy or exclusive boutiques in London. She paid for everything with Lucas's card, even though her fingers were a bit hesitant, then slid the card back into his wallet and put her phone back in her lap.

She glanced up. They were heading out of London now. Thirty minutes had literally passed in a blur.

'Did you get the parrot chairs?'

She shook her head. 'Just some replacement clothes. And some things for my interviews. Thank you for that. I appreciate it.'

'What about a ballgown? Did you get one of those?'

She started to laugh. 'No, I didn't get a ballgown. I didn't even look. Let's worry about that later.'

He shot her a pretend serious glance. 'But if I talk you into a ballgown, then you can't really duck out of the ball. Don't you see my cunning plan here?'

She leaned back against the soft leather of the car seat and took a deep breath. Everything was moving at a million miles an hour. And even though the headlines hadn't been flattering about her, she was starting to push that to the back of her mind.

Lucas was here. He was by her side. And after last night she was even more sure that this was where she wanted to be. But maybe once he realised how much being a duke actually meant, he might look for a girlfriend who had the same social standing. The thought gave her uncomfortable feelings and, for the first time ever, she was glad her mum wasn't around to see those headlines. On any other day she would have absolutely loved for her mum to have the chance to have met Lucas, but that just wasn't to be, and she had to accept that.

She glanced upwards just as they started to reach the outskirts and the area around them became greener. The pale blue sky made her wonder if her mum was up there, and what she might be thinking. Would she be happy for Skye? Or think she was completely out of her depth?

Lucas's phone started to ring again, this time coming through the console on the car. He pressed the accept button and, unfortunately, Mr Bruce's nasal tones came through the speaker.

'Your Grace, we need to have a discussion about your colleague, the young lady, Skye Carter.'

Skye immediately stiffened, all her senses on alert.

'We don't,' said Lucas in a voice she'd only

heard a few times. 'I'm not interested in what you have to say about Skye—unless it's a way to stop the false reporting.'

Mr Bruce cleared his throat. It should have been a completely innocent sound but, for some reason, it had the same smugness and know-it-all manner as everything else he did. He was going to speak again.

Lucas ended the call.

Skye blinked as her eyes filled with tears she was determined not to shed. What on earth were these people going to say about her? There really was nothing to say.

Her heart plummeted. 'What if my potential new employers see the news and think I'm not a good nurse?'

Lucas bristled next to her. She knew this wasn't his fault. He hadn't asked for any of this. But neither had she.

Her thoughts were swirling. Did she have regrets about moving their relationship further on last night? No. But would she have got into a relationship with Lucas in the first place if she'd known there was going to be this kind of fallout? The truth was, maybe not. And that made her uncomfortable.

Because she liked him. She liked him a lot.

Skye wasn't the kind of girl who liked to be

the centre of attention. No one would describe her as a wallflower, but she would never choose to be on the front page of a newspaper.

'I'm sure it will be fine,' said Lucas, but his voice didn't sound quite so convincing.

She sat back into the seat again and tried to think about something else. They had a few days, then it would be Christmas, then it would be New Year. She had no idea what might be involved in the New Year's ball, but Lucas was obviously starting to take his role seriously. He'd met with the accountant. And spoken with the events planner.

As the winding country roads passed by in a welcome flash of white, brown and sometimes green, it seemed as if the countryside had developed into a scene from a Christmas card with snow covering as far as the eye could see.

As they reached Costley Hall, Lucas drew the car to a sudden halt. The huge metal gates were closed, and a number of individuals were skulking around outside. Reporters. Again.

'Must be a slow news day,' he muttered, before phoning the Hall and asking Donald about the gates. The reporters and photographers were around the car quickly, shouting questions through the windows.

A few moments later, the gates slid back and Lucas headed up the driveway, nearly catching a particularly obnoxious reporter with the wing mirror of the car. None of the photographers were stupid enough to be stuck on the wrong side of the gates as they closed again.

Skye let out her breath. 'Is it always going to be like this?'

'Of course not. By tomorrow, I'll be old news. You know what they say about today's news being tomorrow's chip paper.'

She waited until they pulled up at the main door and jumped out, looking down at her scrubs again and wishing she had her own clothes. Lucas grabbed his bag and they walked to the main door. This time, Lucas didn't knock, he just pushed it open and went inside.

Olivia appeared quickly. 'There you are. Those frightful people have been there since this morning. Are you two okay?' She blinked and couldn't hide the fact she looked Skye up and down. It nearly made Skye want to burst into tears.

But it was almost as if Olivia caught that feeling.

'I couldn't get back to my own place to get my things,' Skye explained, trying not to let her voice shake. 'They were outside my flat too. I've been wearing these scrubs since yesterday.'

Olivia walked over and touched her arm. 'Can I make you some tea? Run you a bath?'

Skye had never been good at accepting help, but on this occasion she nodded.

'Come on up to the Duke's suite,' she said. 'I'll start the bath for you, then bring you up some tea.'

'Thank you,' Lucas interjected. 'And our other guest?'

Skye had turned towards the stairs and she looked over her shoulder. 'What other guest?'

Olivia and Lucas exchanged a glance.

'Albert Cunningham has moved in. Well, he's not really, because he's stayed here before. But the hospital wouldn't discharge him without some adaptations in his house. He would have ended up still in at Christmas, so I suggested he come here, where we have some rooms specially adapted while he waited.'

His words made her heart swell.

'Albert's fine,' said Olivia, and Skye could tell she was talking about an old friend. There was a familiarity in her tone. 'The room has everything he needs, and he's using the lift to get up and down. I think he's actually in the library right now.'

'You never told me about Albert,' Skye said, looking at him curiously.

'It was meant to be a surprise, but things just got away from me this morning.'

She nodded, then came back and reached for Lucas's bag. 'I'll need to steal something of yours to put on before I come back down and meet him.'

Lucas gave a nod. 'We've ordered quite a few parcels that will arrive probably later today and tomorrow.'

If Olivia was surprised, she didn't show it. 'I'll let Donald know,' she added simply, then followed Skye up the stairs.

It was nice to be fussed over for once. Olivia found some rose and jasmine bubble bath, and a large dressing gown for Skye. The bath was ready surprisingly quickly and, by the time she came back out, there was a pot of tea and some scones waiting for her.

She looked around the room and smiled,

thinking of the parrot chair and chaise longue and wondering what Olivia would make of them.

Then that deep down feeling surged up again. The one that had been echoed in the news headlines. Was she really good enough to be here? To fit into this grand lifestyle? Her whole London rental could fit into this giant room alone, and that thought made her swallow, her mouth instantly dry.

She walked over to the window and looked over the well-kept beautiful grounds. She was jumping a million miles ahead here. But she knew how she felt about Lucas. She hadn't told him yet, because she was too nervous.

But what if he was having the same thoughts she was? They'd met before either of them had known about his title or estate. What if Lucas was now taking time to contemplate what the future might mean for him, and there wasn't a place in it for Skye?

She sucked in a breath and blinked back tears. That was the trouble with overthinking things, anticipating the worst instead of the best. Their relationship had evolved over weeks, taking the next step when both were ready. He'd been supportive to her, and understanding. And just being in his company made her world feel right.

It was time to stop being paranoid and get back to reality. Get back to how being with Lucas made her feel. She walked back over to the table and sat down.

Lucas appeared at the door. 'Knock, knock.' She instantly smiled, the warm feeling spreading across her body.

He came in and joined her at the table, stealing one of the scones. 'Hey—' she gave his hand a light slap '—get your own!'

He pulled a face. 'I've actually just had one downstairs. But the company up here was too tempting.'

Her smile widened ever further. 'I've just thought of something,' she said.

She looked around the room again. 'Olivia called this place the Duke's suite. She means you—not your father.'

Lucas sat back for a few seconds, as if he was trying to compute what she'd just said. 'My father used the other rooms.' He nodded. 'And it just didn't feel right going in them. She asked me when I spoke to her the other day if I wanted her to prepare rooms for me.'

Skye leaned forward, and she had a teasing glint in her eye. 'Did you warn her about the parrot chair?'

Lucas choked on his scone. When he finally stopped coughing and took a sip of tea, he looked at her. 'I wondered if they might be better in the library. You already declared that your favourite room.'

His green eyes were fixed on hers. She had the weirdest feeling. The kind she'd had as a child, when she tasted sherbet for the first time and it gave her that fizzy sensation, not just on her tongue but all over her body. She nearly didn't say the words that were in her head, but then she just couldn't help it.

'Am I allowed to have a favourite room here?'

She could swear the air crackled around them.

Lucas didn't answer straight away. He just stood up and leaned across the table, his lips connecting with hers.

It wasn't a sweet and tender kiss, nor a madly passionate one. It was solid, safe and reassuring. It gave the message of belonging and for the first time since her mother had died Skye had a feeling of connection and family again.

As his lips parted from hers, he stayed with his face just a few inches from hers.

'You can pick all the rooms you like, and fill this whole place with parrot chairs as far as I'm concerned,' he breathed. 'Just as long as you stay.'

And her world got even brighter.

CHAPTER EIGHT

IT HAD BEEN three days of bliss. Skye was still in awe of Costley Hall. She'd found a cinema and a snooker room, alongside the biggest ballroom that seemed fitting for Cinderella.

Brianna, the event co-ordinator, was scary, but in a good way. Skye admired her organisational skills, attention to detail and passion for her job. Or, more, her passion for the charities she was determined to support. The best laugh was the fact that Lucas seemed in awe of her too and had gone along with most of her plans.

Skye had watched the transformation of the ballroom, from its glittering chandeliers being lowered and cleaned, to the wooden floor being highly polished and the gold and silver decorations being tastefully placed around the room. Brianna supervised all of this with an eternal smile on her face and an endless supply of energy.

In amongst all this, Skye attended three separate interviews. Two with the different GP practices and the third with the trust sponsoring the district nurse training places. The black suit fitted perfectly, as did the shoes, and she'd answered all the questions without any problems. All the interviewers had been completely professional, and no one had made any mention of any of the news stories.

She still wasn't sure of where she wanted to be work-wise, and that made her distinctly uncomfortable. When she'd trained as a nurse and had a placement in A&E, she'd known immediately it was for her. She'd thought that having these interviews might have given her the same sense of belonging and an excitement and urgency for a new role. But that hadn't happened. Yet…

She was just crossing back through the ballroom when Olivia found her. 'Another parcel has arrived. It seems to be books. Donald has put them through in the library for you.'

Skye smiled. The books that she'd ordered wouldn't possibly fit with the much more impressive tomes that were currently in there, but there might be a corner she could find for them.

'I'm feeling a bit like Cinderella with all these parcels arriving,' she admitted, and she wasn't joking. Whilst she knew everything that she'd ordered in the car on the way here, it seemed that Lucas had ordered a bit more for her too. That was the danger of using his card. Now he knew her preferences and sizes, and had added some fun stuff too. Parcel after parcel had arrived, and it was ridiculous how much joy she'd felt in the last few days.

Maybe it was just being away from everything. Costley Hall, while ancient, was still like a little piece of paradise, a different world. Skye had never been in a position where she could just order anything she wanted, and she'd curtailed herself even though Lucas had encouraged her. It just didn't seem right when she came across so many patients where poverty and inequalities were a real factor in their lives. So, her half-hour spending spree in the car had come to an end. These books were the last part.

She still wondered if she really fitted in such a grand place. Lucas hadn't said a single thing to make her feel like that, but inside she still feared she might not be able to live up to what would be expected of anyone who was his girlfriend.

As she approached the library there was a distinctive smell of coffee and the sound of hearty laughter. As she peered around the corner, she saw Albert and Lucas sitting in the high-backed red leather Chesterfield chairs, a box of books perched on a table between them.

Skye put her hand on her hip. 'Are you guys laughing at my book choices?' she said.

Both heads turned towards her and she noticed that Albert already had an open book in his lap.

Lucas lifted his coffee mug and took another sip. 'Albert said they are the only decent books in here for years. He's already claimed one as his own.'

Skye moved into the library and pulled over another chair to join them. 'How are you feeling, you book thief?' she asked Albert.

'Good,' he said, holding up the crime thriller he'd picked. 'But don't plan on hiding any of the others away. I'll read them all.'

Skye laughed out loud as she reached into the box and picked out a pile to stack on one of the nearby shelves. She'd ordered a selection of reading material, some old favourites, others new releases. As she put them on the shelves, she shook her head.

'Okay, we have some more thrillers, some sci-fi, a few non-fiction, a couple of older children's books, some women's fiction, some romance and…' she waved a few floppy books in the air '…these ones are a bit racy—you've been warned,' she said as she stuck them on the shelf.

'Young people,' pooh-poohed Albert. 'You think you invented racy.'

Lucas started to laugh again. Albert relaxed into his chair and looked over at Lucas. 'This would have meant everything to your father—to see you here like this.'

Lucas shifted a little, and Skye knew he was still a bit uncomfortable about all this.

'Have you heard from your mother yet?' asked Albert.

It was a loaded question. They all knew it.

'She's still avoiding me,' Lucas admitted. 'I've asked her numerous questions and she keeps refusing to answer them—or not refusing exactly, just saying she'll let me know… eventually.'

Albert raised his eyebrows and sighed. 'Did you do what I suggested?'

Skye sat back down next to them both. 'Okay, so I'm intrigued. What?'

Albert sighed. 'I told Lucas she'd appear in a heartbeat if her allowance is stopped.'

Lucas glanced at Skye. 'I stopped her payments last week.'

Skye was surprised. 'But wasn't something about that included in the will?' she asked.

'It was,' sighed Albert. 'Ginny had a rock-solid legal agreement with Lucas's father. He couldn't have it stopped. But…' he glanced at Lucas '… Lucas didn't. It might be included as a condition in the will, but I doubt it's enforceable.' He shrugged his shoulders. 'There is another idea, which I didn't like to suggest before now.' There was mischief in his eyes.

'What?' Lucas asked cautiously.

Albert gave a rueful smile. 'You tell her I'm here.'

'What will she do?' Skye asked.

'Probably arrive like a bat out of hell.'

Skye sat back. Albert was a nice and perfectly reasonable man. She couldn't quite understand why Ginny—a woman she hadn't even met—would react in that way.

Albert looked tired. 'I wonder what kind of life you might have lived,' he said as he looked at Lucas, 'if we hadn't lived in such a time of prejudice.'

Skye's skin prickled. Now, she understood.

And it was as if someone had pushed Albert's buttons. 'Your father was in his early forties during the eighties. He lost a very good friend to HIV and, like the rest of the world, he was scared. He got married, tried to settle down and have a family, but Ginny very quickly realised that he didn't love her the way she wanted him to.' He gave a sad sigh. 'She took her opportunity to blackmail him and threatened to expose him to all his older family and friends.' He looked at them both. 'These days, it wouldn't have mattered, and wouldn't have worked. But there was still a lot of prejudice in the eighties. The newspapers would have loved a scoop about the Duke not being conventional and the chance to "out" him. So, he went with what Ginny wanted, even though it meant a risk.'

'A risk?' Lucas's voice was a little hoarse and she knew instantly that he was finding this very emotional.

'Yes,' Albert clarified. 'Ginny implied that there would still be contact between the Duke and you, but she wouldn't agree to it in writing. Demanded full custody. As soon as the papers were signed and she had her money, she vanished in a puff of a smoke, and you with her.'

Albert shook his head. 'You have no idea how hard he tried to find you. He always hoped when you turned eighteen you would get in touch. He had no idea what your mother had told you.' His expression was grave. 'He would have been horrified that you didn't even know of his existence, or who you were.'

Skye was struggling to really understand. She'd always known who her parents were. Her father had died from a heart attack five years ago, which had only made her bond with her mother even stronger. She couldn't imagine having half of her life, or her story, missing, even though she knew lots of people who had lives like that.

'That's terrible. I can't believe she'd do something like that. How could she?'

There was a flash of something in Lucas's eyes. 'Maybe other things were going on that none of us know about.'

Skye was surprised. He hadn't ever said anything particularly affectionate about his mother before. He'd been quite frank about what he thought about her lack of contact. But it was clear that deep down there was still an element of denial there. His mother was the only parent he'd ever known; of course he would have loyalty to her.

Still, the stopping of the payments surprised her. Did it mean that Lucas actually just wanted to see his mother, and this was his way of getting her attention—rather than it actually being about the money?

But, before she could think any further, Lucas reached out and took her hand, obviously surprised by his own snappiness. 'Sorry,' he said in a low voice.

She was a little startled, but that small act of taking her hand seemed to relax him a bit, and she watched as the tension in his shoulders eased and he looked back to Albert with a sincere gaze.

'Albert, tell me more about my dad.'

For a moment Albert said nothing. It was the dad word. The more affectionate term than 'father' that had been banded around a few times. It was the first time Skye had heard Lucas say it. She gave his hand a squeeze back, and settled into her chair to listen.

CHAPTER NINE

THEY WERE IN the kitchen, quietly making tea together. Lucas knew that he'd snapped, but Skye seemed to have accepted his apology. The stories Albert had told them had filled him with melancholy about the life he'd missed out on.

And it wasn't about this place. It wasn't about Costley Hall. Or maybe it was, just a little. It was more about the man. Albert—who accepted he might have a skewed point of view—had described a warm, intelligent, bright man, who might occasionally have been slightly outrageous and enjoyed a good party.

Lucas was trying to get his head around what life might have been like if he'd got to stay in one place, make more friends and spend time with his father. He knew that the glimmer of anger and resentment in him was probably entirely normal, so it was hard for him to understand his earlier reaction when Skye had said something about his mother. He'd been the first to tell Skye she hadn't been around much, or kept in touch, and their relationship was certainly fractured. But he felt as if he could say all these things. So why was it different when it came from someone else's mouth?

A hand brushed his jacket sleeve and he turned around. It was Brianna and her face was flushed.

'Someone is causing a scene. She's along in your suite. Says she's your mother.'

Lucas's heart dropped like a stone. His mother. Of course.

Skye was clearly surprised. 'Lucas?' she asked.

He slipped his hand into hers. 'Time to meet my mother, I guess,' he said in a grim tone as they started down the corridor and up the curved staircase.

Anger thrummed through him. Her answers to his emails had been curt, phone and text messages simply ignored. He had a suspicion of why she was here. And he would actually hate for it to be confirmed.

They entered his suite to see his mother

tossing clothes to the floor. *Skye's* clothes. Toiletries and cosmetics had been flung from the bathroom across the floor. His mother was standing amongst all this mess with a look of fury on her slightly too sun-kissed face, which would have highlighted her wrinkles if they hadn't been Botoxed into non-existence.

'This is my room,' his mother hissed as he made his way into the suite.

It had been five years since he'd seen his mother in the flesh. She was still wearing the same perfume, which hung in the air between them. But the familiar scent brought no fond memories. Just a host of disappointment and bitterness. She was dressed in a bright orange coat and fur hat, looking as if she were about to attend a royal event.

He looked at the mess on the carpet, all Skye's belongings.

'This is my suite,' he said in a low voice. 'And I'd thank you to stop destroying what isn't yours.'

There were two designer suitcases in the room, alongside a huge trunk.

'This isn't your room.'

'It is.' He kept his voice icily cold. He'd dealt with his mother's rages before, but he'd never really understood her hidden resentment or her odd behaviour. 'It's mine, and Skye's.'

'Her?' His mother's voice was incredulous. 'This little money-grabber? What do you actually know about her? Oh, wasn't it convenient that she was around to help you with your new discoveries? Anyone would think she'd planned it.'

Lucas nearly choked. 'Don't be so ridiculous. How could you even think that?'

His mother pointed across the room at Skye. 'Because I looked her up. Of course I did. You became an instant billionaire. Of course she would latch on to you.'

He turned to look at Skye, mainly to reassure her that he knew this was absolute nonsense. But something stopped him. Skye looked shell-shocked. She was staring at his mother in the most curious way. In short, she was horrified.

His mother continued. 'I know her,' she spat. 'She was a nurse at one of the clinics I went to in Harley Street. Who knows what I said under anaesthetic, but she was clearly clever enough to track you down before the lawyers did.'

Skye blinked. Her hands were clasped in

front of her and her arms were trembling. She shook her head and glanced at Lucas.

'Skye?' he asked. He wasn't asking about his mother's accusations. He was asking about the look on Skye's face.

Skye lifted one hand to her face. It was almost as if she was trying to force herself to speak.

His mother kept talking at the top of her voice, twittering on and on about how it was all a conspiracy, and Skye was trying to steal his money, or *her* money.

Lucas lifted his hand and put it on Skye's shoulder. He'd never seen her silent like this before. She was feisty and definitely able to stand up for herself. She'd never let someone treat her like this in A&E.

Unless, of course…no. No, he wasn't even going to go there.

'Skye,' he said quietly, 'are you okay?'

She blinked and stared up at him. 'I do know your mother,' she said in a stiff voice.

He glanced back over his shoulder.

'See!' shouted his mother in glee. 'She looked you up, and saw we were connected. She realised the Duke was dead and that you would inherit everything. She planned this all along. She targeted you from the moment you started at The Harlington.'

There was a flash in his peripheral vision and he realised Albert had entered the room.

It was almost as if there was now another target for his mother. She turned all her attention from Skye onto Albert, treating him with equal venom.

'You're still here! Shouldn't you be dead by now? Haven't you bled this family dry already?'

Albert seemed completely unperturbed by this orange vision with the highest pitched voice Lucas had ever experienced. He sighed. 'Genevieve, a delight to see you, as always.' He gave a gentle shrug of his shoulders. 'Or maybe not,' he added simply.

Lucas felt as if he were in some kind of reality TV show. His mother had always been highly strung and self-centred, but he'd never seen a display like he was currently witnessing. But it was apparent that Albert had seen this kind of behaviour before and couldn't have cared less. He gave a worried glance towards Skye, moved across the room and positioned himself on the parrot chaise longue.

Lucas realised what he was doing. He was deliberately making himself the target. He must have heard Genevieve screeching at Skye and decided to intervene.

Lucas held up his hand again. ‘Enough!’ This time he shouted, gaining his mother’s full attention.

He pointed at her. ‘Don’t you dare come into my home and act like this. You won’t answer my calls or emails. You’ve lied to me for the entirety of my life, and now you think you can appear and make ridiculous claims against the woman I love? Well, no. I won’t stand for it. I don’t know where you came from, but you can just head on back there.’ Rage was flooding his veins, pent-up feelings from years of being virtually ignored by his mother.

He turned back to Skye. Her face was the palest he’d ever seen it.

‘I looked after her post-operatively,’ she said quietly. ‘I do remember her—’ she took a breath ‘—but I didn’t look into anything about her, and I had no idea you were her son.’

It took him a few moments to realise what she was saying.

‘Skye,’ he said, looking into her eyes in confusion. ‘I don’t believe a single word she says. I don’t think for a second you knew we were connected. I don't believe that you knew I was a duke before I did. Don't listen to her, don't listen for a moment.'

He turned back to his mother, who was ranting again at Albert.

He moved across the room quickly. 'You've had years,' he said coldly. 'Years to tell me about all of this. Yes, I get that you were hurt. I get that my father's interests lay elsewhere. But you don't get to come here and speak to my family like that.'

'Family?' she yelled back indignantly. 'I'm your family.'

'Really?' His voice was dangerously low. 'Then when are you going to start acting like it? I had a father. A father you told me was dead. And now he is. And guess what? I don't remember meeting him. You stole a lifetime of memories from me because you were slighted. A lifetime of chances to get to know him. And now I have a wonderful girlfriend. And you seem determined to alienate her too. And Albert—who I understand you might have history with, but who I happen to like, and he can help me fill in the gaps about my father too. So, if you don't understand how I feel about all this, you can leave. And stop living off my father's wealth.'

The elephant in the room had been addressed and there was silence. Genevieve's mouth was open as if she was just about to start again, but had been stopped mid flow. Her face was red, clashing horribly with her orange coat, which she still wore. Albert's eyes were fixed on the floor. He'd done what he'd set out to, and taken the focus off Skye.

'Let's face it, you're not here because you love me, or are worried about me. You're here because I cut off your monthly allowance.'

'It's my money,' his mother shouted, 'not yours!'

Something washed over Lucas. Almost as if Albert had whispered in his ear. Or maybe it was his father?

There was no point fighting with this woman. No point arguing.

'Apparently not,' he said in a low voice. 'So, just leave.'

There was a gasp behind him. Lucas spun round. Skye had a single tear rolling down her cheek.

'You can't ask her to leave,' she said, as if something was caught in her throat.

'Of course, I can. She's spent most of my life absent anyway. I don't need her. I don't want her.'

'Don't say that,' choked Skye. 'You can't say that.'

He was still so angry with his mother that he couldn't take a moment to understand the pain that Skye had in her eyes.

She stepped forward so that only he could hear her speak. 'This is too much,' she whispered, her eyes wide and her voice croaky. Her hand reached up to his cheek. 'The man I love wouldn't do that. He wouldn't tell his mother to leave and cut her off. Stop, Lucas. Think for a minute. I don't have my mother any more, and I would do anything—*anything*—to have her back. You can fix this. You can repair this relationship with your mother. You've both been hurt, but it's time. It's time to sit down and fix this. You have to. Because I don't see a future for us otherwise.'

'What?' He couldn't believe his ears. 'Did you hear what she said about you? What she thinks of you? I'm defending you, and I will always put you first, Skye. Always.'

More tears flowed and her hand lowered from his cheek. 'She doesn't know me, Lucas. She doesn't know me at all. But she does know you. You're her only son. The most important human being on the planet to her. You have to work at this. Families are hard, Lucas.

People don't just grow up in a happy bubble. All families take work. I need to know that you're prepared to work at this, just like you'll be prepared to work at us over the years.'

He looked over his shoulder. His mother was still standing there, stiffly, defiantly, with a hostile look in her eyes. He knew that she would spend her life trying to get between him and Skye. And he couldn't tolerate that. Not for a moment.

He turned back to Skye, but she was gone. Gone from the room. It was as if she already knew what he was going to tell her, and she hadn't waited to find out. Because she knew him. She knew him better than he knew himself.

And she'd already decided she couldn't live like that.

CHAPTER TEN

IT WAS OFFICIALLY the worst Christmas ever.

Things would have been much better if A&E had been crammed with patients. Instead, it was as if the whole world had decided to behave on this day. As she walked into the department, she could almost hear the quietness echo around her.

Being on duty with Lucas today would be torture.

Skye had borrowed the least expensive car in the garage and driven home. Donald hadn't even questioned her tear-stained face, just handed over the keys, explained a few things and put a hand on her shoulder, telling her to drive carefully.

Lucas had phoned and texted but she hadn't answered. She needed time. She needed space.

His mother had been a whirlwind of horror.

Exactly the kind of person anyone wouldn't want in their life. Skye certainly didn't want her in her own life.

But she knew better than to say that.

Families were complicated. All the words Genevieve had said had echoed all the fears that Skye already had in her own head. It was bad enough reading them online, but having someone say them to her face…?

Deep down, she had the worst feeling. It didn't matter how Genevieve had behaved towards her. Well, it did. But Skye had been long enough on this earth to know she had to step back and try and get some perspective.

In one way, she was delighted about the fact that Lucas had stood up for her and told his mother to leave.

But ultimately? It would be destructive and selfish.

If Lucas couldn't see her perspective right now—and she got that—because of how all this had been dumped on him from a great height—it was her job to try and make him see it.

The last thing she wanted to be was the reason that Lucas cut off his last remaining parent. No matter how horrid the woman was.

Skye's mother had been warm-hearted and

considerate—traits Skye wasn't sure that Genevieve possessed. But it didn't matter, because she was still Lucas's mother. And after losing her own mum she was left with that deep down regret of not having another hug or another conversation.

Skye believed that someone would only know how that felt if they'd walked in her shoes. She didn't want Lucas to have regrets—for them to stay together and then, when Genevieve eventually died, for him to have resentment or regret that he hadn't worked things out with her.

If she and Lucas stayed together, she knew, ultimately, that could mean having to tolerate someone in her life who would be difficult, likely interfering and mean at times. But Skye was confident that they would be able to work something out, to lay ground rules, to keep things cordial.

She gulped as she glanced over a set of patient notes. Because, deep down, she was considering something else. If Lucas didn't want to take the time and trouble to attempt to sort things out with his mother, would he want to take the time and trouble to sort things out between them, if they ran into trouble further down the road in their relationship? Or would he just walk away and cut her off, like he'd threatened his mother?

It was a horrible, scary prospect. But one she had to consider.

In between all this, she still had to decide what to do about her career. All three jobs had been offered to her, and she needed to make a decision quickly. Did she want to be a practice nurse or a district nurse? Did she want to stay in London or move to the outskirts and nearer the country? And how, when all this was going on, could she even consider something as silly as Christmas?

Bryn, one of her colleagues, settled into the seat next to her as others gathered around for the handover, which was brief and precise.

Her colleagues greeted the day shift with enthusiasm, mainly because their night shift was now finished and they'd be going home to their families. The department was littered with Christmas chocolates. There were only a few patients in the department so far. A miserable baby with a high temperature, two elderly and confused patients who both had infections, a young homeless man who'd been found freezing in a doorway and was suffering from hypothermia, and a middle-aged woman with chest pain.

Lucas was hovering near the back, staying out of Skye's line of sight. Maybe he didn't want to talk to her. Maybe he'd decided to draw a line under their relationship because she hadn't responded to his texts or messages.

Maybe it had been a wrong decision. Because now, and for the next twelve hours, they were going to have to spend the whole shift tiptoeing around each other, under the watching eyes of their colleagues, who were bound to notice that something was off between them.

It wasn't the first time that Skye wished she could pick up the phone to her mum. She would know what to say about all this. She would know what to say to make Skye feel better.

Christmas might not be her favourite time of year, but Skye took a shaky breath and blinked back tears. What she wouldn't do right now for a giant hug…

There were a few comments. A few jokes about whether he still had time to come to work, or was he too busy counting his money. The truth was, Lucas had expected to be ribbed by his work colleagues. He didn't want people to tiptoe around him. He was more worried about what they might be saying about Skye. The news reports had bothered him—not because he'd believed them, but more because he could see how hurt she'd been by some of the comments from unknown colleagues—even though she'd tried to hide it.

Lucas knew that some of it might just be made up—anything for a headline or a story—but if he caught anyone saying something untoward about Skye he wouldn't hold his tongue for a second.

The last few days at Costley Hall had been awful. All because of his mother.

Up until that point, it had almost felt as if things were clicking into place.

He couldn't pretend to know even half of what was going on at the estate, but he was learning and that was the important thing. He'd made some headway with Brianna, the events co-ordinator, and hoped they could be on the same wavelength. He'd met all the stable staff and gardeners. He enjoyed Albert's company. No one had come out and said it yet, but he knew that Albert had been his father's partner and had lived at Costley Hall, in one way or another, for over twenty years.

But most of all he'd loved being around

Skye. She was warm, friendly and always looking to help in any way she could. Olivia and Donald liked her, and she'd asked about things he hadn't even thought of—such as whether Costley Hall bought their produce from local vendors and supported the nearby village in any way.

He'd spent most days with her constantly in his line of sight. He couldn't help but look at her. Her laughter had filled the air at times. He'd also caught her in a few quiet moments when she was clearly thinking about her mum.

Christmas could be a tough time of year, particularly for those who'd lost someone that they loved. He was conscious of that, and had wanted to make sure he supported her just as much as she'd supported him. But how could he do that now? She hadn't even answered any of his texts or calls.

As for his mother's behaviour? He'd been beside himself with fury. She had refused to leave Costley Hall, screaming and shouting and making demands, insulting Albert and continuing with disparaging remarks about Skye.

When Lucas had gone to try and find Skye

he'd been horrified to realise she hadn't just left the suite—but had left the entire estate.

Donald had told him he'd loaned her a car, and a tiny part of him might have been annoyed, but he knew it was entirely the right thing to do. The direct look that he'd been given by the fearless Donald had been part chastisement and part pity.

As an adult, he could see just how damaging his mother's lifestyle had been for him. It was hard for him to comprehend, because his mother was all he'd known. But most of the time there had been staff looking after him, or 'friends' who'd looked after his welfare more than she'd ever done. Getting accepted into university and moving into halls had been a relief for both of them. There had been an unwritten agreement that he wouldn't be moving back home, as he'd never really had a 'home'. And yet Costley Hall had always been here, and he'd never known it, but she had.

When he'd gone back to his suite, it had seemed that his mother had finally run out of steam.

He'd talked frankly to her, telling her exactly how much he loved Skye and what she meant to him. He'd spoken quietly, sitting at the other side of the table from her as she could hardly meet his eyes.

He'd then pushed back his anger to tell his mother how much he wished he'd known his father, and how nice it had been to meet Albert.

He could tell she was visibly stung by these words. But it was time for complete honesty between mother and son. More words had been exchanged and they'd reached an uneasy truce.

He'd wanted to tell Skye—he'd tried to tell Skye. But the last thing he'd wanted to do was to turn up uninvited at her home.

By the time he'd dealt with his patients, there was a lull in the day. Lucas spent a little time searching for Skye and finally found her in the break room, next to a lopsided Christmas tree and a mound of chocolates and biscuits. He pulled out the tin he'd been given and held it out to her.

'Olivia sent you some baking.'

Skye blinked and held out her hand, taking the tin and pulling off the lid. The smell of baking filled the room instantly.

He saw the edges of her lips hint upwards as she bent over the scones, lemon drizzle cake, tiny Christmas pudding and blackberry and apple tart.

'Wow,' she said simply.

Lucas sat down next to her. He took a deep breath.

'Can I start by telling you that Costley Hall is empty without you and I miss you more than I thought possible?'

He noticed her hand shake as she turned to look at him. There were tears in her eyes.

'Christmas Day can be hard enough. This is the first one without your mum. Am I allowed to hug you?'

Her nod was tiny. It was as if she was scared to move. So he put his arm around her shoulders and let her sink into him.

He reached over with his other hand and took hers in his, gently interlocking their fingers.

'I'm so sorry about how my mother spoke to you. And I know and appreciate you feel differently about all this, because you had a great relationship with your mum.'

Her voice came out croaky. 'But if that's how you treat your mum? What happens if things go bad between us? Will you just walk away then?'

His heart lurched. His thoughts had been

spinning. Wondering if Skye just wanted to walk in the other direction and never see him again. But these words? These words meant there was still a chance for them. And he was going to grab that with both hands—albeit a little gently.

He lifted his hand and stroked her cheek.

'Skye, I love you. We are never going to have the kind of unbalanced relationship that I have with my mother. We're equals. In this together. At least I hope we are. I spoke to her again, you know.'

'You did?' Her blue eyes met his and this time his heart squeezed inside his chest. He never wanted her to feel unsure or upset, like she clearly did now.

'Of course I did.' He sighed. 'She realised how upset I was about you leaving. I told her that I love you, and I plan to spend the rest of my life with you, and she'd better know that she'd crossed a line.'

Skye didn't say anything, just licked her lips.

'I'm always going to have a fractured relationship with my mother, Skye. But I haven't cut her off. I've restored her allowance. I've agreed we'll stay in touch. But the truth is our relationship isn't much more than that.'

Skye put her hand to her chest. 'You don't know what it feels like,' she said shakily. 'To know that you'll never have another conversation with your mum or see her again.'

He nodded. 'I get that. And you're right, I don't understand that. And maybe us talking in the last few days has cleared the air. I don't feel as resentful towards her but—' he paused for a moment '—I don't feel an overwhelming surge of love for my mother either.' He shook his head. 'I'm sad, but it's just never been there. I hear you talk about your mother, and I'm envious. I really am. I'm envious that you two were close and clearly loved each other.' He looked at her for a long moment. 'And I think that might be something we need to talk about.'

She tilted her head. 'What do you mean?'

He lowered his gaze, not wanting to upset her any further. 'You mentioned once about associating The Harlington with memories of your mum. You say you need a career change and something else to focus on. But I'm worried you're trying to run away from how you feel. Run away from the grief about your mum. And I'm worried that if we don't talk about it, you won't ever feel as if you're making the right decision, or in the place you need to be.'

She took a few minutes, clearly thinking about how things were between them.

'I've got something to tell you,' she said a little hesitantly.

His heart gave a flip-flop and he turned to face her, hoping nothing was wrong. 'What?'

She bit her bottom lip, pulled her phone from her pocket and turned it around. The screen was on her email page. 'I got three emails in the last few days, offering me all the jobs.'

'Skye, that's amazing,' he said, leaning over to give her a hug, even though his heart was immediately racing. But he quickly realised the hug was not reciprocated. He leaned back. 'What's wrong? Shouldn't you be celebrating?'

She nodded, and he could see the sheen in her eyes and noticed her swallow as if she had a giant lump in her throat.

'I… I…just don't know.' She gave a sad smile. 'The first person I would normally have told would have been my mum, and—' She didn't fill in the blank because she didn't need to.

He threaded his fingers through hers. 'Are

you happy about any of these jobs? Which one will you take?'

Skye was silent for a few moments, and he could see the uncertainty on her face. He hated this. A new job should make someone excited at taking on a new challenge. Although Skye was certain she was ready to make a move, would she be making the right one? And should he actually tell her he didn't want her to go anywhere? Of course he shouldn't. He had no right to do that.

She gave him the saddest smile. 'Lucas,' she said steadily, 'I need you to give me another few days. I need to sort some things out in my head.'

He swallowed, wanting to say a hundred things but knowing he had to respect her decision. And he would. Because he loved her.

He didn't want to overwhelm her. But he couldn't walk away right now without letting her know how much he cared.

'Of course,' he replied in a low voice. 'You take all the time you need. Because I'll wait,' he said with not a moment's hesitation. 'I'll wait until you're ready.'

He gave a small smile. 'Will you still do me the honour of being my date for the New Year's ball?'

This time her smile was genuine. 'I think I can manage that,' she said, then looked back down to her box of cakes. 'Now,' she said, 'I know from previous experience that you're a cake and scone stealer. So, off you go. Leave me alone to eat cake, drink tea and contemplate life.'

He squeezed her hand one more time and stood, keeping a smile on his face, even though, inside, his heart was breaking.

'You can phone me any time, day or night,' he said as he headed to the door.

Her head gave an almost imperceptible nod and he breathed in slowly and headed back out into the department, giving her the space she needed.

CHAPTER ELEVEN

AS SHE DROVE towards Costley Hall, Skye had a fluttering feeling in her chest, part excitement, part fear. She'd promised to be Lucas's date. But as she swept up the driveway she could see the estate was buzzing with people. Maybe this had been the wrong thing to agree to? There would be no chance of privacy, and Lucas would be tied up with a million responsibilities.

Olivia met her at the door with a nervous smile. 'Go on up to the Duke's suite. He's waiting for you.'

Skye was a bit out of sorts. The Christmas Day shift at the hospital had been fine, nothing too serious. When they'd finished their twelve hours at seven p.m., she'd said a brief farewell to Lucas, gone back to her place, wrapped herself in a duvet on her sofa, had a Chinese meal delivered and watched

Christmas TV. It had blocked out some of the memories that had been circulating in her head—reminding her that this was her first Christmas without any family left. It stung, not having that conversation with her mum on Christmas Day, not having something to unwrap on the day and laugh about. They'd generally always bought something fun for each other, rather than something serious. But that part of her life was gone now, and it was hard to explain to anyone.

But the run-up to New Year's Eve had been harder, and she was wondering if coming to Costley Hall was the right move. In the five years since her dad had died, Skye had always made a point of being with her mum when the clock struck twelve. This was the time of year she always had off, and they'd spent it together, sometimes at her mother's home, one time at a hotel in Scotland, and another in a resort in Tenerife. But the person she'd clinked glasses with at midnight and drank a toast to the New Year had always been her mother, and this time it was as if something dark had settled in the bottom of her stomach. She wasn't quite sure how to explain it to herself, let alone anyone else.

As she arrived at Costley Hall, she knew

deep down that part of what Lucas had said to her was right. She did need a fresh start. But she'd also been running away from her grief. A colleague had given her a card for a counsellor they'd seen when they'd lost a family member, and Skye knew it was time to pull it out and talk to someone. Maybe it would stop these feelings being so overwhelming and give her some new coping mechanisms to try. She could almost hear her mother's voice in her ear, telling her to do it. Telling her not to risk her relationship with a man that she clearly loved.

Because she did love Lucas. She knew she did. She just had to believe that he would always be willing to fight for her, like she would for him. And as she walked up the grand sweeping staircase at Costley Hall, she had to believe she was worth all this.

Today had been a whirlwind. Every time he blinked another person scooted past, preparing the Hall for the grand New Year's Eve charity ball.

Brianna, the event planner, was a wonder, her precision planning evident everywhere that Lucas looked. He had spent most of the day settling in the various children and their families from some of the charities that were represented at the ball tonight. It really was a delight to meet them all, and the whole thing did honestly feel like a family affair. Olivia was always in the background, ready to answer any questions, and Albert had been walking around looking dapper in a navy velvet jacket since just after lunchtime.

He'd barely had a chance to think all day, and that was probably for the best—because any time he did have a chance, his thoughts were fixated on Skye, hoping she would keep her promise and turn up.

When he finally got the signal from Olivia, he went quickly along to the suite, ready to meet her.

He had the biggest grin on his face as Skye walked in, a small overnight bag in her hand. A wave of relief washed over him and he moved beside her, kissing her cheek. 'I have a surprise for you,' he said.

Her nose wrinkled. 'What?'

'This,' he said, waving his hand in the direction of their bed—because that was how he thought of it, *their* bed.

Across it lay three ballgowns. One silver, one green and one a deep red. Skye let out an audible gasp and his heart lurched. She was happy. Thank goodness. He'd asked Brianna for some help, and she'd gone to town, scrolling through online stores and showing her shortlist for Lucas to have the final say.

'Where did they come from?'

'Me,' he replied with a grin. 'I got you three because I wasn't entirely sure which you'd prefer.' His heart was thudding in his chest.

Skye rolled her eyes and swung her bag onto the bed, pulling a black dress from it. She gave him a careful glance. 'I brought the one full-length gown that I actually own.' She held it up. 'It's black,' she said, 'not entirely special—' the hint of a smile was appearing on her lips '—and I bought it five years ago.' She gave him another playful glance. 'I'm not even entirely sure it still fits, but had decided to just breathe in and hope for the best.'

'If you want to wear the black dress, then you can absolutely wear whatever you like,' he said, walking over and touching the fabric, wondering if he might have overstepped.

But Skye walked over to the bed. She touched the skirt of the silver gown, which was adorned with sequins and glimmered under the lights in this room.

'All three are stunning,' she said simply.

He waited, wondering what might come next.

Her blue eyes met his. 'You make me feel like Cinderella,' she whispered.

His arms slid around her from behind. His lips near her ear, he said in a low voice, 'As long as I get to be the Prince, I can live with that.'

She spun around to face him and put her hands around his neck. 'When did you do this?'

'You know that day we were in the car, and you ordered some things?'

She nodded. 'But that was a few weeks ago, before Christmas, just when the news hit.'

He smiled in agreement. 'I know, but I asked you to the ball then, and told you to buy a ballgown.'

'But you could see that I hadn't?'

His green eyes locked with hers. 'I know you were being cautious. Even getting you to buy those beauties was a struggle.' He gestured with his head towards the parrot chaise longue and chair, which had ended up in their suite.

Skye couldn't help but beam. 'They really are magnificent in real life, aren't they?'

'If they're magnificent to you, then they're magnificent to me,' he replied with a grin.

Her head fell back as she laughed, his lips taking advantage of the bare skin at her neck.

'Hey—' she swatted him lightly with her hand '—I'm on a time limit to get ready, and so are you.' She looked at the stunning dresses again. 'I don't even know if any of these will fit yet.'

'Oh, they'll fit,' he insisted as he ran his hands up and down the curves at her waist and hips. Then he grew serious for a moment. 'How are you? I spent all Christmas night worrying about you. I wanted to phone you or text you, but you'd asked me for space so I didn't.' He gave a soft laugh. 'You have no idea how hard I found that,' he admitted.

She gave a slow nod. 'I found it hard too. I always knew the first Christmas without Mum would be like that. I thought work would distract me enough, but…' She took a deep breath, her hands resting on his shoulders. 'You might have been right about talking to someone.'

His heart squeezed for her. 'Do you know someone?'

She pressed her lips together for a moment. 'Someone at work gave me a recommendation. I think it's time to take it.'

He enveloped her in a hug. Part of him felt sorry that he'd been the person to bring this up. But he wanted her to be happy. He wanted her to feel able to move on in life and still have all the wonderful memories of her mum.

She pulled back gently. 'And how's your mum?'

Lucas contemplated the question for a second. 'Ginny is Ginny, and always will be. She's in Spain right now, celebrating New Year with friends. I've made it clear that I consider Costley Hall Albert's home, and if she wants to come and visit, she has to be courteous to him too.'

He could sense a little of the tension leave Skye's body. He reached up and twisted a bit of her hair with one of his fingers. 'You don't know how much I wish I could have had the same kind of relationship with my mum that you did with yours. But I have to accept that she is just not that kind of person and we won't have that kind of relationship. But I'll keep the door open, and I won't cut her off.'

He gave a sad smile. 'The person I'm enjoying a wonderful new relationship with is

Albert. He's an incredible man, with a wicked sense of humour and a unique experience of having to hide who he was for most of his life. I think he takes joy in recounting all the stories about my dad, and is relieved he can finally admit that they loved each other.' He led her over to the chaise lounge so they could both sit down for a moment. 'The other thing you should know is that Albert is one of your biggest fans.'

A smile broke across her face, and he knew she was flattered. 'Well, I'm kind of a fan of Albert too,' she said.

He interwove his fingers with hers. 'Did you decide what you want to do about the jobs you have been offered?' His insides felt as if they were prickling. An idea had hatched in his head, but he wasn't sure whether to mention it or not.

She shook her head and sighed. 'Not yet. I've got pros and cons for each job. All offer me a good opportunity. I've always been a nurse, I've never wanted to do anything else. But the time I had off with my mum made me want to look at other things too. I'm just not in that position really. Like the rest of the world, I need to work to pay my bills.' She sighed and looked around. 'I know that I can't *not* nurse, it's in my blood. It would just be nice to do it a little bit less?' Her final words sounded more like a question, as if she was asking what he thought.

The tiny seed that had been growing in Lucas's head started to emerge into a pink cherry blossom in full bloom. He'd watched her before at Costley Hall. The truth was, before his mother had appeared and caused a scene, it seemed that Skye fitted in even better than he did.

Maybe it was because she had no history or pressure about the place, but she seemed to excel while here. Everyone loved her. She was constantly asking questions and having conversations with the staff, finding out all she could. She was both patient and enthusiastic, and she'd made his time here easier. She'd laughed more here than in any of the time he'd known her. It had been a joy to be around her.

He knew without a doubt how he wanted things to go between them. He loved her. Skye was the first woman he'd ever connected with so much, and the fact she'd been there to share the shock and amazement about the biggest shock of his life just made them seem destined to be.

Everything about Costley Hall was a huge undertaking, and he didn't want to do it alone.

'How about doing something else?' he asked, the question making his throat dry with nerves.

'Like what?' She laughed. 'An airline pilot? A politician? A shopkeeper?'

He gulped. 'How about reducing your nursing hours and helping out at Costley Hall?'

The shock on her face was clear. He held his breath. Was this good shock, or bad?

Skye sat back in her chair and sucked in some air. 'Are you serious?'

'Of course I am. There's going to be so much to do here. I'm probably going to have to consider my hours too. I still want to be a doctor. I didn't train all these years to walk away. But…' he took a breath '… I also have to make sure that Costley Hall is run responsibly and ethically. I have the welfare of the staff to consider, and the grounds and business interests.' He shook his head. 'I can't do this alone, and I can't think of anyone I trust more.'

She sat for another few moments in stunned silence, and then slowly the edges of her lips turned upwards.

'Really?' she asked.

'Really,' he said softly. 'You must know how I feel about you.'

Her blue gaze met his. And held it. Hypnotically, as if they were both in a spell.

'No,' she said. 'Tell me.'

And this was it. The moment that he really told her how he felt. And they weren't in bed. There hadn't just been a romantic meal, or a sunset somewhere.

Lucas reached over and cupped her cheek. 'I love you,' he said tenderly, as his insides flip-flopped around about like a teenager after their first kiss. 'I love being around you, and I want to keep doing that for a very long time.'

Tears flooded into her eyes. She reached up her hand to cover his on her cheek, then dipped her head for a few moments, catching her breath. When she lifted her head again, she was smiling.

'I feel the same,' she said. 'It feels like you appeared at just the right time, to take my mind from other things, and fill a giant gap in my life.'

'Well, I'm glad I was convenient,' he joked.

Her hand clenched his. 'Oh, you're not convenient, Lucas Hastings.' She raised her eyebrows. 'In fact, you're anything but convenient. You've been quite troublesome, actually. It's just as well I think you're handsome, smart and worth the bother.'

She leaned over and kissed him quickly, pulling back in case anyone else might see.

'I'd love to have a role at Costley Hall,' she said, looking thoughtful. 'I do like it here. And I do like the people, and maybe this is the change I need to make in my life.' She took a breath. 'I've always been so self-sufficient that reducing my hours might feel strange for me.'

'You mean, as in your salary?'

She nodded. 'It pays my rent, my bills, for everything. I like the fact that I can make my own way in life.'

He understood what she meant. 'But if you take the job at the GP practice close to here, it would make more sense to live at Costley Hall. It's much closer. You could give up your rental. And don't think you won't get paid for what you do at Costley Hall—of course you will. You're not going to lose any of your income.'

He could say more. He could say that he'd quite happily offer her much more than that, but he wanted to wait for the perfect moment.

Skye looked thoughtful for a few seconds,

then gave a nod, a warm-hearted smile on her face. 'I like the sound of that,' she whispered.

His nose brushed the side of her cheek. 'I like the sound of that too,' he whispered. 'Now, let's get changed. We've got a ball to attend.'

CHAPTER TWELVE

IF SOMEONE HAD told her at the beginning of this year that two of the biggest events of her life would happen, she wouldn't have believed them. But the saddest and happiest parts of her life were coming together.

She ducked into the bathroom and quickly showered, finding appropriate underwear and quickly pulling on each dress in turn. They were all stunning but the silver dress gave her a different kind of sensation—like she could rule the world.

It wasn't a traditional, sticky-out ballgown. It had small cap sleeves, a slightly plunging heart-shaped neckline, then skimmed her hips in a shimmer of silver sequins until it hit the floor. A pair of strappy silver sandals matched it perfectly and by the time she'd applied her make-up, her heart was beating in anticipation.

Was this how it might feel to be lady of the manor, so to speak? She took a few moments, sitting in her parrot chair and running her hand over the velvet, admiring the bright reds, greens and yellows of the parrots on the dark blue material. It was as if someone had flipped a switch and turned her life into something else.

Did she, Skye Carter, really deserve all this?

She closed her eyes and tried to imagine telling her mum about all this, and how happy she would have been to meet Lucas and see the impact he'd had on Skye's life.

She stood up, finding renewed confidence. As she made her way to the top of the stairs she could see Lucas, dressed in his suit, waiting for her. It felt as if her grin was too wide for her face as he slid his arm around her waist.

'Ready to greet our guests?'

Butterflies were in her stomach, but as she looked down into the foyer where their guests were gathering, removing their jackets and getting some refreshments, she could feel the buzz in the air.

The doors were open to the main ballroom,

with its bright twinkling chandeliers and gold and silver decorations.

'A couple of months ago, I was just a doctor,' said Lucas, and she could hear the hint of nerves in his voice.

She put her hand on his chest. 'Lucas Hastings, you've never been *just* a doctor.' She gave him an understanding look. 'But now you're also the Duke of Mercia, and you're going to be wonderful. And tonight will be perfect.'

He kissed her cheek and they descended the stairs together and Skye breathed out, letting the tension she was feeling release throughout her body.

Tonight would be wonderful. And, with Lucas's hand in hers, this place was starting to feel real. Starting to feel like it could be home.

The countdown had begun. Brianna had assembled the crowd from the ballroom at the bottom of the stairs, and even though it seemed as if the eyes of the world were on him, Lucas was finally beginning to feel comfortable in this newly shaped Duke-sized skin.

And he was quite sure the reason he could feel confident about this was because of the woman by his side.

Skye really had no idea how natural she was at all this. Maybe it was the years of experience as a nurse, her ability to read people and assess a situation. But each person she met with ease. There were some people here tonight who were impossibly rich—like he was—but they had clearly never seen, or understood, need or poverty.

There were others from some of the charities who were in treatment, needed support or came from some of the most deprived parts of the country. Lucas was realising how far his father's reach had been, and how he'd worked hard not to think only of his privilege. There were also some staff here to share in the festivities, and some local business owners and people from the nearby village.

There were also a few members of the press. Lucas had baulked at this, but Brianna had reassured him that good press was necessary for the charities and their continued funding. And she'd smiled sweetly and told him he just had to suck it up. She'd patted his shoulder and given him a fond look.

'You're just like your father,' she'd said, and for the first time he'd felt a little pride.

He slipped his arm around Skye's waist as she stood next to him at the top of the stairs.

'You look stunning,' he whispered, dropping a kiss on her cheek. 'And you've been the perfect hostess.'

'I'm learning,' she said with a smile on her face as she looked at the crowd beneath them, and he could feel her tremble slightly.

He raised his glass to the people below as Brianna flicked a switch to flash the lights to get everyone's attention. A few hundred people stopped talking and stared up at him expectantly.

'Thank you everyone for coming this evening. You all know that this is my first official duty as the Duke of Mercia.' A few people whistled and clapped at his use of his title and Lucas smiled.

'It's no secret that this has all been a surprise for me, but I've spent the last few weeks learning about the work my father did at Costley Hall and for the various charities he supported.'

Again, there were a few cheers.

'So, even though I'm new at all this, I want you to know that I'm keen to continue the good work my father did, working with local businesses and supporting all the charities that were dear to his heart.'

From the corner of his eye he glimpsed the

navy smoking jacket of Albert, and the early lift of his glass in support.

'I ask for your patience as I learn this new role, and I will be continuing my work as a doctor.' He turned to Skye. 'I want to start this New Year a little differently from how my father used to do things.' He took a few deep breaths. 'The last few weeks, as I've learned of my new role, and come to terms with what it will mean to be a duke, I have been lucky enough to have someone by my side. Someone I consider to be my best friend.'

Skye's eyes widened, and his smile broadened.

'So, I want to start the New Year by taking a very important step. This job is bigger than one person. Probably even bigger than two, but we'll get to that in time.'

Skye's mouth opened and the crowd cheered.

Lucas put his hand over his heart. 'I've met the person who makes me whole. The person who gives me perspective when I need it, and who has my back. She's the first person I think about in the morning, and the last person I think about at night. I think I'm probably the luckiest man alive that I started work at The Harlington and got to meet the feisty, no-nonsense charge nurse that worked there.'

He dropped down onto one knee and pulled the box from his pocket that he'd taken from the safe earlier.

Skye's hands covered her mouth.

'Skye Carter, I love you with my whole heart. I've never felt connected with someone the way I do with you. I promise to always love you, now and for ever. Will you do me the honour of being my wife?'

The crowd held its breath, along with Lucas, as he waited for his answer. He'd flipped open the black velvet box to reveal the ring he'd found in the family safe earlier. It was a family heirloom. A large single diamond set in yellow gold. He'd worried Skye might find it old-fashioned, or it might not be to her taste. But Albert, his co-conspirator, had told him it didn't matter and he could let her pick what she wanted later. But if he was going to ask the question, he had to have a ring.

Skye finally dropped her hands from her face. Her eyes glittered with tears.

'Yes,' she whispered.

He took the ring from the box, conscious that the crowd below hadn't heard. But as he slid the ring onto her finger, the crowd gave a cheer as he took Skye in his arms.

'You've made me so happy,' he said in a low voice.

Her hand rested on his chest. 'You've made me happy too,' she replied. 'More than you could ever know.'

Lucas glanced at the large clock above the entranceway. He picked up some glasses of champagne that were sitting nearby. 'What's a duke without a duchess?' he shouted jubilantly, and the crowd laughed and cheered again, lifting their glasses to them.

He slid one arm around Skye as he looked down at all the people watching them. He should be nervous, maybe even a little overwhelmed. But he wasn't. And that was because he had Skye by his side.

'Let's have a countdown to the New Year.' He raised his glass, and started counting. 'Ten, nine…'

The crowd beneath him joined in, and he looked into Skye's eyes as they said the last few numbers together, dropping a kiss on her red lips as they reached one.

'Duchess?' she murmured under her breath. 'I hadn't even thought about that.'

He smiled, their lips only millimetres apart and their foreheads touching. 'Sounds kinda nice, doesn't it? How are we going to top this next year? I might have set a dangerous precedent here,' he joked.

But Skye's eyes glistened. 'I like a challenge,' she admitted. 'Maybe we have our wedding next New Year and the one after that...?' Her eyebrows rose as she laughed. 'Leave that one with me. I'll see what I can do.'

And Lucas picked her up and spun her around, kissing her the whole time. When he finally set her down, he grinned.

'All in your hands,' he teased. 'Surprise me.'

* * * * *

6 brand new stories each month

Keep reading for an excerpt of a new title
from the Western Romance series,
WRANGLING A FAMILY by Kathy Douglass

CHAPTER ONE

"LET ME STOP you right there," Alexandra Jamison said, holding up a hand and shaking her head. She needed to stop her friends before they got carried away by this ridiculous idea. "The answer is no."

"Don't say no so fast," Veronica said, her fork suspended halfway between her plate of shrimp scampi and linguini and her mouth. "At least not until you hear the entire plan."

"I've heard enough to know that I don't want any part of it." Alexandra replied.

"Perhaps you don't understand," Kristy said. "Because if you did, you'd realize it made perfect sense."

"I did understand," Alexandra said. Kristy was a sixth-grade math teacher and Alexandra suspected she was about to use her spoon to diagram the plan on her napkin. "We all bought tickets to the Aspen Creek dinner and bachelor auction. Now Veronica wants me to bid on a bachelor."

"It's for a good cause. The money raised will support several local programs for youth and new programs at the library." Veronica Kendrick, the children's librarian, was normally levelheaded, so this loony idea was out of character.

"I have no problem attending," Alexandra agreed. "It's the bidding on a bachelor that I don't want to do."

"Why not?" Marissa asked. Marissa and Alexandra were both nurses at the local hospital. Marissa worked in the ICU and Alexandra worked in pediatrics. They'd become fast friends when Alexandra moved to Aspen Creek five months ago. Marissa introduced her to Kristy and Veronica, and they'd become friends too. They got together regularly for dinner and conversation. Their bimonthly girls' night out had started so normally that Alexandra hadn't expected this at all.

"It'll be fun," Kristy promised.

"How is bidding on some guy I don't know so I can spend the night with him *fun*?"

"You don't have to spend the night with him. It's just a date," Veronica said.

"You know what I meant. Besides, it'll make me look desperate." She hadn't uprooted herself and her child only to have that reputation follow her here. It had been bad enough back home, where someone had started the rumor that she'd gotten pregnant in order to trap her rich, former boyfriend. It hadn't been true, but that hadn't stopped the gossip from spreading like wildfire around the hospital where she worked.

"No it won't. It will make you look like a caring member of the community who appreciates the importance of contributing to charity," Veronica insisted.

"You'll look like someone who wants to have fun," Marissa added.

"And you don't have to bid on a stranger," Kristy added. "You can always bid on someone you know."

Alexandra frowned. "That's even worse. Can you imagine bidding on one of the doctors I work with? That would be too weird."

"So no doctors," Kristy said, making a note on a piece of paper that seemingly materialized out of nowhere.

"Why am I the only one who has to bid on someone?"

"I would love to participate, but I can't," Veronica said.

"I'm the auctioneer. It would be hard to bid and conduct the auction at the same time."

"I suppose not," Alexandra conceded. She looked at Kristy and Marissa. "But what about you two? Neither of you has a steady boyfriend."

"So what? We have busy social lives and date quite a bit. You, on the other hand, only leave the house to work or meet up with us. This will give you the chance to go on at least one date."

"I'm not looking to get involved with anyone right now. I have my daughter to think about. Chloe needs all of my time and attention."

"Nobody is saying that you have to start a relationship. Just have dinner with a nice guy," Marissa said.

"And maybe go to a club," Kristy added, doing a little chair dance.

"That sounds okay in theory. But things have a way of getting complicated really fast. I'd rather not take that chance right now. I still think that you two should bid on someone. It sounds like fun. And it's for charity."

"Don't be so quick to say no. There won't be any complications. And we know plenty of men. Besides, we expect the bidding to go high," Marissa said. "We're going to have to pool our resources in order to win even one date."

"Really?"

"Yes. These aren't just any run-of-the-mill bachelors you'll be bidding on. These are some of the most eligible men in Aspen Creek. And from out of town too—a couple of the guys even live in Denver," Veronica said. As one of the coordinators, she would know.

"Didn't you even look at the list of participants I gave you at lunch yesterday?" Marissa asked.

Alexandra shook her head. "Why would I? The names

wouldn't mean a thing to me. Not to mention that I had no intention of bidding."

While Alexandra was speaking, Kristy rummaged through her purse. Now she pulled out the flyer advertising the Aspen Creek Bachelor Auction, pushed Alexandra's empty plate aside, and set the paper in front of her. "I had a feeling that might be the case, so I circled the names of men you might be interested in bidding on."

"That was such a good idea," Veronica said, rolling her eyes. "Let's see who *you* think Alexandra would like."

"Let's not," Alexandra said. She could have saved her breath. Her friends were too busy looking at the flyer to pay much attention to her.

When Veronica squealed, "Oh no, you didn't," Alexandra couldn't help but glance over to see who they were talking about.

"Who?"

"Dr. Hunt."

"What's wrong with him?" Kristy asked. "I think he's cute."

"We know," Marissa said. "So why are you trying to set Alexandra up with your secret crush?"

"I don't have a crush on him, secret or otherwise. I just appreciate how gentle he is when I bring Twinkie in for his exam."

"Is Dr. Hunt your vet?" Alexandra asked.

Kristy nodded. "Yes. And he's a good one. Twinkie adores him. And you know how cats can be."

Alexandra was a dog person, so she had no idea. But she nodded anyway. "You do talk about him a lot. Maybe you should bid on him for yourself. I'm willing to contribute to the cause if you think he'll go for a lot of money."

"Don't listen to them," Kristy said, waving her hands. "I don't have a crush on him."

"Right," Marissa said, stretching the word over several syllables.

"Who else is on the list?" Alexandra asked, getting into the spirit despite herself. Besides, looking didn't hurt anything. And hearing about the different bachelors would help her to learn more about her neighbors.

"Oh, you really are interested," Kristy teased.

Aspen Creek, Colorado, was a resort town and a very close-knit community. Despite the fact that the population of the town grew significantly during the winter months as vacationers came to ski and participate in other outdoor activities, and less so during the warmer months when people came to fish and hike, the town still managed to keep its sense of community. That was one of the things that had appealed to Alexandra.

"Not really. I'm an outsider. I need these bits of information to get a complete picture of the people in town," Alexandra said quickly. She'd moved to town to help her great-aunt who'd injured her hip. Alexandra's parents wanted to move Aunt Rose in with them in their suburban Chicago home, but she wouldn't hear of it. She loved Aspen Creek and refused to leave the home she'd lived in all of her adult life. As a compromise, Aunt Rose allowed Alexandra and her daughter to stay with her and provide the care she needed. Since Alexandra had just ended a disastrous relationship and wanted to start over fresh, it was the perfect solution for both of them. A man—even one that supposedly came with no strings—was not part of the plan.

"What can you tell me about him?" Alexandra asked, pointing at a random picture. He wasn't one of the ones that had been circled, and she wasn't any more interested in him than she was in the others, but she wasn't above gathering what information she could.

"That's Nathan Montgomery," Marissa said. "I still can't believe he agreed to enter."

"Why? Is he a selfish jerk?"

"Nothing like that. He's generous and supports all the fundraisers. It's just that Nathan's all work and no play. There is no room in his life for anything other than his family's ranch. I would expect him to write a check and be done with it."

"So he's the serious type." Someone who wasn't interested in a relationship was the type of man she'd want to bid on. Not that she was going to bid on anyone.

"That's putting it mildly," Marissa said. "And not at all the type of man I would choose for you. Now Party Marty would be a better fit."

"Party Marty," Kristy said with a smile. "I agree. He would be better."

Veronica nodded. "He'll definitely show you a good time."

A guy named *Party Marty* couldn't be further from what Alexandra wanted. "No. I don't think so."

"So who are you going to bid on?" Veronica asked.

"I told you, I'm not bidding on anyone. I'll be happy to watch the auction." Alexandra took a breath and said firmly, "I'm really not interested in going out with anyone."

"Even though there is no second date? No commitment?" Kristy asked, clearly disappointed.

"Even then. I have enough on my plate right now. So, it's a no for me." Alexandra handed the flyer back to Kristy. "I won't be bidding on anyone."

NATHAN MONTGOMERY GRABBED the crumpled flyer advertising the Aspen Creek Bachelor Auction from his back pocket and held it out to his brother Isaac, so that he could read it. Nathan barely reined in his anger. This nonsense had Isaac's fingerprints all over it.

"What's that?" Isaac asked without looking at it.

"It's a flyer advertising the bachelor auction."

"And why are you showing it to me? I certainly have no interest in it."

"I thought you might find one of the names particularly interesting."

Isaac dropped the saddle he'd been about to place on his horse, snatched the paper from Nathan, and began frantically searching it. "I'm not on here, am I? Savannah is laid-back, but I don't think she would appreciate me going out with another woman, even if it is to raise money for charity."

Savannah was Isaac's fiancée and one of the sweetest people Nathan had met. She'd suffered the loss of her first husband and child and had found happiness with Isaac. Nathan looked at his brother, his suspicion temporarily suspended. "Are you saying you didn't do this?"

"Do what?"

"Enter me in the bachelor auction."

"What? No. Why would I do something like that?"

"As a joke."

"Again, no. Although I have to admit the idea of you strutting your stuff down the catwalk is kind of funny."

"You think so? Well, I don't. I am not interested in anything to do with this shenanigan. But if you didn't do this, who did?"

"Maybe your name was added as a mistake."

"And my picture? No way. Somebody had to intentionally put me on the list."

"Good point. But instead of accusing innocent people, why don't you just call the person in charge and ask how you were added? There's a number right on the flyer."

"Good idea."

"I'm more than just a pretty face and great body." Isaac winked and then flexed, striking a pose. Despite his annoyance, Nathan laughed. Of the three Montgomery brothers, Isaac, the youngest, had gotten the majority of the charm, which had made him popular with the single women of Aspen Creek. Nathan didn't envy him though. He had goals that charm wouldn't help him accomplish. His serious nature and willingness to do the hard work was what had him in line to run the Montgomery Ranch when his father retired. Those qualities might not be what women were looking for, but they were going to help him make the business even more successful than it was now.

Right now, theirs was the biggest beef ranch in the state and enjoyed a superior reputation. But Nathan was eyeing more than Colorado or even the Midwest. Over the next five years, he wanted to expand the operation until they distributed their organic beef across the entire United States.

Being a rancher was in Nathan's blood. From the time he could walk, he'd followed his father around, mimicking everything he did. Nathan learned the business from the bottom up. He'd cleaned stalls, fed cows, participated in cattle drives, and arranged for the stock to be taken to market. The only time he hadn't lived on the ranch had been when he'd gone away to Howard University, earning first his bachelor's and then a master's degree in business. Although he'd enjoyed his time at college, he'd itched to return home to Colorado. Now, unless he was on a business trip or on a weekend getaway, he was on the ranch.

Nathan made a mental note to contact Veronica Kendrick when they were finished moving the cattle from their current grazing site to another. "I wonder what's keeping Miles."

"Probably Jillian or the kids. Besides, we aren't supposed to leave for another five minutes, so technically he's not late."

Nathan nodded. He knew that was true, but he liked to have everything in order ahead of time, just in case an issue arose at the last minute. He didn't like surprises.

"Hey," Miles called, jogging into the stable and heading for his horse. In a minute he'd saddled it and ridden up beside them. He looked at the flyer Nathan was still holding. "Oh, I see you have that. Good. With all of the busyness surrounding the wedding arrangements, I forgot to mention it to you."

"You're the one behind this?" Nathan's fist clenched, crushing the flyer.

"Yes. Is there a problem?"

"You have to ask? Of course there's a problem. Why in the world would you enter me in this ridiculous bachelor auction?"

"If you recall, you had me start attending those Chamber of Commerce meetings. They are such a waste of time. I agreed to go *once* because I was grateful that you babysat the kids so I could spend more time with Jillian. That one time morphed into me going every month."

"And I appreciate you taking that task off my plate."

"You say that as if I had a choice."

"So...what? This is your petty payback? Instead of coming to me with your issue like a man, you signed me up for this bachelor auction?"

"It wasn't like that," Miles objected.

"We all have to do our part to keep the ranch running. It is a *family* business. And the last time I checked you were part of the family."

"The ranch means as much to me as it does to you. And no, this isn't payback. When I have a problem with you, you'll know. But when I mentioned the fundraiser, you didn't let me go into detail. You just said that it was important that Montgomery Ranch be represented in a very visible way. To show that even though we are not geographically a part of Aspen Creek, that we are a part of the town in spirit. That whatever matters to the town matters to the Montgomery family."

Miles was quiet by nature, so this long speech was out of character. And unnecessary. Nathan wound his hand in a "get to the point" gesture. They had a schedule to keep.

"Well, Nathan, the fundraiser is this ridiculous bachelor auction. It was Deborah Lane's idea. But it quickly won the support of most of the women at the meeting. A few of the men even thought it was a good idea and signed up for it on the spot." He shook his head. "They decided to contact the single men in town to see if they were willing to participate. Apparently quite a few were."

"Nobody contacted me." He would have shut down that foolishness in a minute.

"That's because when they asked me if one of the Montgomery men was willing to participate, I said yes. Clearly I'm out. I'm getting married in three weeks. And Isaac is out because he's engaged. That left only you."

"You could have said no."

"Oh, how short your memory is, dear brother. The last time I said no about a fundraiser, you jumped all over me because I made the ranch look like a poor neighbor. I believe your exact words were *always say yes, Miles. Always.*"

"I remember that," Isaac said, not being the least bit helpful. But then, knowing Isaac, he hadn't intended to be. He delighted in being annoying. It was his superpower.

Nathan recalled the conversation too, although he wasn't

going to admit it now. "And somehow you took that to mean I wanted to be bid upon like a cow?"

"Don't turn this on me. I was just following your blanket order. If you want to back out, then that's on you."

"Oh, come on. Why would he want to back out?" Isaac asked. "This is the stuff dreams are made of."

"How do you figure?" Nathan asked. Even Miles looked interested in Isaac's reply.

"Dozens of women willing to spend their hard-earned money for a chance to go out with you. What man wouldn't love that?"

Me, thought Nathan. *I wouldn't.*

But he and Isaac were different. Before Isaac had met Savannah and fallen head over heels in love, his nickname had been Isaac "love 'em and leave 'em happy" Montgomery. He'd dated nearly every woman in town, somehow managing to remain on good terms with all of them.

Nathan had never been as popular with the women as Isaac. But then, nobody was. Being a ladies' man wasn't among Nathan's goals. Not that he was opposed to relationships. They had their place. And time. And now wasn't the time for him to become involved with anyone. The ranch kept him busy and he wouldn't be able to give a woman the attention she deserved.

Not that he hadn't tried on more than one occasion. His last relationship had been a colossal failure. Janet had been a single mother of a six-year-old. He and Billy had been wrecked when the relationship ended, and Billy and his mother had moved to Iowa. But Nathan had learned his lesson—no dating single mothers.

There was an order to things. First he would establish the ranch as the premiere beef ranch in the nation. Then—and only then—would he look for a woman to share his life.

He didn't see what the big rush was to find a woman and get married anyway. After all, he was only thirty years old. There was plenty of time for a relationship in the future.

He'd explained himself to his brothers and parents several times, but they didn't understand. He wasn't going to waste his breath saying it again. "I don't want to lead anyone on."

"Lead them on how? They're bidding on one night. Dinner and maybe some dancing. Or a movie or concert. Nobody is expecting a marriage proposal. Or even a second date," Isaac said.

"Really? If that's all they want, why would they spend all that money for one date?"

"You got me," Miles said. "The whole idea is silly to me. There are plenty of other ways to support a charity. Like writing a check."

"Because it's fun," Isaac said. "You two really are sticks-in-the-mud. I can't believe we're related. Let me break it down for you. Not every date has to lead to a relationship. Sometimes people do things just for the sheer pleasure of it. Like bid on a date at a bachelor auction. Don't read more into it than is there."

"When did you get all logical?" Nathan asked. "You're actually making sense."

"I don't want to be out here all day. Savannah and I have plans for the evening, so I don't have time for you to have an existential crisis over something that doesn't matter. Take the winner to dinner and take her home. Thank her for her time and her charitable donation, and leave. Easy."

"Right?" Miles agreed. "What's the big deal? And it will generate goodwill for the ranch. That's something that's important. If you back out, we'll lose that goodwill and maybe even stir up some bad blood."

"And you definitely don't want to do that," Isaac said.

"No." That was the last thing he would ever want. The ranch was everything.

"Good. Now that it's settled, let's get this show on the road," Isaac said, leading the way from the stable, Nathan and Miles behind him.

As he rode out to the pastures beside his brothers, Nathan tried to convince himself that it was going to be as easy as Isaac claimed.

But he had a sneaking suspicion that the auction was going to be much more complicated than that.